# Redeeming Love

## Francine Rivers

MONARCH
BOOKS

Oxford, UK

Redeeming Love
Originally published in English under the title: Redeeming Love.
Copyright © 1997 by Francine Rivers.
Published by Multnomah Books, an imprint of The Crown Publishing Group, a
division of Random House, Inc., 12265 Oracle Boulevard, Suite 200, Colorado
Springs, Colorado 80921, USA.

All non-English rights are contracted through: Gospel Literature International,
PO Box 4060, Ontario, CA 91761–1003, USA.

First published in the UK by Monarch Books in 2004
(a publishing imprint of Lion Hudson plc),
Wilkinson House, Jordan Hill Road, Oxford OX2 8DR
Tel: +44 (0) 1865 302750  Fax: +44 (0) 1865 302757
Email: monarch@lionhudson.com  www.lionhudson.com

Reprinted 2005, 2006 (twice), 2007, 2009 (twice), 2010 (twice), 2011 (twice).

ISBN: 978-1-85424-659-2

Distributed by: Marston Book Services Ltd, PO Box 269,
Abingdon, Oxon OX14 4YN

Scripture quotations are from:
*New Revised Standard Version Bible* (NRSV)
© Oxford University Press. Used by permission.
Also quoted:
*The King James Version* (KJV) the rights of which are vested
in the Crown's patentee, Cambridge University Press.
Scripture quotations marked (NLT) are taken from
the *Holy Bible, New Living Translation* © 1996.
Used by permission of Tyndale House Publishers, Inc.,
Wheaton, Illinois 60189.

The text paper used in this book has been made from wood independently
certified as having come from sustainable forests.

**British Library Cataloguing Data**
A catalogue record for this book is available
from the British Library.

Printed and bound in Great Britain by Clays Ltd, St Ives plc.

# Dedication

To those who hurt and hunger.

# Disclaimer

*This is a work of fiction. The characters, incidents, and dialogues are products of the author's imagination and are not to be construed as real. Any resemblance to actual events or persons, living or dead, is entirely coincidental.*

*Let anyone among you who is without sin, be the first
to throw a stone at her.*

JESUS, JOHN 8:7

# Child of Darkness

# *Prologue*

*The prince of darkness is a gentleman.*
SHAKESPEARE

NEW ENGLAND, 1835

Alex Stafford was just like Mama said. He was tall and dark, and Sarah had never seen anyone so beautiful. Even dressed in dusty riding clothes, his hair damp with perspiration, he was like the princes in the stories Mama read. Sarah's heart beat with wild joy and pride. None of the other fathers she saw at Mass compared to him.

He looked at her with his dark eyes, and her heart sang. She was wearing her best blue frock and white pinafore, and Mama had braided her hair with pink and blue ribbons. Did Papa like the way she looked? Mama said blue was his favorite color, but why didn't he smile? Was she fidgeting? Mama said to stand straight and still and act like a lady. She said he would like that. But he didn't look pleased at all.

"Isn't she beautiful, Alex?" Mama said. Her voice sounded strange…tight, like she was choking. "Isn't she the most beautiful little girl you've ever seen?"

Sarah watched Papa's dark eyes frown. He didn't look happy. He looked angry. Like mama looked sometimes when Sarah talked too much or asked too many questions.

"Just a few minutes," Mama said quickly. Too quickly. Was she afraid? But why? "That's all I'm asking, Alex. Please. It would mean so much to her."

Alex Stafford stared down at Sarah. His mouth was pressed tight, and he studied her silently. Sarah stood as still as she could. She'd stared at herself in the mirror so long this morning, she knew what he would see. She had her father's chin and nose, and her mother's blonde hair and fair skin. Her eyes were like her mother's, too, although they were even more blue. Sarah wanted

Papa to think she was pretty, and she gazed up at him hopefully. But the look in his eyes was not a nice one.

"Did you pick blue on purpose, Mae?" Papa's words startled Sarah. They were cold and angry. "Because it brings out the color of her eyes?"

Sarah couldn't help it, she glanced at her mother – and her heart fell. Mama's face was filled with hurt.

Alex glanced toward the foyer. "Cleo!"

"She's not here," Mama said quietly, keeping her head high. "I gave her the day off."

Papa's eyes seemed to get even darker. "Did you? Well, that leaves you in a fix, doesn't it, darling?"

Mama stiffened, then bit her lip and glanced down at Sarah. What was wrong? Sarah wondered sadly. Wasn't Papa happy to see her? She had been so excited that she was actually going to be with him at last, even for a little while....

"What would you have me do?" Mama's words were directed at Papa, so Sarah stayed silent, still hoping.

"Send her away. She knows how to find Cleo, I would imagine."

Pink spots appeared on Mama's cheeks. "Meaning what, Alex? That I entertain others in your absence?"

Sarah's smile fell in confusion. They spoke so coldly to one another. Neither looked at her. Had they forgotten she was there? What was wrong? Mama was distraught. Why was Papa so angry about Cleo not being home?

Chewing her lip, Sarah looked between them. Stepping closer, she tugged on her father's coat. "Papa..."

"Don't call me that."

She blinked, frightened and confused by his manner. He *was* her papa. Mama said so. He even brought her presents every time he came. Mama gave them to her. Maybe he was angry that she had never thanked him. "I want to thank you for the presents you – "

"Hush, Sarah," her mother said quickly. "Not now, darling."

Papa flashed Mama a thunderous look. "Let her speak. It's what you wanted, isn't it? Why are you shushing her now, Mae?"

Mama stepped closer and put her hand on Sarah's shoulder.

Sarah could feel Mama's fingers trembling, but Papa bent toward her now, smiling. "What presents?" he said.

He was so handsome, just like Mama said. She was proud to have a father like him.

"Tell me, little one."

"I always like the candies you bring me," Sarah said, feeling warm and proud beneath his attention. "They are very nice. But best of everything, I love the crystal swan."

She smiled again, glowing with joy that Papa listened to her so carefully. He even smiled, though Sarah wasn't sure she liked his smile. It was small and tight.

"Indeed," he said and straightened. He looked at Mama. "I'm so pleased to know how much my gifts mean."

Sarah looked up at her father, thrilled at his approval. "I put it on my windowsill. The sun shines through it and makes colors dance on the wall. Would you like to come and see?" She took his hand. When he jerked away, she blinked, hurt, not understanding.

Mama bit her lip and reached out a hand toward Papa, then stopped suddenly. She looked afraid again. Sarah looked from one parent to the other, struggling to understand. What had she done wrong? Wasn't Papa pleased that she liked his presents?

"So you pass on my gifts to the child," Papa said. "It's good to know what they mean to you."

Sarah bit her lip at the coldness in Papa's voice, but before she could speak, Mama touched her shoulder gently. "Darling, be a good girl and go outside and play now."

Sarah looked up, distressed. Had she done something wrong? "Can't I stay? I'll be very quiet." Mama couldn't seem to say more. Her eyes were moist and she looked at Papa.

Alex bent down to Sarah. "I want you to go outside and play," he said quietly. "I want to talk to your mother alone." He smiled and patted her cheek.

Sarah smiled, utterly enchanted. Papa had touched her; he wasn't angry at all. He loved her! Just as Mama said. "Can I come back when you're done talking?"

Papa straightened stiffly. "Your mother will come and get you when she's ready. Now, run along as you've been told."

"Yes, Papa." Sarah wanted to stay, but she wanted to please her father more. She went out of the parlor, skipping through the kitchen to the back door. She picked a few daisies that grew in the garden patch by the door and then headed for the rose trellis. She plucked the petals. "He loves me, he loves me not, he loves me, he loves me not...." She hushed as she came around the corner. She didn't want to disturb Mama and Papa. She just wanted to be close to them.

Sarah dreamed contentedly. Maybe Papa would put her up on his shoulders. She wondered if he would take her for a ride on his big black horse. She would have to change her dress, of course. He wouldn't want her to soil it. She wished he had let her sit on his lap while he talked to Mama. She would have liked that very much, and she would have been no bother.

The parlor window was open, and she could hear voices. Mama loved the smell of roses to fill the parlor. Sarah wanted to sit and listen to her parents. That way she would know just when Papa wanted her to come back again. If she was very quiet, she wouldn't disturb them, and all Mama would have to do was lean out and call her name.

"What was I to do, Alex? You've never spent so much as a minute with her. What was I to tell her? That her father doesn't care? That he wishes she had never even been born?"

Sarah's lips parted. *Deny it, Papa! Deny it!*

"I brought that swan back from Europe for you, and you throw it away on a child who has no appreciation for its value. Did you give her the pearls as well? What about the music box? I suppose she got that, too!"

The daisies fluttered from Sarah's hand. She sat down on the ground, careless of her pretty dress. Her heart slowed from its wild, happy beat. Everything inside her seemed to spiral downward with each word.

"Alex, please. I didn't see any harm in it. It made it easier. She asked me this morning if she was old enough yet to meet you. She asks me every time she knows you're coming. How could I say no to her again? I didn't have the heart. She doesn't understand your neglect, and neither do I."

"You know how I feel about her."

"How can you say how you feel? You don't even know her. She's a beautiful child, Alex. She's quick and charming and she isn't afraid of anything. She's like you in so many ways. She's *someone*, Alex. You can't ignore her existence forever. She's your daughter...."

"I have enough children by my wife. Legitimate children. I told you I didn't want another."

"How can you say that? How can you not love your own flesh and blood?"

"I told you how I felt from the beginning, but you wouldn't listen. She should never have been born, Mae, but you insisted on having your own way."

"Do you think I wanted to get pregnant? Do you think I planned to have her?"

"I've often wondered. Especially when I arranged a way out of the situation for you and you refused. The doctor I sent you to would have taken care of the whole mess. He would've gotten rid – "

"I couldn't do it. How could you expect me to kill my unborn child? Don't you understand? It's a mortal sin."

"You've spent too much time in church," he said derisively. "Have you ever thought that you wouldn't have the problems you do now if you had gotten rid of her the way I told you. It would've been easy. But you ran out."

"I wanted her!" Mama said brokenly. "She was part of you, Alex, and part of me. I wanted her even if you didn't...."

"Is that the real reason?"

"You're hurting me, Alex!"

Sarah flinched as something shattered. "Is that the real reason, Mae? Or did you have her because you thought bearing my child would give you a hold over me you otherwise lacked?"

"You can't believe that!" Mama was crying now. "You do, don't you? You're a fool, Alex. Oh, what have I done? I gave up everything for you! My family, my friends, my self-respect, everything I believed in, every hope I ever had...."

"I bought you this cottage. I give you all the money you could possibly need."

Mama's voice rose strangely. "Do you know what it's like for me to walk down the street in this town? You come and go when and as you please. And they know who you are, and they know what I am. No one looks at me. No one speaks to me. Sarah feels it, too. She asked me about it once, and I told her we were different from other people. I didn't know what else to say." Her voice broke. "I'll probably go to hell for what I've become."

"I'm sick of your guilt and I'm sick of hearing about that child. She's ruining everything between us. Do you remember how happy we were? We never argued. I couldn't wait to come to you, to be with you."

"Don't — "

"And how much time do I have left with you today? Enough? You've used it up on her. I told you what would happen, didn't I? I wish she had never been born!"

Mama cried out a terrible name. There was a crash. Terrified, Sarah got up and ran. She raced through Mama's flowers and across the lawn and onto the pathway to the springhouse. She ran until she couldn't run anymore. Gasping, her sides burning, she dropped into the tall grass, her shoulders heaving with sobs, her face streaked with tears. She heard a horse galloping toward her. Scrambling for a better hiding place in the vines about the creek, she peered out and saw her father ride by on his great black horse. Ducking down, she huddled there, crying, and waited for Mama to come fetch her.

But Mama didn't come and she didn't call. After a while, Sarah wandered back to the springhouse and sat by the flowered vines and waited longer. By the time Mama came, Sarah had dried her tears and dusted off her pretty frock. She was still shaking from what she had heard.

Mama was very pale, her eyes dull and red-rimmed. There was a blue mark on the side of her face. She had tried to cover it with powder. She smiled, but it wasn't like her usual smile.

"Where have you been, darling? I've been looking and looking for you." Sarah knew she hadn't. She had been watching for her. Mama licked her lacy handkerchief and wiped a smudge from Sarah's cheek. "Your father was called away suddenly on business."

"Is he coming back?" Sarah was afraid. She never wanted to see him again. He had hurt Mama and made her cry.

"Maybe not for a long time. We'll have to just wait and see. He's a very busy and important man." Sarah said nothing, and her Mama lifted her and hugged her close. "It's all right, sweetheart. You know what we're going to do? We're going to go back to the cottage and change our dresses. Then we'll pack a picnic and go down to the creek. Would you like that?"

Sarah nodded and put her arms around Mama's neck. Her mouth trembled, and she tried not to cry. If she cried, Mama might guess she had been eavesdropping and then she would be angry too.

Mama held her tightly, her face buried in Sarah's hair. "We'll make it through this. You'll see, sweetheart. We will. *We will.*"

Alex didn't come back, and Mama grew thin and wan. She stayed in bed too late, and when she got up, she didn't want to go for long walks the way she used to. When she smiled, her eyes didn't light up. Cleo said she needed to eat more. Cleo said a lot of things, carelessly, with Sarah close enough to hear.

"He's still sending you money, Miss Mae. That's something."

"I don't care about the money." Mama's eyes filled up. "I've never cared about it."

"You'd care if you didn't have any."

Sarah tried to cheer Mama up by bringing her big bouquets of flowers. She found pretty stones and washed them, giving them to her as presents. Mama always smiled and thanked her, but there was no sparkle in her eyes. Sarah sang the songs Mama taught her, sad Irish ballads and a few Latin chants from mass.

"Mama, why don't you sing anymore?" Sarah asked, climbing up onto the bed with her and setting her doll in the rumpled covers. "You'll feel better if you sing."

Mama brushed her long blonde hair slowly. "I don't feel much like singing, darling. Mama has a lot on her mind right now."

Sarah felt a heaviness growing inside her. It was all her fault. All her fault. If she hadn't been born, Mama would be happy. "Will Alex come back, Mama?"

Mama looked at her, but Sarah didn't care. She wouldn't call him Papa anymore. He had hurt Mama and made her sad. Ever since he'd left, Mama had scarcely paid attention to her. Sarah had even heard Mama tell Cleo that love wasn't a blessing, it was a curse.

Sarah glanced at Mama's face, and her heart sank. She looked so sad. Her thoughts were far away again, and Sarah knew she was thinking of him. Mama wanted him to come back. Mama cried at night because he didn't. Mama pressed her face into her pillow at night, but Sarah still heard her sobs.

She chewed on her lip and lowered her head, playing distractedly with her doll. "What if I got sick and died, Mama?"

"You won't get sick," Mama said, glancing at her. She smiled. "You're far too young and healthy to die."

Sarah watched her mother brushing her hair. It was like sunshine flowing over her pale shoulders. Mama was so pretty. How could Alex not love her? "But if I did, Mama, would he come back and stay with you?"

Mama went very still. She turned and stared at Sarah, and the horrified look in her eyes frightened her. She shouldn't have said that. Now Mama might guess she'd heard them fighting....

"Don't ever think that, Sarah."

"But – "

"No! Don't you ever ask such a question again. Do you understand?"

Mama had never raised her voice before; Sarah felt her chin quiver. "Yes, Mama."

"Never again," Mama said more gently. "Promise me. None of this has anything to do with you, Sarah." Mama reached out to pull her into her arms and stroke her tenderly. "I love you, Sarah. I love you so much. I love you more than anything or anyone in the whole wide world."

Except for him, Sarah thought. Except for Alex Stafford. What if he came back? What if he made Mama choose? What would Mama do then?

Afraid, Sarah clung to her mother and prayed he would stay away.

A young man came to see Mama.

Sarah watched her mother speak with him while Sarah played with her doll near the fireplace. The only people who came to this cottage were Mister Pennyrod, who brought firewood, and Bob. Bob liked Cleo. He worked at the market and teased Cleo about rump roasts and juicy legs o' lamb. Cleo laughed at him, but Sarah didn't think he was very funny. He wore a soiled white apron covered with blood.

The young man gave Mama a letter, but she didn't open it. She served him tea, and he said thank you. He didn't say very much after that, except to talk about the weather and how pretty Mama's flower garden was. He said it was a long ride from the city. Mama gave him biscuits and forgot all about Sarah.

She knew something was wrong. Mama sat too straight and she spoke very softly. "She's a pretty little girl," the man said, and smiled at her. Sarah looked down again, embarrassed, afraid Mama would send her from the room because he had noticed her.

"Yes, she is. Thank you."

"She looks like you. Pretty as a sunrise."

Mama smiled at her. "Sarah, why don't you go outside and cut some flowers for the table."

Sarah took her doll and went out without a word of argument. She wanted to please Mama. She took a sharp knife from the kitchen drawer and went out to the flower garden. Mama loved roses best. Sarah added spikes of larkspur, red stock, ranunculus, marguerites, and daisies until the straw basket on her arm was full.

When she came back inside, the young man was gone. The letter was open in Mama's lap. Her eyes were bright and her cheeks full of lively color. She smiled as she folded the letter and tucked it into her sleeve. She stood and came to Sarah, lifting her and swinging her around gaily. "Thank you for getting the flowers, darling." She kissed Sarah. When Mama put her down, Sarah put the basket on the table.

"I just love flowers," Mama said. "They're so lovely, aren't they? Why don't you arrange them this time? I need to find something in the kitchen. Oh, Sarah! It's a beautiful, wonderful day, isn't it?"

It was a wretched day, Sarah thought, watching her go. She felt sick with dread. She lifted the big vase down from the table and carried it outside, dumping the wilted flowers on the compost. She pumped fresh water and poured it into the vase. It sloshed on her dress as she carried it back and slid it onto the table again. She didn't trim the stems or remove leaves. She didn't care how they looked and she knew Mama wouldn't even notice.

Alex Stafford was coming back.

Mama returned to the parlor with Cleo. "Oh, darling, I've the most wonderful news. Cleo has made plans to go to the seashore this week and she wants to take you with her. Isn't that grand?"

Sarah's heart beat fast and hard.

"Isn't that sweet of her?" Mama went on brightly. "She has a friend who runs an inn, and he just loves little girls."

Cleo's smile was stiff and cool.

Sarah looked at her mother. "I don't want to go, Mama. I want to stay with you." She knew what was happening. Mama was sending her away because her father didn't want her. Maybe Mama didn't want her now either.

"Nonsense," Mama laughed. "You've never been anywhere but here and you need to see something of the world. You'll like the ocean, Sarah. It's so lovely. And you can sit on the sand and listen to the waves. You can build castles and find seashells. Just wait until you feel the foam tickle your toes."

Mama looked alive again. Sarah knew it was the letter. Alex must have written he was coming to see Mama. She wouldn't want another scene like the last one, so she was putting Sarah out of his way. She watched her mother's glowing face, her heart sinking.

"Come on now, darling. Let's get you ready to go."

Sarah watched her things being folded and stuffed into a carpetbag. Mama couldn't wait to be rid of her. "Where's your doll?" Mama said, looking around. "You'll want to take her along with you."

"No."

"Why not? You're never without your doll."

"She wants to stay home with you."

Mama frowned, but she didn't pursue it. Nor did she change her mind.

Cleo came back for Sarah, and they made the mile walk to town. Cleo purchased the tickets just as the coach rolled in. The driver took charge of the carpetbags, and Cleo lifted Sarah into the coach. When the servant climbed in, she sat across from her and smiled. Her brown eyes were very bright. "We're going to have an adventure, Sarah."

Sarah wanted to jump out of the coach and run home to Mama, but Mama would only send her back again. As the horses set off, Sarah clung to the window, peering out as the familiar houses swept past. The coach rattled over the bridge and traveled on a wood-lined road. Everything familiar to Sarah was quickly gone from sight, and she sank back against the bouncing seat. The further they went, the more desolate she felt.

"We'll stay at the Four Winds," Cleo said, clearly pleased that Sarah seemed content to be quiet. She'd probably expected her to fuss. If she'd thought it would change Mama's mind, she might have done so. She'd never been away from Mama for more than a few hours. But Sarah had known it wouldn't change things. Alex Stafford was coming, so she had to go. She sat still and solemn.

"They've fine food and decent rooms," Cleo told her. "And we'll be close to the sea. You can walk along a little grassy path and come to the bluffs. The surf pounds on the rocks. It's a wonderful sound, and the smell of the salt air is better than anything."

Better than anything...

Sarah liked home and the flower garden behind the cottage. She liked sitting beside the springhouse with Mama, their bare feet dangling in the creek.

Fighting tears, she looked out the window again. Her eyes smarted and her throat became raw from the road dust. The hours passed slowly; the hard pounding of the horses' hooves made her head ache. She was tired – so tired she could scarcely keep her eyes open, but each time she closed them, the coach would lurch or sway sharply, frightening her awake.

The driver stopped the coach once to change horses and make minor repairs. Cleo took Sarah to the backhouse. When Sarah came out again, Cleo was nowhere to be seen. Sarah ran to the coach, then to the stables, and finally to the road, crying out Cleo's name.

"Hush that noise! My heavens, what is the ruckus all about?" Cleo said, hurrying toward her. "One would think you were a chicken without your head the way you're running about."

"Where *were* you?" Sarah demanded, tears streaming down her cheeks. "Mama said we were to stay together!"

Cleo's brows arched. "Well, excuse me, your ladyship, but I was having myself a mug of ale." She reached down and snatched Sarah's hand, leading her back toward the station building.

The station manager's wife was standing in the doorway, drying her hands. "What a pretty little girl," she said, smiling at Sarah. "Are you hungry, sweetheart? You've time for a bowl of shepherd's stew."

Sarah lowered her eyes, timid beneath the woman's scrutiny. "No, thank you, ma'am."

"And polite, too," the lady said.

"Come along, Sarah," Cleo said, giving her a nudge inside.

The lady patted Sarah's back as she ushered her to a table. "You need to put a little meat on your bones, honey. You give my stew a try. I'm said to be one of the best cooks on the line."

Cleo sat down and took up her mug of ale again. "You need to eat something before we leave."

"I'm not hungry."

Cleo leaned forward. "I don't care if you're hungry or not," she said in a low voice. "You'll do as you're told. The driver said it will be another half hour before we can leave, and it'll be three or four more hours before we reach the coast. I don't want to hear you whining that you're hungry then. This is your last chance to eat something until the Four Winds."

Sarah stared at Cleo, struggling not to cry. Cleo sighed heavily, then reached out to pat her face awkwardly. "Just eat something, Sarah," she said. Obediently, Sarah picked up her spoon and began to eat. Mama had said this trip was planned for her, but even Cleo acted as though she were in the way. It was clear Mama had sent her off to get rid of her.

When they set off in the coach again, Sarah was quiet. She sat beside the window and stared out, her small hands clasped in her lap, her back straight. Cleo seemed grateful for the silence, finally dozing off. When she awakened, she smiled at Sarah.

"Smell the sea air?" she asked. Sarah was sitting in the same position she'd been in when Cleo went to sleep, but she knew her dusty face had white streaks from the tears she'd been unable to stop. Cleo just stared at her sadly, then turned to stare out the window.

They arrived at the Four Winds just after sunset. Sarah clung to Cleo's hand while the driver untied their carpetbags. Sarah heard a great roaring like a monster and was afraid. "What's that sound, Cleo?"

"The sea crashing on the rocks. Grand, isn't it?"

Sarah thought it was the most fearsome sound she had ever heard. The wind howled in the trees like a wild beast searching for warm-blooded prey, and when the door to the Four Winds opened, she heard loud laughter and men shouting. Sarah drew back sharply, not wanting to go inside.

"Be careful there," Cleo said, pushing her forward. "Take your bag. I've got my own to carry."

Sarah dragged her bag to the edge of the door. Cleo shoved the door open with her shoulder and went in, Sarah following right behind her. Cleo looked around the room, then smiled. Sarah followed her gaze and saw a man at the bar, arm-wrestling with a brawny sailor. A big man was pouring ale, and he spotted Cleo right away. He leaned over to nudge the man who was arm-wrestling and nodded toward Cleo with a quiet word. The man turned his head slightly, and the sailor, taking advantage of his lack of attention, smashed his arm down on the bar with a shout of triumph. Sarah watched in fear as the beaten man surged to his feet and hit the sailor in the right eye, sending him crashing to the floor.

Cleo laughed. She seemed to have forgotten Sarah, who was

now hiding behind her skirts. Sarah whimpered quietly when the man from the bar made his way to Cleo and gave her a sound kiss, to the shouts of the other men in the room. When he looked past Cleo to stare at Sarah, she thought she would faint from fear. He raised his eyebrows. "A by-blow? You must've taken up with a pretty fellow by the looks of her."

It was a moment before Cleo had her breath back and knew what he was talking about. "Oh, her. No, Merrick. She's not mine. She's daughter of the lady I work for."

"What's she doing here with you?"

"It's a long, sad story I'd rather forget just now."

Merrick nodded and patted her cheek. "How do you like country life?" He smiled, but Sarah didn't think it was a nice smile.

Cleo tossed her head. "It's everything I ever hoped it would be."

He laughed and took her carpetbag. "That's why you're back at the Four Winds, eh?" He took Sarah's bag, too, and grinned boldly, laughing when she drew back from him as though he were the devil himself.

Sarah had never seen anyone like Merrick. He was very big and had black hair and a trimmed beard. He reminded her of the pirate stories Mama told her. His voice was loud and deep, and he looked at Cleo as though he wanted to eat her up. Cleo didn't seem to mind. She paid no attention to Sarah and walked across the room. Sarah followed, too afraid to be left behind. Everyone was staring at her.

"Hey, Stump, give our Cleo a mug of ale!" Merrick shouted to the grizzled barkeeper who welcomed Cleo with a wink and grin. Merrick caught Sarah around the waist and lifted her high, plunking her down on the bar. "And some watered wine for this pale chick." He felt her velvet jacket. "Your mama must be rich, eh?"

"Her papa is rich," Cleo said. "He's also married."

"Oh." Merrick gave Cleo a mocking grin. "So that's how it is. I thought you was after respectable work."

"It is respectable. No one looks down their nose at me."

"Do they know you worked in an alehouse for five years before you decided to improve your station in life?" He slid his hand down her arm. "Not to mention a little work on the side...."

Cleo glanced at Sarah, then brushed his hand away. "Mae knows. She's not one to look down on others. I like her."

"Does this little mite look anything like her?"

"Spitting image."

Merrick chucked Sarah's chin and stroked her cheek. "Eyes blue as violets and hair like an angel. Your mama must be mighty pretty if she's anything like you. I'd like to see her."

Cleo stiffened, and Sarah thought she was angry. She wished Merrick would leave her alone, but he kept stroking her cheek. Sarah wanted to get as far away as she could from this awful man with his black beard and dark eyes and mean grin.

"Leave her alone, Merrick. She's scared enough as it is without you teasing her. This is her first time away from her mama."

He laughed. "She does look a little white around the gills. Come on, mite. I'm harmless. Drink up." He pushed the mug of watered wine to her. "That's it. A little of this and you won't be scared of nothing." He laughed again when Sarah grimaced with distaste. "Is she used to something better?"

"She's used to nothing," Cleo said, and Sarah was more sure now that she was angry. Cleo didn't like it that Merrick was paying so much attention to her. She looked at Sarah, clearly annoyed at the way she was reacting to Merrick. "Don't be such a coward. He's all wind and little else." Old Stump and the others at the bar laughed, Merrick with them.

Sarah wanted to jump down and run away from the loud voices, the laughter, and the staring eyes. She gave a soft sob of relief when Cleo reached out to lift her down, then took her hand, guiding her to a table. She bit her lip when Merrick followed them. He pulled out a chair and sat down. Whenever the mugs got empty, he ordered more. He made jokes, and Cleo laughed a lot. Once he reached under the table, and Cleo pushed him away. But she was smiling, and she was talking more and more. And her voice sounded funny, like the words were all running together.

It was raining outside, and branches scraped against the windowpane. Sarah was tired, her eyelids so heavy she could hardly keep them open.

Merrick raised his mug again. "Mite's dragging her sails."

Cleo touched Sarah's head. "Cross your arms on the table and sleep awhile." Sarah did as she was told, wishing they could leave. Cleo obviously wasn't ready to leave. She seemed to be having a good time, and she kept staring at Merrick and smiling in a way Sarah had never seen her smile before.

"Why'd you have to bring her to the Four Winds?" Merrick said. Sarah kept her eyes closed, pretending she was asleep.

"Because her mama is entertaining her fine papa and they both wanted her out of the way." Cleo's words were cold. "Don't do that."

"Don't?" He laughed low. "You know it's what you came for. What's the matter with those country boys?"

"Nothing. One's after me to marry him."

"Let's go upstairs and talk about why you came back here."

"What am I supposed to do with her? I was so angry when Mae stuck me with her."

Tears pricked Sarah's eyes, and her throat closed up. Didn't anyone want her anymore?

"Seems to me it'd be easy to farm out the pretty little thing. Somebody ought to want her."

"That's what I told Mae, but she says no. She trusts me. The only thing she's got when her man isn't around to play house is this child. About the only thing Mae knows is how to look pretty and how to grow flowers."

"I thought you said you liked her."

"I like her well enough, but anytime His Majesty decides to call, guess who gets stuck with her by-blow. It gets tiresome dragging a child around with you, especially one that doesn't even belong to you."

Merrick chuckled. "Well, why don't we just toss her off the point? Maybe her mama and papa would see it as a favor. Might even give you a bonus."

Sarah's heart pounded.

"That's not funny, Merrick." Cleo's sigh was heavy, annoyed. "I'd better wake her and put her to bed. She's had a long day." She nudged Sarah, who looked up in relief. Cleo took her hand. "Come on. We're going up to bed now. Say goodnight to Mister Merrick."

He grinned. "I'll see you safely upstairs, ladies."

When Cleo opened the door of her old room, Merrick held it ajar and came inside. Sarah looked at Cleo in alarm.

"What're you doing?" Cleo whispered fiercely. "You can't come in here with me. She'll tell her mother, and I'll lose my position."

"I'll take care of that." Merrick bent and pinched Sarah's chin. "You say anything to anybody about me being in this room with Cleo, and I'll cut your little pink tongue out. Understand?" Sarah believed him, and nodded her head. He smiled slightly and let her go. She darted to the corner and crouched there, trembling and feeling sick. "See?" Merrick crowed gleefully. "Nothing to worry about. She won't say a word about us to anyone."

Cleo stared at him, her eyes wide. She looked upset, and Sarah hoped she would tell him to leave. "That was terrible cruel," she said, looking at Sarah. "He didn't mean it, lovey. He was only fooling. Don't believe a word he says."

"You believe it, girl. I wasn't fooling at all." He caught Cleo to him. "Cruel? Cruel would be putting me out when you know I just want to be with you."

She pushed him away. He reached for her again, and she dodged him – but even Sarah could tell the effort was half-hearted. How could Cleo let this man near her?

"I know you, Cleo." Merrick's smile was half-mast, his eyes gleaming. "Why did you come all the way back to the Four Winds? Just to look at the sea again?"

"It's in my blood as much as yours."

Merrick caught hold of her and kissed her. Cleo struggled, trying to pull away, but he held her tightly. When she relaxed against him, he drew back enough to say, "More than that's in your blood."

"Merrick, don't. She's watching – "

"So what?"

He kissed her again, and she fought him this time. Sarah sat frozen in fear. Maybe he would just kill them both.

"No!" Cleo said angrily. "Get out of here. I can't do this. I'm supposed to be taking care of *her*."

He laughed. "I didn't know duty was so important to you." He let her go, but Sarah didn't think Cleo looked glad at all. She looked like she was going to cry. Merrick smiled and turned his back to Sarah. "Come on, mite."

"What're you doing, Merrick?" Cleo demanded when Sarah scrambled to escape him.

"Putting her out. It won't hurt her to sit in the hallway awhile. And don't say no. I know you too well. Besides, she'll be right outside the door. No one's going to bother her." He dragged a blanket and pillow from the bed and motioned to Sarah. "Don't make me come get you."

Sarah didn't dare disobey.

She followed Merrick into the hallway, watching as he dumped the blanket and pillow in the darkened corridor. Something large scurried down the hall and hid in the darkness. She stared at him, wide-eyed.

"You sit right there and don't move. If you don't stay put, I'll find you and take you down to the sea and feed you to the crabs. Understand?"

Sarah's mouth was dry, and she couldn't make any words come out. So she just nodded.

Cleo came to the doorway. "Merrick, I can't leave her out there. I saw a rat."

"She's too small for the rats to bother with. She'll be fine." He patted Sarah's cheek. "Won't you? You stay out here until Cleo fetches you. Don't you move from this spot until she does."

"Y-yes, sir," she stammered, her voice catching in her throat.

"See?" He straightened and turned Cleo around, pushing her back into the room. He closed the door firmly behind them.

Sarah heard Merrick talking and Cleo giggling. Then she heard other sounds as well and she was afraid. She wanted to run away from the sounds they made, but remembered what Merrick had said he would do to her if she moved. Terrified, she covered her head with the dirty blanket and pressed her hands over her ears.

The silence that followed grew heavy. Sarah peeked down the darkened corridor. She felt eyes watching her. What if the rat came back? Her heart was like a drum, her whole body wracked with its beat. She heard soft scratching and drew her legs in tight against her body, staring into the darkness, terrified of what lurked there.

The door clicked open, and she jumped. Merrick came out. She pressed herself back, hoping he wouldn't notice her. He didn't. He had forgotten she existed. He didn't even glance at her as he went down the hall and stairs. Cleo would fetch her now. Cleo would bring her out of this dark corridor.

Minutes passed, then an hour, and another.

Cleo didn't come out for her. Curling in the blanket and pressing against the wall, Sarah waited − as she had waited for Mama that day when Alex had come.

Cleo's head ached when she awakened with the sunlight on her face. She had drunk too much ale last night and her tongue felt swollen. She stretched out her hand, but Merrick was gone. It was like him. She wasn't going to worry about it now. After last night, how could he deny he loved her? She needed coffee. Rising, she washed her face and put on her clothes. Opening the door, she saw the child huddled in the cold hall, her blue eyes darkly shadowed.

"Oh!" Cleo said faintly. She had forgotten all about her charge. Fear and guilt attacked her. What if Mae found out she'd left her daughter in a cold dark corridor for an entire night? She picked Sarah up and carried her into the room. Her little hands were like ice, and she was so white.

"Don't tell your mama," she said tearfully. "It'll be your fault if she lets me go." She grew angry to be put in such a precarious situation, her position dependent on the silence of a child. "Why didn't you come to bed last night the way you were supposed to? Merrick told you to come back inside when he left."

"No, he didn't. He said not to move until you fetched me," Sarah whispered wretchedly, beginning to cry at Cleo's anger.

"Don't lie! I heard him! He didn't say that at all!"

Sarah cried harder, looking confused and frightened. "I'm sorry, Cleo. I'm sorry. I'm sorry." The little girl's eyes were wide and red-rimmed. "Please don't tell Merrick. Don't let him toss me off the point or feed me to the crabs like he said he would."

"Hush! Stop crying," Cleo said, calming down. "Crying doesn't do any good. Has it ever done your mama any good?" Filled with remorse, she pulled Sarah into her arms and held her. "We won't tell anyone. We'll keep it between the two of us."

Merrick didn't come back to the Four Winds, and Cleo got drunk that night. She put Sarah to bed early and went back down to the bar, hoping he would come in later. He didn't. She stayed a little longer, laughing with other men and pretending she didn't care. Then she took a bottle of rum upstairs. Sarah was sitting up in bed, wide awake, her eyes huge.

Cleo wanted to talk. She wanted to vent her spleen on Merrick. She hated him for breaking her heart again. She had let him do it to her so many times before. When would she learn to say no to him? Why had she come back? She should've known what would happen, what always happened.

"I'm going to tell you God's truth, little girl. You listen good." She took a long drink and swallowed down the tears and misery and let the bitterness and anger rise and flow. "All men want to do is use you. When you give them your heart, they tear it to shreds." She drank more, and her voice slurred. "None of 'em care. Take your fine papa. Does he care about your mother? No."

Sarah dug frantically beneath the covers and plugged her ears. So the little princess didn't want to hear the awful truth? Well, that was just too bad. Furious, Cleo dragged the blankets off her. When Sarah scrambled away, she grabbed her by the legs and dragged her back. "Sit up and listen to me!" She pulled the child up and shook her. Sarah squeezed her eyes shut and turned her face away. "Look at me!" Cleo raged, not satisfied until she obeyed.

Sarah stared at her with wide frightened eyes. She trembled violently. Cleo eased her grip. "Your mama told me to take good care of you," she said. "Well, I am going to take care of you. I'm going to tell you God's truth. You listen and you learn." She let go and Sarah sat very still.

Glaring at the little girl, Cleo dropped into the chair by the window and took another swig of rum. She pointed, trying to steady her hand. "Your fine papa doesn't care about anyone, least of all you. And all he cares about your mother is what she's willing to give him. And she gives him everything. He shows up when he pleases, uses her, then rides off to his fine house in town with his aristocratic wife and well-bred children. And your mother? She lives for the next time she'll see him."

She watched Sarah inch back until she was pressed tightly against the peeling wall. As though that would protect her. Nothing protected a woman from the cold hard facts. Cleo gave a sad laugh and shook her head.

"She's such a sweet stupid fool. She waits for him and falls on her face to kiss his feet when he comes back. You know why he went away for so long? Because of you. He can't stand the sight of his own spawn. Your mama cries and begs, and what good's it ever done her? Sooner or later, he's going to get tired of her and toss her into the trash. And you with her. That's the one thing you can count on."

Sarah was crying now, and she reached up to wipe tears from her cheeks.

"Nobody cares about anybody in this world," Cleo said, feeling sadder and more morose by the second. "We all just use each other in one way or another. To feel good. To feel bad. To feel nothing at all. The lucky ones are real good at it. Like Merrick. Like your rich papa. The rest of us just take what we can get."

Cleo was having trouble thinking straight. She wanted to keep talking, but her eyelids were so heavy she couldn't keep them open. She sank lower into her chair and rested her chin on her chest.

All she needed was to rest for a minute. That was all. Then everything would be better....

Sarah watched as Cleo kept mumbling, sagging deeper into the chair, until she went to sleep. She slept loudly, spittle dripping from the corner of her sagging mouth.

Sarah sat in the rumpled bed, shivering and wondering if Cleo was right. But deep inside of her, something told her she was. If her father cared, would he have wanted her dead? If Mama cared, would she have sent her away?

God's truth. What was God's truth?

They left the next morning. Sarah never once glimpsed the sea.

When they arrived home, Mama pretended everything was fine, but Sarah knew something was terribly wrong. There were boxes out, and Mama was packing her things.

"We're going to visit your grandmother and grandfather," Mama said brightly, but her eyes looked dull and dead. "They've never seen you." She told Cleo she was sorry to dismiss her, and Cleo said that was fine. She had decided to marry Bob, the butcher, after all. Mama said she hoped Cleo would be very happy, and Cleo went away.

Sarah awakened in the middle of the night. Mama wasn't in the bed, but Sarah could hear her. She followed the sound of her mother's stricken voice and went into the parlor. The window was open, and she went to look out. What was Mama doing outside in the middle of the night?

Moonlight flowed over the flower garden and Sarah saw her mother kneeling in her thin white nightgown. She was ripping all the flowers out. Handful after handful, she yanked the plants up and flung them in all directions, weeping and talking to herself as she did. She picked up a knife and came to her feet. She went down again on her knees beside her beloved rose bushes. One after another, she cut the roots. Every last one of them.

Then she bent forward and sobbed, rocking herself back and forth, back and forth, the knife still in her hand.

Sarah sank down onto the floor inside and hid in the darkness of the parlor, her hands covering her head.

They rode in a coach all the next day and slept that night in an inn. Mama said little, and Sarah held her doll pressed tightly against her chest. There was one bed in the room, and Sarah slept contentedly in her mother's arms. When she awakened in the morning, Mama was sitting at the window and running the rosary beads through her fingers as she prayed. Sarah listened, not understanding, as her mother repeated the same phrases over and over.

"Forgive me, Jesus. I did it to myself. Mea culpa, mea culpa..."

They rode another day in another coach and came to a town. Mama was tense and pale. She brushed Sarah off and straightened her hat. She took Sarah's hand, and they walked a long, long time until they reached a tree-lined street.

Mama came to a white fence and stopped at the gate. "Lord, please, please, let them forgive me," she whispered. "Oh, please, God."

Sarah looked at the house before her. It was not much bigger than the cottage, but it had a nice porch and pots of flowers on the window sills. Lace curtains hung in all the windows. She liked it very much.

When they reached the door, Mama took a deep breath and knocked. A woman came to answer. She was small and gray and wore a flowered gingham dress covered by a white apron. She stared and stared at Mama and her blue eyes filled with tears. "Oh," she said. "Oh. *Oh...*"

"I've come home, Mother," Mama said. "Please. Let me come home."

"It's not that easy. You know it's not that easy."

"I've nowhere else to go."

The lady looked at Sarah. "I don't have to ask if this is your child," she said with a sad smile. "She's very beautiful."

"Please, Mama."

The lady opened the door and let them in. She showed them into a small room with lots of books. "Wait here and I'll speak with your father," she said and went away. Mama paced, wringing her hands. She paused once and closed her eyes, her lips moving. The lady came back, her face white and lined, her cheeks wet. "No," she said. One word. That was all. No.

Mama took a step toward the door, and the lady stopped her. "He'll only say things that will hurt you more."

"Hurt? How could I be hurt more, Mama?"

"Mae, please, don't…"

"I'll beg. I'll get down on my knees. I'll tell him he was right. He was right."

"It won't do any good. He said as far as he's concerned his daughter is dead."

Mae swept past her. "I'm not dead!" The lady gestured for Sarah to stay in the room. She hastened after Mama, closing the door as she left. Sarah waited, hearing distant voices.

Mama came back after a while. Her face was white, but she wasn't crying anymore. "Come on, darling," she said in a dull tone. "We're leaving."

"Mae," the lady said. "Oh, Mae…" She pressed something into her hand. "It's all I have."

Mama didn't say anything. A man's voice came from another room, an angry, demanding voice. "I have to go," the lady said. Mama nodded and turned away.

When they reached the end of the tree-lined street, Mae opened her hand and looked at the money her mother had placed in it. She gave a soft broken laugh. After a moment, she took Sarah's hand and walked on, tears streaming down her cheeks.

Mama sold her ruby ring and pearls. She and Sarah lived in an inn until the money gave out. Mama sold her music box, and for a while they lived quite comfortably in an inexpensive boarding-house. Finally, she asked Sarah to give back the crystal swan, and with the money they got for it, they lived a long time in a run-down hotel before Mama found and settled them for good in a shack near the docks of New York.

Sarah finally saw the sea. There was garbage floating in it. But still she liked it very much.

Sometimes she would go down and sit on the wharf. She liked the salt smell and the ships coming in loaded with cargo. She liked the sounds of the water lapping at the pillars beneath her and the seagulls overhead.

There were rough men at the docks and sailors who came from around the world. Some came to visit, and Mama would ask

Sarah to wait outside until they left. They never stayed very long. Sometimes they pinched her cheek and said they would come back when she got a little bigger. Some said she was prettier than Mama, but Sarah knew that wasn't true.

She didn't like them. Mama laughed when they came and acted as though she were happy to see them. But when they went away, she cried and drank whiskey until she fell asleep in the rumpled bed by the window.

At seven years old, Sarah wondered if Cleo hadn't been partly right about God's truth.

Then Uncle Rab came to live with them, and things got better. Not as many men came to visit, though they still did when Uncle Rab didn't have any coins to jingle in his pockets. He was big and dull, and Mama treated him with affection. They slept together in the bed by the window, and Sarah had the cot on the floor.

"He's not too bright," Mama said to her, "but he has a kind heart and he tries to provide for us. Times are hard, darling, and sometimes he can't. He needs Mama's help."

Sometimes he just wanted to sit outside the door and get drunk and sing songs about women.

When it rained, he would go to the inn down the road to be with his friends. Mama would drink and sleep. To pass the time, Sarah found tin cans and washed them until they shone like silver. She set them beneath the roof leaks. Then she would sit in the quiet shack with the rain beating down and listen to the music the drops made plinking into the tins.

Cleo had been right about crying, too. Crying did no good. Mama cried and cried until Sarah wanted to cover her ears and never hear her again. All Mama's crying never changed anything.

When the other children mocked Sarah and called her mother names, she looked at them and said nothing. What they said was true; you couldn't argue with it. When she felt the tears coming up, building like a great hard pressure inside her, hot, so hot she thought they would burn, she swallowed them down deeper and deeper until they became a hard little stone in her chest. She learned to look back at her tormentors and smile with cold arrogance and disdain. She learned to pretend nothing they said could touch her. And sometimes she convinced herself nothing did.

The winter Sarah was eight, Mama became ill. She didn't want a doctor. She said all she needed was rest. But she kept getting worse, her breathing more labored. "Take care of my little girl, Rab," Mama said. She smiled the way she had long ago.

She died in the morning, the first sunlight of spring on her face and her rosary beads in her dead-white hands. Rab wept violently, but Sarah had no tears. The heaviness inside her seemed almost too great to bear. When Rab went out for a while, she lay down beside Mama and put her arms around her.

Mama was so cold and stiff. Sarah wanted to warm her. Sarah's eyes felt gritty and hot. She closed them and whispered over and over, "Wake up, Mama. Wake up. Please, wake up." When she didn't, Sarah couldn't stop the tears. "I want to go with you. Take me, too. God, please, I want to go with my mama." She wept until exhaustion overtook her and only awakened when Rab lifted her away from the bed. Men were with him.

Sarah saw they meant to handle Mama and she screamed at them to leave her alone. Rab held her tight, almost smothering her in his foul-smelling shirt, while the others began wrapping Mama in a sheet. Sarah went silent when she saw what they had done. Rab let her go, and she sat down hard on the floor and didn't move.

The men talked as though she weren't there. Maybe she wasn't anymore. Maybe she was different, the way Mama once said.

"I bet Mae was real pretty once," one said as he began sewing the shroud closed over Mama's face.

"She's better off dead," Rab said, crying again. "At least now she's not unhappy. She's free."

*Free,* Sarah thought. *Free of me. If I hadn't been born, Mama would live in a nice cottage in the country with flowers all around. Mama would be happy. Mama would be alive.*

"Wait a minute," said one, and pried the rosary from Mama's fingers and dropped it in Sarah's lap. "I bet she woulda wanted you to have that, honey." He finished the stitching while Sarah ran the beads through her cold fingers and stared at nothing.

They all went away, Mama with them. Sarah sat alone for a long time wondering if Rab would keep his promise to take care of her. When night came and he didn't come back, Sarah went down to the docks and flung the rosary into a garbage scow. "What good are you?" she cried out to the heavens.

No answer came.

She remembered Mama's going to the big church and talking to the man in black. He talked a long time, and Mama had listened, her head bowed, tears running down her cheeks. Mama never went back, but sometimes she would still sift the beads through her slender fingers while the rain spat on the window.

"What good are you?!" Sarah screamed again. "Tell me!" A sailor looked at her oddly as he passed by.

Rab didn't come back for two days and when he did, he was so drunk he didn't remember who she was. She sat cross-legged with her back to the fire, looking at him. He was maudlin, sloppy tears running down his bearded cheeks. Every time he raised the half-empty bottle by its neck, she watched his Adam's apple bob. After a while, he fell over and snored, the rest of the whiskey running through the cracks in the floor. Sarah put the blanket over him and sat beside him. "It's all right, Rab. I'll take care of you now." She couldn't do it the way Mama did, but she would find some way.

Rain drummed against the window. She put out her tin cans and blocked her mind to everything but the sound of the drops plinking into them, making music in the cold, dull room.

She was glad, she told herself, really glad. No one would come knocking at the door. No one would bother them anymore.

Rab was guilt-ridden in the morning. He cried again. "I gotta keep my promise to Mae, else she won't rest in peace." He held his head in his hands and peered at her with bloodshot, sad eyes. "What am I going to do with you, kid? I need a drink. Bad." He looked in the cupboards and found nothing but a can of beans. He opened them and ate half, leaving the rest for her. "I'm going out awhile and think things through. Gotta talk to a few friends. Maybe they can help."

Sarah lay on the bed and pressed Mama's pillow against her face, comforting herself with the lingering scent of her mother.

She waited for Rab to come back. As the hours passed, the trembling started deep inside her.

It was cold; snow was falling. She lit the fire and ate the beans. Shivering, she dragged a blanket from the bed and wrapped herself in it. She sat as close to the grate as she could.

The sun was going down, and the silence was like death. Everything slowed inside her and she thought if she closed her eyes and relaxed, she could stop breathing and die. She tried to concentrate on that, but she heard a man's voice, talking and excited. It was Rab.

"You'll be pleased. I swear. She's a good kid. Looks like Mae. Pretty. Real pretty. And smart."

She was relieved when he opened the door. He wasn't drunk, just lightly in his cups, his eyes bright and merry. He was smiling for the first time in weeks. "Everything's going to be fine now, kid," he said and brought another man into the shack with him.

The stranger was built like the stevedores on the pier, and his eyes were hard. He looked at her and she drew back. "Stand up," Rab said, helping her. "This gent's come to meet you. He works for a man who wants to adopt a little girl."

Sarah didn't know what Rab was talking about, but she knew she didn't like the man who had come with him. He came toward her, and she tried to move behind Rab, but Rab held her in front of him. The stranger cupped her chin and lifted her face, turning it from side to side to study her. When he let go, he took up a handful of her blonde hair and rubbed it between his fingers.

"Nice," he said and smiled. "Real nice. He'll like this one."

Her heart drummed wildly. She looked up at Rab, but he sensed nothing wrong.

"She looks like her mother," Rab said, his voice breaking.

"She's thin and dirty."

"We're poor," Rab said piteously.

Taking some bills from his pocket, the man peeled off two and handed them to Rab. "Clean her up and get her some decent clothes. Then bring her here." He gave him an address and left.

Rab whooped. "Things're lookin' up for you, kid," he said, grinning. "Didn't I promise your mama I'd take good care of you?" He took her hand and walked her quickly to another shack several blocks away. A woman in a thin wrapper answered his knock. Her curly brown hair fell about her pale shoulders and she had circles beneath her hazel eyes.

"I need your help, Stella." After he explained all, she frowned and chewed on her lower lip.

"You sure about this, Rab? You weren't just drunk, were you? It don't sound right somehow. Didn't he give a name or nothin'?"

"I didn't ask him, but I know who he works for. Radley told me. The gent who wants to adopt her is rich as Midas and way up in government."

"Then why's he looking on the docks for a daughter?"

"It don't matter, does it? It's the best chance she's got, and I promised Mae." His voice trembled with tears.

Stella looked at him sadly. "Don't cry, Rab. I'll fix the kid up real pretty. You go get yourself a drink and come back later. She'll be all ready for you." He went, and Stella rummaged through her wardrobe until she found something soft and pink. "I'll be right back," she said and took a bucket to get water. When she came back, she warmed some in a pot. "Now, you wash good. No man wants a dirty girl." Sarah did what she was told, fear growing in her belly.

Stella washed her hair with the rest of the water. "You've the prettiest hair I ever did see. It's just like sunshine. And you've got pretty blue eyes, too."

The woman altered the pink shirtwaist and braided Sarah's hair with blue ribbons. Sarah remembered Mama doing the same thing when they lived at the country cottage. Or had she dreamed that time? Stella put pink paint on Sarah's cold cheeks and lips and rubbed it in gently. "You're so pale. Don't be scared, sweetie. Who'd hurt a pretty little angel like you?"

Rab came back the next day, drunk and no coins jingling in his pocket. His eyes were wide, blank, and full of confused pain. "Hello, kid. I guess this is it, huh?"

She hugged him tightly. "Don't send me away, Rab. Keep me with you. You be my father."

"Yeah? And what am I going to do with a kid, huh?" He pried her loose and looked down at her with a sad smile. "I got enough problems."

"You won't have to do anything. I can take care of myself. I can take care of you."

"How you gonna do that? You ain't old enough to do nothing worth money. You going to steal like me? No. You move in with Money-Pockets and have the good life. Now, come on."

They walked a long time. It was getting dark. Sarah was afraid of the shadows and clung tightly to Rab's hand. They passed saloons filled with loud music and shouting and singing. They went down streets lined with houses, big fancy houses, the likes of which she had never seen before. The lit windows looked like great glowing eyes following her every movement. She didn't belong, and they knew it and wanted her gone. Shivering, Sarah hung close to Rab's side as he asked men directions, showing them the slip of wrinkled paper.

Sarah's legs ached and her stomach growled. Rab stopped and looked up at the big house flanked by others that were similar. "Ain't this a grand place!" He stared in awe.

No flowers. Stone. Cold. Dark. Sarah was too exhausted to care and sat down on the bottom step, miserable, wishing she were back in the shack by the docks with the smell of the sea drifting in on the tide.

"Come on, kid. Couple more steps and you're home," Rab said, pulling her up. She stared fearfully at the huge brass lion head that was on the door. Rab took the ring that was held in its bared fangs and banged it against the door. "Fancy," he said.

A man in a dark suit opened the door and gave Rab a derisive lookover. Rab handed him the paper before he could close the door in his face. The man studied it, then opened the door wide enough for them to enter. "This way," he said coolly.

Inside it was warm and smelled sweet. A wide room opened before Sarah, and in it lay a glorious flowered carpet on a shining wood floor. Above were sparkling jewel lights. She had never seen anything so fine. *Heaven must be something like this,* she thought wonderingly.

A red-haired woman with dark eyes and a full, red mouth came to greet them. She was wearing a beautiful black dress with jet beads winking over her shoulders and full breasts. She looked down at Sarah and frowned slightly. Her eyes flashed at Rab and then met Sarah's again more gently. She bent and extended her hand. "My name is Sally. What's yours, honey?"

Sarah just looked at her and drew back behind Rab.

"She's shy," Rab said apologetically. "Don't mind her."

Sally straightened and looked at him with hard eyes. "You sure you know what you're doing, mister?"

"Sure, I know. This is some place you got here, ma'am. Nothing like the dump we've been living in."

"Up the stairs to your right," Sally said in a dull voice. "First door on the left. Wait there." She reached out before Rab took two steps and stopped him. "Unless you're smart and take my advice. Leave now. Take her home."

"Why would I want to do that?"

"You won't see her again after tonight."

He shrugged. "She ain't mine anyway. Is he here? The big man, I mean."

"He will be shortly, and you'll keep your mouth shut if you've any sense in your head."

Rab headed for the stairs. Sarah wanted to run back out the door, but he had a firm hold on her hand. She looked back and saw the woman in black watching her. She had a pained look on her face.

Everything in the upstairs room was big: the mahogany highboy, the red brick fireplace, the teak desk, the brass bed. A white marble washstand stood in the corner, along with a brass towel rack polished so fine it looked like real gold. All the lamps had jeweled tassels, and the drapes on the windows were blood-red. They were closed tightly so no one could see in. Or out.

"Sit over there and rest, kid," Rab said, patting her back and pointing toward a wing chair. It was exactly like the one Mama used to sit in at the country cottage. Sarah's heart suddenly started to race. Could it be the same one?

What if her father had been sorry? What if he had been

looking for Mama and her all this time and had found out where she was and what had happened? What if he was sorry about all the awful things he had said and wanted her after all? Her heart beat faster and faster as hope and dreams built of desperation and fear filled her.

Rab went to a table near the window. "Will you look at this?" He ran his fingers lovingly over a set of crystal bottles. He took the stopper out of one and sniffed the amber fluid inside. "Oh, my..." With a sigh, he brought it to his lips and tipped it. Gulping half of what was inside, he wiped his mouth with the back of his sleeve. "Closest I'll ever get to heaven." He took the stopper from another and poured a little into the one from which he had drunk. He held them up to see if they were even again, then put them down carefully and fitted the stoppers in place.

He opened the armoire and went through it, tucking something in his pocket. Then he went to the desk and went through it as well, tucking more things into his pockets.

Sarah heard faint laughter. Her eyes were heavy and she rested her head against the wing of the chair. When would her father come? Rab went back to the glass bottles and drank from another two.

"Enjoying my brandy?" came a deep, low voice.

Sarah glanced up in surprise. She stared, her heart sinking. It wasn't her father at all. It was a tall, dark stranger. His eyes glittered, and she thought she had never seen a face so cold, nor so handsome. He was dressed all in black and wore a shiny hat.

Rab shoved a stopper back into the crystal decanter and put it back on the silver tray. "Haven't had anything so fine in a long time," he said. Sarah noticed how his face paled as the man stared at him with those strange eyes. Rab cleared his throat and shifted. He seemed nervous.

The man took off his hat and placed it on the desk. Then he took off his gloves and dropped them into it.

Sarah was so fascinated by the man that she failed at first to notice the other man standing just behind him. She blinked in surprise. It was the same man who had come to the docks and looked her over. She pressed back against the chair. The second man was watching Rab, and his eyes reminded her of the rats in the alley behind the shack. She looked at the fine gentleman and found him looking at her with a faint smile. But somehow that smile didn't make her feel better. It made her insides shiver. Why was he looking at her like that, as though he were hungry and she was something he wanted to eat?

"What's her name?" he asked without taking his eyes from her.

Rab's mouth opened slightly and he looked dumbfounded. "I dunno." He gave an uneasy, befuddled laugh, clearly drunk.

"What did her mother call her?" the man said dryly.

"'Darlin'…, but you can call her whatever you like."

The man gave a short, humorless laugh and dismissed Rab with a contemptuous glance. He studied Sarah carefully. She was scared, so scared she couldn't move when he walked toward her. He smiled again when he stopped, his eyes shining oddly. He took a wad of bills from his pants pocket and removed a gold clip. He counted out several and held them out to Rab without even looking at him.

Rab took them eagerly, counting them again before he stuffed them into his pocket. "Thank you, sir. Oh, my, when old Radley told me it was you lookin' for a daughter, I couldn't believe the kid's luck. And she ain't had much in her life, I can tell you." He rattled on, saying the gentleman's name twice, too drunk and too stupid to see the change in the man's face.

But Sarah saw.

He was furious, but more than that. He looked…. Sarah shivered again. She wasn't sure how he looked, but it wasn't good. She glanced at Rab, feeling panic build inside her again. He rambled on, trying to flatter and cajole the man standing before her, not even noticing the subtle signal being passed from the gentleman to the man behind Rab. A scream tore at Sarah's throat, but it didn't come out. It couldn't. Her voice was as frozen in terror as the rest of her. She watched in horror as Rab kept talking. He didn't stop until the black cord was looped around his neck. His eyes bugged. Choking, he clawed at his neck, drawing his own blood with his dirty fingernails.

Sarah bolted from her chair and ran to the door. She twisted and pulled at the knob trying to escape, but the door wouldn't open. She heard Rab strangling, his feet kicking and scraping as he struggled. She pounded her fists on the wood and screamed.

A hard hand clamped over her mouth and yanked her away from the door. She kicked and bit and fought – and gained absolutely nothing. The man's body was stone, and he caught hold of her arms and held them pinned painfully tight with one hand while the other clamped harder over her mouth.

Rab was silent.

"Carry him out of here," the man holding her said, and she got a glimpse of Rab on the floor, the black cord still around his neck, his face grotesquely distorted. The man who had come to the shack unloosed the cord and slipped it back into his pocket. Pulling Rab up, he draped him over his shoulder.

"Everyone will think he's drunk."

"Before you dump him in the river, go through his pockets and bring back whatever he stole from me," the cold voice said from above her.

"Yes, sir."

Sarah heard the door open and close.

When the man let go of her, she ran to the farthest corner of the room and cowered there. He stood in the middle of the room looking at her for a long time. Then he went to the marble stand and poured water into the porcelain bowl. He wrung out a white cloth and walked toward her. She pressed back as far as she could. He hunkered down and grasped her chin.

"You're much too pretty for paint," he said and began to wash her face.

She shuddered violently at his touch. She looked at the place where Rab had lain. The man tipped her chin back.

"I don't think that drunken lout was your father. You don't look anything like him, and there's intelligence in your eyes." He finished washing the rouge from her cheeks and mouth and tossed the cloth aside. "Look at me, little one."

When Sarah did, her heart pounded until her whole body shook with terror.

He held her face so she couldn't look away. "As long as you do exactly what I tell you to do, we're going to get along fine." He smiled faintly and stroked her cheek, his eyes glowing strangely. "What's your name?"

Sarah couldn't answer.

He touched her hair, her throat, her arm. "It doesn't matter. I think I'm going to call you Angel." Straightening, he took her hand. "Come on now, Angel. I have things to teach you." He lifted her and sat her on the big bed. "You can call me Duke, when you get your tongue back." He took off his black silk coat. "Which you will. Shortly." He smiled again as he removed his tie and slowly began to unbutton his shirt.

And by morning, Sarah knew that Cleo had told her God's truth about everything.

# Defiance

# *One*

*But strength alone, though of the Muses born,*
*Is like a fallen angel: trees uptorn,*
*Darkness, and worms, and shrouds, and sepulchres*
*Delight it; for it feeds upon the burrs*
*And thorns of life; forgetting the great end*
*Of poesy, that it should be a friend*
*To soothe the cares, and lift the thoughts of man.*

KEATS

CALIFORNIA, 1850

Angel pushed the canvas flap back just enough to look out at the mud street. She shivered in the cold afternoon air, that carried with it the stench of disenchantment.

Pair-a-Dice lay in the Mother Lode of California. It was the worst place she could have imagined, a shanty town of golden dreams built out of rotting sails from abandoned ships; a camp inhabited by outcasts and aristocrats, the displaced and dispossessed, the once-pampered and now-profane. Canvas-roofed bars and gambling houses lined mean streets ruled by unmasked depravity and greed, loneliness and grand illusions. Pair-a-Dice was wild jubilation. It wed black despair with fear and the foul taste of failure.

Smiling cynically, Angel saw on one corner a man preaching salvation while on the other his brother, hat in hand, fleeced the godforsaken. Everywhere she looked, there were desperate men, exiled from home and family, seeking escape from the purgatory forged by their own decaying hopes for a future.

These same fools called her a Cyprian and sought solace where they were most assured of finding none – from her. They drew lots for her favors, four ounces of gold, payable in advance to the Duchess, madam of the Palace, the tent brothel where she lived. Any comer could have Angel for one half-hour. Her own meager percentage would be kept under lock and key and guarded by a woman-hating giant named Magowan. As for the rest – those sad unfortunates who lacked the price to sample her talents – they stood knee-deep in a sea of mud called Main Street, waiting for a chance glimpse of "the Angel." And she lived a year in a month in this place that was unfit for anything but business. When would it end? How had all her desperate plans brought her here, to this horrible place of dirt and broken dreams?

"No more right now," the Duchess was saying, ushering several men away. "I know you've been waiting, but Angel's tired, and you want her best, don't you?" Men complained and threatened, pleaded and bargained, but the Duchess knew when Angel had reached the limit of her endurance. "She needs a rest. Come back this evening. Drinks on the house."

Relieved that they were gone, Angel let go of the tent flap and went back to lie on the rumpled bed. She stared bleakly at the canvas ceiling. The Duchess had announced this morning at breakfast that the new building was almost finished and the girls would be moving in tomorrow. Angel was ready to have four walls around her again. At least then the cold night wind would not blow in on her through splits in the rotting sailcloth. She hadn't thought how much four walls meant to her when she paid passage on a barkentine destined for California. Then, all she had been thinking was escape. All she had seen was her chance for freedom. The mirage had dissolved soon enough when she reached the gangplank and learned she was one of three women aboard a ship with 120 vigorous young men, all of whom had nothing on their minds but adventure. The two hard-eyed prostitutes set to work right away, but Angel had tried to stay in her cabin. Within a fortnight, she saw clearly that she had one simple choice: go back to being a prostitute or be raped. What did it really matter anyway? What else did she know? She might as well line her pockets with gold like the others. Maybe then, just maybe, with enough money she could buy freedom.

She survived the rough seas, the foul-tasting lobscouse and hushamagrundy, the cramped quarters, and lack of dignity and decency in the hope that she would have enough money by the time she reached the shores of California to start a new life. Then, amid the excitement of docking, the final blow was struck.

The two other prostitutes set upon her in her cabin. By the time she regained consciousness, they were ashore with all her money and every possession she owned. All that was left to her was the clothes on her back. What was worse, not even one sailor remained aboard to row her ashore.

Beaten and numb with confusion, she sat huddled in the bow of the ship for two days before scavengers came. When they finished taking what they wanted from the deserted ship and her, they brought her to the dock. It was raining hard, and while they argued and divided their booty, she simply walked away.

She wandered for several days, hiding her face and hair beneath a soiled blanket one of the men had given her. She was hungry; she was cold; and she was resigned. Freedom was a dream.

She made her way by working Portsmouth Square until the Duchess, a woman well past her prime but possessed of a shrewd mind for business, found her and talked her into heading for the gold country.

"I've got four other girls, a Frenchie from Paris, a Celestial Ah Toy sold me, and two girls who look like they came off an empty potato boat from Ireland. A little food will fatten 'em up. Ah, but now, you. First time I saw you, I thought there's a girl who can get rich with the right management. A girl with your beauty could make her fortune up there in the gold camps. Those young miners will take the gold out of the stream and fight each other to put it right in your hand."

On an agreement that Angel would turn over eighty percent of her earnings, the Duchess promised to see that she was protected from bodily harm. "And I'll see you have the best clothing, food, and lodgings available."

Angel found the irony laughable. She had fled from Duke and fallen into the hands of Duchess. Just her luck.

For all her seeming benevolence, Duchess was a greedy tyrant. Angel knew she collected bribes to fix the lots, while not a speck of that gold dust found its way into the girls' pouches. The tips left for services well-rendered were divided according to the original agreement. Mai Ling, Ah Toy's Celestial slave girl, tried to hide her gold once, and Magowan – with his cruel smile and ham-sized hands – was sent in to "have a talk with her."

Angel hated her life. She hated the Duchess. She hated Magowan. She hated her own wretched helplessness. Most of all she hated the men for their relentless quest for pleasure. She gave them her body but not a particle more. Maybe there wasn't any more. She didn't know. And that didn't seem to matter to any of the men. All they saw was her beauty, a flawless veil wrapped around a frozen heart, and they were enthralled. They looked into her angel eyes and were lost.

She was not fooled by their endless declarations of love. They wanted her in the same way they wanted the gold in the streams. They lusted for her. They fought for the chance to be with her. They scrambled, grappled, gambled, and grabbed – and everything they had was spent without thought or consideration. They paid to become enslaved. She gave them what they thought was heaven and consigned them to hell.

What did it matter? She had nothing left. She didn't care. An even stronger force than the hatred that feasted on her was the weariness that sucked her soul dry. At eighteen, she was tired of living and resigned to the fact that nothing would ever change. She wondered why she had even been born. For this, she supposed. Take it or leave it. God's truth. And the only way to leave it was to kill herself. Every time she faced that fact, every time she had the chance, her courage failed.

Her only friend was a tired old harlot named Lucky, who was running to fat because of her thirst for brandy. Yet even Lucky knew nothing of where Angel had come from or been, or what had happened to make her the way she was. The other prostitutes thought of her as invulnerable. They all wondered about her, but they never asked questions. Angel made it clearly understood from the beginning that the past was sacred ground no one walked over. Except for Lucky, dumb-drunk Lucky for whom Angel held a fondness.

Lucky spent her off time deep in her cups. "You gotta have plans, Angel. You gotta hope for something in this world."

"Hope for what?"

"You can't get by any other way."

"I get by just fine."

"How?"

"I don't look back, and I don't look forward."

"What about *now*? You gotta think about now, Angel."

Angel smiled faintly and brushed her long, golden hair. "Now doesn't exist."

# *Two*

*She walks in beauty, like the night*
*Of cloudless climes and starry skies;*
*And all that's best of dark and bright*
*Meet in her aspect and her eyes.*

BYRON

Michael Hosea was unloading crates of vegetables from the back of his buckboard when he saw a beautiful young woman walking along the street. She was dressed in black, like a widow, and a big, rough-looking man with a gun on his hip was at her side. All along Main Street, men stopped what they were doing, took off their hats, and watched her. She said not a word to anyone. She looked neither to the right nor the left. She moved with simple, fluid grace, her shoulders straight, her head held high.

Michael couldn't take his eyes off her. His heart beat faster and faster as she came near. He willed her to look at him, but she didn't. He let out his breath after she passed him, not even aware that he had been holding it.

**This one, beloved.**

Michael felt a rush of adrenaline mingled with joy. *Lord. Lord!*

"Something, ain't she?" Joseph Hochschild said. The burly storekeeper held a sack of potatoes over his shoulder and grinned. "That's Angel. Prettiest girl west of the Rockies and most likely prettiest east of the Rockies, too." He went up the steps into his store.

Michael shouldered a barrel of apples. "What do you know about her?"

"No more than anyone else, I guess. She takes long walks. It's a habit of hers. Does it every Monday, Wednesday, and Friday afternoon about this same time." He nodded toward the men along the street. "They all come to watch her."

"Who's the man with her?" A dismal thought occurred to him. "Her husband?"

"Husband?" He laughed. "More like a bodyguard. His name's Magowan. He makes certain nobody bothers her. No one gets within a foot of her unless they've paid their dues."

Michael frowned slightly and went back outside. He stood at the back of his wagon, staring after her. She caught at something deep inside him. There was a grave, tragic dignity about her. As the storekeeper hefted another crate, Michael asked the question burning inside him. "How do I meet her, Joseph?"

Hochschild smiled ruefully. "You have to get in line. The Duchess holds a regular lottery to see who'll have the privilege of seeing Angel."

"What Duchess?"

"The Duchess down there." He nodded down the street in the other direction. "The one who owns the Palace, the biggest brothel in Pair-a-Dice."

Michael felt as though he had been kicked low and hard. He stared at Hochschild, but the man didn't even notice as he toted a crate of carrots inside and upended it into a bin. Michael shouldered another barrel of apples.

*Lord? Did I misunderstand? I must've. This can't be the one.*

"I've put up the ounce of gold a time or two to get my name in a hat," Joseph said over his shoulder. "That was before I found out it took more than that just to get your name in the right hat."

Michael banged the barrel down hard. "She's a soiled dove? A girl like that?" He didn't want to believe it.

"She's not just any old soiled dove, Michael. Angel is something real fine, from what I hear. Special training. But I can't afford to find out for myself. When I've a need, I see Priss. She's clean, does things plain and simple, and she doesn't cost too much hard-earned gold."

Michael needed some air. He went back outside. Unable to help himself, he glanced down the street again at the slender girl in black. She was coming back down the other side of the street and went right past him again. His reaction was worse this time, harder to take.

Hochschild unloaded a crate of turnips. "You look like a bull who just had a club put to his head." His smile was wry. "Or maybe you've been down on your farm too long."

"Let's settle up," Michael said tersely and went inside with the last crate. He needed to get his mind back on business and off of her.

"You'll have enough gold to meet her once we square up," Hochschild said. "More than enough." He emptied the crate and set it aside before putting his scale on the counter. "Fresh vegetables are worth a fortune up here. These young gents get up on the streams and live on little better than flour, water, and salted meat. Then they come into town with swollen, bleeding gums and swelling legs from scurvy and think they need a doctor. All they need is a decent diet and a little common sense. Let's see what we got here. Two barrels of apples, two crates each of turnips and carrots, six crates of squash, and twenty pounds of venison jerky."

Michael told him what he wanted for the wagon load.

"What?! You're robbing me."

Michael smiled slightly. He wasn't green. He had spent the better part of '48 and '49 panning gold and knew what the men needed. True, food was only part of it, but it was a part he could supply. "You'll make twice that."

Hochschild opened the safe behind the counter and took out two sacks of gold dust. He slid one across to Michael and measured a portion out of the other into a hide pouch. Tossing the bigger sack back into the safe, he kicked it shut and checked the handle.

Michael emptied the dust into a belt he had crafted. Hochschild watched, his mouth tipping. "You've got enough for a good time there. Wanna meet Angel? You ought to go down and talk to the Duchess with some of it. She'd usher you right upstairs."

Angel. Just her name affected him. "Not this time."

Joseph saw the set of his jaw and nodded. Michael Hosea was a quiet man, but there wasn't anything soft about him. There was something in his look that made men treat him with respect. It wasn't just his height or the strength of his body, which were both impressive enough. It was the clear steadiness of his gaze. He knew what he was about even if the rest of the world didn't. Joseph liked him, and he had seen clearly enough the effect Angel had on him, but if Michael didn't want to discuss it, he would respect that. "What're you planning to do with all that gold dust?"

"I'm going to buy a couple head of cattle."

"Good," Hochschild said in approval. "Breed 'em fast. Beef is worth more than vegetables."

On his way out of town, Michael drove by the brothel. It was big and fancy. The place was overflowing with men – mostly young, some bewhiskered and some smooth-cheeked – nearly all drunk or well on their way to being so. Someone was fiddling, and men were making up bawdy verses to the tune, each cruder than the last.

*And she lives there,* he thought. *Up in one of those rooms with a bed and little else.* He flicked the reins over his horses and kept on going, frowning heavily.

He couldn't get his mind off her, not all the rest of that day, back down out of the mother lode to his valley. He kept seeing her walking up that muddy street, a slender girl, dressed in black, with a beautiful, pale face of stone. Where had she come from?

"Angel," he said, trying her name on his tongue. Just testing. And he knew, even as he said it, his waiting was over.

"Lord," he said heavily. "Lord, this isn't exactly what I had in mind."

But he knew he was going to marry that girl anyway.

# Three

*I can endure my own despair, but not another's hope.*
WILLIAM WALSH

Angel washed, put on a clean, blue silk wrapper, and sat on the foot of the bed to wait for the next knock on her door. Two more and she could call it a night. She could hear Lucky's laughter in the next room. Lucky was full of laughter and fun when she was drunk, which was most of the time. The woman could lose herself in a bottle of whiskey.

Angel had tried drinking with her once to see if she could lose herself, too. Lucky poured and she tried to keep up. Before long, her head swam and her stomach lurched. Lucky held the chamber pot for her and laughed with sympathy. She said some people could hold their whiskey and some couldn't, and she guessed Angel was one who couldn't. She took her back to her room and told her to sleep.

That night, when the first man had come knocking at the door, Angel told him, in less than polite terms, to go away. Angry, he went to the Duchess and said he wanted his gold dust back. Duchess came up, took one look at Angel, then sent for Magowan.

Angel didn't like Magowan, but she had never been afraid of him. He had never bothered her. He was just there at her side when she went for her walks. He didn't say anything. He didn't do anything. He just made sure no one approached her outside the Palace. She knew it wasn't as much for her own protection as it was for the Duchess. He was there to make sure she came back.

Mai Ling never said what Magowan did to her when he had been sent to her room, but Angel saw the look of fear in the Chinese girl's dark eyes every time he was near. All he had to do was smile at her, and the girl turned white and broke out in a sweat. Angel sneered inwardly. It would take more than words to make her afraid of any man.

That night, when Magowan came in, Angel was only aware

of a dark shape standing over her. "You're not going to get your money's worth," she said. She focused. "Oh, it's you. Go 'way. I'm not going for a walk today."

He ordered her tub filled. As soon as the two servants left, he bent over her again, grinning viciously. "I knew sooner or later we'd have to have a talk." He caught hold of her. Sobering, she struggled, but he lifted her and dumped her into the icy water. Gasping, she tried to get out, but he grabbed her head and forced her under. Terrified by the iron weight of his huge hand, she fought. When her lungs burned for air and she was losing consciousness, he dragged her up. "Enough?" he said.

"Enough," she rasped, dragging in air.

He shoved her down again. She bucked and kicked, clawing for escape. When he pulled her up again, she choked and vomited. He laughed, and she knew he was enjoying it. He stood in front of her, feet planted apart, and reached for her head again. An irrational fury rose, and she swung her fist straight and sure. When he dropped to his knees, groaning, she scrambled out of his reach.

When he came after her again, she screamed. He caught hold of her. She kicked and scratched, gasping with effort. He had a hand at her throat when the door burst open and the Duchess sailed in. She slammed the door behind her and shouted at them both to stop it.

Magowan did as she commanded, but he gave Angel a malevolent look. "I'm going to kill you. I swear it."

"Enough!" the Duchess said, furious. "I heard her scream from the stairway. If the men heard, what do you think would happen?"

"They'd hang him," Angel said, crossing her legs and laughing at him.

The Duchess slapped her. Angel fell back in shock. "Not another word, Angel," the Duchess warned. Straightening, she looked at Magowan again. "I said sober her up, Bret, and have a talk with her. That's all I want you to do to her. Do you understand?" She yanked on the bell cord.

The three waited in pulsating silence. The slap had silenced Angel. She knew Duchess had barely reined in her devil. She also knew after one look at him that another foolish outburst on her part might snap his leash.

When someone knocked discreetly, Duchess opened the door enough to order hot coffee and bread. When she closed the door, she crossed the room and sat down on the straight-backed chair. "I sent you to do something very simple, Bret. You do just what I tell you and nothing more," she said. "Angel's right. They'd hang you."

"She needs a good lesson," Magowan said, eyes black on Angel. All her bravado had evaporated. She'd seen clearly enough that something dark and evil shone in Magowan's eyes. She recognized that look. She had seen it on another man's face from time to time. She had never taken Bret seriously before, but he was serious, indeed. She knew also that fear was the very last thing she could show. It would feed his blood lust until even the Duchess couldn't stop him. So she was calm and still, like a mouse in its hole.

The Duchess looked at her for a long moment. "You're going to behave now, aren't you, Angel?"

Angel sat up slowly and looked back at her with grave, sardonic eyes. "Yes, ma'am." She shivered with cold.

"Give her a sheet before she catches a chill."

Magowan snatched one from the bed and flung it at her. She wrapped the satin around herself like a royal robe and didn't dare look at him. Helpless rage and fear feasted on her.

"Come here, Angel," the Duchess said.

Angel raised her head and looked at her. When she didn't move quickly enough, Magowan grabbed a handful of blonde hair and yanked her up. She gritted her teeth, refusing him the satisfaction of crying out. "When she tells you to do something, you do it," he snarled as he shoved her.

Angel fell to her knees before Duchess.

The woman stroked her hair, and the calculated gentleness after Magowan's brutality destroyed Angel's defiance. "When the tray arrives, Angel, eat the bread and drink every last drop of the coffee. Bret will stay to see that you do. As soon as you're finished, he'll leave. I want you ready to work in two hours."

The Duchess stood and went to the door. She glanced back. "Bret, not another mark on her. She's our best girl."

"Not a mark," he echoed coldly.

He kept his word. He didn't touch her, but he talked – and what he said chilled Angel's blood. She forced the bread and coffee down, knowing the sooner she was done, the sooner he would leave.

"You're going to be mine, Angel. In a week or a month, you'll push Duchess too far or demand too much. And then she'll give you to me on a silver plate."

She had been good since that evening, and Magowan had not bothered her. But he was waiting, and she knew it. She refused to give him the satisfaction Mai Ling did. She always smiled at him mockingly when he came into the room. As long as she did what she was told, Duchess was happy, and Bret Magowan could do nothing.

But the walls were closing in again. More each day. The pressure inside her was building, and the effort to maintain the calm facade was draining her strength.

*One more tonight and I can sleep,* she thought. She held out her hands and looked at them. They were trembling. She was trembling all over. She knew she was losing control. Too much pretending for too long. She shook her head. All she needed was a good night's sleep, and she would be all right tomorrow. *Just one more,* she thought, and hoped he'd be quick.

The knock came and she rose to answer. Opening the door, she took in the man standing there. He was taller and older than most, and well-muscled. Other than that, she noticed nothing special about him. But she felt...what? An odd uneasiness. An increasing of her shakiness. Her nerves were jumping, almost out of control. She lowered her head and breathed slowly, pushing the strange reaction down with every ounce of will she had left.

*One more, and I'm free for the night.*

Despite his twenty-six years, Michael felt like a callow youth, standing outside Angel's open door in the dim lantern light of the brothel hallway. He could scarcely breathe, his heart was racing so fast. She was even more beautiful than he remembered, and smaller. Her slender body was clearly outlined in the blue satin wrapper, and he tried not to look below her shoulders.

She stepped aside so he could enter her room. All Michael saw was her bed. It was made, but visions came to him unbidden and, unnerved, he looked back at her. She smiled slightly. It was a worldly, seductive smile. She knew everything that was in his mind, even what he didn't want there. "What's your pleasure, mister?"

Her voice was low and soft and surprisingly cultured, but she was so direct, he was taken aback. She couldn't have said anything to make him more acutely aware of what she did for her living, or of his own powerful physical attraction to her.

As he entered the room, Angel closed the door behind him and leaned back against it. She waited for him to answer while making a quick assessment of him. Her uneasiness lessened. He wasn't so different from the rest. Just a little older than most, a little broader in the shoulders. He was no boy, but he looked uncomfortable, very uncomfortable. Maybe he had a wife somewhere and was feeling guilty. Maybe he had a good Christian mother and was wondering what she would think about his coming to a prostitute. This one wouldn't want to spend a lot of time with her. Good. The less time, the better.

Michael didn't know what to say. He had been thinking about seeing her all day, and now that he was here in her bedroom he stood mute, his heart beating its way up into his throat. She was so beautiful, and she looked amused. *Lord, what now? I can't even think past what I'm feeling.* She walked toward him, every movement drawing his attention to her body.

Angel touched his chest and heard him suck in his breath. She moved around him, smiling. "No need to be shy with me, mister. Tell me what you want."

He looked down at her. "You."

"I'm all yours."

Michael watched her cross the room to a washstand. Angel. The name fit the way she looked, a flawless, blue-eyed porcelain doll with pale skin and golden hair. Maybe marble was a better description. Porcelain shatters. She looked too hard for that – so hard, he hurt looking at her. Why? He hadn't expected to feel that. He had worried too much about getting past the desire he knew she would arouse in him. *God, give me strength to resist her temptation.*

She poured water into a porcelain bowl and picked up a bar of soap. Everything she did was graceful and provocative. "Why don't you come here and I'll wash you."

He could feel the heat rushing all through his body, most of it ending up in his face. He coughed and felt as though his collar were choking him.

She laughed softly. "I promise it won't hurt."

"It's not necessary, ma'am. I'm not here for sex."

"No. You're here for Bible study."

"I came here to talk with you."

Angel gritted her teeth. Hiding her irritation, she let her gaze drift boldly. He moved uneasily beneath that look. She smiled. "Are you sure you want to talk?"

"I'm sure."

He looked dead certain. With a sigh, she turned to dry her hands. "Whatever you want, mister." She sat on the bed and crossed her legs.

Michael knew what she was doing. He fought the swift desire to take her up on the clear message she kept sending him. The longer he stood silent, the more his mind drew images, and she knew it by the look in her eyes. Was she mocking him? No doubt about that.

"Do you live in this room when you're not working?"

"Yes." She tilted her head. "Where did you think I lived? In a little white cottage at the end of a road somewhere?" She smiled to take the bite from her words. She hated men who asked questions and probed.

Michael studied her surroundings. No personal articles out, no pictures on the wall, no knick-knacks on the small, lace-covered table in the corner, no feminine clothing scattered about. Everything was neat, clean, spare. A modest armoire, a side table, a kerosene lamp, a marble washstand with a yellow porcelain water pitcher, and a straight-backed chair furnished her room. And the bed on which she was sitting.

He got the chair from the corner, set it in front of her, and sat down. Her satin wrap had opened a little. He knew she was toying with him. She swung her foot idly, like a pendulum, sixty seconds to a minute, thirty minutes to a half hour. All the time he had.

*Lord, I'd need a million years to reach this woman. Are you sure this is the one you meant for me?*

Her eyes were blue and fathomless. He could read nothing in them. She was a wall, an endless ocean, a clouded night sky so dark he couldn't see his hand before his face. He saw only what she wanted him to see.

"You said you wanted to talk, mister. So talk."

Michael was saddened. "I shouldn't have come to you like this. I should've found another way."

"What other way is there?"

How was he going to make her understand he was different from the other men who came to her when he came by the same way they did? Gold. He had listened to Joseph and gone to the Duchess, and then he had listened to that woman say Angel was a commodity — a fine, precious, well-guarded commodity. Pay first, then talk. Paying had seemed the easiest, most direct way. He hadn't cared about the price. Now it was clear the easiest way wasn't the best.

He should have found another way, another place. She was too ready to work and not the least bit ready to listen. And he was finding himself too easily distracted.

"How old are you?"

She smiled slightly. "Old. Real old."

He figured that was right. She wasn't talking about years. He doubted much could surprise her. She looked prepared for anything. Yet he sensed something else about her as well, the same way he had the first time he had seen her. There was another layer beneath the one she was showing now. *Lord, how do I get to it?*

"How old are *you*?" she asked, turning his question back on him.

"Twenty-six."

"Old for a gold miner. Most are eighteen or nineteen. I haven't seen many real men lately."

Her lack of subtlety put him on firmer ground. "Why the name Angel? Because of how you look? Or is that your real name?"

Her mouth tightened slightly. The only thing she had left was her name, and she had never told anyone what it was, not even Duke. The only person who had ever called her by her name was Mama. And Mama was dead.

"Call me whatever you want, mister. It doesn't matter." Just because he didn't want what he paid for, that didn't mean she was going to give him anything else.

He studied her. "I think Mara suits you."

"Someone you knew back home?"

"No. It means bitter."

She looked at him then and went very still. What game was this? "Is that what you think?" She lifted one shoulder indolently. "Well, I suppose Mara is as good a name as any." She began to swing her foot back and forth again, ticking off the time. How long had he been here? How long did she have to put up with him?

He kept on. "Where are you from?"

"Here and there."

He smiled slightly at her polite and sultry reticence. "Any here and there in particular?"

"Just here and there," she said. Her foot stopped and she leaned forward. "What about you, mister? What's your name? You from any place in particular? Do you have a wife somewhere? Are you afraid to do what you really want?"

She was leveling all barrels at him, but rather than be taken aback, he felt himself relaxing. This girl was more real to him than the one who had greeted him at the door. "Michael Hosea," he said. "I live in a valley south-west of here, and I'm not married, but I will be soon."

She frowned uneasily. It was the way he was looking at her. The intensity unnerved her. "What sort of name is Hosea?"

His smile became wry. "Prophetic."

Was he making a joke at her expense? "Are you going to tell me my future?"

"You're going to marry me, and I'm going to take you out of here."

She laughed. "Well, my third proposal today. I'm so flattered." Shaking her head, she leaned forward again, her smile cold and cynical. Did he think this was a new approach? Did he think it was *necessary*? "When would you like me to start playing my part, mister?"

"After the ring's on your finger. Right now, I want to get to know you a little better."

She hated him for dragging the game on. The wasted time, the hypocrisy, the endless lies. It had been a long night, and she was in no mood to humor him. "What's to tell? What I do is what I am. All it comes down to is you telling me how you want me to be. But be quick. Your time's almost up."

Michael saw he had made a fine mess of this first meeting. What had he expected? To come in here, talk plain, and walk out with her on his arm? She looked like she wanted to give him the boot. He was angry at himself for being such a naive fool. "You're not talking love, Mara, and I didn't come here to use you."

The steady deepness of his words and that name – Mara – roused her anger even more. "No?" She tilted her chin. "Well, I think I understand." She stood. He was sitting and she moved close, her soft hands combing into his hair. She could feel his tension and relished it.

"Let me guess, mister. You want to get to know me. You want to find out how I think and what I feel. And most of all, you want to know how a nice girl like me got into a business like this."

Michael closed his eyes and clenched his teeth, trying to close out the effect her touch was having on him.

"Do what you're thinking about doing, mister."

Michael put her firmly away from him. "I came to talk with you."

She studied him through narrowed eyes and then yanked her wrapper closed and tied the satin ribbons. She still felt exposed beneath his scrutiny. "You came to the wrong girl. You want to know what you can have, I'll tell you." And she did, explicitly. He didn't blush this time. He didn't even react.

"I want to know *you*, not what you can do," he said roughly.

"If you want conversation, go down to the bar."

He stood. "Come away with me and be my wife."

She gave a harsh laugh. "If you want a wife, send for one by mail, or wait for the next wagon train to cross the mountains."

He came toward her. "I can give you a good life. I don't care how you got here or where you've been before. Come with me now."

She smiled derisively. "For what? More of the same? Look, I've heard it all before from a hundred others. You saw me and fell in love and now you can't live without me. You can give me a wonderful life. What a crock."

"I can."

"It all comes down to the same thing."

"No, it doesn't."

"From my point it does. A half hour is more than enough time for anyone to own me, mister."

"You're telling me this is the life you want?"

What did *want* have to do with anything? "This is my life."

"It doesn't have to be. If you had a choice, what would you want?"

"From you? Nothing."

"From living."

A bleakness settled inside her. *Living?* What was he talking about? She felt battered by his questions and defended herself with an aloof, cool smile. Spreading her hands, she showed off her simple room with its spare furnishings. "I have everything I need right here."

"You've got a roof, food, and fine clothes."

"And work," she said tightly. "Oh, don't you forget my work. I'm real good at it."

"You hate it."

She was silent a moment, wary. "You just drew me on one of my bad nights." She went to the window. Pretending to look out, she closed her eyes and fought for control. What was wrong with her this evening? What was it about this man that got to her? She preferred the numbness to this stirring of emotion. Hope was torment; Hope was an enemy. And this man was a thorn in her side.

Michael came up behind her and put his hands on her shoulders. He felt her tense at his touch. "Come home with me," he said softly. "Be my wife."

Angel shrugged his hands off angrily and moved away from him. "No, thanks."

"Why not?"

"Because I don't want to leave, that's why. Is that a good enough reason for you?"

"If you won't go with me, at least let me get a little closer."

*Finally. Here we go.* "Six steps ought to do that, mister. All you have to do is put one foot in front of the other."

"I'm not talking feet and inches, Mara."

All the feelings slowed inside her and spiraled downward as though they were draining away into a black hole beneath her feet. "Angel," she said. "My name is Angel. Have you got that? *Angel!* And you're wasting my time and your dust."

"I'm not wasting anything."

She sat on the bed again and let out her breath. Tilting her head to one side, she looked up at him. "You know, mister, most men are fairly honest when they come. They pay, take what they want, and leave. Then there are a few others, like you. They don't like being like the rest. So they tell me how much they *care* and what's wrong with my life and how they can fix it." Her mouth curved sardonically. "But eventually they all get past that and get down to what they're really after."

Michael drew in a breath. She didn't mince words. Fine. He could talk plain, too. "I only have to look at you to be made aware of my body. You know pretty well how to feed frailty. Yes, I *want* you, but you're wrong about how much and for how long."

She grew even more uneasy. "You shouldn't feel so bad. It's just the way men are."

"Hogwash."

"Now you're going to tell me about men? That's something I know all about, mister. *Men.*"

"You don't know anything about me."

"Every man likes to think he's different from the last. He likes to think he's better." She patted the bed. "Come here, and I'll show you just how much alike you are. Or are you afraid I might be right?"

He smiled gently. "You'd be more comfortable with me in that bed, wouldn't you?" He came over and sat in the chair, not the least disconcerted. He leaned toward her, his hands loosely clasped between his knees. "I'm not saying I'm any better than any other man who comes to you. I just want more."

"Such as?"

"Everything. I want what you don't even know you have to give."

"Some men expect a whole lot for a couple of ounces of gold dust."

"Listen to what I have to offer you."

"I don't see that what you're offering is any different than what I've got." Someone rapped twice at the door.

Relief swept through Angel, and she didn't bother to hide it. Smirking, she shrugged. "Well, you got your half hour of talk, didn't you?" She stood and walked past him. She took his hat from the hook by the door and held it out to him. "Time to go."

He looked disappointed, but not defeated. "I'm coming back."

"Whatever makes you happy."

Michael touched her face. "Change your mind. Come with me right now. It's got to be better than this."

Angel's heart raced. He looked as though he really meant it. But then, Johnny had looked sincere, too. Johnny, with his charm and glib tongue. When it was all said and done, all he had wanted was to take something away from Duke and then use it. All she had wanted was to get away. They had both failed, and the terrible cost of it had been far too great.

Angel wanted this farmer out of here. "Your gold dust is better spent elsewhere. I haven't got whatever it is you're looking for. Try Meggie. She's the philosopher." She started to open the door.

Michael flattened his hand against it. "You've got everything

I'm looking for. I wouldn't have felt what I did the first time I saw you. I wouldn't feel this certain now."

"Your half-hour is up."

Michael saw she wasn't going to listen. Not this time, anyway. "I'm coming back. All I'll ask for is one honest half-hour of your time."

She opened the door for him. "Mister, five minutes and you'd run like the devil."

# *Four*

*For I do not do the good I want,*
*but the evil I do not want is what I do.*

ROMANS 7:19

Hosea did come back, the next night and the next. Each time Angel saw him, her unrest grew. He talked, and she felt desperation stirring. She knew better than to believe anyone about anything. Hadn't she learned the hard way? Hope was a dream, and reaching for it turned her life into an unbearable nightmare. She wasn't going to get sucked in by words and promises again. She wasn't going to let a man convince her there was anything better than what she had.

Yet, she could not dispel the tension that rose each time she opened her door and found that man standing outside it. He never laid a hand on her. He just painted word pictures of freedom that resurrected the old, aching hunger she had felt as a child. It was a hunger that had never died. Yet each time she had run away to find an answer to it, disaster had fallen upon her. And still, she had kept trying. The last time, the hunger had sent her running from Duke and landed her here in this foul, stinking place.

Well, she had finally learned her lesson. Nothing ever got better. Things only went from bad to worse. It was wiser to adjust and accept and *survive.*

Why couldn't this man get it through his thick head that she wasn't going anywhere with him or anyone else? Why wouldn't he give up and leave her alone?

He kept coming back over and over again, driving her crazy. He wasn't smooth and charming like Johnny. He didn't use force like Duke. He wasn't like a hundred others who paid and played. In fact, he wasn't like anyone she had ever known. That was what she didn't like the most. She couldn't fit Michael Hosea into any mold she knew.

Each time, as soon as he left, she tried to put him out of her mind, but something about him gnawed at her. She found herself thinking about him at the oddest times and had to force herself to think of something else. When she succeeded, others roused him again.

"Who was the man with you last night?" Rebecca asked over supper.

Angel stifled her irritation and buttered her bread. "Which one?" she said and glanced across at the buxom redhead.

"The big, good-looking one. Who else?"

Angel bit into her bread, wanting to enjoy her meal of sourdough bread and venison stew in peace and not be questioned about who went in and out of her room. Who cared what any of them looked like? After a while, they all looked the same anyway.

"Give over, Angel," Rebecca said impatiently. "It's not as though you care. He was with you last night, last one out your door. I saw him in the hallway as I came upstairs. All six feet of him. Dark hair. Blue eyes. Broad shoulders. Every inch of him lean and hard. He walks like a soldier. When he smiled at me, I felt it all the way down to my toes."

Lucky passed on the stew in favor of the bottle of red wine. "If a pock-marked midget from Nantucket smiled at you, you would feel it all the way down to your toes."

"Drink your wine. I wasn't talking to you," Rebecca said contemptuously. She had no patience for Lucky's good-natured insults, and she returned her attention to Angel. "You can't pretend you don't know the one I mean. You just don't want to tell me anything."

Angel glared at her. "I don't know anything. I'd just like to enjoy my meal, if you don't mind."

Torie laughed. "Why shouldn't she want to keep him for herself?" she said, her British accent thick. "Maybe Angel's finally met a man she *likes*." The others laughed.

"Maybe she doesn't want to be bothered, like she says," Lucky said.

Rebecca sighed. "Angel, have a little pity. I've had one untried boy after another for the last month. I'd welcome a man for a change."

Torie pushed her plate away. "If someone like him came to my room, I'd lock him in and keep him there."

Angel poured herself a glass of milk and wished they would all leave her alone.

"That's the second glass you've had," Renee said to her from the end of the table. "Duchess said one glass for each of us because it's so expensive, and you're taking two!"

Lucky smirked. "I told her before supper she could have my share of milk if I could have her share of wine."

"That's not fair!" Renee whined. "I like milk just as much as Angel does! She always gets what she wants."

Lucky grinned. "If you had another glass of milk, it would just turn to more fat around your middle."

As they began to quarrel, Angel wanted to scream and leave the table. Her head was throbbing. Even Lucky's endless needling irritated her, and Rebecca would not give up about that wretched man.

"He must have hit it big to make it to your room three times in as many nights. What's his name? Don't pretend you don't care."

All Angel wanted was to be left alone. "He's not a miner. He's a farmer."

"A farmer?" Torie laughed. "Who are you trying to fool, dearie? He's no farmer. Farmers look dumb as the dirt they plow."

"He said he was a farmer. That doesn't mean he is one."

"What's his name?" Rebecca asked again.

"I don't remember." Did the man have to plague her even when he wasn't around?

"Oh, yes, you do!" Rebecca was angry now.

Angel threw her napkin down. "Look! I don't ask names. I don't care who they are. I give them what they want, and they leave. That's it."

"Then why does he keep coming back?"

"I don't know and I don't care."

Lucky poured another glass of wine. "Rebecca, you're just jealous he isn't coming to your room."

Rebecca glared at her. "Why don't you shut your mouth?

Keep on drinking the way you do, and Duchess will toss you out on your backside."

Unruffled, Lucky laughed. "It's still a pretty good backside."

"If women weren't so scarce, no one would bother knocking on your door at all," Torie sneered.

Lucky was warming to battle. "I'm better drunk than either of you are sober."

Angel ignored the insults being slung back and forth, relieved to be left alone. But now, *he* was on her mind again.

Meggie was sitting next to Angel and hadn't said anything through the whole exchange. Now, she looked at Angel as she stirred a teaspoon of precious sugar into her black coffee. "So, what is this delectable man like, Angel? Has he got any brains?"

Angel gave her a dark look. "Invite him in and find out for yourself."

Meggie arched her brows and leaned back smiling. "Really? I might just do that with all the interest he's stirred among our friends here." She studied her. "You really wouldn't mind?"

"Why should I?"

"I saw him first!" Rebecca said.

Lucky laughed. "First you'll have to knock him out and get someone to drag him into your room."

"Duchess won't like it," Renee said, her thin face waspish. "You know the men pay more for Angel. Though I can't see why."

"Because she looks better dog-tired than you look on your best day," Lucky crowed.

Renee hurled a fork at her, which Lucky dodged easily. It twanged off the wall.

"Please, be quiet, Lucky," Angel said, sure Magowan would come in. Lucky never stopped to think when she was drinking.

"So you really don't care," Rebecca said.

"You can have him with my blessing," Angel said. She didn't want him bothering her anymore. He wanted her. She felt it radiating from his body, but he never did anything about it. He talked. He asked questions. He waited, for what she didn't know. She was tired of trying to think up lies to make him happy. He just asked the same question again in a different way. He wouldn't give up. Each time he came, he was more determined. The last time, Magowan had come back twice and finally shouted through the door that he had better get dressed and get out if he didn't want trouble. Hosea hadn't even unbuttoned his shirt.

And he said the same thing he always did just before he left. "Come away with me. Marry me."

"I already said no. Three times. Don't you ever get the message? No. No. *No!*"

"You're not happy here."

"I wouldn't be any happier with you."

"How do you know?"

"I *know*."

"Put on something you can travel in and come with me. Right now. Don't think about it so much. Just do it."

"Magowan might have something to say about it." But she saw plainly Magowan didn't worry him at all. She wondered then what it would be like to live with a man like this, who didn't seem to be afraid of anything. But then, Duke hadn't been afraid of anything either, and she knew what living with him had been like.

"For the last time, *No*," she said firmly and reached for the doorknob.

He caught her wrist. "What's keeping you here?"

She pulled her wrist free. "I *like* it." She yanked the door open. "Now, get out!"

"I'll see you tomorrow," he said and went out.

Angel had slammed the door and leaned back against it. She always had a splitting headache by the time Hosea left. That night she'd sat on the end of her bed and pressed her fingers against her temples, trying to ease the pain.

The same pain that plagued her now. Pain that only got worse as Hosea's question echoed in her mind. What was keeping her here? Why didn't she just walk out the door?

Her hands balled into fists. She would have to get her gold from the Duchess first, and she knew there was no way the woman would give over all of it at once. Piecemeal, that's what she would get, enough for a few luxuries but not enough to live on. The Duchess couldn't afford to be that generous.

And what if Angel did have enough gold to leave? It could turn out the same way it had on the ship or at the end of the voyage when she had been beaten and left behind for those scavengers to find. Those few days on her own in San Francisco had been the closest thing to perdition she had lived. She had been cold, hungry, afraid for her life. She had looked back on life with Duke with actual longing. Duke, of all people.

Desperation filled her. *I can't leave. Without someone like Duchess, or even Magowan, they would tear me to pieces.*

She didn't want to risk going with Michael Hosea. He was by far a darker unknown.

Michael was running out of gold dust and time. He didn't know how to get through to that woman. He could see her withdraw from him the moment she opened the door. He talked, and she looked through him and pretended to listen, but he knew she heard nothing. She was just waiting for the half-hour to be up so she would have the pleasure of telling him to leave.

*I've got enough dust for one more try, Lord. Make her listen!*

Going up the stairs, he was going over in his mind what he was going to say to her this time when he bumped into a redhead. He drew back with an embarrassed apology. She laid a hand on his arm and smiled up at him. "Don't bother with Angel tonight. She said you'd like me better."

He stared down at her. "What else did Angel say?"

"That she'd see it as a favor to have you taken off her hands."

He clenched his teeth and took her hand away. "Thanks for telling me." He went down the hall. Standing in front of Angel's door, he tried to get control of his anger. *Jesus, were you listening? What am I doing back here? I've tried. You know I have. She doesn't want what I'm offering. What am I supposed to do? Drag her out of here by her hair?*

He rapped twice, the sound echoing loudly down the dim corridor. She opened the door, took one brief look at him, and said, "Oh. It's you again."

"Yes, it's me again." He walked in and slammed the door behind him.

Her brows rose. An angry man could be unpredictable and dangerous. This one could do a lot of damage to her without much effort.

"I'm not getting anywhere with you, am I?"

"It's not my fault you're wasting your gold," she said quietly. "I did warn you the very first night. Remember?" She sat down on the end of the bed. "I haven't misled you."

"I've got to go back to the valley and get some work done."

"I'm not stopping you."

His face was pale and rigid. "I don't want to leave you here in this godforsaken place!"

She blinked at his outburst. "It's not your business."

"It became my business the minute I saw you." Her foot began to swing gracefully back and forth, back and forth, ticking off the time. Asleep with her eyes open. She was self-contained. Nothing showed in her beautiful blue eyes.

"You feel like talking again?" She covered a yawn and sighed. "Go ahead. I'm all ears."

"Am I putting you to sleep?"

She heard the edge in his voice and knew she was getting to him. Good. Maybe a little more would send him on his way. "It has been a long, hard day." She rubbed the small of her back. "And all this talk does get old after a while."

His fuse was lit. "You'd like it better if I joined you on the bed, wouldn't you?"

"At least you could go away feeling you'd finally gotten something for all your gold dust."

Michael's heart beat hard and fast. He went to the window, shaking with anger and physical desire. Drawing the curtain back, he looked out. "Do you like your view from up here, Angel? Mud, slapped-up buildings and tents, men drunk and singing bar-room songs, everyone fighting to survive."

*Angel.* It was the first time he had called her that. For some reason, it hurt. She knew she was finally getting to him. She waited for the rest. He would say his piece, take what he wanted, and leave. That would be the end of it. All she had to do was make sure he didn't take a piece of her out the door.

"Or downstairs?" he said derisively. "Maybe you'd like that better." He let the curtain drop back and faced her. "Does it give you a feeling of power to have me bidding for your favors every night?"

"I don't ask you to do it."

"No, you don't, do you? You don't ask for anything at all. You don't need anything. You don't want anything. You don't feel anything. Why don't I just go on down the hall to that redhead's room? Isn't that it? The one you said could take me off your hands."

So that was it. His pride was hurt. "I just wanted to see you leave town with a smile on your face."

"You want to see me smile? Say my name."

"What is your name? I forgot."

He pulled her up off the bed. "Michael. Michael Hosea." Losing himself, he cupped her face.

*Michael.*

The feel of her skin made him forget why he was there, and he kissed her.

"It's about time." She moved forward against him, setting him on fire. Her hands moved, and he knew if he didn't stop her, he would lose – not just the battle but the whole war.

When she unbuttoned his shirt and slipped her hand in, he jerked back from her.

"Jesus," he said. *"Jesus!"*

Stunned, she looked up at him. It came to her with a shock of clear understanding. "How did you manage to make it to the ripe old age of twenty-six without ever having been with a woman?"

He opened his eyes. "I made a decision to wait for the right one."

"And you really think I'm it?" She laughed at him. "You poor, dumb fool."

She finally got to him.

*Jesus, I misunderstood. This can't be the one you sent for me.*

He could spend the rest of his life trying to make her understand. He wanted to grab her and shake her and call her all kinds of a fool, and all she did was look back at him with that smile on her face, as though she had finally figured him all out. He was labeled and put in a bin.

Michael lost his temper. "If that's the only way you want it, so be it." He slammed out the door and strode down the hall. He went down the stairs, straight across the casino, slapped the swinging doors out of his way and went out. He kept on walking, hoping the night air would cool him down.

*Michael...*

*Forget it! Just forget I ever asked for a wife! I don't need one that badly.*

*Michael...*

*I'll stay celibate.*

**Michael, beloved.**

He kept walking. *God, why her? Tell me that. Why not a gently reared girl, untouched until her wedding night? Why not a God-fearing widow? Lord, send me a plain woman, kind and enduring, someone who would work at my side in the fields, plowing, planting, and harvesting! Someone who'll get dirt beneath her fingernails but doesn't have it already in her blood! Someone to give me children or someone with children already if it's not in your plan for me to have my own. Why do you tell me to marry a harlot?*

**This is the woman I have chosen for you.**

Michael stopped, furious. "I'm no prophet!" he shouted at the darkening sky. "I'm not one of your saints. I'm just an ordinary man!"

**Go back and get Angel.**

"It's not going to work! You're wrong this time."

**Go back.**

"She's good for sex, I'm sure. She'll give me that much, but nothing else. You want me to go back for that? I'm never going to get more from her than one measly half-hour of her time. I go up to that room with hope and come out defeated. Where's your triumph in this? She wouldn't care if she ever saw me again. She's trying to pass me off to the others like a...a – No, Lord. No! I'm just another faceless man in a long line of faceless men in her life. This can't be what you had in mind!" He raised his fist. "And it's sure not what I asked for!"

He raked his hands through his hair. "She's made it plain enough. I can have her any way I want. From the neck down. Excluding the heart. I'm only a man, Lord! Do you know what she makes me feel?"

It started to rain. A cold driving rain.

Michael stood in the dark, muddy road a mile out of town, rain running down his face. He shut his eyes. "Thanks," he said harshly. "Thanks a lot." Hot, angry blood pumped fast through his veins. "If this is your way of cooling me off, it's not working very well."

*Do my will, beloved. I drew you up from the desolate pit, out of the miry bog, and set your feet upon a rock. Go back for Angel.*

But Michael held his anger close like a shield. "Nothing doing. The last thing I want or need is a woman who doesn't feel a thing." He started walking again, this time heading for the livery stable where his wagon and horses were.

"It's a poor time for traveling, mister," the liveryman said. "A storm's coming."

"It's as good as any, and I'm pure sick of this place."

"You and a thousand others."

Michael had to pass the Palace to leave town. The drunken laughter and the piano music grated. He didn't even look at her upstairs window as he drove by. Why should he? She was probably working. As soon as he got back to his valley and forgot about that hell-bound girl, he would feel better.

And the next time he prayed for God to send him a woman to share his life, he would be a lot more specific about the kind he wanted.

Angel was standing at her window when she saw Hosea go by. She knew it was him even with his shoulders hunched against the downpour. She waited for him to look up, but he didn't. She watched him until he was out of sight.

Well, she had finally succeeded in driving him away. It was what she'd wanted from the start.

So why did she feel so bereft? Wasn't she glad she was finally rid of him? He wouldn't be sitting in her room again, talking and talking and talking until she thought she would go crazy.

He had finally called her Angel. *Angel!* She raised a trembling hand and put it against the glass. The cold seeped into her palm and up her arm. She pressed her forehead against the pane and listened to the drumming rain. The sound of it made her remember the shack by the docks and her mother smiling in death.

*Oh, God, I'm suffocating. I'm dying.*

She began to shake and let the curtain fall back into place. Maybe that was the only way out. Death. If she were dead, no one could ever use her again.

She sat on the bed and drew up her knees tightly against her chest. Pressing her head against her knees, she rocked herself. Why did he have to come to her? She had come to accept things the way they were. She had been getting by. Why did he have to destroy her inner stillness? She clenched her hands into fists. She couldn't get rid of the vision of Michael Hosea driving away in the rain.

She had the awful gut feeling she had just thrown her last chance away.

# Five

*Death is before me today. As a man longs
to see his house when he has spent many years in captivity.*

PAPYRUS FROM ANCIENT EGYPT

The storm lasted for days. The rain streaked the glass like tears, washing the grit away and making watery images of the outside world. Angel worked and slept and looked out over the shanties, clapboard buildings, and sagging canvas tents lit by a thousand lanterns until dawn. No green anywhere. Just grays and browns.

Henri would be serving breakfast now, but she wasn't hungry, and she didn't feel like sitting with the others and listening to their squabbles and complaints.

The rain came harder and faster, and with it came memories. She used to play a game with her mother on rainy-day afternoons. Anytime it rained, it grew cold in the shanty, too cold for anyone who didn't have to be there. The men stayed away, warming themselves in a comfortable tavern, and Rab stayed with them. Mama would set Sarah in her lap and wrap the blanket around both of them. Sarah had grown to like storms because then she had Mama all to herself. They would watch the large drops on the glass pane touch and grow and finally slide down into a river on the frame. Mama talked to her about when she was a child. Just the happy things, the good times. Mama never spoke of being turned away by her father. She never spoke of Alex Stafford. But whenever she was quiet, Sarah knew Mama was remembering and hurting all over again. Mama would hug her hard and rock her and hum. "Things will be different for you, darling," she would say, and kiss her. "Things will be different for you. You'll see."

And Angel had seen.

She stopped thinking about the past. She let the curtain drop back in place and sat down at the small, lace-covered table. She stuffed the memories down again. Better the hollow nothingness than the pain.

Hosea won't come back. Not this time. She closed her eyes tightly, her small hand a fist in her lap. Why did she think about him at all? *"Come away with me and be my wife."* Sure, until he tired of her and gave her to someone else. Like Duke. Like Johnny. Life never changes.

She lay down on her bed and covered her face with a pale satin sheet. She remembered the men sewing the shroud closed over her mother's stiffly smiling face and felt empty inside. Whatever hope had once been inside her had drained away. There was nothing left to hold her together. She was caving in.

"I'll make it on my own," she said into the silence around her, and could almost hear Duke laughing: *"Sure you can, Angel. Just like last time."*

Someone knocked on her door, jerking her back from her dark memories. "Can I come in, Angel?"

Angel welcomed Lucky. She reminded her of Mama except Lucky drank to be happy. Mama drank to forget. Lucky wasn't drunk right now, but she was holding a bottle and two glasses.

"You've been keeping to yourself lately," Lucky said, sitting on the bed with her. "Are you all right? You're not sick or anything, are you?"

"I'm fine," Angel said.

"You didn't have breakfast with us." Lucky set the bottle and glasses on the side table.

"I wasn't hungry."

"You're not sleeping well, either. You've got shadows under your eyes. You're just feeling sad, aren't you?" Lucky gently stroked Angel's hair back. "Well, it happens to the best of us, even an old harlot like me." She liked Angel, and she worried about her. Angel was so young – and so hard. She needed to learn to laugh a little at the cards she had been dealt. She was beautiful, and that would always come in handy in this business. Lucky liked to look at her. Angel was a rare flower in this weed patch, something special. The others didn't like her because of it. And because Angel didn't mingle. She was self-possessed.

Lucky was the only one allowed close, but there were rules. She could talk about anything except men and God. She never stopped to wonder or ask why. She was just grateful Angel allowed her to be a friend.

Angel was especially quiet today, her lovely face pale and drawn.

"I brought a bottle and two glasses. You want to try drinking again? Maybe it won't turn out so bad this time. We'll go slower."

"No." Angel shuddered.

"Are you sure you're not sick?"

"Sort of, I guess." She was sick of living. "I was thinking about my mother."

It was the first mention of anything from Angel's past, and Lucky was honored to be trusted with even a tidbit. It was a great mystery among all the girls where Angel had come from. "I didn't know you had a mother."

Angel smiled wryly. "Maybe I didn't really. Maybe it was just my imagination."

"You know I didn't mean it that way."

"I know." Angel stared up at the ceiling. "It's just that sometimes I really do wonder." Had there ever been a cottage with flowers all around and the scent of roses drifting in through a parlor window? Had her mother ever really laughed and sang and run with her across the meadows?

Lucky touched her brow. "You're feverish."

"I have a headache. It'll go away."

"How long have you had it?"

"Ever since that farmer started pestering me."

"Has he been back?"

"No."

"I think he was in love with you. Are you sorry you didn't go away with him?"

Angel tightened up inside. "No. He's just a man like all the rest."

"You want me to leave you alone?"

Angel took Lucky's hand and held onto it. "No." She didn't want to be alone. Not when she had been thinking about the past and couldn't seem to push it away. Not when death was all that was on her mind. It was the rain, the constant, battering rain. She was going mad.

They sat silent for a long while. Lucky poured herself a drink. Tension rippled through Angel as she remembered Mama's drinking herself into oblivion. She remembered Mama's grief and guilt and the endless weeping. She remembered Cleo, drunk and bitter, raging against life and telling her God's truth about men.

Lucky wasn't Mama or Cleo. She was funny and uninhibited, and she liked to talk. The familiar words flowed like balm. If Angel could just listen to Lucky's life story, she might be able to forget her own.

"My mother ran off when I was five," Lucky said. "Have I told you all this?"

"Tell me again."

"My aunt took me in. She was a fine lady. Her name was Miss Priscilla Lantry. She gave up marrying a fine young man because her father was ill and needed her. She nursed the old miser for fifteen years before he died. He wasn't even cold in his grave when my loving mother dumped me on her doorstep with a note. It said, 'This is Bonnie.' And it was signed 'Sharon.'" She laughed.

"Aunt Priss didn't much like the idea of having a child to raise, especially a castoff from her no-good sister. Everyone in the neighborhood thought she was a saint for taking me in." She poured another glass of whiskey. "She said she was going to make sure I grew up proper and not like my mother. If she didn't use a switch on me at least twice a day, she didn't feel she was doing her duty. 'Spare the rod and spoil the child.'"

Lucky plunked the bottle on the side table and pushed her dark hair back from her flushed face. "She drank. Not like I do. She did everything proper. She just sipped. Not whiskey, mind you. Madeira, fine Madeira. She'd start in the morning, a sip here, a sip there. It looked like liquid gold in her pretty crystal glass. She was so mellow and sweet when neighbors came to call." She giggled. "They thought she had such a charming lisp."

She sighed and swirled the amber fluid in her glass. "Meanest woman I ever knew. Meaner than the Duchess. As soon as the guests were out the door and off in their fine carriages, she would start in on me." She began to mimic an elegant southern drawl. "You didn't curtsy when Missus Abernathy came in. You took two biscuits from the tray when I said to take only one. The schoolmaster said you didn't do your arithmetic yesterday."

Lucky drank half her whiskey. "Then she would make me sit and wait while she searched for just the right switch to cut from the willow tree. It had to be as thick as her pointer finger."

She held her whiskey glass up to the lamp and looked through it before she emptied it. "She went to tea one afternoon with the parson's wife. They were going to discuss my enrollment in a young ladies academy. While she was gone, I chopped the tree down. It flattened the roof and fell right into the middle of her fancy parlor. Smashed all her fine crystal. I ran away before she came back."

She laughed softly. "Sometimes I wish I had stayed long enough to see the look on her face when she came home." She held the empty glass and stared at it. "And sometimes I wish I could go back and tell her I'm sorry." She took her bottle and stood, her eyes glazed. "I'd better go to bed and get my beauty sleep."

Angel caught her hand. "Lucky, try not to drink so much. Duchess was talking about kicking you out if you don't slow down on the booze."

"Don't you worry about me, Angel," Lucky said, smiling bleakly. "Last I heard there was still one woman to twenty men out here. The odds are definitely in my favor. You watch out for yourself. Magowan hates you."

"Magowan is a worthless piece of horse dung."

"True, but Duchess has a thing for him, and he's been telling her you're lazy and insolent. Just watch out for yourself. Please."

Angel didn't care. What was the difference? Men would still come and pay to play, until the decent women arrived. Then they'd treat her like Mama. They would pretend they didn't know her when they passed by her on the street. The good women would turn away while the children gawked and asked who she was, only to be cuffed into silence. She would still have work – after dark, of course – until she wasn't pretty anymore or was too sick to be appealing.

If only she could be like one of those mountain men who

went out into the wilderness and stayed there, hunting their food and building their own shelter and never having to answer to another living soul for anything. Just to be left alone, that must be heaven.

She got up and went to the washstand. Pouring water into the bowl, she washed her face, but the coolness gave her no relief. She held the towel over her eyes for a long time. Then she sat at the small table beside the window and looked out through the curtain. She saw an empty buckboard in the street below and thought of Hosea. Why did she have to think of him now?

*What if I had gone with him? Would things have been any different?*

She reminded herself of the one time she had run away with a man. At fourteen, she had still been too inexperienced to recognize Johnny's ambitions. He'd been looking for a meal ticket, and she'd wanted to get away from Duke. As it turned out, neither of them got what they wanted. She closed her eyes tightly at the horror of what Duke had done when he had them brought back. Poor Johnny.

She had been fine before that farmer had come. He was just like Johnny. He held out hope as bait. He painted images of freedom and promised it to her. Well, she had stopped believing the lies. She had stopped believing in freedom. She had stopped dreaming about it...until Hosea came, and now she couldn't get it out of her mind.

She clutched the curtain. "I've got to get out of here." She didn't even care where. Anything else was better.

She had earned enough gold by now to build a little house of her own and quit working for a while. All she needed was the courage to go down and demand it from Duchess. She knew the risk, but it didn't seem to matter anymore.

Pit, the bartender, was polishing and stacking shot glasses when she came downstairs. "Morning, Miss Angel. You want to go for your walk? You want me to see if I can find Bret for you?"

Her courage faltered. "No."

"You hungry? Henri just put something together for the Duchess."

Maybe food would staunch the queasiness. She nodded, and he left the glasses and went out the door at the end of the bar. When he came back, he said, "Henri will bring something out in a minute, Angel."

The small, dark Frenchman brought a tray and uncovered a plate of fried potatoes and bacon. The coffee was lukewarm. He made his apologies and said supplies were low. Angel couldn't eat, anyway. She tried, but the food stuck in her throat. She sipped the coffee instead and tried to drown her fear, but it was there like a hard knot inside her chest.

Pit watched her. "Something wrong, Angel?"

"No. Nothing's wrong." She might as well get it done. Pushing her plate back, she got up.

The Duchess's quarters were on the first floor behind the casino. Angel stood before the heavy oak door, her palms sweating. She wiped her hands on her skirt, took a deep breath, and knocked.

"Who's there?"

"Angel."

"Come in."

The Duchess was dabbing her mouth delicately, and Angel saw what remained of a cheese omelet on her Dresden plate. One egg was worth two dollars, and cheese was very hard to come by at any price. She couldn't even remember the last time she'd had an egg. The deceitful cow. Fear lessened as resentment grew.

The Duchess smiled. "Why aren't you sleeping? You look dreadful. Are you upset about something?"

"You've been working me too hard."

"Nonsense. You're just in one of your moods again." She smoothed the flowing red silk of her lounging gown. It did little to conceal the rolls of flesh gathering around her waist. Her cheeks were puffy, and she was developing a second chin. A pink ribbon held her graying hair back. She was obscene.

"Sit down, darling. I can see you have something unpleasant on your mind. Bret told me you didn't come down for breakfast. Would you like something now?" The Duchess waved an indolent hand magnanimously at a basket of muffins.

"I want my gold."

The Duchess didn't look the least surprised. She laughed and leaned forward to pour herself more coffee. She added cream. Angel wondered where she had gotten it and how much it had cost. Duchess lifted the elegant cup and sipped while studying her over the rim. "Why do you want it?" she asked, as though merely curious.

"Because it belongs to me."

The Duchess gave her a bland, amused look of maternal tolerance. "Pour yourself some coffee, and let's talk about it."

"I don't want any coffee, and I don't want to talk about it. I want my gold and I want it now."

The Duchess tilted her head slightly. "You might ask a little more politely. Did you have an annoying customer last night?" When Angel didn't answer, the Duchess's eyes narrowed. She put the cup back in the saucer. "Why do you need your gold, Angel? What is there to buy up here? More fripperies?" Her expression was amused again, but her eyes held warning. "Tell me what you want, and I'll try to see you have it. Unless it's something completely out of the question, of course."

Like eggs and cream. Like freedom. "I want a little house of my own," Angel said.

The Duchess's face changed, darkening. "So you can go into business for yourself? Are you getting ambitious, my dear?"

"You'll have no competition from me, I assure you. I'll be a hundred miles from here. I just want out. I want to be left alone."

The Duchess sighed and gave her a pitying look. "Angel, we all go through these silly notions. Take it from me. You can't quit. It's too late." She leaned forward and set her cup and saucer down again. "I take good care of you, don't I? If you have reasonable complaints, of course I'll hear you out, but I can't just let you walk away. This is wild country. You wouldn't be safe out there on your own. All kinds of dreadful things can happen to a pretty girl when she's on her own." Her eyes glittered. "You need someone to look out for you."

Angel tipped her chin slightly. "I could always hire a bodyguard."

Duchess laughed low. "Someone like Bret? I don't think you like him the way I do."

"I could get married."

"Married?" She laughed. "You? Oh, that's rich."

"I've been asked."

"Oh, I'm sure you've been asked. Even your drunk little friend Lucky has been asked, but she's also smart enough to know it would never work. A man doesn't want a harlot for a wife. Men say all kinds of foolish things when they're lonely and aching for a woman and there's no one else around. Ah, but they come to their senses quick enough. Besides, you wouldn't like it."

"At least I'd only be working for one man."

The Duchess smiled. "How would you like to wash a man's dirty long johns and cook his meals and clean out his chamber pot? How would you like to do all that and then have to give him whatever he wanted besides? How would you like that? Or maybe you have some idea that he would let you lie around all day and have servants to take care of everything. In another place, you might have managed that. But not here in California, and certainly not now. You would've been smarter to stay where you were."

Angel was silent.

The Duchess's mouth curved. "The trouble comes from you thinking too much of yourself, Angel." She shook her head. "Sometimes you girls make me feel as though I'm dealing with spoiled children. All right, my dear. Let's get to the point of this little visit, shall we? How much more do you want? Thirty percent?"

"Just what I've earned. Now."

The Duchess sighed heavily. "All right, then, if that's the way it has to be. But you'll have to wait. I've invested it for you."

Angel sat very still, frustration and rage building. She clenched her hands. "Uninvest it. I know you have enough gold in your safe right now to square with me." She gestured to the platter. "You have enough to buy eggs and cheese and cream for yourself." She cupped her hands and made a shape. "A sack about this big is all I expect. One of the men you sent my way last night was an accountant, and he made a few calculations for me."

Duchess glared at her. "You, my dear, are speaking like an

ungrateful fool." She stood with injured dignity. "You're forgetting all I do for you. Costs aren't what they were when we started this little operation. Everything has gone up. Your clothing costs a fortune. Silk and lace aren't commonplace in a mining town, you know. Your food costs even more. And this building wasn't put up for free!"

Angel's resentment and bitterness had long since dissolved fear and rational thought. "Is my name on the deed?"

The Duchess stopped. "What did you say?"

"You heard me. Is my name on the deed?" Angel stood as well, past control. "You have cream for your coffee, and eggs and cheese for breakfast. You dress in satin and lace. You even sip from fine china." She picked up a cup and smashed it against the wall. "How many men have I served so you can stuff yourself like a pig and dress up like a grotesque parody of royalty? Duchess from where? Duchess of what? You're nothing but a fat old harlot no man wants anymore!"

The Duchess's face was white with rage.

Angel's heart beat faster and faster. She hated her. "You aren't charging four ounces of gold for my time anymore. How much is the toll these days? Six? Eight? I should have earned enough by now to be free of this place."

"And if you haven't?" the Duchess said very quietly.

Angel jerked her chin up. "Well, a smart girl could do real well for herself."

Duchess became very composed. "A smart girl would never even consider speaking to me in this way."

Angel heard the danger and realized what she had done. She sank down slowly, her heart in her throat.

The Duchess came over to her and touched her hair. "After all I've done for you," she said grievously. "You have a short memory about your first weeks in San Francisco, haven't you?" She cupped Angel's chin and lifted her face. "When I first saw you, you were still showing the marks of a rather nasty beating. You were living in a lousy shack and almost starving." Her fingers tightened painfully. "I picked you up out of the mud and made you into something. You're a princess up here." She let go.

"A princess of what?" she said bleakly.

"You're so ungrateful. I think Bret is right about you. You've become spoiled with special treatment."

Angel was shaking inside. Her unreasoning rage had evaporated. She took the Duchess's hand and pressed it against her cold cheek. "Please. I can't stand anymore of this. I've got to get out of here."

"Maybe you do need a change," the Duchess said, stroking Angel's hair. "Let me think about it. Go upstairs now and rest. We'll talk later."

Angel did as she was told. She sat on the end of her bed and waited. When Magowan walked in without knocking, Angel had her answer. She got up and backed away from him as he closed the door quietly.

"Duchess said you had a lot to say to her a little while ago. Well, little dove, now it's my turn to do a little talking. When I'm done, you'll be as obedient as Mai Ling. And I'm going to enjoy it. I've been waiting for this for a long, long time. And you know it, don't you?"

Angel looked at the closed two-story window, then back at the locked door.

"You won't get past me." He took off his black coat.

Angel's mind flashed back to a tall dark man in a black evening suit. It came to her with sudden finality that there was no way out, not for her. There never had been; there never would be. Everywhere she turned, every time she tried, she was trapped again, worse off than before.

"Don't worry. I won't leave any marks that show. And you'll be working tonight whether you feel up to it or not."

Hopeless rage filled her. She remembered everything ever done to her from the time she was a child in a shack on the docks to now, in this room. It was never going to get any better. This was all she could ever expect of life. The world was full of Dukes and Duchesses and Magowans and men to come line up outside her door. There was always going to be someone to enslave and use her, someone to profit from her flesh and her blood.

There was one way out.

Maybe she had always known it was the only way. She could feel it like a living presence in the room, a force standing beside her, dark and beckoning. And she was finally ready to embrace it. A few well-aimed words, and Magowan would end it for her. She would finally be free – free forever.

Magowan frowned at the look on her face, but she didn't care. She wasn't afraid anymore. She was grinning at him. "What's the matter with you?" Her eyes glowed bright and wild, and she started to laugh. "What're you laughing at?"

"At you. Big man. Duchess's pet dog." She laughed harder at the stunned expression on his face. Her laughter rose, sounding strange and bright in her own ears. It was all so funny, so incredibly funny. Why hadn't she seen it before? Her whole life was a great big joke. Even when Magowan came at her, she couldn't stop laughing about it. Not on the first blow or the second. Or even the third.

After the fourth blow, all Angel heard was the beast roaring in her ears.

# Six

*To have and to hold from this day forward,*
*for better for worse, for richer for poorer,*
*in sickness and in health, to love and to cherish,*
*till death us do part.*

BOOK OF COMMON PRAYER

Michael couldn't get Angel out of his mind. He tried to concentrate on his work and found himself thinking about her instead. Why did she keep eating at him? Why did he have this gut feeling that something was wrong? He worked until past dark every day and then sat before the fire, tormented with thoughts of her. He saw her face in the flames, beckoning to him. To hell itself, no doubt. Or was he getting a taste of that already?

He remembered the tragic air about her as she had passed him that first day, and then reminded himself how hard-hearted she was. He swore he wouldn't go back to her, then did so every night when he slept and Angel haunted his dreams. He couldn't escape her. She danced before him, like Salome before King Herod. He would reach out for her, and she would move back, tantalizing him. *You want me, don't you, Michael? Then come back. Come back.*

After a few days, his dreams turned to nightmares. She was fleeing from something. He ran after her, calling out for her to stop, but she ran on until she came to a ledge. She looked back at him then, the wind whipping her golden hair about her white face.

*Mara, wait!*

She turned away and spread her arms wide and went over.

"No!" Michael awakened with a start, his body streaming sweat. His chest heaved; his heart raced so fast his body shook with it. He raked trembling hands through his hair. "Jesus," he whispered into the darkness. "Jesus, deliver me from this." Why did she haunt him so?

He got up and opened the door, leaning heavily against the frame. It was raining again. He closed his eyes wearily. He hadn't prayed in days. "I'd be a fool to go back," he said aloud. "A fool." He looked out at the dark, weeping sky again. "But that's what you want, isn't it, Lord? And you're not going to give me any peace until I do."

He sighed heavily and rubbed the back of his neck. "I don't see what good will come of it, but I'll go back, Lord. I don't like it much, but I'll do what you want." When he finally went back to bed, he slept deeply and without dreaming for the first time in days.

In the morning, the sky was clear. Michael loaded the wagon and hitched up the team.

When he drove into Pair-a-Dice late that afternoon, he looked up at Angel's window. The drapes were drawn. A muscle jerked in his jaw, and a hard pain tightened his belly. She was probably working.

*Lord, you said do your will, and I'm trying hard. Does it have to hurt so much? I need a woman, and I've waited for your choice. Why did you give me this? Why am I back here again in this camp, looking up at her window with my heart in my throat? She doesn't want anything to do with me.*

Shoulders hunched, he headed down Main Street to take care of business at the mercantile. He needed the gold to get upstairs at the Palace. When he pulled up before Hochschild's Store, he jumped down from his wagon and strode up the steps. A note was stuck in the window. *Closed.* Michael knocked hard anyway. From inside, Hochschild yelled a string of curses that would wither a seasoned sailor. When he threw open the door, his anger vanished.

"Michael! Where've you been? I've been out of everything for weeks and no sight of you." Unshaven, half drunk, his shirt tail hanging, Joseph came outside to look in the wagon. "A full load. Thank heaven. I don't care if it's bug-ridden and rotting; I'll take everything you've got."

"You're the sort of fellow I like doing business with,"

Michael said, smiling slightly. He stacked crates and carried them in two at a time. "You look terrible. Have you been sick?"

Joseph laughed. "Too much to drink. You in a hurry or something? Could you stop long enough for a talk?"

"Not this time."

"You planning to spend everything I give you at the Palace again? It's one of man's afflictions, isn't it? Need of woman."

Michael's jaw stiffened. "How do you come to know so much about my personal business?"

"It wasn't hard when you were still in town after four days last time." Hochschild took one look at Michael, made a silent whistle, and changed the subject. "There was a strike about three miles up river." He gave details. "With all that gold dust coming in I can raise my prices."

Michael slammed the last crate on the counter. Angel's price had probably gone up, too.

Hochschild paid up. He scratched his grizzled cheek. Usually Michael was sociable, but today he looked downright grim. "Got your herd yet?"

"Not yet." He had invested all his hard-earned gold dust in courting Angel last trip. He poured his payment into his belt.

"Rumor has it that Angel's not doing business for a while," Joseph said.

Her name was all it took. Michael felt as though he had been struck in the chest. "Did she earn herself a rest?"

Joseph's eyebrows rose. The remark wasn't like Michael at all. He must have fallen hard and been hurt bad. Shaking his head, he grimaced. "Forget I mentioned her."

He followed Michael outside and watched him jump up onto his wagon. "Town got a pastor just last Wednesday. If you've a mind to hear him, he's preaching at the Gold Nugget Saloon."

Michael was thinking about Angel. He took up the reins. "I'll see you in a couple of weeks."

"You had better rest those horses awhile. Looks like you pushed them pretty hard getting up here."

"I'm heading for the livery stable right now." He tipped his hat and drove down Main Street. It was going to take bribery and fast talking to see Angel tonight. He left the two draft horses and wagon with McPherson and went down into the center of town to rent himself a room at the hotel across from the Palace. For the first time in his life, Michael wanted to get rip-roaring drunk. He went for a long walk instead. He needed time to get his emotions under control and think through what he was going to say to her.

He returned at dusk, no easier in his mind. A crowd was gathered outside the Gold Nugget Saloon listening to the new preacher shouting about these being the end times of Revelation. Michael stood on the outer edge of the crowd, listening. He glanced up once at Angel's window. Someone moved back into the shadows.

He ought to go over now and make his arrangements with the Duchess. His heart raced, and he broke out in a sweat just thinking about it. He would wait a little longer.

Someone touched his back, and he turned to see an older woman looking up at him with bloodshot eyes. Her hair was dark and curly, and she wore a low-cut, garish green dress.

"I'm Lucky," she said. "Angel's friend." She was drunk and slurring her words. "Saw you from across the street." She nodded toward the Palace. "You are the one, ain't you? The one who kept askin' Angel to go 'way with him?"

Anger shot through him like a range fire. "What else did she tell you?"

"Don't get mad, mister. Just go an' ask her again."

"Did she tell you to come down here?" Was she up there laughing at him behind the curtain?

"No." She shook her head sharply. "Angel, she never asks for nothing." Tears filled the woman's eyes, and she wiped her nose on her shawl. "She don't even know I'm talking t' you."

"Well, thanks, Lucky, but the last time I saw her, she could-n't wait until I walked out her door, and it was real clear she hoped I'd never come back."

Lucky looked up at him. "Get her out of there, mister. Even if you don't care anymore, even if Angel don't. Just get her out of there."

Suddenly alarmed, Michael caught her arm as she turned

away. "What's the matter with her, Lucky? What are you trying to tell me?"

Lucky wiped her nose again. "I can't talk anymore. I gotta get back before Duchess misses me." She crossed the street, but instead of going in the front, she sneaked around the back.

Michael looked up at Angel's window. Something was wrong. Very wrong. He strode across the street and went in through the swinging doors. Except for a couple of men playing cards and drinking, the place was almost deserted. The bodyguard wasn't at the foot of the stairs to stop him from going up. The hall was dark and quiet. Too quiet. A man came out of Angel's room, and the Duchess was with him. She saw Michael first.

"What are you doing up here? No one's allowed upstairs until they've dealt with me!"

"I want to see Angel."

"She's not working today."

He looked at the black bag in the man's hand. "What's the matter with her?"

"Nothing," the Duchess answered sharply. "Angel's just taking a few days off to rest. Now get out of here." She tried to block his way, but Michael set her aside and went into the room.

The Duchess grabbed at his arm. "Stay away from her! Doc, stop him!"

The doctor fixed her with a cold glare. "No, ma'am. I won't."

Michael reached the bed and saw her. "Oh, sweet Lord…"

"It was Magowan," Doc said quietly from behind Michael.

"It wasn't my fault!" Duchess said, drawing back in fear from the look on Michael's face. "It wasn't!"

"She's right," Doc said. "If Duchess hadn't come in when she did, he probably would have killed her."

"*Now* will you get out of here and leave her alone?" Duchess said.

"I'll leave, all right," Michael answered. "And I'm taking her with me."

Angel roused to someone's touch. The Duchess was ranting again. Angel wanted the darkness. She didn't want to feel anything, ever again, but someone was there, so close she could feel the warmth of his breath. "I'm going to take you home with me," the gentle voice said.

"You want to take her home, fine. I'll gift wrap her," the Duchess said. "But you're going to pay first."

"Woman, have you no decency?" Another man's voice. "The girl will be lucky to live – "

"Oh, she'll live. And don't look down your nose at me! I *know* Angel. She'll live. And he can't have her for nothing. I can tell you something else. She brought this on herself. The little witch knew exactly what she was doing. She pushed Bret over the edge. She's been nothing but trouble since the day I picked her up out of the mud in San Francisco."

"You can have your gold," came the voice that had pulled her from the darkness. But now it was hard. Angry. Had she done something wrong again? "But get out of here before I do something I'll regret."

The door slammed. Pain exploded in Angel's head, and she groaned. She could hear two men talking. One of them spoke to her. "I want to marry you before we leave together."

Marry her? She gave a whimpering laugh.

Someone took her hand. She thought it was Lucky at first, but Lucky's hand was soft and small. This one was large and hard, the skin rough with calluses. "Just say yes."

She would agree to wed Satan himself if it would get her out of the Palace. "Why not?" she managed.

She drifted on a sea of pain and quiet voices. The room was full of them. Lucky was there, and Doc, and the other man whose voice was so familiar, but she still couldn't place it. She felt someone slip a ring on her finger. Her head was raised gently, and she was given something bitter to drink.

Lucky took her hand. "They're rigging his wagon so he can take you home with him. You'll sleep all the way with the laudanum you drank. You won't feel nothing." She felt Lucky touch her hair. "You're a regular married lady now, Angel. He had a wedding ring on a chain around his neck. He said it belonged to his mother. His *mother*, Angel. He put his mother's wedding ring on your finger. Can you hear me, honey?"

Angel wanted to ask who she had married, but what did it matter? The pain gradually receded. She was so tired. Maybe she would die after all. It would all be over then.

She heard the clink of a bottle against a glass. Lucky was drinking again. Angel could hear her crying. She squeezed Lucky's hand weakly. Lucky squeezed back and sobbed softly. "Angel." She stroked her hair. "What'd you say to make Bret do this to you? Did you *want* him to kill you? Is life really that bad?" She kept stroking her hair. "Hang on, Angel. Don't give up."

Angel sank back into comfortable darkness while Lucky rambled. "I'm going to miss you, Angel. When you're living out there in your cabin with the climbing roses all around, think about me once in a while, will you? Remember your old friend, Lucky."

# Seven

*I am dying of thirst*
*by the side of the fountain.*
CHARLES D'ORLÉANS

Angel awakened slowly to the wonderful aroma of good cooking. She tried to sit up, then gasped in pain. "Easy," a man's voice said, and a strong arm slid beneath her shoulders, raising her gently. She felt something put behind her to support her back and head. "The dizziness will pass."

Her eyes were swollen almost shut, and she could barely make out a man dressed in high boots, dungarees, and a red shirt. He was bending over the fire and stirring in a big iron pot.

Morning light was streaming through a window in front of her. The light hurt her eyes. She was in a cabin not much bigger than her room at the Palace. The floor was wood plank; the fireplace, multicolored stone. Besides the bed, she could make out the fuzzy shapes of a table, four laden shelves, a willow chair, a chest of drawers, and a big black trunk with blankets stacked on top of it.

The man came back and sat down on the edge of the bed. "Do you feel up to eating something, Mara?"

*Mara.*

She froze. Snatches of things came back.... Magowan's beating, voices all around her, someone asking her –

Her heart thudded in her chest. She felt her fingers – there was a ring on one. The throbbing in her head worsened. She swore softly. Of all the men in the world, it had to be *him*.

"It's venison stew. You must be hungry."

She opened her mouth to tell him where to put it when pain shot along her jaw and silenced her. Hosea got up and went back to the fire. When he came to sit down again, he had a bowl and spoon. She saw he meant to feed her. She said something low and foul and tried to turn her head away, but even that simple movement proved too much.

"I'm glad you're feeling better," he said dryly. Pressing her lips together, she refused to eat. Her traitorous stomach growled. "Feed the wolf in your belly, Mara. Then you can try fighting the one you think is at your door."

She gave in. She was starving. The gruel of meat and vegetables he spooned into her mouth was better than anything Henri had ever made. The throbbing in her head lessened. Her jaw ached horribly; her arm was in some kind of sling.

"Your shoulder was dislocated," Michael said. "You've got four broken ribs, a cracked collarbone, and a concussion. Doc didn't know if you had any internal injuries."

Perspiration was dripping down the sides of her face from the painful effort of sitting up. She spoke slowly and stiffly. "So you got me after all. Lucky you. Is this *home*?"

"Yes."

"How did I get here?"

"In my wagon. Joseph helped me rig up a hammock so I could move you out of the Palace."

She looked down at the simple gold band on her finger. She clenched her hand. "How far am I from Pair-a-Dice?"

"A lifetime."

"In miles."

"Thirty. We're northwest of New Helvetia." He offered her the spoon again. "Try to eat some more. You need to put on some weight."

"Not enough meat on my bones to please you?"

Michael made no response.

Angel couldn't tell whether her sarcasm had gotten to him or not. It occurred to her belatedly that she might anger him and this wasn't the best time to do so. She swallowed more soup and tried not to show her fear. He went back to the cooking pot and filled the bowl again. He sat at a small table and ate by himself.

"How long have I been here?" she asked.

"Three days."

"Three *days*?"

"You've been delirious most of it. Your fever broke yesterday afternoon. Can you remember anything?"

"No." She didn't try. "I suppose I have you to thank for saving my life," she said bitterly. He went on eating in silence. "So what's it going to be, mister?"

"What do you mean?"

"What do you want from me?"

"Nothing for a while."

"Just talk. Right?"

He looked at her then, and she felt uneasy at his calm. When he stood up and came toward her, her heart pounded hard and fast. "I'm not going to hurt you, Mara," he said gently. "I love you."

It wasn't the first time a man had said he loved her. "I'm flattered," she said dryly. When he didn't say anything more, she clenched the blanket in her fist. "By the way. My name isn't Mara. It's *Angel*. You ought to get the name right if you're going to put the ring on my finger."

"You said I could call you anything I wanted."

Men had called her by other names than Angel. Some nice. Some not so nice. But she didn't want this man calling her anything but Angel. That's who he had married. Angel. And Angel was all he was going to get.

"The name Mara comes from the Bible," he said. "It's in the Book of Ruth."

"And being a Bible-reading man, you figure Angel is too good a name for me."

"Good's got nothing to do with it. Angel isn't your real name."

"Angel *is* who I am."

His face hardened. "Angel was a prostitute in Pair-a-Dice, and she doesn't exist anymore."

"Nothing's any different now from what it's always been, whatever you choose to call me."

Michael sat on the edge of the bed. "It's a whole lot different," he said. "You're my wife now."

She was shaking with weakness, but she fought back. "Do you really think that makes a difference? How? You paid for me, just like you always did."

"Paying the Duchess seemed the quickest way to get rid of her. I didn't think you'd mind."

"Oh, I don't mind." Her head throbbed.

"You'd better lie down again."

She didn't have the strength to protest when he put his arm around her and removed the support from her back. She felt his hand, rough with calluses and warm against her bare skin as he eased her back. "Don't push it," he said and pulled the blanket up again.

She tried to get a good look at his face and couldn't. "I hope you don't mind waiting. I'm not up to showing any gratitude right now."

She heard the smile in his response. "I'm a patient man."

His fingertips ran lightly across her damp forehead. "I shouldn't have let you sit up so long. You're not up to more than a few minutes at a time." She wanted to argue but knew it was useless. He was bound to know she was in great pain. "What hurts most?"

"Nothing I want you touching." She closed her eyes, wishing she could die so the pain would end. When he touched her temples, she drew in her breath.

"Relax." His caress was neither exploring nor intimate, and she eased. "By the way," he said, "my name is Michael. Michael Hosea. In case you didn't remember."

"I didn't," she lied.

"Michael. Not too hard to remember."

"If you want to."

He laughed softly. She knew she had gotten to him that last night at the brothel. Why had he taken her away from Pair-a-Dice with him? When he had walked out the door, she never expected to see him again. So why had he come back? What use was she to him like this?

"You're tensing up again. Relax the muscles in your forehead," he said. "Come on, Mara. Think about that if you have to think about anything."

"Why did you come back?"

"God sent me."

He was crazy. That was it. He was just plain crazy.

"Try to stop thinking so much. There's a mocking bird outside the window. Listen to it."

His hands were so gentle. She did what he told her, and the pain lessened. He talked to her softly, and she grew sleepy. She had heard all kinds of men's voices before, but none like his. Deep, calm, soothing.

She was so tired, she wanted to die and sleep forever. She could barely keep her eyes open. "You and God better not expect much," she mumbled.

"I want everything."

"Your litany." He could hope all he wanted, and he could ask, too. But all he was going to get was what was left. Nothing. Nothing at all.

# *Eight*

Angel didn't care one way or the other whether she ever got up again. A still darkness lay heavily on her. She had seen a way to end her miserable life and had reached for it in a moment of desperation — and she'd failed again. Rather than find the peace she craved, she found pain. Rather than be free, she was in bondage to another man.

Why couldn't she do anything right? Why did all her plans go awry?

Hosea was the one man she had wanted most to avoid, and now he owned her. She had no strength to fight him. Worse, she had to rely on him for food, water, shelter — everything. Her utter dependency on him chafed bitterly. She was raw with it. And she hated him even more because of it.

Had Hosea been an ordinary man, she would have known how to fight him, but he wasn't. Nothing she said bothered him. He was a mountain of granite. She could not wound him. His quiet determination unnerved her. There was a look about him now that she couldn't describe. He once said he had learned a lot about her during her fever, but he didn't say what. She worried about what "everything" he wanted. Whenever she was awake, he was there. She just wanted him to leave her alone.

Angel felt a trap closing in on her. She wasn't in a fancy brownstone this time. She wasn't in a rotting tent made out of a ship's sail, or a two-story brothel, but it was a trap nonetheless, and this lunatic held the key.

What did he want from her? And why did she sense he was more dangerous than all the other men she had ever known?

After a week, Michael left her in the cabin by herself for a few hours at a time while he went out to work. She didn't know what he did, and she didn't ask. She didn't care. She was relieved he wasn't hovering over her, wiping her brow or spooning soup into her mouth. She wanted to be by herself. She wanted to *think*, and she couldn't do it with him hanging around.

The aloneness she had craved turned to loneliness, and think was all she did. It rained, and she listened to the pounding on the roof...and with the pounding came visions of the shack on the docks, and Mama and Rab. Thinking of Rab led to Duke, and Duke led to all the rest, and she thought she would go mad. Maybe she would start talking to God, too, like this crazy man who had put his mother's wedding ring on her finger.

Why had he done it? Why had he *married* her?

Then, there he would be in the doorway, big, strong, quiet, and looking at her with that way of his. She wanted to ignore him, but he filled the cabin with his presence. Even when he just sat silent before the fire reading the same old worn book, he took over the whole place. He was taking her over with it. Even when she shut her eyes, she saw him there. He was sitting in a chair before the fire, right inside her head.

She didn't understand him any more now than she had at the brothel, but he had changed somehow. He was different. For one thing, he didn't talk a lot. In fact, he talked very little. He would smile at her and ask how she was feeling or if she needed anything and then go about his own business, whatever his business was. Day after day she watched him put his hat on and knew he was going to leave her alone again.

"Mister," she said, determined never to call him by his name, "why did you bring me back here if all you're going to do is leave me alone in this cabin?"

"I'm giving you time to think."

"Think about what?"

"Whatever you need to think about. You'll get up when you're ready." He took his hat from the hook by the door and left.

The morning sunlight streamed in through an open window. A fire burned in the grate. Her stomach was full, and she was warm. She should be satisfied. She should be able to relax and just lean back and not think about anything. Solitude should be enough.

What was the matter with her?

Maybe it was the silence. She was used to sounds attacking her from all sides. Men knocking on the doors, men telling her what they wanted, men telling her what to do, men shouting, men singing, men swearing in the bar below. Sometimes chairs crashed against walls and glasses shattered, and there was always the Duchess telling her how grateful she should be. Or Magowan telling some man his time was up and if he didn't get his pants on and get out, he'd regret it.

But she had never had this silence, this quiet that rang in her ears.

She complained.

"There's plenty of sound," Hosea said. "Just listen for it."

With nothing else to occupy her, she did. And he was right. The silence changed, and she heard sounds breaking through. It was like the rain used to be when she put out the shiny tins in the dark little shack. She began to pick out voices in the chorus around her. A cricket lived under the bed; a bullfrog was just outside the window. A throng of feathered companions came and went outside – robins, sparrows, and a noisy jay.

Finally, Angel stood on her own feet.

When she looked for something to put on, she found nothing. It hadn't occurred to her until then that nothing in the cabin belonged to her. None of her own things were here. Where were they? Hadn't he thought to bring them along? What was she supposed to wear? A scratchy gunnysack?

He had precious little himself from the looks of it. A small chest of drawers yielded an extra pair of worn long johns, a pair of dungarees, and some heavy socks – all far too large for her. An old, battered black trunk was in the corner, but she was too tired to open and rummage through it. Naked and too weak to drag a blanket off the bed to put around herself, she just leaned on the windowsill and drank in the fresh, cold air.

Half a dozen tiny birds flitted from branch to branch in a big tree. A larger bird strutted and pecked at the ground no more than six feet from the cabin. He was so cocky, she smiled. A soft breeze drifted in, and with it a scent so rich, she could almost taste it. The meadowland near Mama's cottage used to smell just like this. She closed her eyes and savored it.

She opened her eyes again and gazed at the stretch of land. "Oh, Mama," she whispered, her throat tightening. Weakness crept up her spine, and her ribs began to ache again. She was shaking and growing light-headed.

Michael walked in and, when he saw her standing naked by the open window, went without a word to take a quilt from the bed. He swung it around her, and she buckled beneath the weight of it. He scooped her up gently.

"How long have you been up?"

"Not long enough to be put back in bed." He held her in his arms like a child, his warmth soaking into her. He smelled of earth and sun. "You can put me down now. But not in bed. I've spent my whole life in bed and I'm sick of it."

Michael smiled. She wasn't going to do anything by halves, even getting on her feet again. He put her in the chair before the fire and added another log.

Pain was shooting along her sides. She clenched the arms of the chair, feeling every spot where Magowan had laid boot and fist. He hadn't missed much. She touched her face gingerly and frowned. "Do you have a mirror?"

Michael took the shiny tin he used for shaving and handed it to her. Aghast, she stared. After a long moment, she held the tin up to him, and he set it back on the shelf.

"How much did you pay for me?"

"Everything I had."

She laughed weakly. "Mister, you're a fool." How could he even look at her like this?

"There's no permanent damage."

"No? Well, at least I have all my teeth. That's something."

"I didn't marry you for your looks."

"Of course you didn't. You married me for my charming nature. Or did *God* tell you to do it?"

"Maybe he figured the horns in your head fit the holes in mine."

Angel rested her head back. "I knew you were crazy the first time I laid eyes on you." She was weary past endurance and thought how much more comfortable she would be lying on her back on that straw mattress again. She might make it to her feet, but one step, and she was going to break her nose again, right on the plank floor.

Michael came to her and lifted her gently, ignoring her protests.

"Mister, I told you I don't want to lie down yet."

"Fine. Sit up in bed."

"What happened to all my things?"

"I forgot them. Besides, what you had wouldn't suit you now anyway. A farmer's wife doesn't wear satin and lace."

"No, I suppose she trots naked up and down your rows of beans and carrots."

He grinned, humor lighting his eyes. "Might be kind of interesting."

Angel could see why Rebecca had been so enamored of him, but good looks made no difference to her. Duke had been a handsome man. A charismatic charmer. "Look," she said tightly, "I want to start getting up and about on my own. *With* something on."

"I'll provide what you need when you need it."

"I need it *now*."

His mouth tipped. "I reckon so," he said with grating calm. He went to the old battered trunk and opened it. He took out a bundle and brought it to her. "These will have to do for a while." Curious, she untied it. The gray wool fell apart, and she realized it was a worn cape. Inside were two linsey-woolsey skirts, one faded brown, the other black; two blouses – one that probably was white once but now was almost yellow – and the other with faded blue and pink flowers. Both would button up to her chin and had sleeves long enough to pass her wrists. Two bonnets matched the blouses. Tucked modestly inside them were two simple camisoles, pantalets, and darned black woolen stockings. Last, she found a pair of down-at-the-heels, high-buttoned black shoes.

She looked up at him in wry disbelief. "I shall be forever grateful for this bounty."

"I know they're not exactly what you're used to, but I think you're going to find these things suit you better than anything you've ever worn."

"I'll try and take your word for it." She fingered the linsey-woolsey.

He smiled slightly. "In another week or two, you'll be up to taking on a few chores."

Her head came up, but he was already on his way out the door. Chores? What chores did he have in mind? Milking a cow? Cooking? Maybe he would expect her to chop the firewood and tote it, along with the water from the creek. And his clothes! He would want her to wash and iron. What a laugh! She was good at one thing and nothing else. He was going to have a real awakening when she started doing *chores*.

He came back in with an armload of firewood.

"Mister, I don't know the first thing about what a farm wife does."

He stacked the wood neatly. "I didn't expect you would."

"Then just what chores did you have in mind?"

"Cooking, washing, ironing, the garden."

"I just told you – "

"You're smart. You'll learn." He put another log on the fire. "You won't be doing anything really heavy until you're able, which you won't be for another month at least."

Really heavy? What did that mean? She decided to take another tack instead. Her mouth curved in a well-practiced smile. "What about the other wifely duties?"

Michael glanced back at her. "When it means something more to you than work, we'll consummate the marriage."

She was taken aback by his frankness. Where was the farmer who blushed and jumped when she touched him? Unnerved, she retreated in anger. "Fine, mister. I'll do whatever you've got in mind. I'll match you hour for hour, day for day since you started taking care of me."

"And when you figure we're square, you'll leave. Is that it?"

"I'm going back to Pair-a-Dice and get what the Duchess owes me."

"No, you're not," he said quietly.

"Yes, I am." She would get her money from the Duchess even if she had to take it out of the old crone's hide. Then she would hire someone to build her a cabin just like this one, far enough away from a town so she wouldn't hear the noise and smell the stench, but close enough that she could get what supplies she needed. She would buy a gun, a big gun, and plenty of bullets, and if any man came around knocking at her door, she would use it, unless she needed some money. Then she would have to let him in to do business first. But if she was careful and smart, she could live a long time on what she had already earned. She could hardly wait. She had never lived all by herself, and it would be heaven.

*You were left to yourself for an entire week,* a small voice mocked her from deep inside, *and you were miserable, remember? Admit it, being by yourself isn't heaven at all. Not when you have so many demons to keep you company.*

"You may have paid a lot of gold dust for me, but you don't *own* me, mister."

Michael studied her with patience. She was small and weak but possessed an iron will. It shone from her defiant blue eyes and the rigid way she was holding herself. She thought she had enough to overcome him. She was wrong. He was doing God's will, and he had plans of his own, plans that kept growing, but he had said all he was going to say for a while. Let her think on it.

"You're right," he said. "I don't own you, but you're not running away from this."

They ate at opposite sides of the room, she on the bed with her plate in her lap and he at the table. The only sound in the room was the crackling fire.

Angel set the plate on the side table. She was shaking violently but was still determined not to lie down. She studied him. Sooner or later, she would figure him out. He was a man, wasn't he? He couldn't be that complex. She would take him apart piece by piece.

"They all have foibles, honey," Sally had told her. "You just have to sort out their messages and find out what it is they want from you. As long as you make them happy, you'll get by just fine. Otherwise, they turn mean."

Like Duke when he was crossed. Angel had known all about Duke after the first night. He liked power. He wanted immediate obedience. She didn't have to like what he wanted to do, as long as she did it. With a smile. Hesitance earned that cold, dark look; protest, a slap; defiance, brute force. Running away earned the end of his lit cheroot. By the time he tired of keeping her all to himself, she had learned one major lesson: to pretend. No matter what she felt, no matter how frightened or repulsed or angry, pretend to like whatever the men wanted and paid to get. And if she couldn't pretend to like it, she had to pretend not to care. She had become real good at that.

Sally understood, but Sally had her own rules.

"You got a bad break when that drunken fool brought you here. Then again, maybe not. Seeing as how your mama was a prostitute too, it weren't likely any folks from uptown would want you, no matter how pretty you are. Whatever mighta been, here's what is, Angel. And here's where you're going to stay."

She'd cupped Angel's chin and forced her to look up. "And I don't ever want to see that look on your face after today. Whatever you feel, you learn to keep it to yourself. Understand? The rest of us have our own sad stories to tell, some worse than yours. You learn to read a man, give him what he pays for, and send him on his way with a smile on his face. You do that, and I'll treat you like the mama you lost. You don't, and you'll think your time with Duke was heaven."

Sally turned out to be a woman of her word, and Angel learned all she ever wanted to know about men. Some knew what they wanted; some only thought they did. Some said one thing when they meant another. Some had guts. More had gall. However or whatever, it all came down to the same thing. They laid down their money for a piece of her. In the beginning, chunk by bloody chunk. After a while, drop by drop. The only difference was whether they quietly slid the money under the silk undergarments discarded on the foot of her bed or laid it in the palm of her hand and looked her right in the eye.

She looked at Michael Hosea. What sort of man was he?

Fingering the worn clothing, she worried her lip. Maybe he

wanted what he bought wrapped up in linsey-woolsey so he wouldn't have to look at it too closely. Maybe he didn't want to see it for what it was. No lantern, please, and keep the ring on your finger so we can pretend this is right. Then I won't have to think what I'm doing is *immoral*. She could play virgin for him. She could even play grateful if it came to that. Oh, yes, thanks a heap for saving me. She could play anything as long as she knew it only had to last a little while.

*Jesus. God. I'm tired of pretending. I'm sick of living like this. Why can't I just close my eyes and die?*

"I've had enough," she said, putting her plate on the side table. More than enough.

Michael had been watching her. "I'm not going to give you anything more than you can handle."

Angel looked back at him and knew he didn't mean chores. "And what about you, mister? Do you think you can handle what I'm going to give you?"

"Try me."

Angel watched him eat his supper. He wasn't worried about anything. Every inch of him told her he knew who he was and what he was about, even if she didn't. And she knew if she didn't get well and get away soon, he would end up taking her apart, piece by piece.

The next morning, Angel dressed as soon as Hosea was out the door. She slipped on the camisole and tied up the frayed ribbons. The fabric was thick and unrevealing, covering her completely. She had never worn anything so simple, so sweet...so cheap.

Who had worn these things before her? What had happened to her? Judging by her clothing, the woman had been prim and hardworking – just like those women who had turned their backs when Mama walked by.

Angel found the buttonhook in the left boot and put the shoes on. They fit well enough to get by. Michael came, and she looked up at him. She raised one brow. "I thought you said you were never married."

"Those things belonged to my sister, Tessie. She and her

husband, Paul, came west with me. She died of fever on the Green River." It hurt to remember burying Tessie in the middle of the road west. Every wagon in the train had gone over her grave so there would be no trace. He and Paul hadn't wanted her dug up by Indians or animals.

He still couldn't get over burying his beloved little sister like that, with no stone or cross to mark the place. Tessie deserved better.

"What happened to her husband? Did he die, too?"

He shrugged off his coat. "His land is at the end of the valley lying fallow. He's panning gold on the Yuba. Paul's never been able to stick to anything for long." His love for Tess had kept him walking a straight road for a while, but when she died, he had gone wild again.

Angel smiled mirthlessly. "So your brother-in-law is another of the multitude raping the streams of California – and anything else to be found."

Michael turned and looked at her.

Angel felt that look and she knew what he was wondering. "If he's a man and he's on the Yuba, he probably made it to the Palace." She saw she had guessed correctly. With a careless shrug, she stabbed deeper. "I couldn't tell you whether he made it to my room. Describe him. Maybe I'll remember."

Her words were hard and cold, but Michael wasn't fooled. She was trying awfully hard to drive him away. He wondered why.

His silence unnerved her. "You needn't worry whether he knows me or not. I'll be gone before he gets back."

"You'll be right here with me, where you belong."

She smiled coolly. "Sooner or later a wagon train of virgins will arrive, all respectable in their dusty, worn-out linsey-woolsey. Then you'll come to your senses. Right about the time you have to say: Meet my wife. I bought her out of a brothel in Pair-a-Dice back in '51."

"It won't matter who comes. I married you."

"Well, that's easy enough to rectify." She slipped the wedding ring off her finger. "See? We're not married anymore." She held it out to him in the palm of her hand. "Simple as that."

Michael searched her face. Did she really believe it was that easy? Just take the ring off, and the marriage is null and void, and everything goes back the way it was? "That's where you're wrong, Mara. We're still married whether you're wearing the ring or not, but I want you to keep it on just the same."

She frowned slightly and did as he said. She turned the ring on her finger. "Lucky said it belonged to your mother."

"It did."

She let her hands drop to her sides. "Just give me the word when you want it back."

"I won't."

She rested her hands in her lap and looked at him indolently. "Whatever you want, mister."

That got to him. "I hate that phrase. Whatever you want. Like you're offering me coffee." Whatever you want. She had offered her body the same way. "We'd better get one thing straight. I married you for better or worse and until death parts us. I made vows before God when I married you, and I'm never going to break them."

Angel knew all about God. Do everything right, or he'd squash you like a cockroach. That was God. She saw the darkness in Hosea's eyes and said nothing.

Mama had believed in God. Mama had had faith. She had opened herself up wide. Our Father who art in heaven was in the same realm as Alex Stafford. Angel wasn't fool enough to open herself up for anyone, least of all *him*. And if this man figured he could make her.... She had learned early that what you don't believe in can't hurt you.

"Do you remember anything about the wedding?" Michael said, startling her from her grim thoughts.

"I remember some man in black talking over me with a voice deader than Jesus."

"You said yes. Do you remember that?"

"I didn't say yes. I said, 'why not?'"

"It will do."

# *Nine*

*Take my yoke upon you and learn from me;
for I am gentle and humble in heart,
and you will find rest....*

JESUS, MATTHEW 11:29

Dressing was all Angel managed to do the first few days out of bed. After a week on her feet, she ventured outside. It gave Michael an odd pang to see her in Tessie's clothes. No two women could have been more different; Tess, sweet and caring, uncomplicated and open; Mara, cold and indifferent, complex and closed. Tessie, dark and muscular; Mara, blonde and slender.

Michael didn't try to fool himself that she'd come outside because she was lonely and wanted his company. She was just tired of being cooped up in the cabin. She was bored.

But Angel was lonely, and because of it she was edgy and defensive when Michael approached. After all, she didn't want him getting any wrong ideas. "When do I start plowing the fields?" she said dryly.

"In the fall."

She glanced up at him sharply.

Michael laughed and brushed the hair back off her shoulder. "You feel up to taking a little walk?"

"How far?"

"Until you say stop." He took her hand, trying not to let it bother him that hers lay like a dead fish in his. Passive resistance. He showed her the corncrib and the gear shed. He took her to the log bridge over the stream where he planned to build the spring-house to store meat and dairy products – when he could afford to buy a cow. He walked her along the pathway to the small barn and showed her the two draft horses. He pointed out the fields he had plowed and planted, and then he took her out into the open meadowland. "I started out west with eight oxen and ended up with the two you see out there."

"What happened to the rest?"

"Indians stole one, and five died in harness. It was hard going," he said. "Animals weren't the only ones dying along the Humboldt Sink." Michael looked down at her and saw how pale she was. She wiped perspiration from her forehead with the back of her hand. He asked if she wanted to head back. She said no. He headed back anyway. She was played out and too stubborn to admit it.

*Lord, is she going to be this bullheaded about everything?*

On the way back to the cabin, Michael showed her where he wanted to put a grape arbor. "We'll sit beneath it on hot days. There's nothing smells better than grapes ripening in the sun. We'll add a bedroom and kitchen and put a porch on the west side, so we can sit in the evenings and watch the sun set and the stars come out. On hot summer afternoons, we'll sip apple cider and watch our corn grow. And children, someday, God willing."

Her stomach dropped. "You've enough work planned out to last a long while."

Michael tipped her chin and looked straight into her eyes. "It'll take us a lifetime, Mara."

She jerked her chin away. "Don't go pinning your hopes on me, mister. I have my own plans, and they don't include you." She went the rest of the way by herself.

The walk had been good for her, but she was exhausted. Still, she didn't want to be inside. She dragged his chair out the door so she could sit in the open. She wanted to feel the warmth of the sun on her face. She wanted to smell the fresh air. A soft afternoon breeze played with her hair, and she could smell the earth, strong and rich. Her muscles loosened, and she closed her eyes.

Michael returned from work to find her sleeping. Not even the bruises darkening her eyes and jaw marred her look of peace. He took a tendril of her hair and rubbed it between his fingers. It was silk. She moved slightly. He looked at the slender column of her white throat and watched the steady pulse there. He longed to lean down and press his mouth to it. He wanted to breathe in the scent of her.

*Lord, I love her, but is it always going to feel like this? Like there's an ache inside me I'll never get over?*

Angel roused. She opened her eyes and started, seeing Hosea standing above her. The sun was behind him, and she couldn't see his face or guess what he was thinking. She pushed her hair back and looked away. "How long have I been sitting here?"

"You looked peaceful. Sorry if I awakened you. You've got some color in your cheeks."

She touched them and felt the warmth. "Add red to the black and blue."

"Are you hungry?"

She was. "You might as well start teaching me to cook." She winced from pain as she got up and followed him inside. She would need to know how to cook for herself when she had a place of her own.

"First thing you have to do is get a good fire laid." He poked the coals into a fiery bed and added more wood. He went out with the bucket and came back with a chunk of salted venison. He cut it into pieces and dropped them into the boiling pot. Angel could smell the pungent herbs as he rubbed them between his palms and dropped them into the bubbling water.

"We'll leave that cooking awhile. Come on outside with me." He took a basket, and she followed him to a vegetable garden. Hunkering down, he showed her how to tell which carrots and onions were ready for harvest. He pulled up a mature potato plant. She didn't want to admit she was astonished. Had anyone asked, she would have said potatoes came from Ireland. The one plant he pulled up produced enough potatoes to last several days.

As Angel straightened, she saw Hosea hunkered down a few feet away, yanking plants up and tossing them aside. A piercing recollection of Mama in the moonlit garden froze her. "Why are you tearing up your garden?"

Michael glanced up at her tone. Her face was white and drawn. He straightened and brushed his hands on his pants. "I'm pulling up weeds. They're choking everything else. I haven't had time to work out here. One of the things I'll ask of you is tending the garden. When you're ready."

He picked up the basket and nodded toward the hills. "There are other foodstuffs growing wild. Chicory, mustard, and miner's lettuce mostly. I'll teach you what to look for. Down the creek a half mile are blackberries. They come ripe in late summer. There are blueberries a half mile up the hill. We've got apples and walnuts as well." He handed her the basket. "You can wash those vegetables in the creek."

She did what he told her and came back to the cabin. Michael showed her how to peel and pare them and left her to it. The meat was boiling in the pot over the fire, and he took an iron hook and slid the pot to the outer edge of the fire. "Stir it once in a while. I'm going out and see to the stock."

The stew didn't seem to be boiling fast enough, so Angel slid the pot back over the fire again. Then it boiled too fast, and she slid it away. She hovered, stirring and sliding, sliding and stirring. The heat and work were draining. She brushed the damp strands of hair back from her forehead. Her eyes smarted from smoke.

Michael came in with a bucket of water. He slammed it down, sloshing it on the floor. "Watch out!" He caught her arm and yanked her back from the fire.

"What're you doing?"

"Your skirt's smoking. In another minute, you would have been in flames."

"I had to get close enough to stir the stew!" The pot lid was banging, the meal boiling over the side and hissing on the red coals. Without thinking, she grabbed the handle. She yelped, swore vilely, and snatched the hook down again.

"Easy!" Michael warned, but she was in no mood to listen. She yanked too hard and dislodged the bar. It clanged and the pot fell, dumping the contents. The fire hissed and sputtered violently. A cloud of smoke billowed and filled the cabin with the horrible stench of burning stew.

She couldn't even do this right! Angel threw the iron hook into the fireplace with the mess and sat in the willow chair. Leaning forward, she held her aching ribs.

Michael opened the two windows and the door, and the smoke began to clear.

Teeth clenched, Angel watched a piece of venison go up in flames. "Your dinner's ready, mister."

He tried not to smile. "You'll do better next time."

She glared up at him. "I don't know anything about cooking. I don't know a weed from a carrot, and if you set me behind your plow, you won't have a straight furrow worth planting." She stood. "You want me to work. Fine. I'll work. The only way I know how. Right there," she said, pointing at his bed. "Right now, if you like, mister. If the bed doesn't suit your fancy, how about the floor, or your stable, or anywhere else you'd like? Whatever you want, just let me know!"

He let out a breath. "It was only a pot of stew, Mara."

She seethed with frustration. "How did a saint like you pick me? Are you testing your faith? Is that it?" She swept past him and went outside.

She wanted to run away but couldn't. Every step hurt. She barely made it to the field before she had to stop and get her breath. He had jarred her when he pulled her away from the fire, and she hurt all over; but the physical pain was nothing to her own self-disgust and humiliation. She was stupid! She didn't know anything! How was she going to manage on her own if she couldn't cook a simple meal? She didn't even know how to build a fire. She didn't know anything necessary to survive.

*You're going to learn.*

"Oh, no, I'm not! I'm not asking for *his* help. I'm not going to owe him anything." She clenched her burned hand into a fist. "I didn't ask him to come back. I didn't ask for any of this!"

She went down to the creek to soak her hand and nurse her grievances.

# Ten

The mess in the fireplace was cleaned up when Angel came back, but Hosea was gone. She expected to feel relief at his absence, but she didn't. Instead there was a hollowness inside her that made her feel she was drifting in empty space. Was he out there somewhere thinking up a suitable punishment for her outburst?

What a fool he must think her. She could bet his sister had known how to build a fire, cook a fine meal, plow a field, and do whatever else needed doing. She'd probably known every wild vegetable plant from the Atlantic to the Pacific, at a distance of a hundred feet. She probably had been able to smell out wild game and then shoot and dress it herself.

Dejected, Angel sat on the floor before the hearth and looked at the barren fireplace. *My life is just like that: a bare, cold, useless hole in a wall.* She was stupid and clumsy. Oh, but she was beautiful. She touched her face. Or she had been.

She got up. She had to *do* something. Anything. She needed light and warmth. She had watched Hosea build a fire often enough. Maybe she could do it herself. She took wood chips and piled them, then laid kindling and small branches. She took the flint and steel from the mantle, but no matter how hard she tried, she could barely strike a spark.

Michael stood in the doorway watching her. He had gone out for her earlier and seen her sitting beside the creek, so dejected she didn't even notice he was there. He stood by, watching over her until she wandered back to the house. He might as well have been invisible. She was so tightly wrapped in herself, her own misery and dark thoughts, that she was blind to everything else. Especially him.

Cursing, she put her fists against her eyes.

Michael put his hand lightly on her hair and felt her jump. "Let me show you how to do it." He hunkered down beside her and held out his hand. She handed him tools. "First of all, you can't expect to get it perfect the first time. It takes practice." Like cooking stew, he wanted to say. Like living a different way of life.

Angel watched him lay the fire and strike the flint. A spark caught, and he blew on it gently until the shavings smoked and began to burn. He added small kindling, then larger branches. Within minutes, the fire was going.

Michael sat back, his forearms resting on his raised knees. He intended to enjoy the fire and Mara's closeness, but she had other ideas. She took the poker and knocked the branches off and scattered the kindling and wood chips. She smashed every last ember.

Kneeling closer, she laid the fire just as he had done. She did it exactly right, then struck the flint and steel. She made a spark, but it didn't catch. She tried again, more resolute, and failed. Her burned hand hurt abominably, but she clutched the tools with such absolute determination that her palms began to sweat. With each failure, her chest ached more, until the pain was so permeating, so deep and disabling, that she sank back on her heels.

"I can't." What was the use?

Michael's heart ached for her. She had never once cried, even when she was out of her mind with fever. And God knew she needed to. "Let go of it, Mara."

"Fine." Angel put the flint and steel between them. "You do it."

"That's not what I mean. You try too hard. You expect to do everything right. It's not possible."

"I don't know what you're talking about. All I want to do is build a fire."

"We don't even speak the same language," he said flatly. He might as well be speaking English to a Spanish-speaking California girl. "It's like fighting me when you don't have to."

She refused to look at him. "Build it again so I can see what I did wrong."

He did as she asked. She watched closely and saw she had done nothing wrong. Why hadn't her fire caught? The hearth was full of blazing light, and he had done it all in but a few moments. Her fire wouldn't even start, but his would last the night.

Angel came to her feet abruptly and stepped away. She hated his competence. She despised his calm. She wanted to destroy both, and she only had one weapon she knew how to use.

She stretched sinuously, aware of his gaze upon her. "I suppose I'll get it eventually," she said and sat on the bed. "My shoulders ache. Would you massage them the way you did before?"

Michael did as she asked. He kneaded the tension from her muscles, increasing his own. "That feels good," she said, and the sultry tone sent his pulse racing. Her hair slipped back and was like silk over his working hands. When he put one knee on the bed, she put her hand on his thigh.

*So that's it,* he thought ruefully. She figured she couldn't build a fire in the grate so she would build one in him instead. It hadn't taken her any time at all to do it. He drew back.

Angel felt his retreat and followed him. She slid her arms around his waist, pressing herself against his straight back. "I know I need someone to take care of me and I'm glad you came back for me."

*Jesus, give me strength!* Michael closed his eyes. When her hands moved, he caught her wrists and withdrew from her embrace completely.

When he turned, Angel was ready. She knew how to act the role. She knew all the words by heart. Soft, broken words...calculated words to tear at his heart, to make him feel his rejection had hurt her. Stir guilt in with the hot blood boiling. Give him reasons and excuses to give in. That last evening in the brothel had already weakened him. He was a lamb ready for the slaughter.

Angel came to him again, shutting down her emotions and using her mind instead. She pulled his head down and kissed him. Michael dug his fingers into her hair and kissed her back.

She used what she knew to wage war against him. She didn't know anything about building fires or cooking stew, but she knew all about this.

He disentangled himself, gripping her shoulders. "You're so relentless," he said, unwilling to surrender.

Angel stared up at him and saw he wasn't fooled. He knew exactly what she was doing and why. She tried to pull away, but he wouldn't let her. "It doesn't have to be the way you know."

"Let go of me!" She struggled frantically. Michael saw she was hurting herself and released her. She stepped well away from him.

"Did all that make you feel any better?"

"*Yes!*" she hissed, lying through her teeth.

"God help me."

She had wanted him to feel more than physical discomfort. She had wanted to annihilate him. She wanted to see him squirm like a worm on a hook. She plunked herself down in the willow chair, her neck stiff, and stared straight ahead.

Michael looked at her bleakly. Her silence screamed profanity at him. She thought she had lost, but did she think he had won? He went outside. *Does this woman have a compromising bone in her body, Lord? Or is this what I've got to look forward to for the rest of my life!? Jesus, she doesn't fight fair.*

**She's fighting you the only way she knows how.**

Michael went down to the creek and knelt, splashing cold water on his face. He stayed on his knees for a long time. Then he went to the barn for the metal washtub.

When he came in, Angel kept her back to him. He set the tub before the fire. She looked from it to him and away again, saying nothing. Had she made him feel dirty? Did he need a bath now to wash her off? He spent the next hour toting water from the well and heating it in the big black pot hanging over the fire. He tossed a bar of soap into the water.

"I'm going for a walk," he said and left.

Surprised, she went to the door and opened it. He kept on going until she lost sight of him in the trees. Frowning, she closed the door. She took off her clothes and stepped into the tub. She scrubbed her hair and body vigorously, poured the warm water down over her to rinse, then stepped out. She wanted to be finished before he came back. He had left a towel draped over the back of the chair, and she rubbed her skin and wrapped her hair. She dressed quickly. She sat down before the fire again and unwound the towel. Her hair was a tangled mess, and she tried to work her fingers through the knots.

Hosea didn't come back for more than an hour.

When the door finally opened behind her, she glanced up at him. His dark hair was wet. She supposed he had bathed in the icy stream, and she felt a twinge of guilt and doubt. He moved about the cabin restlessly. She went on pushing her fingers through her hair, aware of his every movement. He opened the trunk and slammed it shut. As he paced past her, he dropped a brush in her lap. She picked it up and looked at it. Her throat closed up. She looked up at him and slowly began to brush her hair. He stood with his hip resting against the table and watched her. She didn't know what he was thinking. She didn't know what to say.

"Don't ever do that to me again," he said.

He was pale, and she felt something move inside her, curling tight and sinking deep. "I won't," she said and meant it.

Michael sat in the willow chair before the fire, his hands relaxed between his knees. He stared at the flames for a long time. "I guess I got a good taste of what it's been like for you."

She glanced up in surprise. "What do you mean?"

He looked at her. "It doesn't feel good to be used. Whatever the reason."

Something twisted inside her. She held the brush in her lap and stared at it miserably. "I don't know what I'm doing here with a man like you."

"I knew the moment I saw you that I was going to marry you."

"So you told me." She tilted her head. "Look, mister. Let me explain a few facts of life to you. A farmer alone for weeks on end, coming to town. You could've looked at the south end of a northbound mare and known she was the right one for you."

"It was your young, stone-cold face," Michael said. He gave her a rueful smile. "Then the rest of you." His gaze flickered down over her. "You were dressed in black like a widow, and Magowan was with you. I guess he was making sure you didn't run away."

She didn't say anything for a long time. She closed her eyes and tried not to think about any of it, but it was like a foul stench in the room. It lingered. She couldn't get rid of it. It was there under the clean smell of the soap he had given her to use. The foulness was inside her, running in her blood.

"Do you remember when you asked me what kind of name Hosea was and I said prophetic?" She began brushing her hair again slowly, but Michael knew she was listening to him this time. "Hosea was a prophet. God told him to marry a prostitute."

She glanced at him with a mocking smile. "Did God tell you to marry me?"

"Yes. He did."

She was scornful. "He talks to you personally?"

"He talks to everyone personally. Most people just don't bother to listen."

It was better to humor him. "Sorry I interrupted. You were telling me a story. What happened next? Did this prophet marry the prostitute?"

"Yes. He figured God must have a reason. A good reason."

The same as he probably did. "Did this Hosea beat the sin out of her? I suppose she crawled to him on her face and kissed his feet for saving her soul."

"No, she went back to prostitution."

Her stomach dropped. She looked up at him and searched his face. He just looked back at her, solemn, self-contained, enigmatic. "So God isn't so all-powerful after all, is he?" she said quietly.

"God told him to go and get her back again."

She frowned slightly. "Did he?"

"Yes."

"Just because God told him to?" No man would do that.

"Yes, and because he loved her."

She got up and went to look out the window at the darkening sky. "Love? No, I don't think that was his reason. It was his pride. The old prophet just didn't want to admit he couldn't hold onto her all by himself."

"Pride drives a man away, Mara. It drove me away from you that last night in Pair-a-Dice." He should have listened to the Lord and gone back. He should have dragged her out of there no matter how much she kicked and screamed.

Angel looked back over her shoulder at him. "So she stayed with the prophet after that?"

"No. She left him again. He had to buy her out of slavery a second time."

She didn't like his story very much. "Then she stayed?"

"No. She kept leaving. She even had children by other men."

Her chest felt heavy. Defensive, she mocked him. "And he finally stoned her to death," she said wryly, sarcasm dripping. "Isn't that right? He finally sent her to where she belonged." He didn't answer, and she turned her back on him again. "What's your point, mister? Just say it."

"Someday you're going to have to make a choice."

He didn't say any more, and she wondered if that was the end of it. She clenched her teeth. She wasn't going to ask him if the harlot ever stayed with that prophet or if he finally gave up on her.

Michael got up, opened two tins of beans and poured them into a pot. In a few moments they were warm, and he served them. "Sit and eat with me, Mara."

She sat down with him at the table. When he bowed his head and prayed, the anger came up fast inside her again. Trying to ignore him, she began eating. When he looked at her, she gave him a tight, challenging smile. "You know what I think," she said. "I think God had you marry me to punish you for some great sin in your past. Have you lusted after many women, mister?"

"It does plague me on occasion," he said, looking her over with a rueful smile. He ate the rest of the meal in silence.

She envied his peace and self-control. When he finished, she took his plate and stacked it on her own. "Since you did the cooking, I'll wash the dishes." She didn't like the dark, but it was better than staying in the cabin with him. He might start telling her another of his rotten stories. A really nice one this time, something about a leper or someone with running sores.

When she finished the dishes, she sat by the creek for a

while. She was aching all over and knew she had attempted far too much today, but just listening to the water soothed her unsettled nerves.

"What am I doing here?" she said to herself. "What am I doing here with *him*?"

A gentle breeze rustled the leaves of the cottonwood, and she could swear she heard a soft voice. She turned, but no one was there. Shivering, she walked back quickly and saw Hosea leaning against the door frame, waiting for her. His hands were shoved in his pockets. Stepping around him, she entered the cabin and put the dishes away. She was tired and wanted to go to bed.

Stripping off her clothes, she slipped quickly beneath the quilts. Then she lay there thinking about that girl going back to prostitution. Maybe she had a Duchess who had her money, too. Maybe the prophet had driven her half crazy the way this farmer was driving her crazy. Maybe she just wanted to be left alone. Did the prophet ever think of that?

Angel stiffened when Hosea slid into bed beside her. She only had herself to blame. Give them the taste of a kiss and they want the whole meal. Well, the sooner it was done, the sooner she could sleep.

She sat up, brushing her hair impatiently over her shoulder, and looked down at him with grim resolution.

"No."

She was surprised at the look of impatience he gave her. "No?"

"No."

"Look, mister. I can't read your mind. You have to tell me what you want."

"I want to sleep in my own bed with my wife beside me." Taking a strand of her hair, he tugged lightly. "And that's *all* I want."

Perplexed, she lay back down again. She waited for him to change his mind. After a long while, his breathing deepened. She turned her head cautiously and looked at him in the firelight. He *was* asleep. She studied his relaxed profile for a long moment, then turned away from him.

Angel tried to put space between their bodies, but Michael Hosea filled the bed the same way he filled the cabin.

The same way he was beginning to fill her life.

# Eleven

*In the middle of the journey of our life,*
*I came to myself in a dark wood.*

DANTE

Angel moaned as Duke bent over her. He laughed softly. "Did you think you could get away from the Alpha and Omega?"

Someone called to her from a great distance, but Duke kept drowning out the still, soft voice. "You thought four thousand miles was far enough, but here I am."

She strained away from him, trying to hear who was calling her.

Duke pulled her back again. "You belong to me. Oh, yes. Always, and you know it. I'm the only one you'll ever belong to." His breath smelled of the cloves he chewed after smoking his cheroots. "I know what you're thinking, Angel. I can read your mind. Couldn't I always? Hope all you wish, but I will never die. Even when you cease to exist, I'll still live. I am timeless."

She fought him, but he was not substance to be pushed away. He was shadow, covering her, taking her back and down into a deep black hole. She felt her body absorbing him as she fell. He was entering every pore until the blackness was within her, and she tore at her own flesh. "No, no!"

"Mara. *Mara!*"

She awakened abruptly, her mouth open in a silent scream. "Mara," Michael said gently, sitting on the edge of the bed. She tried to still the shaking as he brushed her hair away from her face. "You have a lot of nightmares. What are they about?"

His gentle voice and touch made her relax a little. She brushed his hand away. "I can't remember," she lied, Duke branded into her mind. Would he still be searching for her after all this time? She knew the answer and felt cold. She could still see his face. It was as if she had run from him yesterday and not a year ago. He would find her someday. And when he did...

She could not bear to think about it. She didn't dare go back to sleep. The nightmare would begin again and take the course it always did.

"Mara, tell me what you're afraid of."

"Nothing," she said tightly. "Just leave me alone."

Michael laid his hand on her chest and her muscles tensed. "If your heart beat any harder it would come right out your chest."

"Are you hoping to get my mind on something else?"

Michael took his hand away. "There's more than sex between us."

"There's nothing at all." She turned her back to him.

Michael stripped the quilts off her. "I'll show you what else there is."

"I said leave me alone!" Raw from the nightmare, raw from being with him, she yanked the quilts back up again.

Michael ripped the bedcovers off. Bunching them, he tossed them on the trunk in the corner. "Get up. Now. You're going whether you like it or not."

Angel was frightened of him as he loomed over her. She could sense him trying to reign in his temper.

"We're going to take a little walk," he said.

"Now? In the middle of the night?" It was cold and dark. She gasped as he scooped her up and set her on her feet.

Pulling on his pants, he said, "You can go dressed or naked. It's all the same to me."

She didn't like the shadows in the cabin, and she wasn't going out that door into the darkness. "I'm not going anywhere. I'm staying right here."

She headed for the quilt, but he caught her arm and spun her around. When she cowered and raised her arm to ward off a blow, Michael's anger evaporated. Was that what she expected from him, even after all this time? "I'm never going to hurt you." He got the quilt and swung it around her. He found her shoes and held them out to her. She didn't take them. "You can wear them or walk barefoot. Your choice. But you are going with me."

Angel took the shoes.

"What are you really afraid of, Mara? Why don't we get down to that?"

She threw the buttonhook aside and straightened. "I'm not afraid of anything, least of all a dirt farmer like you."

He opened the door. "Come on, then, if you're so brave."

She could make out the barn, but he took her firmly in hand and headed toward the woods. "Where are you taking me?" She despised the tremor in her voice.

"You'll see when we get there." He kept walking, pulling her along with him.

Angel could barely see anything except shapes. They were menacing and dark, some moving. She remembered Rab hurrying her through the dark night a long time ago and was afraid. Her heart beat faster. "I want to go back." She stumbled and almost fell.

Michael caught and steadied her. "Just once, try trusting me, would you? Have I done anything to harm you?"

"Trust you? Why should I? You're crazy bringing me out here like this in the middle of the night. *Take me back.*" She was trembling and couldn't stop.

"Not until you see what I have to show you."

"Even if you have to drag me?"

"Unless you'd rather ride over my shoulder."

She jerked her hand free. "Go on ahead."

"All right," he said. Angel swung around to go back but couldn't see the cabin or barn through the trees. When she turned around, she couldn't see Hosea either and panicked. "Wait," she cried out. "Wait!"

Michael caught hold of her. "I'm right here." He felt her shaking and drew her into his arms. "I'm not going to leave you in darkness." He tipped her face up and kissed her gently. "When are you going to understand I love you?"

Angel put her arms around him and pressed closer. "If you love me, take me back. We can be warm and comfortable in bed. I'll do whatever you want."

"No," he said roughly, fighting his response to her. "Come with me."

She tried to hold him back. "Wait, please. All right. I am afraid of the dark. Being out here reminds me of – " She stopped.

"Of what?"

"Of something that happened when I was a child." He waited and she bit her lip. She didn't want to talk about Rab or what happened to him. She didn't want to think about the horror of that night. "Please. Just take me back."

Michael combed his fingers into her hair and tilted her head back so he could see her face in the moonlight. She was afraid, so afraid she couldn't hide it.

"I'm afraid, too, Mara. Not of the dark, not of the past – but of you and what you make me feel when I touch you. You use my desire for you as a weapon. What I feel is a gift. I know what I want, but when you press yourself against me, all I can feel is your body and my need. You make me tremble."

"Then take me back to the cabin – "

"You don't hear me. You don't understand anything. I can't take you back. You're not going to have it your way. It's got to be my way or not at all." Michael took her hand. "Now, come on." He walked through the dark woods. Her palms were sweating, but her hand didn't lay in his hand like a dead fish anymore. She was holding on as though her life depended on him.

Angel heard sounds everywhere, a constant ringing and humming that came from all directions and penetrated her head. It was a quiet that was so quiet it screamed. She wanted to be back in the cabin, away from the black, moving things around her. Winged demons, watching and grinning. This was Duke's world.

She was cold and weak from exhaustion. "How much farther is it?"

Michael swept her up in his arms and carried her. "We're almost there." The woods were behind them, the moon above making the hillsides an eerie silver gray. "Just to the top of that hill."

When he reached the crest, he set her on her feet again, and she looked around in confusion. There was nothing. Just more hills and then the mountains in the distance.

Michael watched the night breeze making her pale hair

dance in the moonlight. She huddled into the quilt and glared back at him. "There's nothing here."

"Everything that matters is here."

"All this way for nothing." She didn't know what she had expected. A monument. Something. She sat down, exhausted and shivering from the chill night air. The quilt wasn't enough. Ten quilts wouldn't be enough. The chill was inside her. What did he think he was doing dragging her up this hill in the middle of the night? "What's so special about this?"

Michael sat down behind her. He put his strong legs on either side of her and pulled her back against him. "Just wait."

She wanted to resist his embrace, but she was too cold to fight him. "For what?"

He put his arms around her. "For morning."

"I could have waited for that in the cabin."

He laughed against her hair. Lifting it, he kissed the nape of her neck. "You can't understand until you see it from here." He nuzzled the soft skin beneath her ear. She shivered softly. "Sleep a while if you want." He tucked her more closely against him. "I'll wake you at the right time."

She wasn't sleepy after the long walk. "Do you do this sort of thing often?"

"Not often enough."

They were silent again, but she was not uncomfortable with it. The warmth of his body was coming through her. She felt the weight of his arm across her and the solidness of him bracing her back. She looked at the stars, tiny jewels against black velvet. She had never seen it like this before, so close she felt she could reach up and touch each bright speck of light. The night sky was beautiful. It had never looked like this from a window. And the smell – thick, moist, earthy. Even the sounds around her became a kind of music, like the birds and insects, like the rain plinking into the tin cans in a dingy wharf shack. Then the darkness lightened.

It began slowly, hardly noticeable. The stars grew smaller and smaller, and the black softened. She stood up, hugging the quilt around her, watching. At her back was darkness still, but before her was light: pale yellow growing brilliant, gold-streaked with red and orange. She had watched sunrises before from within walls and behind glass, but never like this, with the cool breeze in her face and wilderness in every direction. She had never seen anything so beautiful.

Morning light spilled slowly over the mountains, across the valley to the cabin and the woods behind, and up the hillside. She felt Hosea's strong hands on her shoulders.

"Mara, that's the life I want to give you."

The morning sunlight was so bright it hurt her eyes, blinding her more than the darkness ever had. She felt his lips against her hair. "That's what I'm offering you." His breath was warm against her skin. "I want to fill your life with color and warmth. I want to fill it with light." He put his arms around her and held her back against him. "Give me a chance."

Angel felt a heaviness building inside her. He had pretty words for her, but words weren't life. Life wasn't that simple, that straightforward. It was tangled and twisted, writhing from birth. She couldn't erase the last ten years, or even the eight before Rab had led her through the streets to the brothel and left her there for Duke to ruin forever. It had started long before that.

She was guilty of being born.

Her own father had wanted her cut out of her mother's womb and thrown away like garbage. Her own father. And Mama would have done it had she known she would lose him over her small defiance. All those years of endless weeping had told Angel that.

No, not a hundred dawns like this, not even a thousand, would change what was. The truth was there forever, just like Duke said in the dream. You can't get away from it. No matter how hard you try, you can't escape the truth.

Her mouth curved into a sad smile, and her soul ached. Maybe this man was all he seemed. Maybe he meant every word he said, but she knew something he didn't. It was never going to be the way he wanted it. It just couldn't happen. He was a dreamer. He wanted the impossible from her. Dawn would come for him, too, and he would awaken.

Angel didn't want to be anywhere around when he did.

# *Twelve*

*Even if you persuade me, you won't persuade me.*

ARISTOPHANES

Michael felt the change in Angel after that night, but it was not a change that made him happy. She retreated and held her distance. Though her bruises were gone and her ribs healed, she was still walking wounded. She wouldn't let him get close. She regained the weight she had lost after Magowan's vicious beating. She grew physically strong, but Michael sensed a deeper vulnerability in her. He gave her work to give her purpose, and the brothel and cabin pallor disappeared. Yet no life shone in her eyes.

Most men would have been satisfied to have such a malleable, hardworking wife. Michael was not. He had not married her to have a drudge. He wanted a woman as part of his life – part of himself.

Every night was a trial. He lay beside her and breathed in the scent of her until his head swam. She made it clear he could use her body whenever and however he wished. She looked at him every night as she took off her clothes. The question in her eyes made his mouth go dry, but he didn't give in. He waited, praying for her heart to soften.

Her nightmares continued unabated. She often awakened shaking, her body drenched with perspiration. In the aftermath, she wouldn't even let him touch her. Only after she went back to sleep could he ease his arms around her and tuck her close. She would relax then, and he knew that on some deeper level she knew she was safe with him.

It was small satisfaction when the natural needs of his body were driving him harder the longer they were together. His mind would create pictures of them making love as it was written in Song of Solomon. He would almost feel her arms around him and taste her honeyed kisses. Then he would come out of the daydream and feel more frustrated and bereft than ever.

Oh, he could have her now if he wanted. She would be accommodating. She would be expert. And he would know, all the while he poured his hope into her, that she was counting the beams in the ceiling or the chores for the next day or anything else that kept her from him. She wouldn't look into his eyes or care that he was dying inside for love of her.

The memory was set in Michael's mind: Angel sitting on the end of the bed at the Palace, swinging her foot back and forth like a pendulum. It would be just the same now if he gave in to his physical desire. It would be Angel, not Mara, just waiting for him to finish so she could consign him to oblivion with all the other men who had ever used her body.

*God, what do I do? I'm going crazy. You're expecting too much of me. Or am I expecting too much from her?*

The answer remained the same: **Wait.**

More than anything, Michael was consumed with the need to hear her say his name. *Just once, Jesus. God, please. Just once. Michael!* An acknowledgment of his existence. Most of the time, she looked right through him. He wanted to be more than someone walking on the periphery of her soul, someone she was convinced would step on her and use her. *Love* to Angel was a foul four-letter word.

*How am I supposed to teach her what love really is when my own instincts are getting in the way? Lord, what am I doing wrong? She's more distant now than she was in Pair-a-Dice.*

**Have patience, beloved.**

Michael's frustrations built, and he started thinking about his father, who had claimed every woman wanted to be dominated.

Michael hadn't believed it then, and he didn't believe it now; but he almost wished he could. Believing that lie would make his life with Angel easier. Every time she looked through him, he thought about his father. Every time she moved close to him in sleep, he knew what his father would say about his self-imposed celibacy.

He heard another voice, dark and powerful and as old as time.

**When are you going to act like a man? Go ahead and take her. Why are you holding back? Take her. She belongs**

to you, doesn't she? Act like a man. Enjoy her body if you can't get anything else from her. What are you waiting for?

Michael wrestled with the voice in his head. He didn't want to hear it at all, but it was there, pushing and pushing at him whenever he was most vulnerable.

Even when he was on his knees in prayer, he could hear it taunting him.

Angel grew restless with time. Something was at work inside her, something slow and insidious and threatening. She liked life in this little cabin. She felt comfortable and safe, except for Michael Hosea. She didn't like the emotions he was beginning to rouse in her, the feelings nibbling at her resolve. She didn't like that he didn't fit any mold she knew; that he kept his word; that he didn't use her; that he treated her differently from any way she had ever been treated before.

He was never angry when she made mistakes. He complimented and encouraged her. He shared his own mishaps with a sense of humor that made her less annoyed with her own incompetence. He gave her hope that she could learn, and pride when she did. She could build a fire now. She could cook a meal. She could identify edible plants from weeds. She was even beginning to listen to the stories he read each evening, not that she believed a single one of them.

*The sooner I get away from him, the better.*

She had unfinished business to take care of back in Pair-a-Dice. Besides, she could have her own little cabin just like this one when she had her share of the gold she had earned. And she wouldn't have to live with any man.

Angel mentally tabulated how much time and money Hosea had spent nursing her back to health and training her for independence. She intended to repay him every hour and ounce before she left.

She took care of his garden. She cooked, swept, washed, ironed, and mended. When he mucked out a stable, she found a shovel to help. When he chopped firewood for the winter, she filled her arms and made neat stacks against the barn.

By the time four months had passed, her skin was brown, her back strong, and her hands rough. She looked in the shiny tin again and saw that her face was back to normal. Even her nose had healed straight. It was time to start making plans to go back.

"Do you suppose those vegetables I've been tending for you would be worth a sack of gold back in Pair-a-Dice?" she asked him one evening over supper.

"Probably more." Michael looked up. "We'll have enough to buy a couple head of cattle."

She nodded, unduly pleased at the thought. Maybe he would buy a cow, and they would have milk. Maybe he would teach her how to make cheese. Angel frowned. What was she thinking? What did it matter to her if he bought a dozen cows? She had to go back and set things right in Pair-a-Dice. She lowered her eyes and ate slowly. The day was coming when she could take off his mother's ring and forget all about him.

Angel washed the dishes and ironed while Michael read the Bible aloud. She didn't listen as she pushed the sadiron around until it was cold and useless. She put it back on the grill. She had lived here with this man for months. She had worked like a slave; she'd never worked this hard back at the Palace. She looked at her hands. Her nails were broken and short, and she had calluses. What would the Duchess have to say about that? She picked up the sadiron again.

She tried to make plans, but her mind wandered to the garden, to the baby birds in a nest outside the bedroom window, to the deep, quiet serenity in Michael Hosea's voice as he read. *What's wrong with me? Why do I feel this heaviness inside again? I thought it was gone.*

**It won't be gone until you go back to Pair-a-Dice and get what the Duchess owes you.**

Yes, that must be it. Until she went back to Pair-a-Dice, everything would be left hanging. The old harridan had cheated her. Angel couldn't let her get away with it.

Besides, Angel reasoned, she ought to be relieved that her time with this farmer was over. But she wasn't. She felt the same way she had the night she had watched him ride out of Pair-a-

Dice, like a hole had been punched in her and her life was running out, not in a rush, but in a slow red trickle staining the dirt at her feet.

**You have to go back, Angel. You must. You'll never be free if you don't. You're going to_ get your money. There will be a lot of it, and you will be free. You can always build another cabin like this one, and it will be all yours. You won't have to share it with a man who expects too much from you. He expects what you don't even have, what you never had. Besides, he's crazy praying to a god who doesn't exist or care and reading a book of myths like it was the answer to everything.**

She worried her lip as she worked. She put the sadiron back on the grill to heat up again. "When are we going back to Pair-a-Dice for supplies?" Thirty miles was a long walk.

Michael stopped reading. He looked up at her. "I'm not going back to Pair-a-Dice."

"Not at all? But why? I thought you sold your produce to that Jew on Main Street."

"Joseph. His name is Joseph Hochschild. And, yes, I did. I decided it's better not to go back. He knows. There are other places. Marysville. Sacramento – "

"You ought to go back and get your money at least."

"What money?"

"The gold you paid for me."

His mouth tightened. "That doesn't matter to me."

She looked at him. "It ought to matter. Don't you care that you were cheated?" She went back to ironing.

Michael watched her and realized she wanted to go back. Even after all this time with him, she was hankering after her life in Pair-a-Dice. His body grew hot and tense. She went on ironing as though nothing were wrong, seemingly blind to his feelings. He wanted to grab her and shake some sense into her.

*Does she have any, Lord? Does she? God, haven't I touched her at all? Have I worked her too hard? Or is she just bored with this quiet kind of life? Jesus, what do I do? Chain her like a dog?*

He thought of something to keep her mind off Pair-a-Dice

for a while. It was a mean, low trick, but the result would keep her on the homestead for a couple more weeks. Maybe she would come to her senses by then.

"I've got a job for you to do tomorrow," he said. "If you're willing."

She had been thinking about leaving tomorrow; but it was a long walk, and she didn't even know which road to take. She doubted he would point her in the right direction. What was she supposed to do? Ask his god? "What is it?" she said tersely.

"There's a black walnut tree in the meadow. The nuts have fallen. I'd like you to go ahead and pick them up. I've got a gunnysack in the barn. You can dump them in the yard to dry."

"Fine," she said. "Whatever you want."

He clenched his teeth. Back to that again. *Whatever you want.* If she said one more word he was going to put his father's theory to the test. "I'm going to check the stock." He went outside to cool off.

He stalked off toward the corral. "How do I get through to this woman?" he said between his teeth. "What do you want from me? Was I just supposed to bring her back and give her time to heal and rest before she went back? Whose will is at work here?"

He couldn't seem to hear the still small voice anymore.

That night, he was worse off than ever. He almost followed the desires of his body rather than his heart and mind, but he knew what was expected. He got up and went down to the creek. The cold water helped, but it was no cure for what ailed him.

*Why are you doing this to me, Lord? Why did you give me this bullheaded, maddening girl? She's turning me inside out.*

Angel knew when he left the bed. She wondered where he was going. She missed his warmth. When he came back, she pretended to be asleep, but rather than get back into bed with her, he sat in the willow chair before the fire. What was he brooding about? Cattle? His crops?

He was asleep in the chair when she got up in the morning. Angel shrugged off his old shirt and gathered her clothing. When she turned slightly and saw him staring at her, she knew what was wrong. She had seen that look on men's faces often enough to know what it meant. Was that all that ailed him? Well, why hadn't he said so?

She straightened, lowering her arms slowly so he could look at her. She gave him her old smile.

A muscle jerked in his cheek. He stood, took his hat from the hook by the door, and went out.

She frowned, perplexed.

Angel prepared his breakfast and waited for him to come in. When he did, he ate without so much as a word. She had never seen him in such a foul mood before. He looked at her darkly. "Have you decided whether you're going to pick those nuts?"

Her brows flickered up. "I'll pick them. I didn't know you were in such a hurry." She scraped her chair back and went out to the barn for the gunny-sack. It took several hours to fill it. She dragged her load back and dumped the nuts. She shook out the sack, proud of her work.

Michael was splitting logs. Pausing, he wiped his brow with the back of his hand and nodded toward the heap. "Is that all?"

Her smile evaporated. "Isn't this enough?"

"I thought there'd be more."

She stiffened. "You mean you want *all* of them?"

"Yes."

Tight-lipped, she went back. "Maybe he's part squirrel," she muttered under her breath. Maybe he figured on selling them along with the vegetables and smoked venison. Stubborn and angry, she kept at it right through the noon meal. *Let him fix something to eat for himself. If he wants nuts, he's going to get nuts.*

It was near dusk when she dumped the last sack in the barn. Her back was a mass of pain. "I sniffed all through the leaves and couldn't find anymore," she told him. She longed for a long, hot soak, but the thought of toting one bucket of water made her give up that idea.

He smiled. "We've got enough there to share with neighbors."

Share? "I didn't know we had any neighbors," she said angrily, pulling a wayward strand of blonde hair out of her mouth.

She hadn't done all this work for a bunch of strangers. Let them pick their own nuts.

*What do you care, Angel? You're not going to be here.*

"I'm going to wash up and fix supper," she said and headed for the creek.

"Do that," Michael said. He grinned and jabbed the pitchfork into the hay again. He started to whistle.

Half an hour later, Mara stormed back. "Look at this!" She held her hands for him to see her blackened palms and fingers. "I've used soap. I've used grease. I've even rubbed with sand. How do you get this stuff off?"

"It's the dye from the hulls."

"You mean they're going to stay like this?"

"For a couple of weeks."

Her blue eyes narrowed. "Did you know this would happen?"

He smiled slightly and pitched hay into a stall.

"Why didn't you tell me?"

Michael leaned on the pitchfork. "You didn't ask." Her stained hands balled into fists and her face filled with angry color. She didn't look indifferent or aloof anymore. He added fuel to the fire already blazing. "The nuts still have to be peeled and dried before we can sack them again. Then you and I'll have all winter long to crack 'em."

He saw the heat coming into her face; she was ready to explode. "You did it on purpose!"

His own temper was just beneath the surface, so he held his silence.

"How am I supposed to go back now with my hands looking like this?" She could just hear the Duchess laughing at her dung-colored hands. She could just imagine the remarks.

Michael's mouth curved wryly. "You know, Mara, if you were really that set on going back to Pair-a-Dice, you'd have been on your way weeks ago."

She blushed, which only added to her fury. She hadn't blushed in years. "Why this?" she demanded hotly. "You got your money's worth out of me!"

He heaved the pitchfork into the haystack. "I haven't gotten anything from you yet, lady. Nothing *worth* anything."

Fury made a red haze before her eyes. "Maybe you're just not man enough to take it the usual way!" She swung around and started out of the barn, calling him a foul name under her breath.

Michael's own temper erupted. He caught up with her and swung her around. "Don't mutter it under your breath, Mara. Come on! Say it to my face. Let's get your real feelings for me out in the open."

She yanked free of him. She screamed names up at him. She knew plenty. She saw his anger and jerked her chin up, daring him. "Go ahead and hit me. Maybe it'll make you a man!"

"Not likely, but that's what you want, isn't it? Another beating. More hard knocks." He was afraid of his own rising emotions, the hot surging blood that made him almost call her challenge. He was shaking with the power of it. "It's the only thing you know, and you're too full of your own stubborn pride to find out if there's anything else in the world!"

"Don't make me laugh! You think you're any different from the rest? I'm quit of this place. I've matched you hour for hour. You've had your gold's worth of work out of me."

"Hogwash. You're just running because you're scared, because you're beginning to *like* it here." She swung at him, but he blocked her hand. She swung again, and he caught her wrist. "Finally I have your full attention!" He let her twist free. "At least you're looking *at* me instead of *through* me."

Angel spun away and marched across the yard. She went into the cabin and slammed the door. Michael expected to see something come crashing through the window, but nothing did.

His heart was pounding like a locomotive. He let out his breath and pushed his fingers back through his hair. It was going to be open warfare from here on out. Well, so be it. Anything was better than her apathy. He went back to his work.

When he came in, Mara seemed calm enough. She glanced at him and gave him a sweet smile as she ladled stew into a bowl and set it on the table for him. One cautious taste and he knew there was enough salt in it to pickle him. The biscuits had sand in them, and when he looked into his mug of coffee, he saw half a dozen flies floating on the steaming surface. He laughed and pitched the coffee out the door. What else had she cooked up for him? "Why don't we discuss what's really bothering you?"

Angel folded her hands on the table. "I've only got one thing to say. I am not going to stay here with you forever." He just looked at her with that faint, enigmatic smile on his face that made her want to use a club on him. "I'm not," she said again.

"We'll take one day at a time, beloved." He took a can of beans from the shelf and opened them. Her eyes were hot enough to fry a steak. He leaned his hip against the counter and ate his cold meal.

She glared up at him. "I don't belong here, and you know it."

"Where do you think you belong? Back in that bordello?"

"That's my choice, isn't it?"

"You don't even know you've got a choice yet. You think there's only one way to go, and that's straight downhill to hell."

*"I know what I want."*

"Then would you mind telling me?"

"I want to get out of here!" She got up and went outside, too angry and frustrated to look at him.

Michael set the can down and came to lean in the doorway. "I don't believe you."

"I *know*, but I don't see that what I want is any of your business." He laughed, but it wasn't in amusement. She glared back at him, her eyes glittering in the moonlight. "What *everything* did you have in mind when you brought me here?"

Michael didn't answer for a long moment. He wondered if he could make her understand. He wondered if he could even put it into words. "I want you to love me," he said and saw the derision in her face. "I want you to trust me enough to let me love you, and I want you to stay here with me so we can build a life together. That's what I want."

Her anger dissolved at his sincerity. "Mister, can't you understand that's impossible?"

"Anything's possible."

"You don't have any idea who and what I am other than what you've created in your own mind."

"Then tell me."

**Go ahead, Angel. Tell him.** He could never even guess at the things that had been done to her or that she had done. Oh, she could tell him. Level the gun. Both barrels. Point-blank. Straight for his heart. Annihilation. That would put a quick end to everything. Why was she holding back?

Michael came outside. "Mara," he said. His gentle voice was like salt on her wounds.

"My name *isn't* Mara. It's Angel. *Angel.*"

"No, it isn't. And I'll call you by what I see. Mara, embittered by life; Tirzah, my beloved who stirs a fire in me until I feel like I'm melting." He moved toward her. "You can't keep running away. Don't you see that?" He stopped right in front of her. "Stay here. Stay with me. We'll work things through together." He touched her. "I love you."

"Do you know how many times I've heard those words before? I love you, Angel. You're such a pretty little thing. I love you, sweetheart. Oh, baby, I love you when you do that. Say you love me, Angel. Say it so I believe you. As long as you do what I tell you, I'm going to love you, Angel. I love you, love you, love you. I'm sick to *death* of hearing it!"

She stared at him angrily, but the look on his face defeated her. She hugged herself tightly. *Don't think. Don't feel anything. He'll destroy you if you do.* She tried to focus on something else.

The night sky was so clear, stars everywhere and a moon so big it seemed to be a single silver eye staring down. Her mind and emotions still boiled. She tried to call up her defenses, but they had dispersed. She wanted to be up on that hilltop, seeing the sunrise again. She remembered his words: *"Mara, that's the life I want to give you."* Who was he kidding? She knew it could never happen, even if he still didn't.

Her eyes burned. "I want to go back to Pair-a-Dice as soon as possible."

"Am I getting too close?"

She swung around. "I am not staying here with you!" She

tried to calm down and reason with him. "Look, mister, if you knew even half of what I've done, you'd have me headed back for Pair-a-Dice so fast – "

"Try me. Go ahead and see if it makes a difference."

Angel withered at the thought. She had opened Pandora's box and couldn't get it closed again. The horrible, grotesque memories rose from the dead. Her father. Mama dead, clutching her rosary. Rab with the cord around his neck because he knew Duke was not the moral, upstanding citizen the public thought he was. Duke raping her over and over again. The dozens of men in the years that followed. And the hunger, the endless, aching hunger inside herself.

Michael could see her face white in the moonlight. He didn't know what she was thinking, but he knew she was tormented by her past. He reached out to touch her cheek. "I wish I could open your mind and climb inside with you." Maybe the two of them could fight off the darkness that was trying to swallow her whole. He wanted to hold her, but she had withdrawn from him already. *God, how do I save her?*

Angel looked up at him and saw the sheen of moisture in his eyes. Shock ran through her. "Are you crying? For me?" she said weakly.

"Don't you think you're worth it?"

Something inside her cracked. She writhed inside to escape the feeling, but it was there nonetheless, growing with the light touch of his hand on her shoulder, with every soft word he spoke. She was sure if she put her hands against her heart, her palms would come away covered with her own blood. Was that what this man wanted? For her to bleed for him?

"Talk to me, Amanda," he whispered, "Talk to me."

"Amanda? What's this name supposed to mean?"

"I don't know, but it sounds like a gentle, loving name." He smiled slightly. "I thought you might prefer it to Mara."

He was a strange man given to strange ways. What had become of her defenses? Where was her defiance and anger? her resolve? "What do you want to hear, mister?" she said, meaning to sound amused and failing. What could she tell a man like him that he would even understand?

"Anything. Everything."

She shook her head. "Nothing. Ever."

Michael cupped her face tenderly. "Then just tell me what you're feeling right now."

"Pain," she said before she thought better of it. She pushed his hands away and went back into the cabin.

She was cold, and desperate to get warm. She knelt down before the fire, but even its warmth couldn't permeate. She could lie in the coals and still not melt the chill attacking her.

**Run away from him, Angel. Run away now –**
*Stay, beloved.*

Voices warred in her head, pulling at her very soul.

Michael came inside and sat down beside her on the floor, watching quietly as she drew up her knees and hugged them against her chest. He knew she was trying to shut him out again. He wasn't going to help her succeed this time. "Give your pain to me," he said.

Surprised, Angel looked at him. She was in a wilderness with this man. She was desperate to find a familiar road, some known landmark to guide her away. She couldn't remember the last time she had even felt close to tears. And she had no tears, not anymore. Hosea perplexed her.

"I've done everything for you but the one thing I know best." She searched his eyes. "Why not?" His expression changed, and she felt a softening toward him. He was vulnerable, and oddly she felt no desire to attack his defenses. "Are you afraid? Is that what holds you back? Do you think I'd make fun of you because you've never been with a woman before?"

Michael took a strand of her hair and rubbed it between his fingers. Where were all his rational answers now? "I suppose it's entered my mind. But more than that, I need to know why."

"Why what?" she asked, not understanding.

"Why you would make love with me."

"Why?" She would never understand this man. All the men she had ever known would expect her to "thank" them if they had given her so much as a box of candy or a bouquet of flowers. This man had kept her alive and nursed her back to health. He had taught her things that would help her live on her own. And now he wanted to know why she offered her body to him. "Would gratitude be enough reason?"

"No. It wasn't in my hands whether you lived or died. That was up to the Lord."

Angel turned her head away. "Don't talk to me about your god. He didn't come back for me. *You* did." She put her forehead against her raised knees and said nothing more.

Michael started to speak, but the voice held him back.

***Michael, there is a time for all things.***

He sighed inwardly, heeding the message. She wasn't ready to listen to the why and wherefore. It would be acid, not salve. And so he held his silence.

*Lord, please guide me.*

The fire crackled, and Angel began to relax just listening to the soothing sounds. "I wanted to die," she said. "I couldn't wait, and just when I thought I had, there you were."

"Do you still want to die?"

"No, but I don't know why I want to live, either." The siege of emotion passed. She turned her head slightly and looked at him again. "Maybe it has something to do with you. I don't know anything anymore."

Joy leaped inside Michael but only briefly. She looked hurt, not happy; confused, not certain. He wanted to touch her and was afraid if he did, she would take it the wrong way.

***Comfort my lamb.***

*If I touch her now, Lord…*

***Comfort your wife.***

Michael took her hand. Her whole arm stiffened, but he didn't let go. He turned her hand over in his and smoothed his fingers down over her blackened palm and fingers so that his large hand covered hers. "We're in this together, Amanda."

"I don't understand you," Angel said.

"I know, but give me time and you will."

"No, I don't think I ever will. I don't know what you want

Francine Rivers 143

from me. You say everything and take nothing. I see the way you look at me, but you've never treated me as a wife."

Michael turned the gold band on her finger. She was his wife. It was time he did something about it. If she didn't know the difference between having sex and making love, he would have to show her. *Oh, God, I am afraid, afraid of the depth of my physical desire.* Most of all he was afraid he would not know how to please her.

*Lord, help!*

Angel watched him looking at the ring on her finger. "Do you want it back?"

"No." He wove his fingers with hers and smiled at her. "I'm just as new at being married as you are." A calm settled over him, and he knew everything would be all right.

Angel looked away. Married men had come to her plenty of times, and she knew what they had to say about it. Their wives didn't understand them. They married for convenience and progeny. They were bored with the same woman and needed a little change, like having steak for dinner instead of stew, fish instead of chicken. Most said their wives didn't enjoy sex. Did they think she did?

"What I know about marriage isn't encouraging, mister."

"Maybe not." Michael kissed her hand. "But I believe marriage is a contract between a man and woman to build a life together. It's a promise to love one another no matter what comes."

"You know what I am. Why would you make a promise like that to me?"

"I know what you were."

She felt an ache inside her. "You'll never learn, will you?"

Leaning over, Michael tipped her face toward him and kissed her. She didn't pull away, but she wasn't moved either. *Lord, I could use a little help down here.* He shook as he combed his fingers into her hair and kissed her again.

He was so tentative, Angel relaxed. She could handle this. She could handle him just fine. She could even help him along.

Michael drew back. He wasn't going to allow his desire to

become rampant. He wasn't going to embrace sex and lose sight of love, no matter how much more comfortable she would be with that.

"My way, not yours. Remember?" He stood up.

Angel watched him in confusion. "What do you know about it?"

"We'll have to wait and see."

"Why do you make things difficult for yourself? It all comes down to the same thing. It won't be *my* way or *your* way. It'll just be the way it is."

A sexual act was what she meant, and he didn't know how to show her it was meant to be a celebration of love.

All Angel saw was his determination. She stood slowly and joined him. "If it has to be your way, fine. It'll be your way." In the beginning.

Michael looked into her eyes and saw no hardness. Neither did he see understanding. He wasn't sure which part of himself to listen to anymore. He was hard pressed by his physical nature. She was so beautiful to him.

"Let me help you," she said and took his hand.

Michael sat in the willow chair, his heart in his throat as she knelt before him and pulled off his boots. He was losing control fast. Standing, he moved away from her. He unbuttoned his shirt and shrugged it off. As he undressed, Michael kept thinking about Adam in the Garden of Eden. How had he felt the first time Eve came to him? Scared half to death, yet surging with life?

When Michael turned, his wife stood naked before the fire, waiting for him. She was breathtaking, just as Eve must have been. Michael came to her in wonder.

*Oh, Lord, she is so perfect, like no other creation in the world. My mate.* He swung her up into his arms and kissed her.

As he stretched out beside her on their marriage bed, he marveled at how she fit him, flesh to flesh, molded for him. "Oh, Jesus," he whispered, awestruck by the gift.

Angel felt him shaking violently and knew it was due to his long, self-imposed celibacy. Strangely, she was not repulsed. Instead, she felt an alien sense of sympathy. She pushed the feelings away, blocking him out of her mind – and was surprised when he drew back from her and searched her eyes, his own filled with so much she turned her face away.

**Think of your money in Pair-a-Dice, Angel. Think of going back and getting it from the Duchess. Think of having something for yourself. Think of being free. Don't think about this man.** It had worked for her in the past. Why not now? **Come on, Angel. Remember how you used to close your mind? You've done it before. Do it again. Don't think. Don't feel. Just play the part. He'll never know.**

But Michael wasn't like other men, and he did know. He didn't have to die to realize she had brought him to the edge of heaven and slammed the gates in his face.

"Beloved," he said, turning her face back to him. "Why won't you let me get close to you?"

She tried to laugh. "How close do you want to be?" She could feel the difference in this man right through her pores and sought to protect herself from him.

Michael saw the flatness in her blue eyes, and it broke his heart. "You keep shutting me out. Tirzah, stay with me."

"Is it Tirzah now?"

*Oh, Jesus, help me.* "Stop running from me!"

Angel wanted to cry out, "Not from *you*! From *this*. From the mindless, selfish grasping for pleasure. Theirs and yours, not mine. Never mine." But she didn't. Instead she challenged him in anger.

"Why do you have to talk?" She struggled, but he was unyielding. Why did he have to keep intruding on and interfering with her thoughts, breaking her concentration? He kept confusing her feelings, stirring them into a boiling mess. He held her and looked into her eyes and was aware of her, and something deep within her shifted.

Her panic grew, and she closed her eyes.

"Look at me, beloved."

"Don't."

"Don't what? Don't love you? Don't become part of you? I *am* part of you."

"This way?"

"In every way."

"No," she said, struggling.

"Yes!" He gentled. "This can be beautiful. It doesn't mean what you've been taught. It's a blessing. Oh, my love, say my name...."

How could he think this could be anything but vile and simple? She knew everything there was to know about it. Hadn't Duke taught her? Hadn't all the rest? So this farmer wanted to know what it was really like. Well, she would show him.

*"Don't."* His rasped command confused her.

"Don't you want me to please you?"

"You want to please me? Say my name." His breath mingled with hers. "You said you wouldn't say no to anything I asked of you. Remember? I want you to say my name. Anything, you said. Can't you keep your word?" His calm left. *"Say it!"*

"Michael," she ground out.

He cupped her face. "Look at me. Say it again."

"Michael." Was he satisfied now? She waited for his triumphant grin and instead saw his adoring eyes and heard his tender voice.

"Keep on saying it...."

When it was over, Michael held her close, telling her how much he loved her and of the pleasure he found in her. He was no longer hesitant, no longer the least unsure, and with his growing assurance, her own doubts expanded.

Some unknown and unwelcome emotion opened deep inside Angel. Something hard and tight began to soften and uncurl. And as it did, the dark voice arose.

**Get away from this man, Angel. You've got to get out of here! Save yourself and flee. Flee!**

# Thirteen

*But if we hope for what we do not have,*
*we wait for it patiently.*

ROMANS 8:25

When Michael went out to do his morning chores, Angel headed up the hill to the road. The faint trail Michael had cut with his wagon during his journeys to camp markets was difficult to follow. On a road less traveled, Angel was soon lost. Everything looked so unfamiliar, she was disconcerted. Was she still walking in the right direction, or had she come full circle and was back near Hosea's homestead where she had started?

The sky was darkening, heavy gray clouds closing together. Angel pulled the shawl more tightly around her, but the thin wrap did little to ward off the chill in the air.

She headed for the mountains, reasoning that Pair-a-Dice was up there somewhere, and heading that way gave her a better chance of reaching it. Besides, going east would take her away from Michael Hosea. The farther away from him, the better.

Things had changed between them. It wasn't that he had finally had sex with her. It was something else, something deeper and more elemental, something beyond her understanding. She wasn't sure what it was, but she knew if she was ever going to call her life her own, she had to get away from him. *Now.*

But where was the road to freedom? She hunted in vain.

She saw a creek and, thirsting, she went to it. Dropping to her knees, she scooped up water and drank deeply. Looking around, she wondered if this was the same stream that ran through Michael's land. If so, surely crossing it and climbing that hill would bring her back to the road again.

The stream looked shallow, the current calm. She had forgotten to bring the buttonhook. Annoyed, she worked at the shoes until she could pull them off. Pulling the skirt up, she bunched it in front and tucked the shoes into the folds for safe keeping before she waded into the stream.

Rocks bit into her tender feet, and the water was so cold it hurt. Though she picked her way carefully, she slipped on a mossy stone and dropped a shoe. Swearing, Angel reached for it and slipped again, falling this time. She struggled quickly to her feet, but she was already soaked. Worse, both shoes were floating downstream. She took off the shawl and tossed it on the far bank.

One shoe filled with water and sank. Angel retrieved it easily and stuffed it securely inside her shirtwaist. The other shoe had lodged in the branches of a fallen tree. She plodded through the water toward it.

The rushing stream deepened and the current tugged, but she knew she couldn't walk all the way to Pair-a-Dice barefooted. She had to have that shoe. Determined to get it, Angel pulled her skirt higher and waded closer.

When the bottom sloped sharply, she caught hold of a branch and leaned out to reach the shoe. Her fingers brushed it once, and the branch snapped. Crying out, she slid down sharply, cold water closing over her head.

The current dragged her thrashing into the hollow beneath the tree. Clawing at the trunk, she pulled herself up and gasped in air. Her skirt caught. She clung with all her strength to the fallen tree and kicked her skirt loose. She grabbed the vines close by. The blackberry thorns cut into her palms, but she held on and pulled herself to the safety of the bank, collapsing there. She was shaking violently from fright and cold.

Angry, she threw rocks at the shoe until it broke free and was swept along with the current. It lodged in the reeds not far away, where she had no difficulty retrieving it.

Cold, weary, and miserable, she pulled on the sodden shoes and climbed the hill, sure she would find the road.

She didn't.

It began to rain, a few drops at first, then more, plastering her hair to her head and soaking through the shirtwaist. Cold, stiff, and exhausted beyond pain, Angel sat down and put her head in her hands.

What was the use? So what if she did make it to the road? She couldn't walk all those miles. She would never make it. She was already exhausted, aching, and hungry, and she couldn't even find her way.

Who would be there to give her a ride back to Pair-a-Dice? What if it was someone like Magowan?

Thoughts of Michael's warm hearth, a heavy quilt, and food tormented her. She hadn't thought to bring any food with her. Her stomach was already knotted with hunger.

Dejected but resolved, Angel got up and went on.

After another mile, her feet hurt so badly, she took off the shoes and tucked one in each skirt pocket, unaware when they dropped out along the way.

When Michael came in for breakfast and found Angel gone, he saddled his horse and went looking for her. He blamed himself for not expecting it. He had seen the look in her eyes when he made her say his name last night. He had smashed through her defenses for one brief instant, and she hadn't liked it.

He followed the road to where she left it and trailed her to the stream. He found Tessie's shawl. He spotted a shoe print on the bank and followed her trail up the hill.

It began to rain. Michael was worried. She would be soaked and cold and probably frightened. It was clear she didn't know where she was or where she was going.

He found her shoes. "Lord, she's heading away from the road." He galloped to the top of the knoll and looked for her. He could see her in the distance, walking across a field of grass. He cupped his hands. "Mara!"

She stopped and turned. He could tell even at this distance by the set of her shoulders and the tilt of her head that she had made up her mind to leave him. He rode slowly toward her. When he was within a hundred yards, he dismounted and walked toward her. Her face was dirty, her shirtwaist torn. He saw bloodstains on her skirt. The look in her eyes made him hold his tongue.

"I'm leaving," she said.

"Barefooted?"

"If I have to."

"Let's talk it over." When he put his hand beneath her elbow, she drew back sharply and slapped him in the face.

Michael stumbled back a step, astonished. He wiped the blood off his mouth and stared at her. "What was that for?"

"I said I am leaving. You can drag me back, and I'll leave again. However long it takes you to get it through your thick head."

Michael stood silent. His anger burned hotter than his cheek, but he knew anything he said now he would later regret.

"Do you hear me, Michael? This is a free country. You can't make me stay." He still said nothing. "You don't own me no matter what you paid the Duchess!"

Patience, God said. Well, patience was wearing thin. Michael wiped the blood off his lip. "I'll give you a ride to the road." He walked to his horse.

Angel stood, mouth ajar. He glanced back at her. She lifted her chin but didn't move. "You want a ride or not?" Michael said.

She went to him. "So, you've finally come to your senses."

He lifted her to the saddle and then swung up behind her. When he reached the road, he took her arm and slid her off the horse. She stood looking up at him, bemused. He unlooped the canteen and tossed it to her. She caught it against her chest. He took the shoes out of his coat pocket and dropped them at her feet.

"That way is Pair-a-Dice," he said. "It's thirty miles, uphill all the way, and Magowan and the Duchess are waiting for you at the end of it." He nodded in the opposite direction. "That way is home. One mile downhill, fire and food and me. But you'd better understand something right now. If you come back, we're picking up where we left off last night, and we're still playing by my rules."

He left her standing alone in the road.

It was after dark when Mara opened the cabin door. Michael glanced up from his reading but didn't say anything. She stood there for a moment, pale, strained, and covered with road dust. Mouth tight, she came in.

"I'll wait for spring," she said bitterly and dropped his empty canteen on the table. She sank down on a stool as though every muscle in her body hurt, but she remained too stubborn to seek the warmth of the fire.

From the look on her face, it was clear she was waiting for him to mock her.

Michael got up and ladled stew from the iron pot. He took a biscuit from the pan. Setting both before her, he smiled ruefully. A small frown flickered across her brow as she glanced up.

Obviously famished, she ate. He poured her coffee. She sipped at it while watching him fill a pan with hot water. When he leaned his elbow on the mantle and looked at her, she lowered her head and went back to eating her supper.

"Sit over here," he said when she finished. She was so tired she could hardly get up, but she did what he told her. He knelt and set the pan of water at her feet and eased the shoes off.

All the way back, she had imagined him gloating and taunting, rubbing her face in her own broken pride. Instead, he knelt before her and washed her dirty, blistered feet. Throat burning, she looked down at his dark head and struggled with the feelings rising in her. She waited for them to die away, but they wouldn't. They stayed and grew and made her hurt even more.

His hands were so gentle. He took such care. When her feet were clean, he kneaded her aching calves. He cast the dirty water outside and poured more, setting the pan in her lap. He took her hands and washed them as well. He kissed her stained, scratched palms and worked salve in. Then he wrapped them with warm bandages.

*And I hit him. I drew his blood....*

Angel shrank back ashamed. When he raised his head, she looked into his eyes. They were blue, like a clear spring sky. She had never really noticed before. "Why do you do this for me?" she said thickly. "Why?"

"Because, for some of us, one mile can be farther to walk than thirty." He brushed the dust and tangles from her hair, undressed her, and put her to bed. Undressing, he lay down beside her. He said nothing and asked nothing.

She wanted to explain. She wanted to say she was sorry. The words just would not come. They stuck like hot rocks in her chest, weighing her down deeper and deeper.

*I don't want to feel this. I can't let myself feel this way. I can't survive it.*

Michael turned on his side and propped his head up on his hand. He stroked the hair back from her temples. She was back in his tiny cabin and looked more lost than ever. Her body was like ice. He pulled her close to share his warmth.

Angel didn't move when he kissed her. If he wanted sex, he could have it. All he wanted. Anything. For tonight, anyway.

"Try to sleep," he said. "You're home and safe."

*Home.* She took a long shuddering breath and closed her eyes. She had no home. Her head rested on his chest, and the steady beat of his heart soothed her. She remained like that for a long time, but for all her exhaustion, sleep would not come. She drew away and lay on her back staring up at the ceiling.

"Will you talk about it?" Michael said.

"About what?"

"Why you left."

"I don't know."

Michael traced the side of her face. "Yes, you do."

She swallowed heavily, fighting emotions she couldn't even identify. "I can't put it into words."

He curled a strand of her pale hair around his finger and tugged gently. "When I made you say my name, you couldn't pretend nothing was happening between us, could you? Was that it? I wanted to get inside you, inside your heart," he said huskily. "Did I?"

"A little."

"Good." He traced her face with one finger again. "A woman is either a wall or a door, beloved."

She gave a bleak laugh and looked at him. "Then I guess I'm a door a thousand men have walked through."

"No. You are a wall, a stone wall, four feet thick and a hundred feet high. I can't get over you all by myself, but I keep trying." He kissed her. "I need help, Tirzah." Her lips softened, and she touched his hair. Aroused, he drew back. He knew how exhausted she was.

"Roll over," he said softly, and she did. He tucked her body into his own and put his arm around her. He brushed his lips against her hair. "Go to sleep." She sighed in relief. It only took a few moments for the weariness to catch up with her.

She lay in the safety of Michael's arms and dreamed of a high, thick wall. He was there below her, planting vines. As soon as they touched the soil, they grew, spreading the green life up the sides and working their strong tendrils between the stones. The mortar was crumbling.

Michael lay in the darkness, wide awake. He would have to give up hoping he could break through her barriers. *But how do I reach her, Lord? Tell me how!*

He closed his eyes and slept peacefully, forgetting the enemy who was loose in the world. The battle was not yet won.

Paul was coming home.

# Fourteen

*Judge not, that ye be not judged. For with the judgment you pronounce you will be judged, and the measure you give will be the measure you get.*

JESUS, MATTHEW 7:1–2

Paul dumped his meager gear and stood on the hillside. He saw Michael working in the field and cupped his hands to his mouth to shout. Michael left the shovel to meet him halfway down the hill. They embraced. Paul almost wept at the feel of those strong, sure arms.

"Oh, I'm glad to see you, Michael," he said, his voice graveled with fatigue and emotion. The relief was so great he had to fight back unmanly tears. He withdrew and rubbed his face self-consciously. He hadn't shaved in weeks, and his hair had grown long. He hadn't changed his clothes in a month. "I must look – " He gave a bleak laugh. "It was awful." Hard work for little or nothing, drinking to forget, women to remember, and fighting just to stay alive.

Michael put his hand on his shoulder. "You'll look a lot better after you clean up and have a good meal." Paul was too tired to protest when Michael went up the hill and shouldered his load. "How was it on the Yuba?"

Paul grimaced. "Dismal and *cold.*"

"Did you find what you were looking for?"

"If there's gold in them thar hills, I never saw much of it. What I found was barely enough to keep body and soul together." He looked toward his end of the valley and thought of Tess. The last few days had been filled with thoughts of her and how they had dreamed of coming to California and building a place of their own. Losing her was what had driven him into the gold country. Every time he thought about her, he felt the pain coming up again.

*Oh, Tessie. Why did you have to die?*

His eyes burned and filled up against his will. He needed her so much. He didn't know what he was doing anymore. His life had lost meaning when she died.

"Are you home for good?" Michael asked.

Afraid to trust his voice, Paul cleared his throat. "I don't know yet," he admitted flatly. "I'm just played out." He was too bone-weary to think about what he was going to do tomorrow. "I wouldn't have survived winter in the mountains. I wasn't even sure I could make it home." Now that he was, he felt the old ache again. Thank God, he could spend the winter with Michael. He was looking forward to long hours of intelligent conversation. All the men on the streams talked about was gold and women. Michael talked of many things, big things that filled a man's head and gave him hope.

He had headed for the streams to make his fortune the quick way. Michael had gone with him but only stayed a few months. "This isn't what I want from life," he said and tried to talk Paul into going back to the land. Pride had made Paul stay. It was cold, disillusionment, and hunger that brought him back. Not hunger for food or even riches, but a deeper hunger of the spirit.

Michael put his hand on his shoulder. "I'm glad you're home." He grinned. "There are fields to plant, brother, and the workers are few."

Michael always made it easy. Paul smiled wryly. "Thanks." He fell into step beside him. "It wasn't anything like I expected out there."

"No pot at the end of the rainbow?"

"Not even a rainbow." He was feeling better already. He would stay. Better to break soil than your back. Better to muck out a stable than stand in freezing water trying to find a few meager specks of gold in a rusting pan. The quiet, dull farmer's life was what he needed right now. The sameness and routine of every day. Watching something grow from the earth, rather than ripping something out of it.

"Anything happen around here while I was gone?" He could see Michael had done some building and cleared another section of land.

"I got married."

Paul stopped dead and stared at him. He swore. "You didn't."
He realized as soon as the words were uttered how bad they
sounded. "Sorry, but I haven't seen a decent woman since we got
here." He saw an odd look on Michael's face and tried to make
amends. "She must be something if you married her." Michael
had always said he was waiting for just the right one.

Paul tried to be happy for him, but he wasn't. He was jealous. All this time he had been on the road home, looking forward
to sitting in front of the fire and talking to Michael, and now
Michael had a wife. What rotten luck.

He needed Michael's advice. He needed his friendship. His
brother-in-law had a way of listening and understanding things
you didn't even say. He could bring a lightness to the heaviest
times, a feeling that everything would come out the way it was
intended, and for good. Michael raised hope, and God knew how
much he needed hope right now. He expected to come back and
find everything the same.

Women had been chasing after Michael for as long as he
could remember. Why did one have to catch him now?
"Married," Paul muttered.

"Yes, married."

"Congratulations."

"Thanks. You sound real happy about it."

Paul winced. "Ah, Michael. You know I'm selfish." They
walked again. "How did you manage to find her, anyway?"

"Just lucky."

"So tell me about her. What's she like?"

Michael nodded his head toward the cabin. "Come and
meet her."

"Oh, no. Not like this," Paul said. "One look at me and she'd
be sure the neighborhood went to seed. What's her name anyway?"

"Amanda."

"Amanda. Nice." He grinned wickedly. "Is she pretty,
Michael?"

"She's beautiful."

She could be the plainest of women, but if Michael loved
her, he would see her as beautiful. Paul didn't intend to make any

judgments until he saw her for himself. "Let me put up in the barn tonight," he said. "I'm dead on my feet, and I'd like to meet your wife after I've cleaned up."

Michael brought him a blanket, soap, and a change of clothes. Paul was too tired to even get on his feet. All he could do now was lean back against the wall, feet outstretched. Michael came back again with a hot meal. "You should eat something, old man. You're skin and bones."

Paul smiled weakly. "Did you tell her there was a filthy beggar in the barn?"

"She didn't ask." He pitched hay. "Burrow into this with the blanket and you'll be warm enough tonight."

"It'll be like heaven after hard ground for so many months." It was the first roof over his head in weeks. He tasted the stew and raised his brows. "You got yourself a good cook. Thank her for me, would you?" He wolfed down the rest and wilted into the hay. "I'm tired. I don't think I've ever been so tired." He couldn't keep his eyes open anymore. The last thing he saw was Michael bending down to cover him with a thick blanket. All the tension he had carried for months left him.

Paul awakened to a horse whinnying. He was stiff and sore when he got up. Stretching, he went to look out the barn door. Michael was digging a hole for a fencepost. He leaned against the wall watching him for a long while. Then he went back to the hay and got the borrowed clothing.

He bathed down at the creek so he wouldn't offend Michael's wife. He shaved off his beard. Shrugging into Michael's red wool shirt, he went to help him.

Michael stopped work and leaned on his shovel. "I wondered when you were going to wake up. You've slept two days clean through."

Paul grinned. "Just goes to show you panning gold is harder work than putting up fences."

Michael laughed. "Come on back to the house. Amanda will have breakfast ready."

Paul was beginning to look forward to a woman being

around. He expected someone like Tess at the hearth, someone quiet and sweet, good-natured and devout. He came in behind Michael, eager to meet her. A slender girl stood before the fire, her back to them. She was wearing a skirt exactly like the one Tess had worn walking the Oregon Trail. The same shirtwaist, too. Odd. He frowned slightly. She bent to her cooking pot, and he was quick to notice she had a nice backside. When she straightened, he noticed her tiny waist and a long, thick golden braid that reached it. So far so good.

"Amanda, Paul's here."

When she turned around, Paul felt his stomach drop into his worn boots. He stared in disbelief, but she was there staring right back, that high-priced prostitute from Pair-a-Dice. He glanced at Michael and saw him smiling as though she was the sun and moon and all the stars in the heavens.

"Paul, I'd like you to meet my wife, Amanda."

Paul stared at her and didn't know what to do or say. Michael was standing beside him, waiting, and he knew if he didn't say something nice real soon, things would go from bad to worse. Paul forced a stiff smile. "Sorry to gape at you, ma'am. Michael said you were beautiful." And she was that. Just like Salome and Delilah and Jezebel.

What was Michael doing married to a woman like this one? Did he know she was a prostitute? He couldn't. The man had never set foot in a brothel in his life. He had never had a woman. Not that the chance hadn't been presented often enough. Against all reason and natural drives, Michael had set his mind to wait for the right one. And now, look what he got for all his purity. *Angel!*

What story had the witch concocted? What was he going to do about it? Should he tell Michael now?

Michael was looking at him strangely.

Angel smiled. It wasn't a friendly smile. Her eyes were a gorgeous blue, but they had become deathly cold. She knew he recognized her, and she was letting him know that she didn't care. And if she didn't care, then it was clear she hadn't married Michael for love.

He smiled back. Colder than she. *How'd you get your claws into him?*

Angel saw the world in one man's eyes, and she felt every stone cast. Her smile tipped up a little more on one side. This man she understood. He probably had never had the dust to make it up the stairs. "Coffee, gentlemen?"

Michael looked between them and frowned. "Sit down, Paul."

Paul sat and tried to keep his eyes off her. The silence stretched tight. What could he say?

Michael leaned back slightly. "Now you're rested, you can tell us about the Yuba."

Paul did talk, out of desperation. Angel served him a bowl of porridge and a mug of coffee. He thanked her stiffly. She was beautiful, *too* beautiful – a cold, defiled, alabaster goddess.

She didn't sit with them or speak. Paul figured she already knew more about the Yuba than he did. Only the men with the best strikes could have afforded her services. What was she doing here? What sweet little lies had she whispered in Michael's ear? What would happen when he found out the truth? Would he throw her out? It would serve her right.

Paul asked about the farm and let Michael do the talking for a while. He needed to think, or at least try to. He stole glances at Angel. How could Michael not know? How could he not suspect? What would a beautiful girl like her be doing in the gold country? It wouldn't make sense to a thinking man.

But then, one look into a pair of clear blue eyes like hers and a man could be lost. Michael wasn't a philanderer. He was honest and loving. She could tell him anything, and he would believe her. A girl like her would make mincemeat out of him. *I've got to tell him the truth. But how? When?*

Michael got up to pour himself more coffee, and Paul looked at Angel. She looked back at him, her chin tilted slightly, her blue eyes mocking. She was so sure of herself, he almost blurted the truth out right then, but the words stuck in his throat when he looked at Michael's face.

Angel took down her shawl from a hook by the door. "I'm going to get some water," she said, picking up the bucket. "I'm sure you two have lots to talk about." She looked right at him before she went out the door.

It struck him like a blow in the face. *She doesn't even care if I tell him.*

Michael was looking at him solemnly. "What's on your mind, Paul?"

He couldn't make the words come. He gave a hoarse laugh and tried to retrieve his old teasing manner, but he couldn't do that either. "Sorry, but she took the breath right out of me. How did you meet her?"

"Divine intervention."

Divine? Michael was in the black pit of Sheol and didn't even know it. He had fallen head over heels for a devil with blue eyes and waist-length blonde hair and a body that would tempt a man into sin and death.

Michael stood. "Come on outside and I'll show you what I've done since you went off to seek your fortune."

Paul saw Angel washing his clothes. Nice touch. Did she think doing him a favor would keep him quiet? She didn't look their way. He might not be able to spill the truth about her to Michael, but he sure wasn't going to let her off easily.

"Give me just a minute with your wife, would you, Michael? I've made a poor impression staring at her the way I was. I'd like to thank her for breakfast and for washing my clothes."

"Do that. Then meet me down at the creek. I'm building a springhouse. You can help."

"I'll be along in a minute." Paul headed for Angel. He looked her up and down again, and this time there was no mistake. She was wearing Tessie's clothes. He felt hot fury all over. How could Michael give them to her? He walked up just as she finished shaking out his worn long johns. He expected her to turn around, but she didn't. She knew he was there; he was sure of it. She was just ignoring him.

"Hello, Angel," he said, thinking that might bring her about quick enough. She turned, but her expression was cool and self-possessed. "*Angel*," he said again. "That's your real name, isn't it? Not Amanda. Correct me if I'm wrong."

"I guess I'm found out, aren't I?" She draped his long johns over the line Michael had put up for her. "Should I remember you?"

Brazen hussy. "I suppose faces all begin to look alike in your business."

"And everything else." She looked him over and laughed. "Hard luck on the streams, mister?"

She was worse than he expected. "Does he know who and what you are?"

"Why don't you ask him?"

"Doesn't it even bother you what it'll do to him when he finds out?"

"Do you think he'll fall to pieces?"

"How did someone like you get your hooks into him?"

"He trussed me up like a goose and brought me back here in his wagon."

"A likely story." Her look of boredom infuriated him. "What do you think he'd do if I told him I'd seen you before, in a brothel in Pair-a-Dice?"

"I don't know. What do you think he'd do? Stone me?"

"Pretty sure of your hold over him, aren't you?"

She picked up the empty basket and rested it on her hip. "You tell him whatever you want, mister. It doesn't make a lot of difference to me." She walked away.

On the way to Michael, Paul made up his mind to tell him, but when he reached him, he couldn't follow through with it. He spent all day working beside Michael and couldn't get the courage up. When they headed back, Paul declined supper. He said he was too tired to eat. He went to the barn instead and ate the last of his jerky. He didn't want to sit across the table from her. He couldn't keep up the pretense that he was pleased his best friend was married to a deceiving harlot. He shoved his things into his pack, slung it over his shoulder, and headed to his own place at the end of the valley.

Standing in the open doorway of the cabin, Michael saw him go. He rubbed the back of his neck and turned away.

Angel looked at Michael and felt the tension building inside her again. She sat in the willow chair he had made for her and watched him close the door and come sit before the fire. He took up his boots and began rubbing beeswax into them to make them waterproof. He didn't look at her. He didn't have much to talk about tonight, and he hadn't taken the Bible down to read. Clearly, last night was forgotten. "You're wondering, aren't you?" she said. "Why don't you just ask?"

"I don't want to know."

"Of course, you don't," she said dryly. Her throat was tight and raw. "I'll tell you anyway, just to clear the air. I don't remember him, but then that doesn't mean a thing in my business, does it? I didn't remember you, either, even after a couple of visits." She looked away.

Michael knew it wasn't the whole truth, but it hurt none the less. "Don't lie, Amanda. Can't you get it through your head I love you? You're my wife now. Whatever happened before, it's in the past. Leave it there."

The lull was over. The storm was on them in a fury.

"Two weeks ago, you wanted to hear everything about me. Do you still want to know *everything*?"

*"Leave it be!"*

She stood up. Keeping her back to him, she ran a shaking hand along the mantle. "You still don't understand, do you? Even if I wanted things to work, others out there won't let it happen. Like your fine upstanding brother-in-law." She smiled dryly and looked up at the wall. "Did you see his face when he recognized me?"

"I'm sorry he hurt you."

She swung around, glaring at him. "Is that what you think?" She gave a short laugh. "He can't hurt me. And neither can you." She wasn't going to give either of them the chance.

Paul spent a day cleaning his cabin and thinking what to do about Angel. He had to go back and talk to Michael about her. He couldn't remain silent. Michael had every right to know about her deception. Once he knew all the facts, he would do the right thing and toss her out. Like a cat, she would land on her feet.

The marriage could be annulled. It probably hadn't even been performed by a sanctified reverend, so it wouldn't count anyway. Michael could put the whole bad experience behind him. With wagon trains pouring into California, he was bound to find another woman, one that would make him forget Angel.

Michael came over and chopped wood with him. They talked, but it wasn't the way it had been. Paul had too much on his mind, and Michael was strangely pensive. "Come on over for supper," Michael said before he left, but Paul couldn't stand the thought of eating with Angel across the table.

Michael looked annoyed with him. "You've hurt Amanda's feelings."

Paul almost laughed. Hurt? That hardened harlot? Not likely, but he knew exactly what she was doing. She was driving the wedge between him and Michael. She was out to destroy their friendship. Well, if she wanted to play rough..."I'll be over tomorrow."

Angel was outside beating blankets on a line when he arrived. She paused and looked straight at him. She wasted no time flinging the gauntlet in his face. "He's working down at the stream on the springhouse. Why don't you get it off your chest before it eats you alive?"

"You're betting I won't, aren't you?"

"Oh, I think you will. You can hardly wait."

"Do you love him?" he sneered. "You think you could make him happy? Sooner or later, he's going to see you for what you really are."

Her hand whitened on the stick. Shrugging, she turned away.

"You don't care about anything, do you?"

"Should I?" She began beating the blanket again.

Paul wanted to grab her and swing her around so he could lay his fist into her arrogant face. "You're just asking for it." He headed straight for the stream.

All the stiffness went out of her as Angel watched him go. She sat down weakly on a stump, refusing to acknowledge the feelings coursing through her.

"You came just in time," Michael said, straightening and wiping the sweat from his forehead with the back of his arm. "Give me a hand with these planks, will you?"

Paul helped him place the notched log, planed flat on one side. "Michael, I've got to talk to you about something," he said with a grunt as the log banged into place. Michael gave him a dark look he could not decipher. The heat of his own anger made him plunge ahead. "It's got nothing to do with what happened on the Yuba or why I can't make up my mind whether to stay. It's got to do with something else. It's got to do with your *wife*."

Michael straightened slowly and looked at him. "Why do you feel you have to say anything?"

"Because you have to know." He could still see her arrogant face. "Michael, she's not who you think she is."

"She's exactly who I think she is, and she's *my wife*." He bent to his work again.

She really must have gone to work on him the past day. Furious, Paul slammed the next log into place. He looked back across the yard at her. She stood in the doorway of Michael's cabin. In Tessie's clothes. He wanted to go over there and rip them off her. He wanted to beat her and chase her right out of this valley. Michael, of all people, tricked. Michael with his high ideals and strength of character. Michael with his purity. It was inconceivable. It was obscene.

"I'm not going to leave it alone. I can't." Michael wasn't even looking at him. Paul caught his arm. "Listen to me. Before she was your wife, she was a prostitute. Her name's Angel, not Amanda. She worked in a brothel in Pair-a-Dice. She was the highest-priced soiled dove in the whole town."

"Take your hand off my arm, Paul."

Paul did. "Aren't you going to say anything?" He had never seen Michael so angry.

"I know all about it."

Paul stared at him. "You *know*?"

"Yes." Michael bent for another log. "Take the other end, would you?"

Paul did so without even thinking. "Did you know before or after she got the ring on her finger?" he asked cynically.

"Before."

Paul banged the log into place. "And you still married her?"

Michael straightened. "I still married her, and I'd marry her again if I had it to do over." A simple statement, calmly and quietly delivered, but his eyes were burning with wrath.

Paul felt like he had been punched, hard. "You're besotted with her. Michael, she has you fooled." He had to try to reason with him. "It happens. You haven't seen a woman in months and then you do, and she's got pretty blue eyes and a beautiful body, and you lose your head over her. So enjoy her for a while, but don't try and convince yourself she'll make a decent wife. Once a prostitute, always a prostitute."

Michael clenched his jaw shut. Almost Angel's own words about herself. "Stop judging."

"Don't be a fool!"

"Shut up, Paul. You don't know her."

He laughed at that. "Oh, I don't have to. I know enough. You're the one that doesn't know. How much experience have you had with women like her? You see everything and everyone through your own set of principles, but the world isn't like that. She's not worth the pain she'll bring you. Listen to me, Michael! Do you want a woman who's been with a hundred men being the mother of your children?"

Michael stared at him. Was this what Angel had put up with all her life? Condemnation and blind hatred? "I think you'd better stop right there," he said tightly.

But Paul wouldn't. "What would your folks say if they knew about her? Would they approve? What about the neighbors when they start arriving? *Good* people. *Decent* people. What're they going to think when they find out your pretty little wife was a high-priced prostitute?"

Michael's eyes darkened ominously. "I know what *I* think and what God thinks, and that's all that matters. Maybe you ought to get your own life in order before you examine hers."

Paul stared at him, smarting. Michael had never used that

tone of reproach on him before, and it hurt. Couldn't he see he was only trying to help; he was only trying to prevent him from being destroyed by that worthless woman? "You're like my own brother," he said thickly. "You saw me through the worst times in my life. I don't want to see you destroyed by some conniving witch who's got your heart so twisted around her little finger you don't even know you're heading for disaster!"

A muscle jerked in Michael's jaw. "You've said enough!"

But all Paul could see was a prostitute in his beloved Tessie's clothes. "Michael, she's nothing but *dung!*" He didn't even see the fist coming. He didn't even know what happened. Pain spread along his jaw, and he was lying on his back, Michael standing over him, fists clenched, face livid.

Michael caught him by the front of his shirt and yanked him to his feet, shaking him like a rag doll. "If you love me as you claim to, then you love her as well. She's part of me. Do you understand? She's part of my flesh and my life. When you say things against her, you say them against me. When you cut her, you cut *me*. Do you understand?"

"Michael — "

*"Do you understand?"*

It was the first time in his life Paul had been afraid of his brother-in-law. "I understand."

"Good," Michael said and let him go. He moved away, his back to Paul, trying to control his anger.

Paul rubbed his bruised chin. She was the cause of this dissension between them. It was her fault. *Oh, I understand all right, Michael. Better than you do.*

Michael rubbed the back of his neck and looked at him. "I'm sorry I hit you." He let out his breath and came back. "I need help, not hindrance. She's in pain you can't even begin to understand." He made a fist, his face tormented, his eyes filling with tears. "And I love her. I love her enough to die for her."

"I'm sorry."

"Don't be sorry. *Be silent!*"

And Paul was, while they worked, but his mind was yelling the whole while. He was going to help Michael the best way he knew how. He was going to drive her out. Somehow. The sooner, the better. He would find a way.

Michael broke the tension. "You're going to have to go to town and lay in supplies for winter. I haven't got enough to stake you."

"I haven't any gold dust."

"I have a little laid by. It's yours. You can use my horses and wagon."

Paul felt ashamed. But why should he? He was only trying to keep Michael from being hurt. Michael was a thinking man. He would come to his senses. His big problem was overlooking defects of character in others. He looked at a harlot and saw someone worthy of love.

Paul seethed. Already she was coming between them. Already she was breeding contention. He had to think of some way to flush Angel out of her comfortable hole and send her back where she belonged. And he had to do it before she broke Michael's heart into little pieces.

They set the last plank into place. The inside walls were up. Michael said he could manage the roof on his own. He put his hand on Paul's shoulder and thanked him for the help, but the tension was heavy between them.

"You'd better head for Pair-a-Dice tomorrow. Tell Joseph I'll settle up with him in a few weeks. He'll see you get everything you need."

"Thanks." Pair-a-Dice. Maybe he could find out a little more about Angel and her weaknesses when he got there. The Duchess would want her best girl back, and she could always send that big hulking giant who guarded her like she was the crown jewels to get her.

When Michael came in at dusk, Angel didn't ask what Paul had to say. She put supper on the table and sat down with him, back straight, head up. He still hadn't said anything. He was probably thinking everything over, examining and weighing. So let him.

The heaviness was back inside her, and she pretended it didn't matter. He didn't matter. When Michael looked at her, she tilted her chin and looked straight back. *Go ahead and say what's on your mind, mister. I don't care.*

Michael put his hand over hers.

Pain gripped her heart, and she yanked her hand from beneath his. She couldn't look at him. Taking her napkin from the table, she shook it gently before meticulously placing it on her lap. When she raised her head again, he was looking at her. His eyes, oh, his eyes.

"Don't look at me like that. I told you before, I don't care what he thinks of me, and he can say anything he wants. It's all the truth. You knew it. And it doesn't matter. He's not the first man who's looked down his nose at me, and he won't be the last." She remembered Mama walking down the street, and the men who had come to the shack walking right on by like they didn't know her at all.

"I might believe you if you weren't so angry."

Angel raised her chin. "I'm not angry. Why should I be angry?" She had no appetite, but she forced herself to eat anyway, just so he couldn't make something of it. She cleared the dishes. Michael put another log on the fire.

"Paul will be gone a couple of days. He needs supplies. He'll be over tomorrow morning for the horses and wagon."

Angel lifted her head slightly, thinking. She poured water into the basin and washed the dishes. Michael wouldn't take her back where she belonged, but she knew Paul would. Just to save poor Michael from himself.

Something squeezed tight inside her at the thought of leaving Michael. She forced herself to think instead of the satisfaction she would feel when she faced the Duchess again and demanded her money. She could always enlist the bartender's help if she had to. He was as big as Magowan and had plenty of practice with his fists. As soon as her gold was safely in her hand, she would be free. *Free!*

Her chest hurt, and she pressed her hand against it.

Michael pulled her close again that night, and she didn't resist. After a few minutes, he drew back shaking, bathed in sweat. He could hardly get his breath. "What are you trying to do?"

"Be good to you," she said and used everything she knew to give him the pleasure he deserved.

Paul came at dawn for the wagon and horses. Michael helped him hitch up the team. He gave him gold dust and a letter for Joseph Hochschild. "I'll look for you in four or five days."

"I spotted a buck on the way over. A big one."

"Thanks," Michael said. As soon as Paul was on his way, he came back into the cabin and took the gun down from the rack above the mantle. "Paul spotted a buck on the way over. I'm going to see if I can't get us some more meat for winter."

Angel had wondered all night how she would manage to get away without Michael knowing. Now, here was her answer. She waited for him to be out of sight, then slipped the ring off her finger. She put it on his Bible where she knew he would find it. Grabbing the shawl and swinging it around her shoulders, she hurried out.

The wagon couldn't have gone too far. Lifting her skirt, she ran to catch up with it.

Paul heard her call. He drew rein and waited, wondering what she wanted. She was probably going to tell him to bring something back for her with Michael's gold. Or maybe she was going to beg him to leave things alone. Well, let her. A lot of good it would do her.

Angel was flushed and breathless when she reached him. "I need a ride back to Pair-a-Dice."

He covered his surprise with a curt laugh. "So you're running out on him already."

She smiled derisively. "Were you hoping I would stay?"

"Get on up," he said, not even reaching out a hand to help her.

"Thanks," she said dryly and climbed onto the wagon seat with him.

Paul had spent the better part of last night wondering what to do about Michael's soiled bride, and here she had solved the problem for him. He hadn't thought she would leave so easily. No bribe. No threats. She was going of her own free will. He clicked the reins, and they set off.

Paul glanced at her as she dabbed her face with the hem of Tessie's shawl. It was all he could do not to tear it off her. "How do you think Michael's going to feel when he finds you gone?"

She looked straight ahead. "He'll get over it."

"You don't care about his feelings much, do you?" She didn't say anything. He looked straight ahead and then at her again. "You're right. He'll get over you. In a few years' time, California will have plenty of suitable girls for him to choose from. Women have always been after Michael."

She looked off toward the forest as though she could care less. Paul wanted to cut her so deep she would bleed the way Michael was going to when he found she had deserted him without so much as a backward glance. Hadn't he warned him? But she ought to feel something. It was only right.

He was curious. "What made you decide to leave?"

"No particular reason."

"I suppose you got bored with the quiet life Michael leads. Or is it just having the same man all the time?" She didn't respond. Michael would see now he was right about her. In time, he would accept what a mistake he had made. Women loved Michael. Besides his good looks, he combined a strength and tenderness that attracted them like flies. He would marry again if he was that ready, and he wouldn't have to wait long. The next one would sure be better than this one.

"The Duchess'll be glad to see you back again. I hear you were bringing in a fortune to her coffers. She never would say where you went."

Angel raised her head slightly and gave him a cloying smile. "Don't feel you have to make polite conversation."

He grinned coldly. So he was getting to her a little. He dug deeper. "I guess talking isn't all that important in your business, is it?"

Angel felt the fury rise inside her. Sanctimonious pig. If it weren't so many uphill miles to Pair-a-Dice, she would get off this wagon right now and walk, but she wasn't fool enough to think she could make it. Let him peck at her all he wanted. She could take one day of riding on a high seat with a lowbrow hypocrite. She'd think about her gold. She would think about her own little cabin in the woods. She would think about never having to look at another man like him again.

Paul didn't like being ignored, especially by someone like her. Who did she think she was anyway? He snapped the reins and picked up the pace. He hit every hole in the road, bouncing and jarring her. She had to hold on tight to keep her balance and not be pitched out. He enjoyed her discomfort. She pressed her lips tight but made no complaint. He kept the hard pace until the horses tired and he had to slow down again.

"Feel any better now?" she said, mocking him.

He loathed her more with each mile.

When the sun was straight overhead, he pulled off the road and jumped down. He unhitched the team and let them graze. Then he strode off into the woods. When he came back, he saw her heading for the trees on the other side. She moved as though she were in pain.

His saddlebag was under the front seat. Inside he had an apple, beef jerky, and a can of beans. He ate them with relish. She glanced at him once when she came back and went to sit down in the shade of a pine. He tore off a piece of beef jerky with his teeth and chewed while studying her. She looked tired and hot. She was probably hungry, too. Tough luck. She should have thought to bring something with her.

Paul opened his canteen and drank deeply, corking it again when he was finished. He looked at her and frowned heavily. Annoyed, he got up and walked over to her. Swinging the canteen back and forth in front of her face, he said, "Do you want a drink? Say please if you want one."

"Please," she said quietly.

He tossed the canteen into her lap. She uncorked it, wiped off the mouth, and drank. When she finished, she wiped the mouth again, corked it and held it up to him. "Thanks," she said. Nothing showed in those blue eyes.

Paul went back and sat down beneath the tree and finished

the beef jerky. Angry, he started on the apple. When he finished half, he looked her way. "Hungry?"

"Yes," she said simply, not looking at him this time.

He tossed what was left to her. Getting up, he went for the horses and hitched them to the wagon. Glancing back, he saw her picking the needles and dirt out of the half-eaten apple before she took a bite. Her cold, silent dignity made him uncomfortable.

"Let's go!" He sat waiting for her impatiently.

She winced as she climbed up onto the wagon seat with him. "How'd you meet Michael?" he said as he snapped the reins and they started off again.

"He came to the Palace."

"Don't make me laugh! Michael wouldn't set foot in that stink hole. He doesn't drink and he doesn't gamble, and he's sure never consorted with prostitutes."

She smiled, taunting. "Then how do you think it all came about, mister?"

"I imagine a girl with your gifts would think of something. You probably met him at the mercantile and told him your family had died on the trail west and you were all alone in the world."

She laughed at him. "Well, mister, you needn't even wonder anymore. Now that I'm gone, you can have Michael to yourself all winter long."

His knuckles whitened on the reins. Was she making some sort of foul insinuation? Did she doubt his manhood? Yanking the reins, he pulled the wagon off the road and stopped.

She stiffened, wary. "Why are you stopping?"

"You owe me something for the ride."

She went very still. "What did you have in mind?"

"What have you got?" He wanted to rub her raw. "I guess you figure when someone does you a favor, you don't owe them anything. Right?" She looked away. He caught her arm tightly, and she looked at him again, her face pale. He glared into her cynical blue eyes. "Well, you do. You *owe* me for this ride." He let her go abruptly.

She didn't turn away this time. She just sat looking at him, face smooth and expressionless.

"You know, I never made it upstairs at the Palace," he said, stabbing deeper. He untied the leather cord in her hair. "I didn't have enough dust to even get my name in the hat." He tugged it free. "I used to wonder what it'd be like to make it to *Angel's* inner sanctum."

"And now you want to know for yourself."

Paul wanted to make her squirm. "Maybe."

Angel felt the spiraling begin inside her. Going down, like water in a sinkhole. She had forgotten that everything cost something. She let her breath out and tilted her head slightly. "Well, we might as well get it done." She got down from the wagon seat.

Paul stared. He jumped down on the other side and came around to stand in front of her. She was white and tired, and he wasn't sure whether she was bluffing or not. Did she think she could walk thirty miles? He wasn't going to give her the chance to change her mind and go back. "What do you figure on doing?"

"Whatever you want, mister." She took off the shawl and draped it over the side of the wagon. "Well?" Her smile mocked him.

Did she think he couldn't? Furious, he grabbed her arm and propelled her a hundred feet off the road, into the shadows of a thicket. He was rough and quick, his sole desire to hurt and degrade her. She didn't make a sound. Not one.

"Didn't take you long to fall back into old ways, did it?" He glared down at her in disgust.

Angel stood up slowly and brushed leaves from her skirt. She picked them out of her hair.

Paul was filled with distaste. "It doesn't even bother you, does it? You've got the morals of a snake."

She raised her head slowly and smiled a cold, dead smile.

Uncomfortable, he strode back to the wagon. He couldn't wait for this trip to be over.

Angel could feel the shaking start. She tied her camisole and buttoned up her shirtwaist, shoving it into the skirt. The trembling became worse. She went into the trees where Paul couldn't see her and dropped to her knees. Clammy sweat broke out on her forehead. She felt cold all over. Closing her eyes, she fought the nausea. *Don't think about it, Angel. It doesn't matter if you don't let it. Pretend it didn't happen.*

Her fingers dug painfully into the tree bark, and she vomited. The coldness passed, and the shaking stopped as she stood up. She stood for a long moment waiting for the calm to come.

"Hurry up!" Paul shouted. "I want to get there before dark."

Chin up, she walked back to the road.

Paul glared down at her from the wagon seat. "You know what, Angel? You're overrated. You aren't worth more than two bits."

Something burst inside her. "And what are you worth?"

His eyes narrowed. "What do you mean?"

She came closer and snatched the shawl from the side of the wagon. "I *know* what I am. I never pretended to be anything else. Not once. Not ever!" She put her hand on the edge of the wagon seat. "And here you are, borrowing Michael's wagon and his horses and his gold and using his wife." She laughed at him. "And what do you call yourself? His *brother.*"

His face went from white to red, then white again. He clenched his fist and looked as though he wanted to kill her. "I ought to leave you here. I ought to let you walk the rest of the way."

Calm now, in complete control, Angel climbed up onto the wagon seat and sat beside him. She smiled and smoothed her skirt. "You can't now, can you? I've paid you."

They didn't speak another word the rest of the way.

# Fear

# Fifteen

*Then Peter came and said to him, "Lord, how*
*often shall my brother sin against me and*
*I forgive him? Up to seven times?" Jesus said to him,*
*"I do not say to you up to seven times, but up to*
*seventy times seven.*

MATTHEW 18:21–22

The Palace was gone.

Angel stood shivering in the falling snow, mud up to her ankles, and stared at the blackened rubble of what was left. She looked around and saw that the streets were quiet and half deserted. Several buildings were half torn down, the boards and shingles already loaded on wagons. What was happening?

Across the street was an open saloon. At least the Silver Dollar was still in business. She remembered the proprietor, Murphy. He always came up the back stairs. When Angel entered the swinging doors, the few men inside stopped talking and stared. Murphy was at the bar.

"Well, I'll be! If it ain't Angel!" He grinned broadly. "I didn't recognize you in those rags. Max! Get the lady a blanket. She's wet and half frozen. Hey, gents, look who's back! Little lady, you are a sight for sore eyes. Where you been, sweetheart? Word was you got married to some farmer." He laughed as though it were a great joke.

Murphy was loud, and Angel wanted to tell him to shut up. "What happened to the Palace?" she asked quietly, trying to still the shaking inside her.

"Burned down."

"I can see that. When?"

"Couple of weeks ago. It was the last bit of excitement we had in these parts. Town's dying, in case you hadn't noticed. The gold that's left in these parts is too hard to get out. Another month or two and Pair-a-Dice is going to be stone-cold dead. I'll have to move with the strikes or go broke like some have already done. Hochschild saw what was coming and tore his mercantile down weeks ago. He's in Sacramento now, raking in the dust."

She tried to still her impatience and raise her waning hope. "Where's the Duchess?"

"Duchess? Oh, she's gone. Left right after the fire. Sacramento, San Francisco. Don't rightly know where. Someplace bigger than this, you can bet."

Angel's heart sank as all her plans disintegrated. Max gave her a blanket, and she wrapped it around herself to ward off the growing chill. Murphy kept on talking. "She didn't have a thimble to spit in after Magowan burned the place down around her. Fire killed two of her girls."

She glanced up sharply. "Which girls?"

"Mai Ling, that little Celestial flower. I'm going to miss her."

"Who was the other girl?"

"The drunk. What was her name? Can't remember. Anyway, both of them were trapped upstairs when the blaze started. Nobody could get them out. You could hear them screaming. Gave me nightmares for days afterward."

*Oh, Lucky. What am I going to do without you?*

"Magowan tried to get away," Murphy said. "Made it about five miles before we caught up with him. Brought him back and hanged him right out there on Main Street. Raised him like a flag. Took him a long time to die. He was the meanest – "

Angel left the bar and sat down at a table. She needed to be alone and get control of her emotions.

Murphy came over with a bottle and two glasses. He stayed and poured her a whiskey. "You look down on your luck, honey." He poured another drink for himself. His eyes were dark and bright as he looked her over. "You got nothing to worry about, Angel. I've got a spare room upstairs." He glanced around at the men. "You could be back in business in five minutes on a simple say-so." He leaned closer. "All we got to work out is the split. How about sixty for me, forty for you? You'll get room, board, clothes, whatever you want. I'll take good care of you."

The shaking began inside her again. Angel cupped the glass of whiskey between her hands and stared bleakly into the amber liquid. All her prospects were gone. She had no gold, no clothes other than the ones on her back, no food, and no place to stay. She was back where she had started in San Francisco. Except it was winter now and snowing.

*There's never going to be a cabin.*

Murphy leaned forward. "What do you say, Angel?"

She looked up at him and smiled bitterly. He knew she couldn't say no.

*I'm never going to be free.*

"Well, what do you say?" He ran his finger back and forth on her arm.

"Fifty-fifty, and they pay me," she said, "or we don't do business."

Murphy leaned back, brows flicking up. He studied her for a long moment and then laughed. Downing his whiskey, he nodded. "Fair enough. Providing you give me whatever I want for free. After all, it is my place, isn't it?" He waited, and when she made no argument, he smiled. "Right now, honey." He stood. "Hey, Max! Take over for me. I'm going to show Angel her new digs."

"She's staying?" a man called, looking like Christmas had finally come.

Murphy grinned. "She's staying."

"I'm next! How much?"

Murphy named a high price.

Angel drank the glass of whiskey. Shuddering, she stood as Murphy pulled back her chair. *Nothing is ever going to change.* Her heart beat slower and slower as she went up the stairs. By the time she reached the top, she couldn't feel her heart beating at all. She couldn't feel anything.

*I should have stayed with Michael. Why didn't I stay with Michael?*

**It would never have worked, Angel. Not in a million years.**

*It did for a while.*

**Until the world caught up. The world has no mercy, Angel. You know that. It was a desert dream. You just left before he was finished using you. Now you're back where you belong, doing what you were born to do.**

What did any of it matter? It was too late to think about what-ifs. It was too late to think about why. It was too late to think about anything.

Murphy wanted the works.

When he left, Angel got out of bed. She blew out the lamp. Sitting in the darkened corner, she hugged her knees against her chest and rocked herself. The pain that had begun when Paul showed up in the valley bloomed and expanded and consumed her. Eyes tightly closed, she made no sound, but the room was filled with silent screaming.

The days ran together. Nothing much had changed. Instead of the Duchess, Angel now had Murphy; instead of Magowan, there was the more manageable Max. Her room was smaller and her clothing less grand. The food was tolerable and plentiful. Men were still the same.

Angel sat on the bed, leg crossed and swinging back and forth as a young miner undressed. His hair was still wet and slicked back, and he smelled strongly of harsh soap. He didn't have much to say, which was fine, because she didn't want to listen. This one wouldn't take long. Closing down her emotions, closing down her mind, she went to work.

The door crashed open, and someone yanked the young man away. Angel drew in a sharp breath as she recognized the face of the man above her. "Michael!" She pushed herself up. "Oh, *Michael...*"

The young man thudded on the floor. He came to his feet. "What're you doing?" Swearing, he lunged. Michael hit him and sent him back against the wall. Hauling him up, he hit him again and sent him flying backwards through the open door to crash and sag against the outer wall. Michael snatched up the miner's things and heaved them out on top of him. Kicking the door shut, he turned.

Angel was so relieved at the sight of him she wanted to fall at his feet, but one look at his face and she shrank back.

"Get dressed." He didn't wait for her to move as he grabbed up her discarded clothing and tossed it at her. *"Now!"*

Heart pounding, she fumbled with the clothing, frantically trying to think of a way to escape him. Before she was fully clothed, he yanked her off the bed, opened the door, and shoved her into the corridor. He hadn't even allowed her to put her shoes on.

Murphy was coming. "What do you think you're doing? I told you to wait downstairs. That man paid. You can wait your turn."

"Get out of my way."

Murphy spread his feet and balled his fists. "You think you can get by me?"

Angel had seen Murphy in action before and was sure Michael was no match for him. "Michael, please – " Michael shoved her roughly to one side and stepped in front of her.

Murphy came at him, but Michael moved so fast, Murphy was down before he knew what hit him. Michael caught her wrist and pulled her along again. Before they reached the stairs, Murphy was up. He grabbed her arm and yanked back so hard, she cried out in pain. Michael let go, and she fell against the wall. Murphy came at him again, and this time Michael sent him straight down the stairs.

When Michael bent over her, Angel drew back from him. "Get up!" he bellowed. She didn't dare disobey. He took her arm and shoved her ahead of him. "Keep walking and don't stop."

Max charged Michael when they reached the bottom of the stairs. Michael used the man's momentum to lift and heave him across a poker table. Two more men came at him, and he pushed her out of the way just before they hit him. The three went crashing back over a faro table. Chips, cards, and men scattered. Two more entered the fracas.

"Stop it!" she screamed, sure they would kill him. Frantic, she looked for something to use as a weapon to help, but Michael wasn't down long enough. He kicked one man off of him and was on his feet. She stared, mouth agape, as he fought. He stood his ground, punching hard and fast as the other men came at him. Swinging around, he brought one foot up straight into a man's face. She had never seen anyone fight the way he did. He looked as though he had been doing it all his life instead of plowing furrows and planting corn. He hit square and he hit hard, and those he hit stayed down. After a few minutes, the men weren't so eager to come at him.

Michael stood ready, eyes blazing. "Come on, then," he grated, daring them. "Who else wants to get between me and my wife? *Come on!*"

No one moved.

Kicking a turned table out of his way, Michael strode toward Angel. He didn't look anything like the man she had come to know in the valley. "I told you to keep walking!" He grabbed her arm and swung her toward the doors.

His wagon was right outside. Michael caught her up in his arms and tossed her onto the high seat. She had no time to think of escape before he was beside her. He took the reins and snapped them. She had to hang on for dear life. The pace he set was grueling. He didn't slow until they were several miles out of Pair-a-Dice, and when he did, it was out of care for the horses and not her.

Angel was afraid even to look at him. She was afraid to say a word. She had never seen him like this before, even that one time when he had lost his temper in the barn. This was not the quiet, patient man she thought she knew. This was a stranger bent on vengeance. She remembered Duke lighting his cheroot and broke out in a cold sweat.

Michael wiped blood from his lip. "Make me understand, Angel. Tell me why."

*Angel.* There was a death knell in the name. "Let me off this wagon."

"You're coming home with me."

"So you can kill me?"

"Jesus, are you listening to her? Why'd you give me this stupid, stubborn woman?"

*"Let me off!"*

"Not a chance. You're not skipping out of this. We have some things to settle."

The look in his eyes was so full of violence, she jumped. She hit heavily and rolled. Regaining her breath, she clambered to her feet and ran.

Michael drew back hard on the reins and veered the wagon off the road. He jumped down and started after her. "Angel!" He could hear her footsteps fleeing into the woods. "It's getting dark. Stop running before you break your neck!"

She didn't stop. She tripped over a root and fell so hard she knocked her wind out. She lay gasping on the ground and could hear Michael close behind. He was walking fast, slapping branches out of his way until he spotted her.

Angel scrambled to her feet and ran from him in terror, heedless of the branches that slapped her face. Michael cut her off and caught her shoulders. Stumbling, she took him down with her. He turned his body so he landed first and tried to roll her. She kicked and twisted, fighting for freedom. Flinging her onto her back, he pinned her down. When she tried to claw his face, he caught her wrists and held them against the ground.

"That's enough!"

She lay panting for breath, her eyes enormous. Getting his breath back, he yanked her to her feet. The minute he loosened his hold, she tried to run again. He swung her back and took a blow. He almost hit her back, but he knew if he hit her once, he wouldn't stop. He let go of her, but each time she tried to flee, he swung her back. Finally, she attacked, slapping, hitting, and kicking at him. He blocked her blows, all without retaliating.

When she sagged, Michael pulled her into his arms and held her tightly. Her whole body was shaking violently. He could feel the fear radiating from her. And rightly so. His rage frightened him. If he had hit her back once, he would have killed her.

He had almost gone out of his mind when she left him.

He searched on foot until he found the wagon marks and realized what had happened. She had left with Paul. She was on her way back to Pair-a-Dice. He went home, hurt and furious at them both. The long wait for Paul's return from town had been the closest thing to hell he had ever experienced. Why had Paul done it? Why hadn't he sent her home instead of taking her with him?

But Michael knew.

Paul brought the wagon and horses back. He said Hochschild moved to Sacramento and that was why it had taken him so long. It was clear he wasn't going to volunteer any information about Amanda. Michael asked straight out. Paul had little to say other than yes, he had driven her back to Pair-a-Dice.

"It was her idea to leave. I didn't talk her into it," Paul said, pale and scared. What struck Michael hardest was the guilt etched deeply into his grieving face. He didn't have to ask anything more. He knew what else had happened on the road. Or in Pair-a-Dice.

"Michael, I'm sorry. I swear it wasn't my fault. I tried to tell you what she was – "

"Get out of my sight, Paul. Go home and stay there." And he did.

Michael almost didn't come and get her back after that. She deserved whatever she got. She went looking for it, didn't she? He wept. He cursed her. He had loved her, and she betrayed him. She might as well have stuck a knife in his guts and twisted it.

But at night, in the dark, he remembered those first days when she had been so sick and he had been given a glimpse of her soul. She had said a lot in her delirium, drawing pictures of the wretchedness of her life. Did she even know any better? He remembered Paul's reaction to her, and her own anger. He had seen her hurt, though she had denied it fiercely. He had to go and get her back. She was his wife.

*Until death do us part.*

He prepared himself for anything on the way to Pair-a-Dice, but when he walked into that room and saw for himself what she was doing, he had almost lost all reason. If he hadn't seen her eyes or heard the way she said his name, he would have killed them both. But he had seen and heard it – for one brief, unguarded instant he'd known what she really felt. Relief. Relief so profound it stopped him cold.

But it didn't mean the instinctive rage at her betrayal wasn't still there, bubbling just below the surface.

Michael shuddered and drew back from her. "Come on," he said tightly. "We're going home." He took her hand and started back through the woods.

Angel wanted to resist but was afraid. What was he going to do to her now? In this mood, could he be as brutal as Duke? "Why did you come for me?"

"You're my wife."

"I left the ring on the table! I didn't steal it."

"That didn't change a thing. We're still married."

"You could've just forgotten about it."

He stopped and glared at her. "It's a lifetime commitment in my book, lady. It's not an arrangement you nullify when things get a little tough to bear."

She searched his face in confusion. "Even after you just found me – " He started walking again, pulling her along with him. She didn't understand him. She didn't understand him at all. "Why?"

"Because I *love* you," he said thickly. He swung her around in front of him, his eyes tormented. "That simple, Amanda. I *love* you. When are you going to understand what that means?"

Her throat tightened, and she hung her head.

They walked the rest of the way in silence. He lifted her onto the wagon seat. She shifted over as he pulled himself up beside her. She looked at him bleakly. "Your kind of love can't feel good."

"Does your kind feel any better?" She looked away. He unlooped the reins. "Right now love doesn't have an awful lot to do with feelings," he said grimly. "Don't misunderstand. I'm as human as the next man. I *feel* all right. I feel plenty right now, a lot I wish I didn't." He shook his head, his face strained with hurt and anger. "I felt like killing you when I walked in that room, but I didn't. I feel like beating sense into you right now, but I won't." He looked at her with dark eyes. "And no matter how much it hurts, and no matter how much I feel like hurting you back for what you've done, I'm not going to." He snapped the reins and set off again.

Angel tried to shove her feelings down, but they kept coming up, choking her. She clenched her fists, fighting it. "You knew what I was. You *knew*." She wanted him to understand. "Michael, it's all I've ever been. It's all I'm ever going to be."

"That's pure, unadulterated horse manure. When are you going to stop wallowing in it?"

She looked away, shoulders sagging. "You just don't understand. It's never going to be the way you want it to be. It can't be! Even if there ever could have been a chance, that's gone now. Don't you see?"

His eyes impaled hers. "Are you talking about Paul?"

"He told you?"

"He didn't have to. It was written all over his face."

Angel offered no defense. She offered no excuses. Shoulders limp, she stared straight ahead.

Michael saw she took the whole blame on herself, but she and Paul were both going to have to deal with it. So was he. He faced the road again and was silent for a long time. "Why did you go back? I just don't get it."

She closed her eyes, searching for a good enough reason. She could find none and swallowed hard. "To get my gold," she said bleakly. Admitting it aloud made her feel small and hollow.

"What for?"

"I want a little cabin in the woods."

"You've already got one."

She could hardly speak past the lump of pain in her chest. She pressed her hand against it. "I want to be free, Michael. Just once in my whole life. *Free!*" Her voice broke. She bit her lip and clutched at the side of the wagon seat so hard the wood dug into her hands.

Michael's face softened. The anger vanished but not the hurt, not the sorrow. "You are free. You just don't know it yet."

It was a long, quiet ride back to the valley.

# Sixteen

*The mind is its own place,*
*and in itself can make a heav'n of hell, a hell of heaven.*

MILTON

Michael couldn't get it out of his head. She made no apology. She gave no excuses. She just sat, wordless, back straight, head up, hands clenched in her lap as though she were going into battle instead of going home. Would she rather reject his gift and live in eternal darkness than open her mind and heart to him? Was her pride the only thing that mattered?

He didn't understand.

Angel sat in silent torment. She struggled against the emotions tearing at her, remorse, guilt, confusion. They became a solid mass, a hardened lump growing in her throat and chest, like a cancer spreading pain into every limb. She was afraid. The hope she thought long-since dead was resurrected. She had forgotten the small light that had sometimes flickered inside her as a child. Something would strike its spark, and it would grow – until Duke crushed it.

She tried to crush it now with logic.

Nothing could be the same. Whatever might have grown between her and Michael was ruined. She knew that. The moment Paul had used her, she had thrown her last chance away.

*I did it to myself. I did it to myself. Mea culpa. Mea culpa.*

Her mother's words haunted her, unbearable memories of a forsaken life. Why was she feeling this small light again when she knew it would only be destroyed in the end? Just as it always had been. Hope was cruel. Only the aroma of sustenance before a starving child. Not milk. Not meat.

*Oh, God, I can't hope for anything. I can't. I won't survive if I do.*

But it was there, a tiny spark glowing in the darkness.

As they reached the valley at first light, Angel felt the building warmth of the sun on her shoulders and remembered Michael dragging her with him through the night to face the sunrise. "That's the life I want to give you." She hadn't understood then what he offered. She had not comprehended until she walked up the stairs at the Silver Dollar Saloon and sold her soul into slavery again.

**It's too late, Angel.**

*Then why is he bringing me back? Why didn't he just leave me in Pair-a-Dice?*

**Duke brought you back, too, didn't he? Several times.**

She had always seen retribution in Duke's dark eyes. He had made her suffer. Yet it had been easier to take what he did to her than to watch the suffering he brought on others who dared aid her. Like Johnny – before Duke dispatched him forever.

But Michael wasn't like Duke. She had never seen that sheen of calculated cruelty in his eyes. She had never felt it in his hands.

**There's a price for everything, Angel. You know that. You've always known.**

What kind of price would he require for bringing her back from hell? What price for saving her from her own folly?

She shook inside.

Michael swung the wagon around in the yard in front of the cabin and tied the reins securely. Angel started to climb down, but his hand clamped her wrist. "Sit tight." His voice was heavy, and she sat silently awaiting his command. When he came around to lift her down, she closed her eyes, afraid to look into his. He set her on the ground gently.

"Go into the house," he told her. "I'm going to see to the horses."

Angel pushed the cabin door open and felt her whole being permeated with a sense of relief. *I'm home.*

**For how long, Angel? Long enough to make you suffer before he casts you out again?**

She couldn't let herself think of that right now. She entered and looked around for changes. Everything was so familiar, so plain, so dear. The rough table, the willow chairs before the fireplace, the bed made out of the wagon bed, the worn quilts his sister had made. Angel moved to lay a fire and make the rumpled bed.

Picking up a red wool shirt, she pressed her face into it and inhaled the scent of Michael's body. He was the earth and sky and wind. Her breath stopped.

*What have I done? Why did I throw it all away?*

Paul's words came back: *"You're not even worth two bits."* It was true. She was a prostitute and that's all she would ever be. It hadn't even taken a day for her to fall right back into her old ways.

Trembling, she folded the shirt carefully and tucked it away in his drawer. She had to stop thinking. She had to get by as she had always done before. But how could she now? How?

Her desperate mind worked for answers and none came. *I'll do whatever he wants for as long as he wants if he'll let me stay. If he'll only let me.*

Though she had no appetite, she knew Michael would be hungry when he came in. She took great care with breakfast. While the porridge cooked, she dusted and swept. An hour passed, then another. Still Michael didn't return.

What was he thinking? Was his anger growing? Had he already changed his mind about bringing her back here? Would he kick her out now? Where would she go if he did?

Memories of Duke made her stomach twist.

*He's not like Duke.*

**Every man is Duke when betrayed.**

Her mind circled like a bird searching for carrion. Her self-defenses roused and took up arms against Michael. No one had forced him to come after her. If he was hurt about what he had seen, he had only himself to blame. It wasn't her fault he walked in when he did. It wasn't her fault he came at all. Why didn't he just leave her alone in the first place? She had never tried to fool him. What did he expect? He knew from the beginning what he was getting. He knew what she was.

*What am I?* her mind cried out. *Who am I? I don't even have a name of my own anymore. Is there even a piece of Sarah left?*

She kept seeing his eyes, and the hot heaviness of her own heart was unbearable.

Finally, she could bear it no more and went out to find him. He wasn't in the field, though the horses were grazing. He was nowhere to be seen. Finally, she entered the barn quietly and saw him. He was sitting, head in his hands, weeping. Her heart sank as she watched, and the ease she sought became an even heavier burden.

*I've wounded him. I might as well have taken a knife and stabbed it into his very heart. It would have been better if Magowan had killed me. It would have been better if I had never been born.*

Hugging herself, she went back to the cabin and sank to her knees before the fire. It was her fault. All the *ifs* flooded her: If she had never left Duke...if she had never gotten on that barkentine...if she hadn't sold herself to any passerby on the muddy streets of San Francisco or gone with Duchess...if she had ignored Paul...if she had stayed here and never left...if she hadn't gone back to Pair-a-Dice or gone up those stairs with Murphy. *If, if, if...*the endless, twisting, downward staircase.

*But I did all of it. I did. And now it's too late, and Michael sits crying while I haven't a tear for anything.*

She held herself and rocked back and forth. *Why was I ever born? Why?* She stared down at her hands. *For this?* She could feel the filth of her trade covering them. Her whole body was fouled, inside and out. Michael had taken her straight out of the abyss and offered her a chance – and she had thrown it away. Then he came again and took her straight from her soiled bed to his home, and staying true to her own stupidity, she had spent the whole morning cleaning the cabin and had not once thought to cleanse herself.

Searching frantically she found soap and ran for the creek. Stripping off her clothing and heedlessly casting it aside, she waded in. The icy air and water bit her flesh, but she didn't care. All she wanted was to be clean, to wash it all away, everything from as far back as she could remember.

Maybe right to the very moment of her conception.

Michael rose and hung up the harnesses. He came out of the barn and walked slowly back to the cabin. What could become of a marriage so fouled by sexual betrayal?

*She never loved me in the first place. Why should I expect her loy-*

*alty? She never really promised it. I made her say the vows. She never said a word about being sorry, Lord. Not one word in thirty miles. Have I made a mistake? Was it your voice I heard, or was it my own flesh? Why are you doing this to me?*

He should have left her in Pair-a-Dice.

**She is your wife.**

*Yes, but I don't know if I can forgive her.*

The image of her in bed with another man was branded in his mind. He couldn't get it out of his head.

*I loved her, Lord. I loved her enough to die for her, and she did this to me. Maybe she's beyond redemption. How do you forgive someone who doesn't even care enough to want to be forgiven?*

**What does she want, Michael?**

*Freedom. She wants freedom.*

The cabin was neat; a cozy fire was burning. The table was set and his breakfast ready. Only Angel was missing. Michael swore for the first time in years. "Let her go back! I don't care. I'm sick of the struggle." He kicked the pot free of the iron bar. "How many times am I supposed to go after her and bring her back?"

He sat for a while in the willow chair, but his anger just kept building. He would go find her again, and this time he would give her a good piece of his mind. He would tell her if she wanted to leave so badly, he'd even give her a ride back. Slamming out of the cabin, he stood outside, arms akimbo, wondering which way she had run off this time. He scanned the landscape and, with some surprise, spotted her standing naked in the creek.

He strode down the bank. "What are you doing? If you wanted a bath, why didn't you tote water to the house and warm it?"

In a sudden, uncharacteristic act of modesty, she turned her back to him, trying to hide herself. "Go away."

He stripped off his jacket. "Come on out of there. You'll catch pneumonia. If you want a bath that badly, I'll tote the water."

"Go away!" she screamed, dropping to her knees and hunching over.

"Don't be a fool!" He waded in and caught hold of her,

yanking her to her feet. Her fists were full of gravel. Her breasts and belly were raw from scrubbing. "What are you doing to yourself?"

"I have to wash. You didn't give me the chance – "

"You've washed enough." He tried to put the jacket around her, and she pulled away.

"I'm not clean yet, Michael. Just go away and leave me alone."

Michael grabbed her roughly. "Will you be finished when you've stripped your skin off? When you've bled? Is that it? Do you think doing this to yourself will make you *clean*?" He let go of her, afraid he would do her physical harm. "It doesn't work that way," he said through gritted teeth.

She blinked and sat down slowly, the icy water swirling around her waist. "No, I guess not," she said softly. Her tangled wet hair hung limp around her white face and shoulders.

"Come back inside," he said and helped her up. She came without resistance this time, stumbling as they reached the bank. When she bent for her clothing, he pulled her along without them. Half shoving her into the cabin, he slammed the door.

Yanking a blanket from the bed, he threw it to her. "Sit down by the fire."

Angel pulled the blanket around her shoulders and sat. She didn't raise her head.

Glancing back at her, Michael poured her a cup of coffee. "Drink this." She did as he told her. "You'll be lucky if you don't get sick. What are you trying to do? Make *me* feel guilty you went back to prostitution? Make *me* feel guilty for dragging you out of that brothel again?"

"No," she said quietly.

He didn't want to pity her. He wanted to shake her until her teeth fell out. He wanted to kill her.

*I could. God, I could kill her and be glad of it!*

**Seventy times seven.**

*I don't want to listen to you. I'm sick of listening. You ask too much. It hurts. Can't you understand? Don't you know what she's done to me?*

**Seventy times seven.**

His eyes were hot with tears, his heart pounding like a war drum. She looked like a bedraggled child. Shadows lay dark beneath her blue eyes. Let her suffer. She deserved it. There was a mark on her neck that made him sick. She put her hand over it and turned her face away from him. He could almost see her shrinking. Maybe she had a tiny bit of conscience left. Maybe she did feel a little shame. Oh, but it'd wear off soon enough, and she'd be ready to cut him to ribbons again.

*I can't help how I feel, Lord. If I thought she could love me, maybe –*

**As you have loved me?**

*It's not the same. You're God! I'm only a man.*

"You shouldn't have come for me," she said dully. "You should never have come near me in the first place."

"That's right. Blame me." Maybe she was right. He felt sick. Clenching his hand, he glared down at her. "I said vows, and I'm going to stick by them no matter how much they're choking me now."

She looked up at him with bleak eyes. "You don't have to." She shook her head.

"It'll work. I'll make it work." *Didn't you promise, Lord? Or was I imagining it? Was she right all along and it was just sexual attraction?*

"You're only fooling yourself," Angel said. "You just don't understand. I never should've been born."

He laughed derisively. "Self-pity. You're drowning in it, aren't you? You're a blind fool, Angel. You can't see what's right in front of your face."

**Nor can you.**

She stared into the fire. "I'm not blind. I've had my eyes open all my life. You don't think I know what I'm saying? You don't think it's true? I heard my own father say I was supposed to be aborted." Her voice broke. She regained control and went on more quietly. "How can a man like you understand? My father was married. He already had enough children. He told Mama she just wanted a hold over him. I never knew if that was true. He sent her away. He didn't want her anymore. Because of me. He stopped loving her. Because of me."

She kept on in that quiet, agonized voice. "Mama's parents were decent people in a good neighborhood. They wouldn't take her in, not with an illegitimate child. Even her church turned her away." The blanket fell open, and Michael stared down at the reddened marks on her skin. There were lines of red where she had torn at her own flesh.

*Jesus, why are you doing this to me?*

It was easier retreating into anger than seeing into her tortured soul.

"We ended up on the docks," she said, emotionless now. "She became a prostitute. When the men left, she'd drink herself to sleep while Rab went out and drank the money away. She wasn't very pretty anymore. She died when I was eight." She looked up at him. "Smiling." Her own mouth curved. "So you see. It *is* true. I shouldn't have been born. It was all a terrible mistake from the beginning."

Michael sat down heavily, tears at the surface again, but not for himself this time. "What happened to you then?"

She bowed her head and clasped her hands tightly together. She didn't look at him. It was a long, heavy silence before she spoke very quietly. "Rab sold me to a brothel. Duke has a thing for little girls."

Michael shut his eyes.

She looked up at him. Of course he was repulsed. What man wouldn't be at the thought of a child fornicating with a grown man? "That was just the beginning," she said dully, lowering her head, unable to look at him. "You can't even begin to imagine what happened from there. Things done to me. Things *I* did." She didn't tell him it was a matter of survival. What did it matter? She had chosen to obey.

He looked at her through his tears. "You think you're to blame for all of it, don't you?"

"Who else? Mama? She loved my father. She loved me. She loved *God*. A lot of good love ever did her. How can I blame her for anything, Michael? Should I blame Rab? He was just a poor, dull-witted drunk who thought he was doing the best for me. They killed him. Right there in the room, in front of me, because he knew too much." She shook her head. He didn't have to know everything.

"You're not to blame, Amanda."

*Amanda*. Oh, God. "How can you still call me that?"

"Because it's who you are now."

"When will you ever understand?" she cried out in frustration. "It doesn't matter who does things to you. You can't pretend they didn't happen." She clutched the blanket around her, hugging herself. "You take it all into yourself. What's happened is what I am. You said it yourself and you're right. I can't wash it away. I can't get clean. I could strip my skin off. I could drain my blood. It wouldn't make any difference. It's like a foul stench I can't get rid of no matter how hard I try. And I've tried, Michael. I have. I swear to you. I've fought and I've run. I've wanted to die. I almost succeeded with Magowan. Almost. Don't you see? Nothing matters. Nothing ever made any difference. I'm a prostitute, and that's what I was meant to be."

"That's a lie!"

"No, it isn't. It isn't."

He leaned toward her, but she drew back, hugging herself even more tightly and looking away. "Amanda, we'll make it through this," he said. "We will. I swear a covenant with you."

"No, we won't make it. Just take me back." When he shook his head, she pleaded. "*Please.* I don't belong here with you. Find someone else."

"Better than you, you mean?"

Her face was white as death, her pain stark and raw. "Yes."

Michael reached out to put his hand on her shoulder, but she withdrew from him. He knew why now, and it pierced him to the core that she thought she was so unclean he shouldn't even touch her.

"Do you think I'm such a saint?" he said hoarsely. Only moments ago he had denied love and God himself and even longed to kill his own wife. What was the difference in murder by hand or thought? His fleshly nature had relished thoughts of retribution, even lusted for it.

He went down on his knees and held her shoulders. "I should

have run all the way to Pair-a-Dice," he said thickly. "I shouldn't have waited for Paul to come home with his tail between his legs."

She raised her head and looked him straight in the eyes, wanting to end it quickly, once and for all. "I gave him sex just to pay for the ride back."

The pain of those words hit him hard, but he didn't give up on her. Michael lifted her chin. "Look at me, Amanda. I'm never taking you back. Not ever. We belong together."

"You're a fool, Michael Hosea. A poor, blind fool." She shivered violently.

Michael got up to get her a dry blanket. When he turned, her eyes were on him, and they were filled with fear. "What is it?" he said, frowning. "Do you think I mean to harm you?"

She closed her eyes tightly. "You want what I don't have. I can't love you. Even if I was able, I wouldn't."

He hunkered down, took the damp blanket from her and covered her with the dry quilt. "Why not?"

"Because I spent the first eight years of my life watching my mother do penance for loving a man."

He tipped her chin. "The wrong man," he said firmly. "I'm not the wrong man, Amanda." He straightened and dug in his pocket. Kneeling down before her, he dug beneath the quilt and found her hand. He slipped his mother's wedding ring back on her finger. "Just to keep it official." He touched her cheek tenderly and smiled.

She hung her head and pulled her hand back beneath the heavy folds of wool. She clenched it against her breasts and felt every self-inflicted scratch and bruise, but far worse was the feeling blooming inside her.

The spark was becoming a fire.

Michael took a cloth and dried her hair. When he finished, he pulled her close and cradled her in his arms. "Flesh of my flesh," he whispered against her hair. "Blood of my blood."

Angel closed her eyes tightly. His desire for her would diminish with time. He would stop loving her the same way her father had stopped loving Mama. And if she let herself love Michael the way Mama had loved Alex Stafford, he would tear her heart out.

*I don't want to weep myself to sleep on a rumpled bed and drink my life away.*

Michael felt her trembling. "I can't send you away without cutting myself in half," he said. "You're already part of me." He brushed his lips against her temple. "We'll start over. We'll put what's happened behind us."

"How can we? What's done is done. It's all inside me, carved in stone."

"Then we'll dig it out and bury it."

She gave a bleak, humorless laugh. "You'll have to bury *me*."

His heart lightened. "All right," he said. "We'll baptize you." Not just with water but with the Spirit, if she would ever allow it. He kissed her hair and held her. It was ironic how close he felt to her now, closer than he ever had before. He stroked her hair back. "I learned a long time ago we've control of little in this world, Amanda. It doesn't belong to us. It's out of our hands. Like being born or being sold into prostitution at eight. All we can change is the way we think and the way we live."

She gave a shuddering sigh. "And you've made up your mind to keep me with you for a while."

"Not for a while. Permanently. I'm hoping you'll make up your mind to stay." He caressed her skin tenderly. "Whatever anyone else has said and done to you, it's up to you now to make the decision. You can *decide* to trust me."

She searched his face uncertainly. "Just like that?"

"Yes. Just like that. One day at a time."

She studied him for a moment, then nodded. Life had been too unbearable the other way not to try Michael's.

Stroking her cheek with his thumb, he kissed her mouth. Her lips softened beneath his, and she clutched the front of his shirt. When he raised his mouth from hers, she rested her cheek against his chest. He felt her body relax completely into his.

Michael closed his eyes. *Lord, forgive me. You said go to her, and I let pride stand in my way. You said she needed me, and I didn't believe. You said love her, and I thought it would be easy. Help me. Open my heart and mind so that I will love her as you have loved me.*

The fire crackled softly, and a steady warmth built within

Michael as he held his young wife; and sometime within the space of a shuddering sigh, he ceased thinking of her as Angel – the harlot he loved and who had betrayed him – and saw her instead as the nameless child who had been broken and was still lost.

# Seventeen

*You are our letter…written not in ink,*
*but with the Spirit of the living God,*
*not on stone tablets, but on tablets of human hearts.*

2 CORINTHIANS 3:2–3

*Forgiveness* was a foreign word. Grace inconceivable. Angel wanted to make up for what she had done, and she sought to do it by labor. Mama had never been forgiven, not even after a thousand Hail Marys and Our Fathers. So how could Angel be forgiven by a single word?

She worked to make it up to Michael. When she was finished with her own chores, she sought him out and asked for more to do. If he plowed, she walked behind him and pulled up the rocks, toting them to the stone wall growing between the fields. When he downed trees, she hacked off the branches with a hatchet, piled and tied them into bundles and stacked them inside the barn to dry for kindling. When he split wood, she stacked it. She even took up a shovel to help him dig up stumps.

He never asked her to do anything, so she looked for things to do for him.

By nightfall, she was exhausted but could not sit idle. Idleness made her feel guilty. Rather than pleasing him, she found he withdrew from her more each day. He was quiet, watchful, pensive. Was he already regretting his impulsiveness at bringing her back?

One evening, she struggled with her weariness as he read. His voice was deep and rich, and she drifted, exhausted, fighting to keep her eyes open. He closed the book and put it back on the mantel.

"You're working too hard."

She pushed herself up straighter and looked at the mending in her hands. Her hands were shaking. "I'm just not used to this kind of work yet."

"You've enough to do without thinking you have to take on half of what I do as well. You're dead on your feet."

"I suppose I'm not very good company."

When Michael put his hand on her shoulder, he felt her wince. "You ache all over from toting those rocks yesterday, and this morning you were shoveling manure from that stall."

"I needed it for the garden."

"Tell me and I'll take care of it!"

"But you said the garden was my responsibility."

There was no use in talking to her. She was set on doing penance. "I'm going to go out and walk awhile. Go on to bed."

He went up to the hill and sat, forearms resting on his knees. "So what do I do now?" Nothing was the same as it had been. It was as though they both walked side by side, never touching, never talking. She had cut herself wide open and poured her insides out to him the night he brought her home. Now she lay bleeding to death and wouldn't allow the healing to come. She hoped to please him by working like a slave when all he wanted was her love.

He raked a hand back through his hair and held his head. *So, what do I do, Lord? What do I do?*

**Tend my lamb.**

"How?" Michael said to the night sky.

Entering the cabin quietly, he saw she was asleep in the chair. He lifted her gently and put her to bed. She looked so young and vulnerable. How far was she removed from the child raped at eight? Not far enough. No wonder she had never seen sex as having anything to do with love. How could she? He knew he didn't know the half of what she had gone through. He knew the only one who could mend a ruptured soul was God, and she wanted no part of him.

*How do I teach a hurt child to trust you when the only father she knew hated her and wanted her dead? How do I teach her the world isn't all bad when the priest turned her mother away. Lord, she was sold into bondage to a man who sounds like Satan himself. How do I convince her there are good people in the world when everyone she has ever known used her and then condemned her for it?*

Michael lifted a strand of her pale hair and rubbed it between his fingers. He hadn't made love to her since bringing her home. He wanted to. His body yearned for her. But then he would remember her lifeless voice as she said, "Duke has a thing for little girls," and his desire evaporated.

*What was she thinking all those times we were together? Was I just like all the others, taking my pleasure at her expense?*

She had always seemed so strong. And she was. Strong enough to take unspeakable abuse and survive. Strong enough to adapt to anything. Strong enough to lock herself away inside walls she thought would make her safe. What choice had she then? How could she even comprehend what he offered her now?

*She was just a child, Lord. Why did you let it happen? Jesus, I don't understand. Why? Aren't you supposed to protect the weak and innocent? Why didn't you protect her? Why didn't you help her? Why?*

How was Angel any different from Hosea's wife, Gomer, sold to the prophet by her own father? A child of prostitution. An adulteress. Was Gomer ever redeemed by her husband's love? God had redeemed Israel countless times. Christ had redeemed the world. *But what about Gomer, Lord? What about Angel? What about my wife?*

**Tend my lamb.**

*You keep saying that, but I don't know how. I don't know what you mean. I'm not a prophet, Lord. I'm a simple farmer. I'm not up to the task you've set for me. My love hasn't been enough. She's still there in the pit, dying. I reach for her, but she won't take my hand. She'll kill herself trying to earn my love when it's hers already.*

**Trust in me with all your heart and lean not on your own understanding.**

*I'm trying, Jesus. I'm trying.*

Dejected, Michael sat down on the edge of the bed. Tessie's skirt slid off and landed in a heap on the floor. He picked it up and looked at the threadbare fabric. Frowning, he tossed it back on the bed. He picked up the faded shirtwaist and looked at it. He rubbed it between his fingers. The first time he had come to Angel in her upstairs room, she had been in satin and lace. Now he dressed her in rags. Not even her own but those of his dead sister.

Not once had Amanda asked for anything to replace them, and he had been too caught up in his own bleak thoughts and labor to give time to it. Well, that was going to change. They weren't so far away from Sacramento that they couldn't make a trip to see Joseph, who would be well stocked with his merchant's sharp mind on the coming influx of families.

Michael went to Paul and asked him to watch over the stock while he and Amanda were away. At the mention of her name, Paul paled. "You brought her back?"

"Yes. I brought her home."

Paul fell silent, his face stiff, when Michael reminded him she was his wife. Paul agreed to take care of things.

"I'll settle up with Joseph while we're in Sacramento," Michael said.

"Thanks just the same, but I'll make my own arrangements."

Michael hesitated, then nodded. He felt the rift between them growing wider. Paul and his insufferable, stiff-necked pride. Paul and his guilt.

Michael loaded the wagon with sacks of potatoes, boxes of onions, and crates of winter apples while Amanda stood in the barn doorway, hugging her shawl around her shoulders. She didn't ask any questions.

"Paul's going to watch the stock," Michael said as he pulled the canvas top over the produce.

"I can do that. You didn't need to ask him."

"You're going with me." That clearly took her aback. He smiled. "Make some extra biscuits this evening. We'll pack a couple cans of beans and be on our way in the morning."

They left at sunrise. Amanda said very little on the way. They stopped for a noon meal and started off again, driving until dusk before Michael made camp a hundred yards off the road. It was cold, the sky clear. Amanda gathered wood while Michael dug a wide pit and pitched a lean-to over it. After they ate supper, he shoveled hot coals into the earthen hollow. He spread a layer of dirt over them, then pine bows and canvas before the blankets. Angel sank into the bed gratefully, her body aching from the bouncing wagon.

A coyote howled and she edged closer to Michael. He put his arm around her and she pressed against him, fitting him like a puzzle piece. He turned to her and kissed her, his fingers digging into her hair, but after a moment he withdrew and lay back staring up at the stars.

Angel moved away. "You don't want me anymore, do you?"

He didn't look at her as he spoke. "I want you too much. I just can't stop thinking of what it must have been like for you as a child."

"I should never have told you anything."

He turned his head to her. "Why not? So I could keep on taking my pleasure and never understand the cost to you?"

"It doesn't cost me anything, Michael. Not anymore."

"Then why did I have to force you to say my name?"

She couldn't answer that.

Michael turned toward her and tenderly caressed her face. "I want your love, Amanda. I want you to feel the pleasure I feel when I touch you. I want to please you as much as you've pleased me."

"You always want too much."

"I don't think so. I think it's just going to take time. It's going to take us getting to know one another better. It's going to take trust."

Angel stared up at the star-studded sky. "I knew soiled doves who fell in love. It never worked."

"Why not?"

"Because they became obsessive just like Mama and they were just as miserable." Angel counted herself lucky she lacked the ability to love. She thought she did once, but it was only an illusion. Even Johnny had turned out to be only a means of escape.

"You're not a prostitute anymore, Amanda. You're my wife." Michael smiled ruefully and toyed with a tendril of blonde hair. "You can love me as much as you want and feel safe."

Falling in love meant you lost control of your emotions and your will and your life. It meant you lost yourself. And Angel couldn't risk that, even with this man.

"What do you feel when I touch you?" he asked, running a fingertip down her cheek.

She looked at him. "What do you want me to feel?"

"Forget what I want. What goes on inside you?"

She knew he would wait until she answered, and she knew he would know if she lied. "I don't really feel anything, I guess."

Frowning, he kept touching her face. He loved the feel of her soft, smooth skin. "When I touch you, my whole body comes alive. I feel the warmth all through me. I can't even describe how wonderful it feels when we make love."

She looked away again. Did he have to talk about it?

"We've got to find a way to help you like it just as much as I do," he said, and lay back beside her again.

"Does it matter that much? Why should it matter at all whether I feel anything or not?"

"It matters to me. The pleasure is meant to be shared." Michael put his arm around her. "Come here. Just let me hold you."

She turned to nestle her head against his shoulder and relaxed. She put her arm across his broad chest. He was so warm and solid. "I don't know why it bothers you," she said. It never bothered anyone else what she thought or felt, just as long as she did what she was supposed to do.

"It bothers me because I love you."

Maybe he just didn't understand the facts of life. Maybe he was functioning under some illusion. "Women aren't supposed to really enjoy sex, Michael. It's all an act."

"Did someone tell you that?"

"A few."

"A man or woman?"

"Both."

"Well, I know that's not the way the Lord intended it to be."

She laughed derisively. "God? You're so naive. Sex is the great original sin. He threw Adam and Eve right out of the Garden because of it."

So she did know something about the Bible. Probably from her mother. And she had her theology twisted. "Sex had nothing to do with why they were cast out. Eve's sin was trying to be God. That's why she wanted the apple, so she would know all and be like the Lord. She was deceived. Adam was weak and went along with what she said rather than follow what God had told him."

Angel drew away slightly and stared up again. She wished she hadn't brought up the subject. "Whatever you say. You're the expert."

He smiled. "I studied the Scripture before we were together that first time."

She glanced at him in surprise. "Your Bible told you what to do?"

He laughed. "Knowing *what* to do wasn't the problem. It was the *how* I worried about. Song of Solomon told me a man and woman's passion is intended to be mutual." His smile dissolved and he looked troubled. "A shared blessing."

Angel moved out of his embrace and looked up at the stars. It made her uncomfortable when he started talking about God. The great I AM hovering and watching her. Mama said God could see everything, even when the lantern was extinguished, even when you were in bed with someone. She said God even knew what you were thinking. The great "Spy in the sky", eavesdropping on her every thought.

Angel shivered. The vast darkness of the night sky frightened her. Every sound seemed amplified and ominous. There really wasn't anyone up there, was there? It was all in Mama's head. It was all in Michael's.

Wasn't it?

"You're shaking. Are you cold?"

"I'm not used to sleeping in the open."

Michael drew her closer and pointed out Orion's belt, the Big Dipper, and Pegasus. Angel listened to the deep resonance of his voice. He was not uneasy with the darkness or the sounds, and after a while, in his arms, she wasn't either. Long after he slept, she lay awake looking at the pictures he had drawn in the night sky, but it was God she dared not contemplate.

They set off just past dawn the next morning. As they came down out of the foothills, the grass was a brilliant green from the fall rains. Massive oak trees dotted the landscape. A stage came up the hill, horses in full gallop. Michael leaned protectively toward Angel as it roared past, splattering mud up as it went.

As they reached the outskirts of Sacramento, Angel was amazed at what she saw. A year ago she had traveled through a swarming tent-and-clapboard settlement with the Duchess, Mai Ling, and Lucky. Now it was a booming metropolis with a look of permanence. Streets were thronged with wagons and men on foot. Some men looked prosperous in their suits while others appeared to have just arrived from the goldfields, packs and shovels on their hunched backs. There were even some women in dark linsey-woolsey dresses and woolen capes. A few had children with them.

As Michael drove down a wide street, Angel saw a grand hotel front, two eateries, half a dozen saloons, a barber shop with men standing in line outside, and a real estate office. On the next block were a construction company and a haberdashery with a display of denim pants, heavy overcoats, and wide-brimmed hats. To Angel's left stood a miner's variety store, a theater, and an assayer's office. On the other was a two-story building advertising bailing and barbed wire, nails and horse shoes. More mining supply shops and a seed store followed, flanked by a wagon-wheel and barrel warehouse. An apothecary advertising plasters had more than a dozen men lined up on the boardwalk.

Another stage rolled by, kicking up more mud.

"Paul said Joseph was down near the river," Michael said, turning down another street. "Makes it easier for him to get his merchandise from the ships coming up the American from San Francisco."

Michael saw how the men noticed Angel all along the drive through town. She was a rare gem in a city of mud. They would stop and stare, some thinking to remove their hats despite the rain that had begun. Angel sat beside him, back straight, head up, completely unaware. Reaching back over the seat, Michael got the blanket. "Wrap yourself in this. It'll keep you dry and warm." She unbent enough to glance at him, but he saw the uneasiness in her expression as she put the blanket around her shoulders.

Angel saw ships' masts ahead of them. Michael turned up a

street that ran along the river. Hochschild's store, which was next door to a big saloon, was twice the size of his mercantile in Pair-a-Dice. The sign over the door boasted, "Everything under the sun." Michael drove the wagon up front and set the brake. Jumping down, he came around and lifted Angel from the high seat, carrying her across the mud to the boardwalk.

Two young men came out of the mercantile. They stopped talking when they saw her. Whipping their hats off, both stared like poleaxed mules, neither noticing Michael stomping the mud off his boots. When he glanced over, he smiled and took her arm. "If you gentlemen will excuse us." They stammered apologies and moved out of the doorway.

Spotting a Franklin stove near the back of the store, Angel told Michael she would get warm while he conducted his business. She glanced to where Joseph was, up a ladder, taking canned goods from a high shelf and dropping them to an assistant who boxed them for a waiting customer. She noticed the two young men come back inside the store as Michael wove his way past several tables displaying tools, household goods, jackets, and boots to reach the counter.

"What sort of grocer are you? Not a potato in the place."

Joseph looked down with a start, then grinned broadly from his perch. "Michael!" He came down the ladder with quick agility and extended his hand. Ordering his assistant to finish the order, he took Michael aside. He glanced once in her direction and then looked again with obvious surprise. Michael turned and looked back at her with a smile and said something to Joseph as he winked at her.

Looking away, she stood as close to the stove as she could. One of the young men came over to stand with her. She ignored him, but she could feel him staring at her. The other joined him. She drew her shawl more tightly around herself and gave them both a cold look, hoping they'd take the hint and leave her alone. They looked thin, their coats patched.

"I'm Percy," one said. He was smooth cheeked like the other, but his skin was darkly tanned. "I just got back from the Tuolumne. Sorry to be staring, ma'am, but it's been a month of

Sundays since I've seen a lady." He nodded toward his companion. "This is my partner, Ferguson."

Angel looked at Ferguson, and he blushed. She rubbed her arm, trying to ease the chill, and wished they would go away. She didn't care who they were, where they came from, or what they had been doing. Her silence was meant to discourage them, but Percy took it as encouragement and talked about his home in Pennsylvania, the two sisters, three younger brothers, and mama and papa he had left behind.

"I've been writing and telling them how good the land is," he said. "They're thinking of coming out and bringing Ferguson's family with 'em."

Michael was coming toward them, his expression inscrutable. Angel was afraid he might think she was drumming up business. He put his hand beneath her arm possessively but smiled. Percy introduced himself and Ferguson again. "Hope you don't mind us talking to your wife, sir."

"Not at all, but I was about to offer you both some work helping me unload my wagon." They accepted with alacrity, and Angel was relieved to see the back of them. She glanced up at Michael to judge his mood. He smiled. "They were harmless and lonely," he said. "If they'd been looking at you like a piece of meat, I might have felt like busting some heads. But they weren't, were they?"

"No." She gave a faint, mocking laugh. "One said it was a long time since he had seen a *lady*."

"Well, you are a married lady." He nodded toward some tables. "Joseph has some cloth I want you to look over. Pick what you like." He led her between tables stacked with mining gear and stopped at one piled high with bolts of cloth. "Enough for three dresses." He went to help the boys unload.

Thinking what Michael might like, she selected one of dark gray linsey-woolsey and another of brown. When he came back, he didn't look pleased by her selections. "Just because Tess wore brown and black, doesn't mean you have to." He cast the bolts onto another table and yanked a bolt of light blue linsey-woolsey from the bottom. "This would suit you better."

"It's more expensive."

"We can afford it." He took out another bolt of light rust and a muted yellow plaid to match. Next he pulled out a forest green and a flower-patterned gingham. Joseph brought out two more bolts of flowered cotton. "I just got these. More on the way. I'm stocking up as I can. Husbands are bringing their wives and children now." He nodded and smiled at her. "Hello, Angel. It's a pleasure seeing you again. I've got a box of buttons, a bolt of white lawn, and two of red flannel, too, if you're interested in taking a look."

"We are," Michael said. "She needs wool stockings, boots, gloves, and a good coat." Joseph went off to see to it. Michael took up a bolt of blue-and-white gingham. "What do you think of this for curtains?"

"It would be pretty," she said and watched him stack it with the other bolts of cloth. Joseph came back with the buttons and gave them to her to make selections. "How long will it take you to get us a stove?" Michael asked.

"Got a shipment coming in anytime. Tell me how big a stove you want, and I'll hold it for you."

Michael gave him the dimensions, and Angel put her hand on his arm. "Michael, it's too big," she whispered. "Besides, we've got the fireplace."

"A stove's more efficient and doesn't burn as much wood. It'll keep the cabin warm through the night."

"But how much is it?"

"Don't argue with him, Angel. At the price he's asking for his potatoes and carrots, he can afford a stove."

"As long as you don't mark up your stoves the way you mark up your vegetables," she retorted.

The men laughed. "Maybe I ought to let my wife do the bargaining," Michael said. When he said he wanted a set of dishes, Angel went back to stand by the Franklin stove. If he meant to spend every penny he had to his name, it was none of her business.

Joseph asked them to stay for supper and insisted they spend the night in his own quarters. It was the least he could do after emptying Michael's coffers. "There's not a hotel room to be had in the whole township, what with the men coming down out of the mountains to winter here," Joseph said, ushering them upstairs. "Besides, it's been a long time since you and I have had a conversation." He slapped Michael on the back.

The upstairs apartment was well furnished and comfortable. "I bought everything for next to nothing. Fellow from the East came sailing in loaded to the beam with Chippendale and fancy sofas, thinking he was going to outfit the new millionaires in their mansions. He also had a ton of mosquito netting and enough Panama hats to last the population along the isthmus a decade." He welcomed them into a neat parlor that overlooked the river. A Mexican cook served a savory meal of roast beef and potatoes on elegant china. Joseph poured a fine imported tea for them. Even the knives, forks, and spoons were silver.

Joseph did most of the talking. "I think I've just about convinced my family to leave New York and come west. Mama said the only way she'll agree is if I'll take a wife."

Michael grinned across the table at him. "Did you tell her to bring you one?"

"I didn't have to. She already had one picked out and packed up, ready to come west."

Dinner finished, Joseph poured coffee. The two men talked politics and religion. Neither agreed with the other's viewpoint, but the conversation continued amicably unabated. She was drowsy. She didn't care that California had become a state or that mining companies were taking over the gold country or that Joseph insisted Jesus was a prophet and not the Messiah he was waiting for. She didn't care if the river was rising with the rain. She didn't care if a shovel cost three hundred dollars while a new plow cost seventy.

"We've put Angel to sleep," Joseph observed, adding another log to the fire. "The second bedroom is right through that door." Joseph watched Michael lift his wife tenderly and carry her in. He swirled the coffee in his cup and finished it. He had been watching Angel since spotting her by his Franklin stove. She was one of those rare beauties that caught a man's breath no matter how many times he had seen her before.

When Michael came back in and sat down, Joseph smiled. "I'll never forget the look on your face the first time you saw her. I thought you were crazy when I heard you married her." Good men were often destroyed by obsessions with fallen women, and he had worried about Michael. Joseph had never known a more mismatched pair. A saint and a sinner. "You seem pretty much the same."

Michael laughed and took up his cup. "Did you expect me to change?"

"I expected her to feast on your heart."

Michael's smile altered, hinting at pain. "She does," he said and tipped his cup.

"She's changed," Joseph said. She didn't have the glow of a woman in love. There was no sparkle in her eyes or flush to her cheeks. But there was something different about her. "I can't put my finger on it exactly. But she doesn't look as hard as I remember."

"She never was hard. It was pretense."

Joseph didn't argue, but he remembered well the beautiful soiled dove who walked Main Street every Monday, Wednesday, and Friday. He had come out to watch her like all the others, enraptured by her pale, perfect beauty. But she was hard all right, hard as granite. Michael was just seeing her through the eyes of a man who loved her far more deeply than a woman like her deserved. But then, maybe it was Michael's kind of loving that was changing her. God knew Angel would never have come across a man like Michael before. Not in her trade. He would be something new to her. Joseph laughed silently at himself.

Michael had been something new to *him*, too. He was one of those rare men who lived what he believed, not once in a while, but every hour of every day, even when the going wasn't easy. As gentle a man as he was, as tender as was his heart, there was nothing weak about Michael Hosea. He was the strongest-minded man Joseph had ever met. A man like Noah. A man like the shepherd-king, David. A man after God's own heart.

Joseph prayed Angel wouldn't rip that heart out of him and leave him destroyed for the rest of the human race.

# Eighteen

*So whatever you wish that men
would do to you, do so to them.*
JESUS, MATTHEW 7:12

Wagon loaded with their purchases, Michael and Angel started for home early the next morning. Michael made a stop at the seed store and purchased what he needed for spring planting. On the way through town, he stopped again at a small building. He came around the wagon and lifted her down. Angel hadn't realized he intended to go to church until he was almost to the door and she heard singing. She pulled her hand from his and shook her head. "You go ahead. I'll wait out here."

Michael smiled. "Give it a try. For me." He took her hand again. When they went inside, her heart pounded so fast she thought she was choking on it. Several people glanced up and stared at her. She could feel heat pouring into her face as more people noticed their late arrival. Michael found space for them to sit.

Angel clenched her hands in her lap and kept her head down. What was she doing in a church? A woman down the row leaned forward to look at her. Angel stared straight ahead. Another in the row in front looked back over her shoulder. The place seemed full of women – plain, hardworking women like those who had turned their backs on Mama. They would turn their backs on her, too, if they knew what she was.

One dark-haired lady in a doe brown bonnet was studying her. Angel's mouth went dry. Did they know already? Did she bear the mark on her forehead?

The preacher was looking straight at her and talking about sin and damnation. Sweat broke out on her, and she felt cold. She was going to be sick.

Everyone stood and started singing. She had never heard Michael sing before. He had a deep, rich voice, and he knew the words without the hymnal offered by the man next to him. He belonged here. He believed all this. Every word of it. She stared forward again and looked into the dark eyes of the preacher. *He knows, just like Mama's priest knew.*

She had to get out! When they all sat down again, that preacher would probably point straight at her and ask what she was doing in his church. In a panic, she pressed past all those down the row. "Let me by, please," she said, frantic to get out. Everyone was staring at her now. One man grinned at her as she hurried toward the back door. She couldn't get her breath. She leaned against the wagon and fought down the nausea.

"Are you all right?" Michael said.

She hadn't expected him to follow her. "I'm fine," she lied.

"Would you just sit by me?"

She turned and looked up at him. "No."

"You don't have to take part in the service."

"The only way you'll get me back inside that place is to drag me."

Michael studied her strained face. She hugged herself and glared up at him.

"Amanda, I haven't been in a church in months. I need the fellowship."

"I didn't say you had to leave."

"Are you all right?"

"Yes," she said and reached up to the wagon seat. Michael lifted her. She felt steadier at his touch. Regretting her harshness, she wanted to explain, but when she turned, he was already disappearing into the church. She felt bereft.

They were singing again, loud enough to be heard clearly outside. "Onward, Christian soldiers, marching as to war...." It was a war. A war against God and Michael and the whole world. Sometimes she wished she didn't have to fight anymore. She wished she were back in the valley. She wished it were the way it had been in the beginning, just her and Michael. She wished Paul had stayed in the mountains. Maybe things would have worked then.

Not for long. Sooner or later, the world comes charging in. **You just don't belong, Angel. You never will.**

When the service finally ended, others came out ahead of Michael. Every one of them looked straight at her where she sat on the wagon seat, waiting for him. Several women stopped to talk together in a small group. Were they talking about her? She kept watching the door for Michael. When he appeared, he was with the minister. They spoke for a few minutes and then shook hands. Michael came down the steps, and the dark-suited man looked at her.

Her heart started pounding again. She could feel the sweat breaking out on her skin as Michael strode toward her. He stepped up, took the reins and set off without a word.

"It didn't even look like a real church," she said as he drove down the hill toward the river road. "There was no priest."

"The Lord isn't bound by denomination."

"My mother was Catholic. I didn't say I was."

"So why're you so afraid to be inside a church?"

"I wasn't afraid. It made me sick. All those hypocrites."

"You were scared to death." He took her hand. "Your palms are still sweating." She tried to pull her hand free, but his tightened. "If you're convinced there's no God, what are you afraid of?"

"I don't want any part of some great eye in the sky who's waiting for a chance to squash me like a bug!"

"God doesn't condemn. He forgives."

She tore her hand free. "The way he forgave my mother?"

He looked at her with that maddeningly quiet assurance. "Maybe she never forgave herself."

His words were like a blow. Angel stared straight ahead. What was the use where Michael was concerned? He didn't understand anything. It was as though the poor fool had never even lived in this world.

He decided to press it. "You think maybe that could've been part of it?"

"Whatever my mother believed, it doesn't mean I belong in a church any more than she ever did."

"If Rahab, Ruth, Bathsheba, and Mary belonged, I think there might be a place for you."

"I don't know a single one of those women."

"Rahab was a prostitute. Ruth slept at the feet of a man she wasn't married to, on a public threshing floor. Bathsheba was an adulteress. When she found she was pregnant, her lover plotted the murder of her husband. And Mary became pregnant by Someone other than the man she was betrothed to marry."

Angel stared at him. "I didn't know you made a habit of running with fast women."

Michael laughed. "They're named in the lineage of Christ. In the beginning of the book of Matthew."

"Oh," she said blandly and gave him a resentful glance. "You think you can march me right into a corner, don't you? Well, tell me something. If all that garbage is true, why didn't the priest speak to my mother? It seems she fit right in to such exalted company."

"I don't know, Amanda. Priests are only men. They're not God. They come with their own personal prejudices and faults just like anyone else." He snapped the reins lightly over the horses' backs. "I'm sorry about your mother, but I'm worried about you."

"Why? Are you afraid if you don't save my soul, I'll go to hell?"

She was mocking him. "I think you've had a good taste of it already." He snapped the reins again. "I don't plan on preaching at you, but I don't plan on giving up what I believe, either. Not to make you comfortable. Not for anything."

Her fingers tightened around the brace. "I didn't ask you to."

"Not in so many words, but there's a certain pressure brought to bear on a man when his wife is sitting and waiting outside in a wagon."

"How about when a man drags his wife into church?"

He glanced at her. "I guess you've got a point. I'm sorry."

She looked straight ahead again and bit her lip. Letting out a shaky breath, she said, "I couldn't stay inside, Michael. I just couldn't."

"Not this time, maybe."

"Not ever."

"Why not?"

"Why should I sit with the same children who called me foul names? They're all the same. It doesn't matter whether it's the docks of New York or a muddy hillside in California." She gave a bleak laugh. "There was a boy whose father visited Mama at the shack. He was real regular. His son would call Mama and me names, obscene names. So I told him where his father was on Wednesday afternoons. He didn't believe me, of course, and Mama said I had done a terrible, cruel thing to him. I couldn't see how the truth would make things worse, but a few days later, out of curiosity I guess, that boy followed his father and found out for himself it was true. I thought, now there, he knows, and he'll leave me and Mama alone. But no. He *hated* me after that. He and his nice little friends used to wait at the end of the alley, and when I would go to market for Mama, they would throw garbage on me. And every Sunday morning I would see them in mass, all scrubbed and dressed up and sitting by their papas and mamas." She looked up at Michael. "The priest *spoke* to them. No, Michael. I won't sit in a church. Not ever."

Michael took her hand again and wove his fingers with hers. "God had nothing to do with it."

Her eyes felt strangely hot and gritty. "He didn't stop it either, did he? Where's the mercy you're always reading about? I never saw any given to my mother." Michael was silent for a long time after that.

"Did anyone ever say anything nice to you?"

Her mouth curved into a wry smile. "A lot of men said I was pretty. They said they were just waiting for me to grow up." Her chin jerked up and she glanced away.

Her hand was cold in his. For all her defiance, he felt her pain. "What do you see when you look in the mirror, Amanda?"

She didn't answer for a long time, and when she did, she spoke so softly, he almost didn't hear. "My mother."

They stopped by a stream. While Michael unharnessed the horses and hobbled them, Angel laid out the blanket and opened the basket. Joseph's cook had supplied them with bread, cheese, a bottle of cider, and some dried fruit. When Michael finished eating, he stood and put his hand up on an overhanging branch. He seemed in no hurry to hitch up his horses and get back on the road.

Angel watched him. His blue wool shirt pulled taut across his shoulders, and his waist was lean and hard. She remembered Torie's fascination and was beginning to understand. She liked to look at him. He was strong and beautiful without being threatening. When he glanced back at her, she looked away and pretended to be busy putting the things back into the basket.

Michael shoved his hands into his pockets and leaned back against the massive trunk. "I've been called a few names in my time, too, Amanda. Most of them hurled by my own father."

She looked up at him again. "*Your* father?"

He looked out over the river. "My family had the biggest plantation in the district. The land was passed down from my grandfather. We had slaves. I didn't think much about having them when I was a boy. It was just the way things were. Mother told me that they were our people and we were to take care of them, but when I was ten, we had a bad year, and my father sold off some of the workers. When they were taken away, one of our house slaves disappeared. I can't even tell you her name. My father went after her. When he came back, he had two bodies strapped over a horse, hers and one of the workers he had sold. He dumped the bodies in front of the slave quarters and strung them up so they had to see them every time they went out to the fields. It was a gruesome sight. He had turned the dogs loose on them."

He put his head back against the bark of the massive old oak. "I asked him why he had to do that, and he said it was to make an example of them."

She had never seen him so pale, and a new emotion stirred inside her. She wanted to go to him and put her arms around him. "Did your mother feel the same way he did?"

"My mother wept, but she never said a word against my father. I told him the first thing I would do when he died was free our slaves. It was the first beating he ever gave me. He said if I was so enamored of them I could live with them for a while."

"Did you?"

"For a month. Then he ordered me back to the house. By then, my life had really changed. Old Ezra brought me to the Lord. Up until then, God was just a Sunday morning exercise my mother carried out in the parlor. Ezra showed me how real God is. My father would have sold him if he hadn't been so old. He freed him instead. It was a worse fate. The old man had nowhere to go, so he moved out into the swamps. I used to go out and see him every chance I got and bring him what I could."

"And your father?"

"He tried other ways of turning my thinking around." His mouth curved wryly. "He wanted me to know the full privileges of ownership." He looked at her. "A beautiful, young slave girl of my own to use any way I wanted. I told her to go, but she wouldn't. My father had ordered her to stay. So I left." He laughed softly and shook his head. "That's not completely honest. Actually, I fled. I was fifteen, and she was more of a temptation than I could handle."

Michael came and hunkered down in front of her. "Amanda, my father wasn't all bad. I don't want you to think that of him. He loved the land, and he did take care of his people. Other than that one time, he was decent to the slaves he owned. He loved my mother and my brothers and sisters. And he loved me. He just wanted everything his own way. And there was something about me from the very beginning.... I didn't fit the mold. I knew someday I'd have to cut out on my own, but it was a long time before I had the courage to leave everyone I loved behind, especially when I didn't know where I was going."

She raised her eyes to his. "Do you ever think about going back?"

"No." There was no doubt in his expression.

"You must have hated him."

He looked at her solemnly. "No. I loved him, and I'm grateful he was my father."

"Grateful? He treated you like a slave, took away your inheritance, your family, everything. And you're *grateful*?"

"Without all that, I might never have come to know the Lord, and in the end, my father had more reason to hate me,"

Michael said. "When I left, Paul and Tess came with me. Tessie was special to him. Very special. And now she's dead."

Angel saw the tears in his eyes. He didn't try to hide them.

"She would have liked you," he said, reaching out and touching her cheek. "She could see into people." Without thinking, Angel put her hand over his, moved by his sadness. His smile made her heart twist. "Oh, beloved," he said. "Your walls are coming down."

She took her hand away. "Joshua blowing his horn."

He laughed. "I love you," he said. "I love you very much." He drew her into his arms and lay back with her in the grass. Rolling her beneath him, he kissed her gently at first, then more thoroughly. She felt a quickening inside her, a soft, warm curling in her belly, yet she felt neither threatened nor used. When he drew back slightly, she saw the look in his eyes. *Oh.*

"Sometimes I forget what I'm waiting for," he said huskily. He stood, drawing her up with him. "Come on. I'll hitch up the horses."

Bemused, Angel folded the blanket and put the basket back beneath the seat. Resting her arms on the side of the wagon, she watched Michael bring the horses back. There was power in the way he moved. As he harnessed the horses, she watched the strength of his shoulders and hands. Straightening, he turned to her. He lifted her to the high seat and stepped up beside her. When he took the reins he smiled at her, and without the least hesitation, she found herself smiling back.

It began to rain as they traveled. Michael stopped to put up the canvas while she wrapped herself in the blanket. When he sat with her again, he put a second blanket around them both. She felt comfortably snug next to him.

Five miles down the road, they came upon a broken-down covered wagon. A haggard man and woman were trying to raise it enough to put on a repaired wheel. Nearby, sheltered beneath a massive oak, a dark-haired girl hugged four small children around her.

Michael pulled the team off the road. "Fetch those children and have them sit in the back of the wagon," he said to Angel as he got down. She went for them. The oldest girl looked but a few years younger than she. Her dark hair was plastered about a pale face dominated by wide brown eyes. When she smiled, she was pretty.

"You'll all be dryer if you sit in the back of the wagon," Angel said. "We have another blanket."

"Thank you, ma'am," the girl said, taking up the invitation immediately as she hurried the children to the wagon's shelter. Full of trepidation, Angel climbed up into the back with them. She handed the girl a blanket, and she draped it around her shoulders while tucking the four smaller children in close to her like a mother hen.

She smiled at Angel. "We're the Altmans. I'm Miriam. This is Jacob – " she looked at the tallest boy, whose eyes and hair were like hers – "he's ten. And Andrew – "

"I'm eight!" the boy volunteered somberly.

Miriam smiled again. "This is Leah," she said, snuggling the bigger girl close and then kissing the smallest, "and Ruth."

Angel looked at the cold, wet group huddled together beneath a single blanket. "Hosea," she said self-consciously. "I'm...Mrs. Hosea."

"Thank the Lord you came when you did," Miriam said. "Papa was having trouble with that wheel, and Mama is just about done in." She took the blanket off herself and settled it around the four children. "Would you watch over the children, Mrs. Hosea? Mama's been ill for the past three hundred miles, and she shouldn't be out in the rain."

She jumped down from the wagon before Angel could protest. Angel looked at the children again and saw they were all staring at her with wide, curious eyes. A few moments later, Miriam returned with her mother. She was a worn, dark-haired woman with stooped shoulders and shadowed eyes. The children closed around her protectively.

"Mama," Miriam said, an arm around her, "this is Mrs. Hosea. This is my mother."

The woman smiled warmly and nodded. "Elizabeth," she said with a smile. "God bless you, Mrs. Hosea." Tears gathered in the tired eyes, but she didn't let them fall. "I don't know what we would've done if you and your husband hadn't come along." She put her arms around her four children while Miriam peered out to see if the men needed assistance. "Everything's going to be fine. Papa and Mr. Hosea are fixing the wagon. We'll be on our way soon."

"Do we have to go to Oregon?" Leah whimpered.

Pain flickered in the woman's face. "Let's not think about it right now, dear. We'll take one day at a time."

Angel fumbled in the basket. "Are you hungry? We've bread and some cheese."

"Cheese!" Leah said, her small face brightening, the long journey to Oregon forgotten. "Oh, yes, please."

Tears did come then, and Elizabeth wept. Miriam stroked her and murmured to her. Mortified, Angel didn't know what to say or do. Not looking at the weeping woman, she cut slices of cheese for the smaller children. Elizabeth coughed again, and her crying stopped. "I'm so sorry," she whispered. "I don't know what's wrong with me."

"You're worn out," Miriam said. "It's the fever," she told Angel. "She hasn't had any strength since it hit her."

Angel held out a wedge of cheese and bread, and Elizabeth touched her hand tenderly before taking it. Little Ruth pushed off her mother's lap and stood in front of her. Angel felt alarmed and then surprised when the child reached out and touched the golden braid that had slipped over her shoulder and hung to her waist. "Angel, Mama?" Heat flooded Angel's face.

Elizabeth smiled through her tears. Her soft laugh was full of pleasure. "Yes, darling. An angel of mercy."

Angel could not look at them. What would Elizabeth Altman say if she knew the truth? She got up and went to the back of the wagon to peer out. Michael had raised the Altmans' wagon, and the man was fitting the wheel. She wanted to get out of the wagon, but the rain was coming now in sheets – Michael would just send her back. Every muscle in her body was taut when she looked back at Elizabeth with her adoring children all around her.

Miriam took her hand, startling her. "They'll have it fixed

in no time," she said. Her eyes flickered with surprise and embarrassment when Angel pulled her hand free in haste.

Mr. Altman appeared at the back of the wagon, rain running off his hat.

"Is everything all right, John?" Elizabeth said.

"It'll be good for a ways." He tipped the brim of his hat to Angel as Elizabeth made the introduction. "We're much obliged to you and your husband, ma'am. I was almost done in until your husband came." He looked to his wife again. "Mr. Hosea's invited us to winter at his place. I said yes. We'll head for Oregon in spring."

"Oh," Elizabeth said, the relief clearly apparent.

Angel's lips parted. Winter at Michael's? Nine people in a fifteen-by-fifteen foot cabin? Elizabeth touched her, and she jumped. She sat stunned as the woman thanked her before John lifted her out. The boys and girls followed, then Miriam, who touched her shoulder in passing and flashed her a warm, excited smile. Teeth gritted, Angel sat huddled in her blanket in the back of the wagon, wondering what on earth Michael thought he was going to do with all these people. He climbed into the seat, soaked to the skin, and she handed him the spare blanket as they set off again.

"We'll let them have the cabin," he said.

"The cabin! Where are we supposed to sleep?"

"In the barn. We'll be comfortable and warm."

"Why don't *they* sleep in the barn? You built the cabin." She didn't much like the idea of sleeping anywhere but in that nice, snug bed with the fire close by.

"They haven't slept in a house in over nine months. And that woman's sick." He nodded ahead. "I've been thinking. There's a good strip of land bordering Paul's. Maybe I can talk the Altmans into staying. It'd be a good thing having another family in the valley." He glanced at her with a smile. "You could use women friends around."

Friends? "What do you suppose I have in common with them?"

"Why don't we wait and find out?"

They camped beside an outcropping of granite that gave them shelter from the rain. Michael and John hobbled the horses and pitched a tent while Angel, Elizabeth, and Miriam set up camp. The children gathered enough wood to last the night and brought some of it to Miriam, where she and the others were gathered in the tent. She opened a small flap at the ceiling. "Learned this from the Indians," she said with a grin as she built a fire inside a wash tub right inside the tent. Amazingly, the smoke went up and out the hole.

Elizabeth looked so worn out, Angel insisted she lie down. Michael brought some of their supplies in, and she put together a meal. Still awake, Elizabeth was silent, watching her. Troubled, Angel glanced at her, wondering what she was thinking.

"I feel so useless," Elizabeth said tremulously, and Miriam bent to stroke her face gently.

"Nonsense, Mama. We can manage. You rest." She gave her an impish grin. "When you're better, we'll let you do it all by yourself again." Her mother smiled at the tender teasing. "I'll get some heavier wood," Miriam said and went out. She came back with a large chunk and stacked it with the kindling. "The rain's letting up."

Elizabeth pushed herself up. "Where are the boys?"

"Papa's got them. Leah and Ruth will stay put right here. You've no need to worry. Now, lie down again, Mama." She looked at Angel. "She's always worried about Indians," she whispered. "A little boy wandered away from the wagons a hundred miles shy of Fort Laramie. There was no trace of him. Ever since then, Mama's been terrified one of us would be kidnapped." She glanced back at her mother resting on the pallet. "She'll get better now that she can rest."

Miriam warmed her hands over the fire, smiling across at Angel. "Whatever you're cooking, it smells good." Angel kept stirring without comment. "How long have you been in California?"

"A year."

"Oh, then you didn't marry Michael until you came here. He said he arrived in '48. Did you come overland?"

"No. By ship."

"Is your family in the valley Michael's been describing to my father?"

Angel had known the questions would come and that making up lies would only tie her into tighter knots. Why not get it over with now, and then the girl would let her be? Maybe if they all knew the truth, they'd winter someplace else. Certainly that woman wouldn't want to sleep in the same bed where a prostitute had slept. "I came to California alone. I met Michael in a brothel in Pair-a-Dice."

Miriam laughed and then, seeing Angel meant what she'd said, fell silent. "You're serious, aren't you?"

"Yes." Elizabeth was looking at her with an indefinable expression. Angel's gaze fell, and she kept stirring.

Miriam didn't say anything for a long moment, and Elizabeth closed her eyes again. "You needn't have said anything," Miriam said finally. "Why did you?"

"So you wouldn't have any shocking surprises down the road," Angel said bitterly, her throat tight.

"No," Miriam said, "I was prying again, that's why. Mama says it's one of my failings — always wanting to know everyone else's business. I'm sorry."

Angel kept stirring, troubled by the girl's apology.

"I'd like to be friends," Miriam said.

Angel glanced up in surprise. "Why would you want to be friends with me?"

Miriam looked surprised. "Because I like you."

Taken aback, Angel stared at her. She glanced at Elizabeth. The woman was watching them, a tired smile on her face. Blushing, Angel looked at the girl and said softly, "You don't know very much about me other than what I just told you." She wished now she hadn't said anything.

"I know you're honest," Miriam said with a rueful laugh. "Brutally so," she added more seriously. A thoughtful look came into her eyes as she studied Angel.

The boys came in, and with them a blast of cold air. The girls awakened and Ruth started to cry. Elizabeth sat up and held her close, admonishing the boys to quiet their excited chatter.

John came in and with one word hushed them. Angel saw Michael just behind him. When he smiled at her, her relief was physical. Then she worried what he would say when he found out she had blurted out the truth.

Wet coats shrugged off, the men hunkered by the fire while she served beans into the bowls Miriam passed out. When everyone had their meal, John bowed his head, his family taking his lead. "Lord, thank you for delivering us today and bringing us Michael and Amanda Hosea. Watch over our lost loved ones, David and Mother. Please give Elizabeth renewed strength. Keep us all well and strong for the journey ahead. Amen."

John asked questions about land, crops, and the California market while Jacob and Andrew asked for second helpings of beans and biscuits. Angel wondered when Michael would be ready to return to their wagon. She felt Miriam watching her. She didn't want to know what questions were running through the girl's head now that she'd had time to think about it.

"The rain's stopped, Papa," Andrew said.

"Shouldn't we go to our own wagon now?" Angel whispered to Michael.

"Stay here with us," John said. "We've room enough. With the fire going, it's warmer in here than it'd likely be in your wagon."

Michael accepted, and Angel's heart dropped as he went for their blankets. Excusing herself quickly, she went after him. "Michael," she said, searching for words to convince him they should sleep in the wagon and not in the tent with the Altmans. He reached out and pulled her close, kissing her soundly. Then he turned her back toward the tent, saying next to her ear, "Sooner or later you'll learn there are people in the world who don't want to use you. Now, buck up your courage and go back in there and get to know a few."

Pulling her shawl tightly around herself, she ducked back inside the tent. Miriam smiled at her. Angel sat self-consciously near the fire and didn't look at anyone as she waited for Michael to come back. The two boys pleaded for their father to read from *Robinson Crusoe*. John took a worn leather volume from a pack and began to read while Miriam laid out the bedding. little Ruth, thumb still tucked in her mouth, dragged her blanket from where it was placed and put it next to Angel. "I wanna sleep here."

Miriam laughed. "Well, I think you'd better ask Mr. Hosea, Ruthie. He might want to sleep there, too."

"He can sleep on the other side," Ruthie said, clearly staking her claim.

Miriam came over with two quilts and handed one to Angel. Bending, she whispered, "See? She's likes you, too."

Feeling an odd pang in her stomach, Angel glanced around at them. Michael came in with more blankets. "Storm's coming. If we're lucky, it'll blow itself out by morning."

As the others slept, Angel lay awake beside Michael. The wind howled, and the rain pelted against the tent. The sound of the storm and the smell of the wet canvas reminded her of her first weeks in Pair-a-Dice.

Where was Duchess? And Megan and Rebecca? What had happened to them? She tried not to think about Lucky dying in the fire. She kept remembering her saying, "Don't forget me, Angel. Don't forget me."

Angel couldn't forget any of them.

When the rain ceased, Angel listened to the breathing of the sleepers around her. Turning slowly onto her side, she looked at them. John Altman lay beside his frail wife, his arm curled protectively around her. The boys slept nearby, one sprawled on his back, the other curled on his side with the blanket over his head. Miriam and Leah were curled together like spoons, Miriam's arm around her sister.

Angel's eyes came to rest on Miriam's sleeping face. This girl was a new entity.

Angel hadn't known many *good* girls. Those on the docks had been warned away by their mothers. Sally had said once that good girls were dull and critical and that's why when they grew up and married, their husbands frequented brothels. Miriam was neither dull nor critical. She had poked good-humored fun at her father all evening while seeing to her ailing mother. Her sisters and brothers clearly adored her. Only Jacob balked when she told him what to do, and one glance from his father ended that. When it was time for the children to settle down, it was Miriam who tucked them in and prayed with them quietly while the men talked.

*"I'd like to be friends."*

Angel closed her eyes. Her head ached. What would she and Miriam have to talk about? She hadn't a clue, but it seemed she was going to be faced with it. The men had already developed an easy rapport. Both loved the land. John Altman talked about Oregon as though it were another more desirable woman, and Michael talked about the valley in the same way. "Papa," Miriam had said in amused exasperation, "you were convinced California was paradise until we rolled down out of the Sierras."

He shook his head. "It's more crowded here than in Ohio. The whole territory is crawling with fortune hunters."

"All those good boys from good homes," Miriam said, and a dimple showed in one cheek. "Maybe even a few from Ohio."

"Gone wild," John Altman remarked grimly.

Miriam poked his shoulder. "You'd be panning for gold in a stream, too, Papa, if you didn't have all of us to watch over. I saw the gleam of greed in your eyes when that gentleman was telling you about making a good strike on the American." She included Michael and Angel. "The man owns a big store now with goods to the rafters. He said he arrived in California with little more than a shovel and the clothes on his back."

"One chance in a million," John told her.

"Oh, but think of it, Papa," Miriam went on dramatically, a hand to her heart and her dark eyes sparkling with mischief. "You and the boys could pan and work the Long Tom while Mama and I run a little cafe in the camp and serve all those poor, dear, downtrodden, handsome young bachelors."

Michael laughed, and John tugged his daughter's braid.

The Altmans fascinated Angel. They all liked each other. John Altman was clearly in charge and would tolerate no disrespect or rebellion, but it was clear he was not held in fear by his wife and children. Even Jacob's brief rebellion had been handled with good humor. "Whenever you don't listen, there's going to be stern discipline," his father said. "I'll supply the discipline, and you'll supply the stern." The boy capitulated and Altman ruffled his hair affectionately.

What if they did decide to stay in the valley? Angel massaged her throbbing temples. What did she have in common with them? Especially a young, doe-eyed virgin? When she had blurted out her past profession and how she and Michael had met, she had fully expected the girl to be shocked and leave her alone. The last thing she expected was that look of questioning concern and an offer of friendship.

Angel felt movement beside her and opened her eyes against the pain in her head. Ruthie snuggled against her seeking warmth in her sleep. Her thumb had slipped out of her mouth. Angel touched the smooth pink cheek – and suddenly she saw Duke's enraged face swimming before her eyes. She felt the slap across her face again. "I told you to take precautions!" She could feel him grabbing her by her hair as he dragged her up from the bed so that his face was right in hers. "The first time was easy," he said through his teeth. "This time I'm going to make sure you never get pregnant again."

When the doctor came, she had kicked and fought, but it had done no good. Duke and another man strapped her to the bed. "Do it," Duke ordered the doctor and stood by watching to make sure he did. When she started to scream, they put a strap in her mouth. Duke was still there when the ordeal was over. Consumed in pain and weak from loss of blood, she'd refused to look at him.

"You'll be fine in a few days," he told her, but she knew she would never be all right. She called him the foulest name she knew, but all he did was smile. "That's my Angel. No tears. Just hate. It keeps me warm, my sweet. Don't you know that yet?" He kissed her hard. "I'll be back when you're better." He patted her cheek and left.

The black memory tortured Angel as she gazed at little Ruth Altman. She wanted desperately to leave the tent but was afraid if she got up she would awaken the others. Staring up at the canvas ceiling, she tried to think of something else. The rain started again, and with it came all her old ghosts.

"Can't sleep?" Michael whispered. She shook her head. "Turn on your side." When she did, he drew her back against him, tucking her into his body. The child shifted, snuggling deeper into the quilts and pressing into Angel's stomach. "You've got a friend," Michael murmured. Angel put her arm around Ruth and closed her eyes. Michael put his arm around both of them. "Maybe we'll have one like her someday," he said against her ear.

Angel stared into the fire in despair.

# Nineteen

Michael settled the Altmans comfortably in the cabin and shouldered his own trunk. Angel followed him to the barn, biting off any protest. She could see his mind was set. What in the world was he was going to get out of this deal? Why do this for total strangers?

The rains came day after day. After the first few nights, Angel found comfort in the sounds of the owl in the rafters and the soft stirring of mice in the hay. Michael kept her warm. Sometimes he would explore her body, rousing alien sensations that unnerved her. When his own desire became too great, he drew away and talked about his past and especially the old slave he still loved. In those quiet, unthreatening moments, Angel found herself telling him what Sally had taught her.

Head propped up on his hand, Michael toyed with her hair. "Do you think she was right about everything, Amanda?"

"Not by your rules, I guess."

"Whose do you want to live by?"

She thought before answering. "My own."

Outside the confines of the barn and Michael's protective arms, Angel was affectionately accosted by Miriam. At every turn, the girl undermined Angel's determination to remain aloof. Miriam made her laugh. She was so young and full of innocent mischief. What Angel could not comprehend was why this girl should want to be *her* friend. She knew she should discourage her, but Miriam grew obtuse at her rebuffs and continued to tease and delight her.

Starved of any family life as a child, Angel did not know what was expected of her when she and Michael spent evenings in the cabin with the family. She sat quietly and observed. She was captivated by the respectful camaraderie between John and

Elizabeth Altman and their five children. John was a hard man who seldom smiled, but it was clear he adored his children – and that he had a special affection for his eldest daughter, despite their constant arguing.

Dark-eyed Andrew and his father were much alike in appearance and manner. Jacob was gregarious and given to practical jokes. Leah was solemn and shy. Little Ruth, open and bright, was the darling of the whole family. For some reason Angel could not contemplate, the child adored her. Perhaps it was her blonde hair that drew Ruthie's infatuation. Whatever it was, every time she and Michael came in to join the family, Ruthie sat at her feet.

It amused Miriam. "They say dogs and children can always pick a tenderhearted person. Can't argue with that, now, can you?"

For a full week after they moved in, Elizabeth was too weak to get out of bed. Angel cooked and took care of the household duties while Miriam saw to her mother and the children. Michael and John dug up stumps in the field. When they came in for supper, John sat with his wife and held her hand, talking to her softly while the children played pick-up sticks and string games.

Watching John, Angel was reminded of all those weeks Michael had cared for her after Magowan's beating. She remembered his tender care and consideration. He had tolerated her worst insults with quiet patience. He was in his own element with these people. She was the one who didn't belong.

Angel couldn't help but make comparisons. Her father had hated her enough even before she was born to want her thrown away like so much trash. Her mother had been so obsessed with him that she had almost forgotten she had a child. From her life with harlots, Angel was used to women who worried incessantly about the shape of their bodies and whether they were beginning to age. She was used to women who fussed with their hair and clothing and talked about sex as easily as the weather.

Elizabeth and Miriam were new and fascinating to her. They adored one another. They spoke no harsh words, were clean and neat without being preoccupied about their appearance, and talked about everything but sex. Though Elizabeth was too weak to do any work, she organized and orchestrated Miriam's and the children's days. At her urging, Andrew made a fish trap to set up in the creek. Leah fetched water. Jacob weeded the vegetable garden. Even little Ruth helped, setting out the dishes and utensils and picking wild flowers for the table. Miriam washed, ironed, and mended clothes while overseeing her siblings. Angel felt useless.

Once Elizabeth was up, she assumed full command. Unpacking her Dutch oven and pans, she took over the cooking. The Altmans had replenished their own supplies in Sacramento, and she made delicious meals of fried salt pork with gravy, baked beans sweetened with molasses, cornbread, and stewed jackrabbit with dumplings. When the fish trap worked, she fried the trout in seasonings. She skillet-baked johnnycakes while she spit-roasted two ducks. Most days, she made sourdough biscuits for breakfast. As a special treat, she soaked dried apples and made a pie.

She sighed one evening as she set the food on the table. "Someday we'll have another cow and have milk and butter again."

"We had one when we left home," Miriam said to Angel, "but the Indians took a liking to her near Fort Laramie."

"I'd give Papa's watch for a spoonful of plum jam," Jacob said, making his mother laugh and cuff him lightly.

Following supper, it was the Altman family custom to have devotions. John frequently asked Michael to read the Bible. The children were bright and full of questions. If God created Adam and Eve, why did he let them sin? Did God really want them running around Eden *naked*? Even in winter? If there was only Adam and Eve, who'd their children marry?

Eyes twinkling, John settled back to smoke his pipe while Elizabeth tried to answer the endless questions. Michael shared his own opinions and beliefs. He told stories rather than read them. "You'd make a fine preacher," John said. Angel almost protested and then realized he meant it as a compliment.

Angel never joined in the discussions. Even when Miriam asked her what she thought, she shrugged it off or turned the question back on the girl. Then, one evening, Ruthie went straight to the heart of the matter. "Don't you believe in God?"

Unsure how to respond, Angel said, "My mother was Catholic."

Andrew's mouth fell open. "Brother Bartholomew said they worship idols." Elizabeth blushed bright red at his comment, and John coughed. Andrew apologized.

"No need," Angel said. "My mother didn't worship any idols that I remember, but she prayed a lot." Not that it ever did her any good.

"What'd she pray for?" irrepressible Ruthie asked.

"Deliverance." Determined not to become part of a religious discussion, she took up the materials Michael had purchased for her new clothing. There was a still silence in the cabin that made Angel's skin prickle.

"What's *deliv'rance* mean?" Ruthie asked.

"We'll talk about it later," Elizabeth hushed her. "Right now, you children have school work to do." She got up and took out the children's school books. Angel looked up after a moment and saw Michael's gentle gaze on her. Her heart fluttered strangely. She wished for the cool, quiet darkness of the barn and no one noticing her, not even this man who had come to matter entirely too much.

She returned her studious attention to the cloth in her lap. How should she start? Never having made her own clothing before, she didn't know how to begin. She kept thinking of all the money Michael had spent and was afraid to cut into it and ruin it.

"You look glum." Miriam grinned. "Don't you like to sew?"

Angel could feel the color mounting in her cheeks. She was humiliated by her own ignorance and inexperience. Of course, Elizabeth and Miriam would know exactly what to do. Any *decent* girl would be able to make a shirtwaist and skirt.

Miriam suddenly looked aggrieved, as though she realized she had drawn attention where she shouldn't have. She gave Angel a tentative smile. "I don't enjoy it much myself. Mama is the seamstress in our family."

"I'd love to help you," Elizabeth volunteered.

"You've enough to do already," Angel said roughly.

Miriam brightened. "Oh, let Mama do it for you, Amanda. She loves to sew, and she hasn't had much to work with over the past year." Not waiting for an answer, she took the material from Angel and handed it over to her mother.

Elizabeth laughed, looking delighted. "Do you mind, Amanda?"

"I suppose not," Angel said. She gave a start of surprise when Ruthie climbed up into her lap.

Miriam grinned. "She only bites her brothers."

Angel touched the dark, silky hair and was enchanted. Little Ruth was soft and cuddly, with pink cheeks and bright brown eyes. Angel felt her heart grieve. What would her own child have looked like? She blotted out the horrible memory of Duke and the doctor and savored Ruthie's affection. The child chattered like a little magpie, and Angel nodded and listened. Glancing up, Angel encountered Michael's gaze. *He wants children*, she thought, and the thought hit her solid in the pit of her stomach. What if he knew she couldn't have them? Would his love for her die then? She couldn't hold his gaze.

"Papa, would you play the fiddle for us?" Miriam asked. "You haven't played in so long."

"Papa, *please*," Jacob and Leah begged.

"It's packed away in the trunk," he said, eyes shadowed. Angel expected that to be the end of the discussion, but Miriam was dogged.

"No, it's not. I unpacked it this morning." John gave his daughter a dark look, but she only smiled, knelt down beside him, and put her hand on his knee. "Please, Papa." Her voice was very gentle. "'For everything there is a season, and a time for every matter under heaven.' Remember? 'A time to weep, and a time to laugh; a time to mourn, and a time to dance.'"

Elizabeth had stilled where she stood, her hands on the fabric spread out over the supper table. When John looked at her, his eyes were dark with pain. Her own were swimming in tears. "It has been a long time, John. I'm sure Amanda and Michael would enjoy hearing you."

Miriam nodded to Leah, who fetched the instrument and

bow, then held them out to her father. After a long moment, he took hold of them and laid them in his lap.

"I tuned it this afternoon while you were out in the field," Miriam admitted as he ran his fingers across the strings. Then, lifting it, he set it beneath his chin and began to play. At the first few notes of the tune, Miriam's eyes flooded with tears, and she sang with a high, pure voice. When he finished playing, he laid the fiddle on his lap again.

"That was beautiful," he said, plainly moved. He touched his daughter's hair. "For David, hmm?"

"Yes, Papa."

Elizabeth raised her head, tears running down her cheeks. "Our son," she told Angel and Michael. "He was only fourteen when – " Her voice broke, and she looked away.

"He sang alto," Miriam said. "He had a wonderful voice. He far preferred lively songs, but 'Amazing Grace' was his favorite hymn. He was so full of life and adventure."

"He was killed near the Scott's Bluff," Elizabeth managed. "His horse threw him when he was chasing a buffalo. He hit his head."

No one said anything for a long time. "Gramma died at the Humboldt Sink," Jacob said finally, breaking the silence.

Elizabeth sat down slowly. "We were the only family she had left, and when we decided to come west, she came with us. She was never very well."

"She wasn't sorry, Liza," John said.

"I know, John."

Angel wondered if Elizabeth was sorry. Maybe she never wanted to leave home. Maybe all this was John's idea. Angel looked between the two of them and wondered if John wasn't thinking the same thing, but when Elizabeth regained her composure and looked across the cabin at her husband, there was no resentment in her expression. John lifted the fiddle again and played another hymn. Michael joined in the singing this time. His rich, deep voice filled the cabin, and the children were in awe of him.

"Well, now!" Elizabeth said, smiling in delight. "The Lord blessed you indeed, Mr. Hosea."

The boys wanted to sing road songs, and their father obliged. When they exhausted their repertoire, Michael told them about Ezra and the slaves who sang in the cotton fields. He sang one he remembered. It was deep and mournful. "Swing low, sweet chariot, comin' for to carry me home...." Michael's voice pierced Angel's heart.

Angel was tense when she and Michael finally returned to the barn loft. The *what-ifs* went around and around in her head. What if Mama had married a man like John Altman? What if she herself had grown up in a family like that? What if she had come to Michael whole and pure?

But it hadn't happened that way, and wishing didn't make it any better.

"You'd have done very well in the Silver Dollar Saloon," she said, striving for lightness. "The singer they had wasn't nearly as good as you. He used some of your same tunes," she added wryly, "but the lyrics were different."

"Where do you think the church got most of their music in the first place?" Michael chuckled. "Preachers need recognizable tunes to get their congregations singing along." He put his arms behind his head. "Maybe I could've won a few converts."

He was teasing her, and she didn't want to soften any more toward him. He made her heart ache as it was. When she looked at him, her nerves felt raw. "The lyrics I could sing for you are offensive." She felt his thoughtful silence as she undressed and slipped beneath the blankets. Her heart was pounding so fast she wondered if he could hear it. "And don't try to teach me yours," she said. "I'm not singing praises to God for anything."

He didn't turn away from her as she hoped. He gathered her in his strong arms and kissed her until she could scarcely breathe. "Not yet, anyway," he said. His hands fanned the spark inside her until it was a flame, but he didn't quench it. He gave her the space and freedom she thought she wanted and let it burn.

Within a few days, Elizabeth had a yellow plaid shirtwaist and rust skirt ready for fitting. Angel was hesitant to undress, embarrassed at the poor state of Tessie's worn undergarments. "It needs another tuck here, Mama," Miriam said, pulling in an inch at the skirt-waist.

"Yes, and a little more fullness in the back, I think," Elizabeth said, fluffing the material at the back of the skirt.

Angel was disturbed that they would go to so much work on her behalf. The less they did, the less she would owe. "I'm going to be working in the garden in these clothes."

"You needn't look like a drudge doing it," Miriam said.

"I don't want this to be a bother to you." The dress was lovely as it was. It didn't need to be a perfect fit.

"A bother?" Elizabeth said. "Nonsense. I haven't had so much fun in months! You can take the dress off now. Be careful of pins."

As Angel removed the dress and reached quickly for Tessie's worn clothing, she saw Elizabeth's pitying glance at the shabby camisole and threadbare pantalets. If she had her things from the Palace, these ladies would be impressed. They had probably never seen satin and lace undergarments from France, or silk wraps from China. Duke had dressed her only in the finest. Even Duchess, cheap as she had been, wouldn't have thought to dress her so crudely. But no, she had to appear to them in underwear made from used flour sacks.

She wanted to explain that the things weren't hers, that they belonged to Michael's sister, but that would only raise questions she was loathe to answer. And worse, it might reflect badly on Michael. She didn't want them thinking ill of him. She didn't know why it mattered so much, but it did. She dressed quickly, stammered out a thank-you, and escaped to the garden.

Where was Michael? She wished he were close by. She felt safer when he was. She felt less alone and out of her element when he was in sight. He and John had been in the field digging stumps this morning, but they were nowhere in sight now. The horses weren't in the corral. Perhaps Michael had taken John hunting.

Young Leah was gathering miner's lettuce from around the oaks, and Andrew and Jacob were fishing. Angel bent to her weeding and tried not to think about anything.

"Can I play here?" Little Ruth asked, standing on the gate. "Mama's washing and says I'm being a pest."

Angel laughed. "Come in, sweetheart."

Ruthie sat in the pathway where she was working and talked incessantly as she pulled up the weeds Angel showed her. "I don't like carrots. I like green beans."

"So there you are," Miriam said, swinging the gate open. "I told Mama I knew where to find you," she said, wagging her finger at her baby sister. Stooping over, she chucked Ruthie's chin. "You know better than to leave her and not say exactly where you're going."

"I'm with Mandy."

"*Mandy?*" she said, straightening, her eyes dancing over Angel. "Well, *Mandy's* working."

Angel lifted the small carrot from the basket. "She's helping."

Miriam sent Ruthie to report back to Mama and knelt to work with Angel. "It suits you better," she remarked, thinning bean plants.

"What does?" Angel asked tentatively.

"Mandy," Miriam said. "Amanda just doesn't seem right somehow."

"My name was Angel."

"Really?" Miriam said, raising her brows dramatically. She shook her head, eyes twinkling. "Angel doesn't fit you either."

"Would 'Hey-you' do?"

Miriam chucked a dirt clod at her. "I think I'll call you Miss Priss," she decided. "By the way," she added, tossing weeds into the bucket. "I wouldn't be so embarrassed about your unmentionables." At Angel's startled response, she laughed. "You should see *mine!*"

A few days later, Elizabeth gave Angel something wrapped in a pillowcase and told her not to take it out in front of anyone. At Angel's curious look she blushed and hastened back to the cabin. Curious, Angel went into the barn and dumped out the contents. Picking the things up, she found a beautiful camisole and pantalets. The cutwork and embroidery were exquisite.

Clutching the lovely things in her lap, Angel felt the heat pouring into her cheeks. Why had Elizabeth done this? Out of pity? No one had ever given her anything without expecting something back. What did Elizabeth want? Everything she had was Michael's. She didn't even belong to herself anymore. Shoving the things back into the pillowcase, she went outside. Miriam was toting water from the creek, and Angel intercepted her.

"Give these things back to your mother, and tell her I don't need them."

Miriam set the buckets down. "Mama was afraid you'd be offended."

"I'm not. I just don't need them."

"You're angry."

"Just take these things back, Miriam. I don't want them." Angel thrust them at her again.

"Mama made them especially for you."

"So she could feel sorry for me? Well, tell her thank you very much and she can wear them herself."

Miriam was affronted. "Why are you so determined to think the worst of us? Mama's only intent was to please you. She's trying to say thank you for giving her a roof over her head after months of living in that miserable wagon!"

"She needn't thank me. If she wants to thank someone, tell her to thank Michael. It was *his* idea." She immediately regretted her harsh words when the girl's eyes filled up with tears.

"Well, then, I suppose *he* can wear the camisole and pantalets, can't he?" Miriam snatched up the buckets again, tears running down her pale cheeks. "You don't want to love us, do you? You've set your mind against it!"

Angel smarted at the hurt in Miriam's face. "Why don't you keep them for yourself?" she said more gently.

Miriam was not mollified. "If you're of a mind to hurt my mother, then you do it yourself, Amanda Hosea. I won't do it for you. You go tell her you don't want a gift she made for you because she loves you like you're one of her own children. And that's exactly what you are, isn't it? Just an idiotic child who doesn't know something precious when it's staring her right in the face!" Her voice broke, and she hurried away.

Angel fled back to the barn.

Clutching the camisole and pantalets, she sat with her back against the wall. She hadn't thought a few cutting remarks from a naive girl could hurt so deeply. Flinging the things away from her, she pressed her fists against her eyes.

Miriam came in quietly and picked them up. Angel waited for her to leave with them, but she sat down instead.

"I'm sorry I spoke so crossly to you," she said meekly. "I'm far too outspoken."

"You say what you think."

"Yes, I do. Please accept Mama's gift, Amanda. She'll be so hurt if you don't. She's worked on these things for days, and it took her all morning to get up nerve enough to give them to you. 'Every young bride should have something special,' she said. If you give them back, she'll know she's offended you."

Angel drew her knees up tightly against her chest. She felt trapped by Miriam's entreaty. "I would have gone right past all of you on the road that day." Grimacing inwardly, she held Miriam's gaze. "You knew, didn't you?"

Miriam smiled slightly. "You don't really mind now we're here, do you? I don't think you knew what to make of us at first. But that's changed, hasn't it? Ruthie saw through you right away. Contrary to what you may believe, she doesn't take to everyone she meets. Not the way she has to you. And I love you, too, whether you like it or not."

Angel pressed her lips together and said nothing.

Miriam took the camisole and pantalets and folded them onto her lap. "What do you say?"

"They're very lovely things. You should keep them."

"I already have some tucked away in my hope chest. Until I'm a new bride, flour sacks will do very nicely."

Angel could see she wasn't going to get anywhere with this girl.

"You don't know what to make of us, do you?" Miriam said. "Sometimes you look at me so strangely. Was your life so very different from mine?"

"More different than you could ever imagine," Angel said bleakly.

"Mama said it's good to talk things out."

Angel arched a brow. "I wouldn't think to discuss my life with a child."

"I'm sixteen. Hardly that much younger than you."

"Age hasn't anything to do with years in my business."

"It's not your business anymore, is it? You're married to Michael. That part of your life is over."

Angel looked away. "It's never over, Miriam."

"Not when you carry it around like so much baggage."

Angel gave her a startled look. She laughed mirthlessly. "You and Michael have a lot in common." He had told her the same thing once. Neither one of them could understand. You didn't just walk away and say things had never happened. They *had*, and they left deep, raw, gaping wounds. Even when the wounds healed, there were scars. "'Just walk away and forget,'" she mocked. "It's never that simple."

Miriam toyed with a blade of hay and changed the subject. "I imagine it would take a great deal of effort, but wouldn't it be worth it?"

"It always catches up with you."

"Maybe you just don't have enough faith yet in Michael."

Angel didn't want to discuss Michael, especially with a nubile girl like this one, who was far better suited for him than she was.

"I was walking the other morning and saw a cabin," Miriam said. "Do you know who lives there?"

"Michael's brother-in-law, Paul. His wife died coming west."

Miriam's dark eyes were alight with curiosity. "Why doesn't he ever come to visit Michael? Are they feuding?"

"No. He's just not very friendly."

"Is he older or younger than Michael?"

"Younger."

Her smile was playful. "How much younger?"

Angel shrugged. "In his early twenties, I guess." She could see where this was going and didn't like it. Miriam reminded her of Rebecca, the prostitute who'd been so intrigued with Michael.

"Is he handsome?" Miriam persisted.

"I suppose to a virginal young girl anyone without warts and buckteeth would be handsome."

Miriam laughed. "Well, I *am* sixteen. Most girls are married by now, and I haven't even a beau on the horizon. Naturally, I'm interested in who's available. I have to find a groom so I can wear all those pretty unmentionables Mama's made for me and packed away in my trunk."

Thinking of this sweet girl with Paul disturbed Angel greatly. "Pretty things don't mean very much, Miriam. They really don't. Wait for someone like Michael." She could scarcely believe she had said it.

"There's only one Michael, Amanda, and you've got him. What's Paul like?"

"The opposite of Michael."

"So that would mean…ugly, weak, glum, and irreverent?"

"It's not funny, Miriam."

"You're worse than Mama. She won't tell me the least little thing about men."

"There's not much to know. They all eat, defecate, have sex, and die," Angel said without thinking.

"You really are bitter, aren't you?"

Angel winced inwardly. This girl couldn't possibly understand. Not without having experienced Duke. She should have kept her thoughts to herself rather than blurt them out without forethought. What could she say? *"I was raped at eight by a grown man? When he got tired of me, he turned me over to Sally, and she taught me how to do things a nice girl couldn't even imagine?"*

This girl should stay innocent, find a young man, marry him as a virgin, bear his children, and have a family just like the one she came from. She didn't need to be polluted.

"Don't ask me anything about men, Miriam. You wouldn't like what I would tell you."

"I hope a man looks at me someday the way Michael looks at you."

Angel didn't tell her that men had been looking at her like that for longer than she cared to remember. It didn't mean anything at all.

"Papa says I need a strong man who'll keep a firm hand on me," Miriam said. "But I want a man who needs me, too. I want someone who can be tender as well as strong."

Angel studied Miriam as she sat dreaming in the stall about her Prince Charming. Maybe things would have been different if Michael had met Miriam first. How could he have helped but love her? She was vivacious, unsullied, and devout. Miriam had no ghosts. No devil on her back.

Miriam stood and brushed the hay from her skirt. "I'd better stop dreaming and help Mama with the wash." She bent and put the camisole and pantalets on Angel's lap. "Why don't you try these things on before you make up your mind?"

"I wouldn't hurt your mother for anything, Miriam."

The girl's eyes teared up. "I didn't think you could." She left.

Angel leaned her head back. Right from the first, Duke had bought her a wardrobe full of frilly frocks and white lace pinafores and filled her dresser drawers with satin ribbons and bows. Most of her clothes had been made in Paris.

"*Be grateful,*" Sally had told her, bathing and dressing her meticulously for Duke's impending visit. "Try to remember you'd be starving on the docks if not for Duke. Say thank you and mean it. Be *happy* for him. If you become too difficult, Duke will find another little girl who'll be good, and what do you think will happen to you then?"

The warning still sent chills through her. At eight, Angel had thought Duke would order Fergus to strangle her with his thin black cord and throw her into the alley where she would be eaten by rats. So she tried to be grateful, but it never worked. She feared Duke and loathed him. Only later had her terrible dependence on his good will made her think she loved him. It hadn't taken long to learn the truth.

Duke still haunted her. He still owned her soul.

*No, he doesn't. I'm in California. He's four thousand miles away and can't find me.* She was with Michael and the Altmans, and she could decide to change her life. Couldn't she?

She looked at the pristine garments in her lap. Elizabeth

didn't want anything from her. Unlike Duke, she gave a gift freely without expecting anything back.

Duke's words mocked her from deep within. *"Everybody wants something, Angel. Nobody gives you anything without expecting something back."*

Closing her eyes, she saw Elizabeth's sweet, pensive face. "I don't believe you anymore, Duke."

**Don't you?**

Rebelling against the echo of his voice, she stood up swiftly and stripped off her clothing. She put on the new camisole and pantalets. They fit her perfectly. She hugged herself in them. She was going to dress and find Elizabeth and thank her properly. She was going to pretend that she was pure and whole and not let the nightmares of the last ten years destroy it for her.

Not this time. Not if she could help it.

# Twenty

*Of all base passions,*
*fear is most accurs'd.*
SHAKESPEARE

Michael worried about Amanda's growing attachment to the Altman family. John still talked about Oregon as though it were heaven, and spring was closing in fast. As soon as the weather stayed clear, John would be ready to move on. Michael knew he couldn't count on John's women holding him back. Good land was the only way to change his mind.

Young Miriam clearly adored Amanda like a sister, and Ruth was her constant shadow. Elizabeth thought her youngest's attachment to Amanda was endearing, but Michael saw danger in it. Amanda was opening her heart a little more each day. What would happen to her if the Altmans pulled up stakes and left?

He straightened from digging around the stump and looked back toward the cabin. Amanda was toting two buckets from the creek. Elizabeth had a fire going and a big washpot over it, and Miriam was sorting through the basket of wash. Little Ruth skipped along beside Amanda, chattering gaily.

*What she needs is a child of her own, Lord.*

"She really took to her, didn't she?" John said, resting on the pick handle and watching Ruthie and Amanda.

"Sure did."

"Something worrying you, Michael?"

He slammed his boot onto the shovel and slung the dirt aside. "You head north with your family and you're going to break my wife's heart."

"Not to mention Liza's. She's adopted your wife, if you had-n't noticed."

"There's good land right here."

"Not as good as in Oregon."

"You're not going to find what you're looking for in Oregon or anyplace else."

Michael talked to Amanda that night about selling off a portion of their own land to the Altmans. "I wanted to discuss it with you before mentioning it to him."

"It won't make any difference, will it? He spent the whole evening talking about Oregon. He can't wait to leave."

"He hasn't seen the west end of the valley yet," Michael said. "He may change his mind after that."

Angel sat up, her heart twisting at the thought of Miriam and Ruth riding away to Oregon. "What's the use? Once a man's made up his mind about something, there's nothing can change it."

"John's looking for good farmland."

"John's looking for the pot at the end of the rainbow!"

"So we'll give it to him." Michael sat up behind her and drew her back against him. "He wants the best for his family. The west end is the best we've got."

"All he ever talks about is Oregon. Elizabeth doesn't want to go. Neither does Miriam."

"He thinks the Willamette Valley is Eden."

Angel jerked out of his arms and stood up. "Then he should've gone there in the first place instead of stopping here." She held herself in tightly and leaned against the wall, looking out at the cabin. It was dark, the lantern extinguished. The Altmans were all sleeping. "I wish they'd never come here. I wish I hadn't met any of them."

"They aren't gone yet."

She looked back at him, her face white in the moonlight. "Is Oregon that wonderful? Is it Eden like he thinks it is?"

"I don't know, Tirzah. I've never been there."

*Tirzah.* His desire for her was in that name. Angel felt tingling warmth run down into her belly when he said it. *Tirzah.* She tried not to think about what it meant, but when she heard the hay rustle softly as he arose, her heart jumped. She looked up at him as he came close and could hardly draw a breath. When he touched her, she felt a rush of warmth and was afraid. What was this power he had over her?

"Don't give up hope," he said, feeling her stiffen as he drew her into his arms. He wanted to tell her they could have a child of their own, but there was time enough for that, and this wasn't it. Not yet. "John might change his mind when he sees what we're offering."

She didn't think John would even agree to look, but he did. The two men rode away the next morning just after dawn. Angel saw Miriam running across the yard, her shawl thrown carelessly about her shoulders. She swung the barn door open and came halfway up the ladder, calling to her. "Mandy, I want to see the west end of the valley, too. It's only a few miles, from what Michael said."

Angel came down the ladder. "It's not going to make any difference."

"You're as bad as Mama. We're not packed and rolling yet."

Miriam talked most of the way, coming up with all sorts of outlandish plans of how to prevent her father's exodus. Angel knew on a month's acquaintance that if John Altman said, "Go," Elizabeth and Miriam would.

"There's Papa and Michael," Miriam said, "but who's that man with them?"

"Paul," Angel said, steeling herself. She hadn't seen him since that miserable ride back to Pair-a-Dice, and she had no desire to face him now. But what excuse could she possibly use for turning back?

Miriam didn't even notice her trepidation, curiosity spurring her ahead. The three men spotted them. Michael waved. Angel gritted her teeth. She had no choice but to go ahead. She wondered what form Paul's attack would take this time.

Michael came to meet her. She forced a smile and kept her chin up. "Miriam wanted to come."

He kissed her cheek. "I'm glad she dragged you along."

The men had been digging. Miriam scooped up some dirt. She crumbled it in her hand and smelled it. Her eyes shone as she looked at her father. "It's rich enough to eat."

"Couldn't do much better."

"Even in Oregon, Papa?"

"Even in Oregon."

With a squeal Miriam catapulted into his arms, laughing and crying. "Wait'll Mama hears!"

"Your mother is to know nothing about it. Not until we've built a cabin for her. Promise me."

Miriam wiped the tears away. "One mention of Oregon, Papa, and I'll spill the beans."

Angel glanced at Paul. His gaze brushed hers. It was full of silent, seething hatred. She drew her shawl more tightly around her. She had drawn a good amount of his blood that day on the road. She had put the knife in as deeply as she could. He looked at her again, longer this time. A wounded animal, enraged and dangerous.

"Paul is handsome," Miriam said on the walk back. "Such dark, brooding eyes."

Angel said nothing. Just before he'd ridden away, Paul had tipped his hat to her. No one but she had noticed, nor had they seen the expression in his eyes – an expression that consigned her to Hades.

The men began work the next morning. Paul met them with his ax and adze. Michael located four large stones for the foundation. They began felling trees.

Jacob learned the secret the third day when he followed Miriam with the lunch. He was sworn to silence and set to work. By the time Michael and John returned with him, the boy was too tired to speak.

"What are you doing to him?" Elizabeth asked. "He can barely keep his head out of the stew."

"Clearing land is hard work."

Angel worked with Elizabeth. She wanted to avoid Paul, but even more, she wanted more time with Elizabeth and Ruthie. Elizabeth sensed it and asked her to watch over the children while she baked. Angel learned tag, hide-and-seek, blindman's bluff and leapfrog. She stood on the creek bank and skipped rocks with Ruthie and Andrew. Most of all, she thought about how precious little time she had left with them.

"The children follow her about like chicks," Elizabeth told John. "She's like a big sister to them."

Miriam took Angel aside. "The walls are up." Then, "The roof's set." Angel heard each report with sinking heart. "Paul's made enough shingles to cover the roof." Then, "Michael and Paul are working on the fireplace." In a few days, the cabin would be finished, and the Altmans would leave. Two miles began to seem like two thousand.

Paul would be their nearest neighbor. How long before he poisoned their affection?

The weather was clear and warming. "There's no reason to take further advantage of the Hoseas' hospitality," John said. "It's time we found a place of our own." He told Elizabeth to start packing.

Pale and tight-lipped, Elizabeth set to work.

"I've never seen her so angry," Miriam said. "She hasn't said a word to Papa since he said we were leaving. Now it's pure cussed stubbornness that keeps him from telling her."

Angel helped Miriam load the wagon. Andrew filled the water barrel hanging from the side, and Jacob helped John hitch up the horses. When Elizabeth came and embraced her, Angel couldn't speak.

"I shall miss you dearly, Amanda," Elizabeth whispered brokenly. She patted her cheek like one of her children. "Take good care of that man of yours. There aren't many around like him."

"Yes, ma'am," Angel said.

Miriam squeezed her hard and whispered, "You're a wonderful actress. You really look like you're saying good-bye to us for good." Little Ruth was inconsolable and clung to Angel until she thought her heart would break. Why wouldn't they just go and be done with it? Miriam took Ruthie and whispered something that silenced the child, then lifted her into the back of the wagon with Leah. Ruth looked at Angel, and her face was glowing. All the children knew the secret now.

"I'll give you a hand up, Liza," John said.

She didn't look at him. "Thank you, but I think I'll walk awhile."

As soon as they started off, Michael went to saddle his horse. Angel stood in the yard, watching the wagon roll away. She missed them already and could feel the gap widening like a chasm she couldn't cross. She kept remembering Mama sending her off with Cleo to the sea. She went into the house and packed a basket with sweet biscuits and winter apples. Nothing was going to be the same.

Paul was at the cabin when the two of them arrived. He had a side of venison roasting on the spit. Angel hung up the curtains Elizabeth had made for Michael's cabin while the men talked. Michael went out to see if he could spot the Altmans yet. Angel felt Paul's cold gaze on her back.

"I bet they don't know anything about you, do they, Angel?"

She turned and faced him. He wouldn't believe the truth if she told him. "I like them very much, Paul, and I wouldn't want them to be hurt."

He sneered. "Meaning you hope I'll keep your sordid past a secret."

She saw it was no use appealing to him. "Meaning you'll do what you think you have to," she said dully. How long before he made them see her for what she really was? It would be very little time at all before they realized the animosity he held toward her, and they would wonder and ask why. What could she tell them? *"He wanted me to pay for a ride, and I gave him the only currency I had"?*

Why had she ever let herself get involved with these people? Why had she allowed herself to like them? She knew it was a mistake from the beginning.

"Love is debilitating," Sally had said.

"Have you ever been in love?" Angel had asked.

"Once."

"Who was it?"

"It's Duke." She gave a bitter laugh. "But I've always been too old for him."

A cold voice broke into her thoughts. "Scared, aren't you?" Paul's smile was stone cold. Angel went outside. She couldn't breathe in the cabin. The pain was beginning already. It was the same pain she felt the day she heard her father say he wished she had never been born, the same pain when Mama died, the same when she learned of Lucky's death. She had even felt pain the first time Duke gave her to another man.

Everyone to whom she drew close left her. Sooner or later they walked away. Or died. Or lost interest. Love someone, and it was a guarantee. Mama, Sally, Lucky. Now Miriam, Ruthie, and Elizabeth.

*How could I forget what it felt like?*

**Because Michael fed you hope, and hope is deadly.**

Sally told her once that you had to be like a stone because people would chip away at you, and that stone had to be big enough that they would never reach the very heart of you.

Angel saw Michael standing in the sunlight, strong and beautiful. Her heart twisted inside her. He of all of them had chipped away the most, and sooner or later, he would walk out of her life and leave a hole where her heart had been.

He came to her, and when he saw the look on her face, his eyes darkened. "Did Paul say something to hurt you?"

"No," she rasped. "No. He didn't say anything."

"Something's upset you."

*I'm falling in love with you. Oh, God, I don't want to, but I am. You're becoming the air that I breathe. I'm losing Elizabeth and Miriam and Ruthie. How long will it be before I lose you, too?* She looked away. "Nothing's upset me. I'm just worried what Elizabeth will say to all this."

It wasn't long before she had her answer. The wagon came over the rise and drew close. Elizabeth stared in disbelief, looking from the cabin to John, who jumped from the wagon seat, a broad grin on his face. Then Elizabeth wept and threw herself into John's arms, telling him he was a wretch and she adored him.

"You should apologize, Mama," Miriam laughed. "You've been horrid to him ever since we left the Hoseas'." John took his wife's hand, and they headed out for a walk to see their land.

Miriam set right to work in the cabin, but it wasn't long before she stopped and looked at Angel. "You and Paul aren't on friendly terms, are you?"

"Not very," Angel said. Ruth tugged her skirt, and Angel lifted her, setting Ruth on her hip.

"Oh, no, you don't." Miriam dried her hands and took Ruth and set her down again. "Mandy has to help me make a cake, and she needs both hands to do it. Don't stick your lip out at me, young lady." She turned her around and gave the little girl's bottom a light swat. "Michael's right outside. Ask him to give you a piggyback ride." She set out the bowls and glanced at Angel. "Now, tell me what it's all about."

"What?"

"You know what. You and Paul. Was he in love with you before you married Michael?"

Angel gave a sardonic laugh. "Hardly."

Miriam frowned. "He didn't approve."

"Doesn't," Angel said. "With good reason."

"Name one."

"You needn't know everything, Miriam. You know far more than is good for you already."

"If I asked him, would he tell me?" she challenged.

A wince of pain crossed Angel's face. "Probably."

Miriam brushed a strand of hair from her eyes and left a smudge of flour across her cheek. "Then I won't ask."

Angel adored her. One minute she was a child like Ruth, full of excitement and mischief, and the next a woman with a mind of her own. "Don't think too badly of him," she said. "He was looking out for Michael." She gave the sifter a last tap and set it aside. "I knew a girl once who received a chunk of amethyst as a gift. It was beautiful. Bright purple crystals. The man told her it came from a stone egg he had cracked open and part of the outer shell was still on it. Gray, ugly, and smooth." She looked at Miriam. "I'm like that, Miriam. Only it's inside out. All the loveliness is here." She touched her braid and her flawless face. "Inside, it's dark and ugly. Paul saw that."

Tears welled into Miriam's eyes. "Then he didn't look hard enough."

"You're very sweet but very naive."

"I'm both and neither. I don't think you know me half as well as you think you do."

"We know one another as well as we're going to."

The day grew so warm and pure that Miriam laid out blankets for a picnic. Angel saw Michael and Paul talking. Her stomach tightened as she thought of the horrible things Paul could gleefully relate to Michael about her cold-blooded behavior on the road. The grotesqueness of it nauseated her. How would Paul see what had happened between them? As a straight-forward business proposition? a wanton act without feeling? No wonder he saw only black foulness inside her, the leprosy of her soul. She had shown him nothing else.

She watched Michael covertly, hungering for his glance in her direction just to show things were all right, but he was intent on what Paul was saying.

She tried to calm her heart. Michael had seen her in a worse place than Paul could imagine, and still he took her back. Even after she deserted and betrayed him, he fought for her. She would never understand him. She had thought men like him were weak, but Michael wasn't. He was quiet and steady, unyielding, like a rock. How could he still look at her with anything but loathing after all she had done? How could he love her?

Maybe the reality of *Angel* hadn't caught up with him yet. When it did, he would look at her the same way Paul did. What he saw now was clouded by his own fantasy of a woman redeemable.

*But it's all a lie. I'm just playing another role. Someday the dreamer will awaken, and life will fall back into the old pattern again.*

As she talked and worked with Miriam, she pretended nothing bothered her. The dark inner silence grew, familiar and heavy, weighing her down inside. She shored up the cracks in her walls and girded herself for the coming attack. Yet every time she looked at Michael, she weakened.

But the past kept catching up with her, no matter how far she ran. Sometimes she felt as though she were on a road and could hear the hard beat of the horses' hooves coming, as though a coach were coming straight at her but she couldn't get out of the way. In her mind she could see it racing toward her, and within it were Duke, Sally, Lucky, Duchess, and Magowan. And there on the high driver's seat were Alex Stafford and Mama.

And they were all going to run her down.

Elizabeth and John returned. Angel saw the way John touched his wife tenderly and noted how Elizabeth blushed. Angel had seen that same look on other men's faces, but they hadn't smiled into her eyes just that way. With her, it had been business.

The cabin was overcrowded, and she went out into the field of mustard flowers to sit down. She wanted to empty her mind. She wanted the anguish to go away. Ruthie joined her. The mustard weeds were taller than she, and Ruthie thought it a great adventure to make paths in the golden forest. Angel watched her dropping blossoms and chasing a white butterfly. Her heart squeezed tight and small.

Tonight, she and Michael would walk away, and that would be the end of it. She wouldn't see Ruthie anymore. Or Miriam. Or Elizabeth. Or the others. She hugged her knees tightly against her chest. She wished Ruthie would come back and want to be held. She wanted to cover her sweet face with kisses; but the child wouldn't understand, and she couldn't explain.

Ruth did come back, eyes bright with childish excitement. She plopped down beside Angel. "Did you see, Mandy? The first butterfly."

"Yes, darling." She touched her silky dark hair.

Ruth gazed up at her with wide, sparkling brown eyes. "Did you know they come from *worms*? Miriam told me."

She smiled. "Is that so?"

"Some are fuzzy and pretty, but they don't taste good," Ruth said. "I ate one when I was little. It was awful."

Angel laughed and lifted Ruth to her lap. She tickled Ruthie's tummy. "Well, then, I don't suppose you'll eat another one, will you, little mouse?"

Ruth giggled and bounced up again to pick more mustard flowers. She tugged one plant up by the roots. "Now that we have a cabin, are you and Michael going to come live with us?"

"No, sweetheart."

Ruth looked at her in surprise. "Why not? Don't you want to?"

"Because now we each have cabins of our own."

Ruth came back and stood in front of her. "What's the matter, Mandy? Don't you feel good?"

Angel touched her baby-soft hair. "I feel fine."

"Well, then, will you sing me a song? I've never heard you sing."

"I can't. I don't know how."

"Papa says *anybody* can sing."

"It has to come from inside, and I don't have anything left inside."

"Really?" Ruth said, amazed. "How did that happen?"

"It all just drained out."

Ruth frowned, studying Angel critically from head to foot. "You look fine to me."

"Looks can be deceiving."

Still perplexed, Ruth sat in her lap. "Then I'll sing to you." The words and tunes were all mixed up, but Angel didn't care. She was content to have Ruthie on her lap and the fragrance of mustard flowers strong about her. She rested her head on Ruthie's and held her close, not noticing Miriam until she spoke.

"Mama wants you, punkin."

Angel lifted Ruth off her lap and gave her a light pat to send her off again.

"Why are you cutting us off?" Miriam asked, sitting down with her.

"What makes you think I am?"

"You always do that. Ask a question instead of answer one. It's very annoying, Amanda."

Angel stood and brushed dust from her skirt.

Miriam stood with her. "You won't answer or look me in the eye, and now you're running away."

Angel looked at her squarely. "Nonsense."

"What do you think is going to happen? Do you think that, just because we have a cabin of our own now, the friendship is over?"

"We'll all be very busy with our own lives."

"Not *that* busy." Miriam reached out to take her hand, but Angel walked away, pretending not to notice.

"You know, sometimes you can hurt yourself more by trying to keep yourself from being hurt!" Miriam called after her.

Angel laughed it off. "Words from a sage."

"You're impossible, Amanda Hosea!"

"Angel," she said under her breath. "My name's Angel."

Everyone gathered at the blankets when Elizabeth, Miriam, and Angel brought out the food. Angel pushed her food around so the others would think she was enjoying the meal, but her throat closed every time she took a small bite.

Paul looked at her coldly. She tried not to let it bother her. It was his own weakness that made him hate her so much.

She remembered a few young men who paid for her services and came face-to-face with their own hypocrisy when they were putting their pants and boots on and getting ready to walk out the door. It suddenly dawned on them what they had done. Not to her. That didn't matter one way or the other. But to themselves.

"Haven't you forgotten something?" she would say, wanting to drive the knife straight into their hearts any way she could. They *ought* to know. First the red flags in their pale cheeks, then the dark, loathing in their eyes.

Well, she had driven the blade straight and sure into Paul, but she knew now she was the one impaled. It would have been better if she had walked all the way to Pair-a-Dice that day. Maybe then Michael would have caught up to her before it was too late. Maybe Paul wouldn't hate her so much. Maybe she would not have so much to regret.

Her whole life was one huge regret, right from the beginning. *"She should never have been born, Mae."*

Michael took her hand, and she started. "What are you thinking about?" he asked quietly.

"Nothing." Warmth spread through her at his touch. Disturbed, she drew her hand away. He frowned slightly. "Something's bothering you."

She shrugged, not meeting his eyes.

He studied her thoughtfully. "Paul isn't going to say or do anything to hurt you."

"It wouldn't matter if he did."

"If he hurts you, he hurts me."

His tone caught her full attention. She had intended to hurt Paul and had hurt Michael instead. Not once had she thought that day of what it would do to him. She thought only of herself and her anger and her hopelessness. Maybe she could make some amends. "It's nothing to do with Paul," she assured him. "It's just that truth always catches up."

"I'm counting on that."

Michael watched Amanda throughout the day. She withdrew further and further into herself. She worked with Elizabeth and Miriam but said very little. She was preoccupied, in full retreat, building her walls again. When Ruthie took her hand, he saw the pain in Amanda's eyes and knew what she expected. He couldn't promise it wouldn't happen. Sometimes people became too caught up in the problems of day-to-day living to notice the pain in someone else.

Young Miriam noticed. "She's here, but she isn't. She won't let me close, Michael. What's wrong with her today? She's acting the same way she did when we first came to your place."

"She's afraid of being hurt."

"She's hurting herself now."

"I know." He wasn't going to reveal her past or discuss his wife's problems.

"Paul doesn't like her. That's part of it. She's not a prostitute anymore, but she expects everyone to look at her and treat her like one."

Rage shot through him. "Did Paul tell you that?"

She shook her head. "She told me the first night and loudly enough for Mama to hear." Tears filled her eyes. "What are we going to do about her, Michael? The way she holds Ruthie breaks my heart."

Michael knew Miriam was going to have plenty to do in helping John and Elizabeth get this place going. He couldn't ask her to make frequent visits to his place so Amanda would know the affection was real and not a matter of convenience, and the girl was already looking on Paul like he was a Greek god come down from

Olympus, despite his flaws. He knew Paul found the girl attractive, as well. It was clear in the studied way he avoided her. Whatever way it went, Miriam's loyalties were going to be put to a hard test.

John took out his fiddle. No quiet mournful hymns this time, but Virginia reels. Michael caught hold of Angel and whirled her around. Being in his arms was heady stuff.

Angel's heart raced. She could feel heat pouring into her face and didn't dare look up at him. Jacob danced with his mother while Miriam danced around the clearing with Ruth. John lifted his booted foot and gave Andrew a shove toward his sister Leah. Paul watched, leaning indolently against the cabin wall. He looked so alone, Angel pitied him.

"It's the first time I've danced with you," Michael said.

"Yes," she said breathlessly. "You're very good."

"And that surprises you." He laughed. "I'm good at a lot of things." His arm tightened around her, speeding up her pulse even more.

Jacob came and bowed to Angel, and Michael relinquished her with a grin. She glanced around the yard, and they danced. It only took one look at Miriam to know she wanted to dance with someone other than her baby sister or younger brothers. But Michael had danced with Elizabeth, Leah, and Ruth, and left Miriam alone. An unpleasant sensation stirred in Angel's belly. Why did Michael avoid Miriam? Was he afraid to get too close to her? When he came back to claim her from Jacob, she pulled her hand away. "You haven't danced with Miriam. Why won't you dance with her?"

He frowned slightly and caught firm hold of her hand, pulling her into his arms. "Paul will get around to it."

"He hasn't danced with anyone yet."

"And he won't feel the necessity if I step in for him. I'd hazard a guess he's thinking about Tessie. He met her at a dance. It'll dawn on him soon that young Miriam needs a partner."

Paul did dance with Miriam, but he was stiff and grim and hardly spoke a word to her. Miriam was clearly perplexed. As soon as the dance was finished, he said good night and went for his horse.

"We'd better head for home, too," Michael said.

Miriam embraced Angel and whispered, "I'll be over in a few days to visit. Maybe you'll tell me what's eating that man."

Angel lifted little Ruth and held her tightly, kissing her smooth, baby cheek and nuzzling her neck. "Good-bye, darling. Be good."

Michael lifted Angel onto the saddle and swung up behind her. His arm held her firmly as they headed home in the moonlight. Neither spoke the whole way. Angel was overwhelmingly aware of his body against hers and was confused by the sensations running through her. She wished she were walking.

When she spotted the cabin through the trees, she was relieved. Michael dismounted and reached up for her. Leaning toward him, she rested her hands on his strong shoulders. Her body brushed his as he lifted her down, and she felt life coursing through her, wild, exhilarating, and unfamiliar.

"Thank you," she said stiffly.

"You're welcome." He grinned, and her mouth went dry. When he didn't take his hands from her waist, her heart beat faster and faster. "You've been very quiet all day," he said, pensive again.

"I've nothing to say."

"What's bothering you?" he asked, pushing the thick braid back off her shoulder.

"Nothing."

"We're on our own again. Could that be it?" He tipped her chin and kissed her. Angel felt her insides melting, her knees weakening. When Michael lifted his head, he touched her face tenderly. "I'll be in shortly."

Pressing her hand against her quivering stomach, she watched him lead the horse away. What was happening to her? She went inside the cabin and set to work on the fire. Once it was going, she looked around for something else to do to keep her mind off Michael, but everything was tidy. Elizabeth had even restuffed the mattress with fresh straw. Herbs hung from a beam and filled the cabin with their sweet, fresh scent. A jar of mustard flowers was on the table, undoubtedly placed there by Ruth.

Michael shouldered their things in from the barn. "Pretty quiet around here with the Altmans gone, isn't it?"

"Yes."

"You'll miss Miriam and Ruth most." He set the trunk back in the corner. She was bending over the fire. He put his hands on her hips and she straightened. "They love you."

Her eyes flickered. "Let's talk about something else, shall we?" she said and stepped away from him.

He caught her shoulders. "No. Let's talk about what's on your mind."

"There's nothing on my mind." He waited, obviously unsatisfied, and she drew in a ragged breath. "I knew better than to get close to them." She pushed his hands away and hugged her shawl about her.

"You think they love you less now that they're living in their own place?"

She glared at him defensively. "Sometimes I wish you'd just leave me alone, Michael. That you'd just send me back where I came from. It'd be so much easier all the way around."

"Because you're *feeling* now?"

"I *felt* before, and I got over it!"

"You adore Miriam and that little girl."

"So what?" She would get over it, too.

"What're you going to do when Ruth comes over here with another fistful of mustard flowers? Show her the door?" he asked harshly. "She's got feelings, too. So does Miriam." He saw by her expression that she didn't think they would come at all. He took her in his arms, holding her there even when he felt her resistance. "I've prayed unceasingly that you might learn to love, and now you have. Only you fell in love with them instead of me." He laughed softly in self-mockery. "There were times when I wished I'd never brought them here. I'm jealous."

Her cheeks burned, and she couldn't still her racing heart no matter how hard she tried. If he knew the power he had over her, what would he do with it? "I don't want to fall in love with you," she said, pushing away.

"Why not?"

"Because you'll just end up using it against me." She saw she had angered him.

"How?"

"I don't know. The truth is, maybe you wouldn't even know you're doing it."

"Whose truth are we talking here? *Duke's?* Truth sets you free. Were you ever free with him? Even for a single minute? He filled your head with lies."

"And what about my father?"

"Your father was selfish and cruel. That doesn't mean every man in the world is the same as him."

"Every man I've ever known is."

"Does that include me? What about John Altman? What about Joseph Hochschild, and a thousand others?"

Her face jerked in pain.

Seeing her torment, he gentled. "You're a bird who's been in a cage all your life, and suddenly all the walls are gone, and you're in the wide open. You're so afraid you're looking for any way back into the cage again." He saw the emotions flicker across her pale face. "Whatever you choose to think now, it's not safer there, Amanda. Even if you tried to go back now, I don't think you could survive that way again."

He was right. She knew he was. She had reached the end of enduring it even before Michael claimed her. Yet, being here was no assurance.

What if she couldn't fly?

# Twenty-one

*As a hart longs for flowing streams,*
*so longs my soul for thee.*

PSALM 42:1

The land awakened with the coming of spring. The hillsides were splashed with purple lupines and golden poppies, red paintbrushes and the white of wild radish. Angel found something strange stirring inside her as well. She felt it first while watching Michael turn the earth in the vegetable garden. The movement of his muscles beneath the shirt sent a rush of warmth through her. He only had to look at her, and her mouth went dry.

At night, they lay side by side, hardly touching, tense and silent. She felt the distance he put between them and honored it. "This is getting harder to do," he said cryptically, and she didn't ask him what he meant.

Her own loneliness grew. It had to do with Michael, and the ache grew worse, not better, with time. Sometimes when he would finish reading at night and raise his head, she wouldn't be able to breathe for the look in his eyes. Her heart would beat wildly, and she would look away, afraid he would see the deep longing she felt. Her whole body spoke of it. It sang inside her like a loud chorus, filling her head with thoughts of him. She could hardly speak when he asked her a simple question.

How Duke would laugh. *"Love is a trap, Angel. Stick to pleasure. It doesn't require any great commitment."*

She wondered now if Michael wasn't the answer to all things for her. Contemplating that, she was afraid. At night, when he turned to her in his sleep, his strong body brushing hers, she would remember the way he used to make love to her – with joyous abandon, exploring her body as he did the land he owned. She had felt nothing then. Now, the lightest touch made her senses spin. His dreams were becoming her dreams.

Michael opened his hand more each day, but she was frozen

in fear. Why couldn't they leave things as they were? Let her stay *this* way. Let her still be inside herself. Let things be as they had been. Still, Michael kept pushing, gently relentless, and she held back in fear because all she could see ahead was a great unknown.

*I can't love him. Oh, please, I can't!*

She couldn't be more than her mother, and Mae hadn't been able to hold on to Alex Stafford. All her love hadn't been enough to keep him from riding out of her life like the wind. Angel could still see his dark figure, cape flying, as he galloped down the road and out of her mother's life. Had he even come in person to tell Mama to pack and get out? Or had he left it to that young lackey to do it for him? She didn't know. Mama never said, and she never asked. Alex Stafford was sacred ground Angel had never dared walk over. Only Mama spoke his name, and only when she was drunk and despondent, and it had always grated like salt on a raw wound. "Why did Alex leave me?" Mama had wept. "Why? I don't understand. *Why?*"

Mama's grief had been so great, but her guilt had been even greater. She had never gotten over what she had given up to have *love.* She had never gotten over *him.*

*But I paid him back in spades, Mama. Can you hear wherever you are? I smashed him into tiny pieces the way he smashed you. Oh, the look on his face.*

Angel covered hers.

*Oh, Mama, you were so beautiful and perfect. You were so devout. Did your rosary beads ever help you, Mama? Did hope? Love never did anything but bring you pain. And it's doing the same to me.*

Angel had sworn she would never love anyone, and now it was happening in spite of her. It stirred and grew against her will, pushing its way through the darkness of her mind to the surface. Like a seedling seeking the light of the spring sun, it came on. Miriam, little Ruth, Elizabeth. And now Michael. Every time she looked at him, he pierced her heart. She wanted to crush the new feelings, but still they came, slowly finding their way.

Duke was right. It was insidious. It was a trap. It grew like ivy, forcing its way into the smallest cracks of her defenses, and eventually it would rip her apart. If she let it. If she didn't kill it now.

**There's still a way out,** came the dark voice, counseling her. **Tell him the worst of what you've done. Tell him about your father. That'll poison it. That will stop the pain growing inside you.**

So she decided to confess everything. Once Michael knew everything, it would be finished. The truth would drive a wedge in so deep between them, she would be safe forever.

Michael was chopping wood when she found him. He had his shirt off, and she stood silently watching him work. His broad back was already tanned, and hard muscles moved beneath the golden skin. He was power and beauty and majesty as he swung the ax in a wide arc, bringing it down hard, splitting the log clean through. The two halves banged off the block. As he bent to set up another, he saw her.

"Morning," he said, smiling. Her stomach fluttered. He looked pleased and surprised to see her watching him.

*Why am I doing this?*

**Because you're living a lie. If he knew everything he would detest you and cast you out.**

*There's no reason for him to know.*

**Would you rather someone else told him? Then it will be even worse.**

"I have to talk to you," she said weakly. All she could hear was the pounding of her heart in her own ears and that dark voice driving her on in desperation.

Michael frowned slightly. She was tense, worrying away at a gather in her skirt. "I'm listening."

Angel felt hot and cold all over. She should do it.

**Yes. Do it, Angel.**

She had to do it. Her palms were damp. Michael took his handkerchief from his back pocket and wiped the sweat from his face. When he looked at her, her heart sank.

*I can't do it.*

**Yes, you can.**

*I don't want to.*

**Fool! You want to end up like your mother?**

Michael studied her. She looked pale, small beads of perspiration breaking out on her forehead. "What's wrong? Are you feeling ill?"

**Tell him and get it over with, Angel! It's what you really want, to make him let you go now while you can still bear it. If you wait, it'll only hurt worse. He'll cut your heart out and carve it up for dinner.**

"I've never told you the worst I've done."

His shoulders stiffened. "It's not necessary for you to confess everything. Not to me."

"You ought to know. You being my husband and all."

"Your past is your own business."

"Don't you think you should know what sort of girl you've got living with you?"

"Why the attack, Amanda?"

"I'm not attacking. I'm being *honest*."

"You're pushing again. Pushing hard."

"You should know that – "

"I don't want to hear it!"

" – I had sex with my own father."

Michael let out a sharp breath as though she had punched him hard. He stared at her for a long moment, a muscle jerking in his cheek. "I thought you said he walked out of your life when you were about three."

"He did. He came back into it later, when I was sixteen."

Michael felt sick. *God. God! Is there a sin this woman hasn't committed?*

*No.*

*And you ask that I love her?*

*As I have loved you.*

Why had she done it? Why couldn't she keep some burdens on herself? "Did it make you feel better to throw that in my face?"

"Not much," she said dully. She turned and headed for the house, sickened at herself. Well, it was done. Finished. She wanted to hide. Her strides lengthened. She would pack a few things and be ready to leave.

Michael was shaking with anger. The idyll was over. The storm had hit.

*As I have loved you, Michael. Seventy times seven.*

Michael cried out and sank the ax deeply into the chopping block. He stood breathing heavily for a long moment, then snatched up his shirt and shrugged it on as he strode toward the cabin. He hit the door open and saw her pulling things from the dresser he had made for her after the Altmans left.

"Don't leave it at that, Amanda. Tell me the rest of what you've done. Get it off your chest. Dump it on me. Give me all the gory details."

*Michael, beloved.*

*No! I'm not listening to you right now! I'm going to have it out with her once and for all!*

When she didn't stop what she was doing, he caught Angel's arm and swung her around. "There's more, isn't there, Angel?"

The name was a slap in her face. "Enough, wasn't it?" she said in a tiny voice. "Or do you really need more?"

He saw the emotions she was so desperate to hide, but even that didn't calm him. "Let's get all the dirty laundry out in the open at once."

She drew her arm away from his disturbing touch and took his challenge. "All right. If that's the way you want it! There was a short while when I thought I was in love with Duke. Amazing, isn't it? My whole life seemed to depend on him. I told him everything. Everything that hurt. Everything that mattered. I thought he'd fix it for me."

"And he used what he knew against you instead."

"You guessed it. I never gave a single thought to Duke's life outside the brownstone or what people he had for friends. Not until he came back with one he wanted me to meet. 'Be nice to him, Angel. He's one of my oldest and dearest friends.' And in walks Alex Stafford. When I looked at Duke, I could see him laughing at both of us. Rich, isn't it? Duke knew how much I hated Stafford for what he did to my mother. He just wanted to see what I'd do about it."

"Did your father know who you were?"

Angel gave a bleak, broken laugh. "My father just stood there staring at me like I was a ghost. And you know what he said? I reminded him of somebody he used to know."

"Then what?"

"He stayed. The whole night."

"Did you ever stop to think – "

"I *knew* what I was doing, and I did it anyway! Don't you understand yet? I did it with *relish*, just waiting for that moment when I'd tell him who I was." She couldn't hold his gaze. She was trembling violently and couldn't stop. "When I did, I told him what became of Mama, too."

Michael's anger evaporated. She was silent so long, he touched her. "And what did he say?"

She moved back again, swallowing convulsively. Her eyes were huge and tormented. "*Nothing.* He said nothing. Not then. He just looked at me for a long time. Then he sat down on the edge of the bed and cried. He *cried.* He looked like an old, broken man. '*Why,*' he said to me, 'Why?'" Her eyes felt hot and grainy. "And I told him Mama used to ask me the same thing. He asked me to forgive him, and I told him he could rot in hell." The shaking stopped, and she felt cold inside, dead. When she looked up at Michael, he was just standing there, quiet and still, watching her and waiting for the rest of it.

"You know what else?" she said dully. "He shot himself three days later. Duke said it was because he owed money to everybody, including the devil himself, but I know why he did it." She closed her eyes, ashamed. "I know."

"I'm sorry," Michael said. How many more nightmares did she have locked away inside her?

She looked up at him. "That's the second time you've apologized for something you've got nothing to do with. How can you even look at me?"

"The same way I can look at myself."

She shook her head and pulled her shawl tightly around herself. "One more thing," she said. "It'll make a difference." Michael stood like a soldier going into battle. "I can't have children. I got pregnant twice. Both times Duke had a doctor take the baby. The second time he told the doctor to make sure I could never get pregnant again. *Never*, Michael. Do you understand?" She saw he did.

He stood, stunned. Alternately hot and cold. Her words had gone straight through his breastplate.

She put her hand over her face because she couldn't bear the look on his.

"Anything else?" he asked quietly.

"No," she said, her mouth jerking. "I think that about does it."

Michael didn't move for a long moment. Then he took the shirtwaists she had laid out. He jammed them back into the drawer and banged it shut. Then he walked out the door.

He was gone so long, she went to look for him to ask what he wanted her to do. He wasn't in the fields or in the barn. He wasn't down by the creek. She wondered if he had gone to the Altmans. Maybe he had ridden over to see Paul to tell him he was right about her, more than right.

The horses were in the corral.

She kept thinking of her father, and she was afraid.

She thought hard and realized one other place he might have gone. She put on a coat and took a heavy blanket from the bed and headed for the hill where he had taken her to see the sunrise. Michael was there, sitting with his head in his hands. He didn't look up when she reached him. She put the blanket around his shoulders. "Do you want me to leave? I know where the road is now." Coaches even went by on occasion. "I could find my own way back."

"*No*," he said hoarsely.

She stood looking at the sunset. "Do you ever get the feeling God is playing some horrible joke on you?"

"No."

"Then why, when you love him the way you do, would he do such a thing to you as this?"

"I've been asking him."

"Did he say?"

"I already know." He took her hand and pulled her down to sit beside him. "To strengthen me."

"You're strong enough already, Michael. You don't need this. You don't need *me*."

"I'm not strong enough for what's yet to come."

She was afraid to ask him what he meant. When she shivered, he put his arm around her. "He hasn't given us a heart of fear," he said. "He'll show me the way when the time comes."

"How can you be so sure?"

"Because he always has before."

"I wish I could believe." Crickets and frogs were making a cacophony around them. How could she have ever thought there was silence out here? "I can still hear Mama weeping sometimes," she said. "At night, when the tree branches scrape against the window, I can hear the tink of her bottle against a glass and almost see her sitting on that rumpled bed, staring out at nothing. I liked rainy days best."

"Why?"

"Men didn't come so often when the weather was bad. They'd stay away where it was warm and dry and drink up all their money, like Rab." She told him how she collected tin cans in the alley and polished them, putting them out to collect the drips from the leaky ceiling. "My own private symphony."

A breeze came up. Michael brushed a wayward strand of hair from her face and tucked it behind her ear. She was quiet, drained; he was pensive. "Come on," he said and stood. He pulled her up and held her hand as they headed home. When they entered the cabin, he rummaged in the utensils drawer. "I'll be back in a while. There's something I want to do in the barn."

She set to work on dinner, needing to keep busy so she wouldn't have to think. Michael was driving nails into the cabin eaves. Was he tearing the place down around her? She stepped to the door while drying her hands and peered out. He was hanging metal scraps, utensils, nails, and a worn horseshoe.

Stepping down a ladder rung, he ran his hand along the line of things. "Your own private symphony," he said and smiled at her. Speechless, she watched him carry the ladder back to the barn.

She went back inside and sat down because she was too weak to stand. She destroyed his dreams, and he made her wind chimes.

When he came in, she served him supper. *I love you, Michael*

*Hosea. I love you so much I'm dying of it.* The breeze stirred the wind chimes, filling the cabin with pleasant ringing. She managed a frail thank-you. He didn't seem to expect more. When he finished eating, she ladled hot water from the big iron pot over the fire to wash dishes.

Michael took her wrist and turned her toward him. "Leave the dishes." When he began to loosen her hair, she could scarcely breathe.

She was trembling and embarrassed. Where was her calm, her control? He was shattering it with tenderness.

Combing his fingers into her hair, he tilted her head back. He saw the fear in her eyes. "I promise to love and cherish you, to honor and sustain you, in sickness and in health, in poverty and in wealth, in the bad that may darken our days, in the good that may light our way. Tirzah, beloved, I promise to be true to you in all things until I die. And even beyond that, God willing."

She stood staring at him, shaken to the core. "And what have I to promise you?"

His eyes lit with gentle humor. "To obey?" He lowered his mouth to hers.

When he kissed her, Angel was lost in a wilderness of new sensations. It had never felt like this, warm and wonderful, exciting and right. None of the old rules applied. She forgot everything she had ever learned from other masters. She was dry ground soaking in a spring rain, a flower bud opening to the sun. Michael knew and gently coaxed her with tender words flowing over her like the sweet balm of Gilead healing her wounds.

And she flew, Michael with her, into the heavens.

Earthbound once more, Michael smiled. "You're crying."

"I am?" She touched her cheek and found a single tear.

"Don't look at me like that," he said, kissing her. "It's a good sign."

But when Michael awakened in the morning, Angel was gone.

# Humility

# Twenty-two

*Because a thing seems difficult for you,
do not think it impossible.*

MARCUS AURELIUS

The jangle of pots and pans on the side of Sam Teal's wagon reminded Angel of the wind chimes Michael had hung for her. Closing her eyes, she could see Michael's face. *Beloved. Oh, beloved.* She couldn't let herself think of him. She had to forget. Better to think of what love had brought Mama and keep her head straight.

The old peddler beside her hadn't stopped talking since he picked her up on the road at dawn. She was thankful for the barrage. He hadn't sold any of his stock on this trip to the mountains. His food supplies were low, and his rheumatism was paining him something fierce. Best thing that had happened to Sam Teal in the last month was seeing a pretty little thing like her sitting on a stump by the road. Sam was clean and trimmed but worn out and bent over. Most of his hair was gone. As were his prospects. But he had kindly eyes beneath gray beetled brows. As long as she listened, she didn't have to think.

"Who you running from, missy?"

She pushed a loose strand of blonde hair back from her face and forced a non-committal smile. "What makes you think I'm running from someone?"

"The way you keep looking back over your shoulder. You looked mighty worried back there when I found you. I figured you must be running away from your husband."

"How did you know I was married?"

"You're wearing a wedding ring."

She covered her hand quickly and blushed. She had forgotten to take the ring off. She turned it on her finger and wondered how she was going to get it back to Michael.

"Did he mistreat you?"

Michael wouldn't think of it. "No," she said dully.

He gave her a curious look. "Must've done something to make you run away."

She looked away. What could she say? *"He made me fall in love with him?"* If she told this old man that Michael had never done anything but treat her with the greatest kindness and consideration, he would start asking questions. "I don't want to talk about it, Mr. Teal." She twisted the ring 'round and 'round her finger and wanted to weep.

"Sam. Call me Sam, missy."

"My name's Angel."

"Just take the ring off and throw it away if it'll make you feel better," he said.

She would never do that. The ring had belonged to Michael's mother. "I can't get it off," she lied. She would have to find a way to send it back to him.

"Were you on your way to Sacramento?"

Sacramento was as good a place as any to start over. "Yes."

"Good. I'm on my way there. I'll be stopping off at a few more mining camps along the way and see if I can't sell some stock." He urged the tired horse on. "You look wore out, missy. Why don't you climb back in my wagon and sleep? Bed folds down from the side," he told her. "Just pull that latch."

She was exhausted and thanked him for the offer. She lowered the bed down and curled up on it, but sleep eluded her. The wagon rolled and bounced along, and her mind spun. She kept thinking about Michael. He wouldn't understand why she left him, and he would be angry. She was so full of confusion. Something inside her tugged at her to go back and talk to Michael, to tell him what she was feeling. She knew that in that lay madness. Hadn't Mama poured out her emotions on Alex Stafford? Hadn't she professed her love over and over again? All love had done was destroy her pride and shame her.

She couldn't stop thinking about last night. Being with Michael had made her feel replete, not empty. She had felt a rightness in Michael's arms, a sense that this was exactly where she belonged.

**Your mother felt the same way about Alex Stafford, and look how that turned out.**

She moaned softly and curled tighter.

If Sam Teal hadn't come by when he did, she might have weakened and gone back. And she would have clung to Michael the same way Mama clung to her father. Sooner or later Michael would tire of her the same way Alex Stafford tired of Mama.

She thought distance would ease the pain, but it kept getting worse. Her mind and body, her very essence, longed for him.

*Why did I ever meet him? Why did he ever come to Pair-a-Dice? Why did he have to be standing on the street when I walked by that day? Why did he come back to the brothel after I drove him away?*

She could see his eyes, full of passion and tenderness. *"I love you,"* he'd said. *"When are you going to understand I'm committed to you?"*

*"He said he loved me,"* Mama had wept. *"He said he'd love me forever."*

Angel could feel the tears building and fought them down. All right. She had fallen in love with Michael and shed a tear, but she had been smart enough to flee before things got too bad. She had brought more this time than just the clothes on her back. She would put it all behind her. She would go east, west, north or south. Whatever she wanted.

"I'll make it," she whispered. "I'll make it on my own."

**Doing what?** A voice mocked.

"Something. I'll find something."

**Sure you will, Angel. Doing what you do best.**

"I'll find some other way to live. I won't go back to that."

**Yes, you will. What else do you know? Was it really so bad? You had food and shelter, beautiful clothes, adoration....**

The dark voice kept cadence with the steady clop of the tired horses on the dusty road. When she slept, she dreamed of Duke again. He was doing all the things he used to do. And Michael wasn't there to stop him.

Sam Teal awakened her. He shared his grub with her and told her he would be coming into a camp soon. "I'm going to give it another try. If I don't sell some of these wares, I'll be busted when I get back to Sacramento. All this gear's on consignment. I don't get a penny if I don't sell something. Maybe the Good Lord'll be with me this time."

He took her empty tin plate, and she watched him take it down and wash it in the creek. The Good Lord hadn't done anything for this poor old man. No more than he'd done for her. Sam Teal gathered his things together and packed them back in the wagon. He was waiting beside it and handed her up as though she were a lady.

"You'd better stay hidden inside," he advised. "Some of these young gents can get pretty woolly when they see a lady." He gave her a wry, apologetic smile. "And I'm too old to fight for you."

She touched his hand and climbed into the back.

When they arrived in the camp, she listened to Sam hawk his wares. Men hooted insults and ridiculed his horse and wagon. They made disparaging remarks about his merchandise. They made worse remarks about him. Sam was dogged. More insults were hurled, and still he kept on, swearing to the quality of what he had to offer. The men were having fun tearing this poor old man down. She could hear in Sam Teal's voice that his last hope was dwindling. She knew how that felt. She knew how the soul could hurt.

"One pan's all anybody needs up here," someone called. Someone called Sam a fool. Angel frowned. Maybe he was one, but he didn't deserve this. All he wanted was to make an honest living.

Angel drew back the curtain and came out. Her appearance silenced the men in the crowd immediately. "What're you doing?" Sam whispered. He looked scared to death. "Go back inside, missy. These gents are *mean*."

"I know," she said. "Let me have that pan, Sam."

"You can't beat them all off."

"Let me have the pan."

"What're you going to do with it?"

"Sell it," she said. She took the pan from his hand. "Sit down, Sam." Nonplussed, he did as she told him. She stepped around him and held the pan up, running her hand over it as though it was an object of great worth. "Gentlemen, Sam knows his merchandise, but he doesn't know anything about cooking." She smiled slightly and saw the grins coming.

Some laughed as though she were making a ribald joke. She talked about chicken and dumplings, fried salt pork and gravy, scrambled eggs and bacon. When they were fairly drooling, she quietly discussed the necessity of having a quality pan to bring about a good meal. She talked of the fine cast iron, the distribution of heat, the easy handling. Sam had said it all before, but this time the men listened raptly.

"Besides all the wonderful meals you can prepare in this pan, it has other uses. When you run out of bullets and need to protect your claim, you have a weapon." She made a mocking swing at a man who was pushing too close. The men laughed. She laughed, too, playing them. "So what do you say, gentlemen? Do I have a buyer?"

"Yes!" Men started pushing forward to get closer to her. They would have bought a dented tin can from her. A fight broke out in the middle. While it was going on, she leaned toward Sam and asked him what his cost was. He named a modest amount. "Oh, I think we can do much better than that," she said and waited for the two brawlers to be separated before she named her price. Someone complained loudly, making the others pause.

Angel smiled and shrugged, her attitude saying that she didn't care whether they bought anything or not. She hung the pan back on the side of the wagon and sat down. "Let's go, Sam. You were wrong about these gentlemen. They don't know quality when they're looking at it."

His mouth was agape. Several men protested. She looked back at them. "You said we're asking too much," she said. "Frankly, I see no sense in trying to talk you into something your own intelligence should tell you is necessary. Sam?" She handed him the reins. A miner held the horse's harness and told her to hold on, he had a pan to buy before she took off.

Angel gave in graciously and sold every pan on the wagon.

The crowd didn't start dispersing until Sam took the reins

and drove down the road out of town. He was grinning and chuckling. "You got a talent for this, missy."

"Well, I've got something," she said dryly. It wasn't so much what you said as how you said it and the look in your eyes as you talked. Selling a frying pan wasn't any different from selling herself. And she knew all about how to do that.

She cooked their evening meal while Sam Teal counted his gold. She served him and then sat down to eat. When she set her plate aside, he tossed her something. She caught it, startled. "What's this?" she asked, holding a leather pouch.

"Your share of what we earned today."

She glanced up in surprise. "But the pans were yours."

"And they'd still be hanging on my wagon if you hadn't spoken up. You need a grubstake. Now you've got one." He took an extra blanket and slept under the wagon.

They headed for Sacramento at first light. They arrived at noon the second day. There was a race going on, and Sam just managed to get his wagon to one side as three riders thundered by. The street filled in after them with wagons and men. Angel could see buildings going up everywhere. The air rained with the sound of hammers and lumber wagons rolling.

"First there was the fire," Sam said as he drew the wagon into the traffic. "Then the flood. Lost most of the buildings down by the river." He snapped the reins. "Have you got family here?" he asked her.

"Friends," Angel prevaricated, pretending interest in the bustling activity.

"Can I take you anywhere in particular?" Sam asked, clearly worrying about her.

"No. Anywhere is fine. I'll find my own way. Sam, don't worry about me. I can take care of myself."

Sam pulled up before a big hardware store. "This is the end of the line for me." He helped her down and shook her hand. "I'm grateful for your company, missy, and for your help at that last camp. I think my traveling days are over. Time I stood behind a counter. Maybe I'll set up shop and find myself some pretty little sales ladies."

Angel wished him luck and made a quick departure. She walked along the boardwalk, stepping around men who lifted their hats to her. She didn't look at anyone, her mind busy trying to figure out what she would do now that she was in Sacramento. She passed a saloon, and the riotous music sent her mind reeling back to the Silver Dollar and the Palace. It seemed a lifetime ago, but the reminder brought it too close for comfort.

She ended up near the river. The irony of it made her smile bitterly. Hadn't Mama ended up on the docks? And here she was gravitating toward the pier with the ships coming in. She watched people coming down the plank and crates being unloaded.

Walking on, she saw buildings going up all along the street, replacing the ones that had been swept away in the flood. A couple of buildings were still in business. One was a big saloon. Angel knew if she walked through those swinging doors, she would be working in one of those upstairs rooms within the hour.

Aimlessly, she continued down the street. What was she going to do? The gold Sam Teal had given her was enough to last a week or two. But what about after that? She needed to find a way to make a living for herself, and the thought of going back to prostitution was unbearable.

*I can't do it anymore. Not after Michael.*

**Michael's just a man like any other.**

*No. Nothing like the rest.*

A tall man with dark hair came out of a store and her heart lurched. It wasn't Michael but another man with his coloring and build. He was laughing with several other men as they crossed the street.

She had to stop thinking about Michael. The first thing she had to do was find a place to stay, but everything she passed looked too rough or too expensive. Her mind kept betraying her and turning back to Michael. What was he doing right now? Was he looking for her, or had he given up and gone back to work in his field? She passed another brothel.

**Go on in, Angel. They'll take care of you. You'll have a room of your own and food.**

Her palms perspired. It was late afternoon and getting cold.

How long had she been wandering? She moved back as a man came out. He looked at her in surprise. "Sorry, ma'am," he said, tipping his hat. He was swaying on his feet. "You shouldn't be standing outside a place like this."

"My husband's inside," she said, grasping at the first thing she could think of to get rid of him.

"Your husband?" He looked her over and shook his head. "What's he doing inside with someone like you at home? What's his name?"

"His name? Oh. It's Charles." As soon as the man went back through the swinging doors, shouting up the stairs for the nonexistent Charles, she hurried on, crossing the street and heading up another. Men stared as she raced past them. She spotted a freshly painted sign: *Hochschild's General Mercantile*, and headed straight for it like a beacon in the darkness.

A heavyset elderly woman came out with a broom and swept the steps and boardwalk. Unsmiling, she worked diligently, swishing dirt onto the street and rapping the broom against the boards. She glanced up when Angel stepped onto the boardwalk. "Men," she muttered with a faint smile. "Can't even use the boot scraper before tracking their mud into the store." Her gaze dropped to the tied bundle in Angel's hand. Angel gave a self-conscious nod and went inside. She looked for Joseph, but he was no where to be seen.

"Can I help you find something?" the woman asked, standing just inside the door, broom held like a rifle at rest.

"Carpetbags," Angel said. "A small one."

"Right over here," the woman said and led her to a shelf against the wall. "This one's nice." She took one and handed it to Angel. Another woman, dark-haired and robust, came out from behind the back curtain and set a box down on a counter. She wiped perspiration from her forehead. "Joseph," she called back, "would you bring out that crate for me, please? I can't lift it."

Angel wished she hadn't come here. Why hadn't she given it a thought before plunging in? Joseph was fond of Michael. What would he say about her running off the way she had? She couldn't expect any help from him. And who were these women with him? Hadn't he said something about his mother coming and bringing him a wife?

"Do you like it?" the woman asked her.

"What?" Angel stammered. She had to get out of here.

"The carpetbag," the woman said, curious now.

"I've changed my mind." She handed it back. Joseph came through the curtain with the crate and saw her immediately. His face split with a wide smile, and she saw his quick glance around the store for Michael. Angel turned quickly and started for the door, bumping into the elderly woman. "Excuse me," she stammered, trying to steady her as she brushed past.

"Angel! Where you going? Wait!"

Angel didn't. Joseph slammed down the crate, swung over the counter, and caught up with her. "Hold up," he said, his hand clamping on her shoulder. "What's going on?"

"Nothing," she said, her face hot. "I just came in to look at a carpetbag."

"So look to your heart's content. Where's Michael?"

She gulped. "Home."

Joseph frowned. "What's happened?"

She tilted her chin. "Nothing's happened."

His mother came to stand with them, the broom still in her hand. "Who is this young woman, Joseph?" She was studying Angel with new and disapproving interest.

"The wife of a friend of mine," he said without looking away from Angel. She wished he would stop probing her with his shrewd eyes. His hand gripped her elbow. "Come over here and sit down and tell me what this is all about." He dispensed with introductions quickly. "My wife, Meribah, and my mother, Rebekkah."

"Would you like some coffee?" Meribah asked, and Joseph said yes she would. He waved his mother off, and she went back to her sweeping, watching them surreptitiously.

"I shouldn't have come here," Angel said flatly.

"Does Michael know where you are?"

"Of course he does," she lied.

"So," he said, a multitude of statements in that one simple

word. He sat down on a barrel, still not letting go of her arm. "You ran out on him, didn't you?"

She pulled her arm free and drew herself up in self-defense. "It wasn't working out."

"No?" He didn't say anything for a long moment. "That's not too unexpected, I guess, but it's a shame."

Her defiance flagged. "Got any ideas what a reformed soiled dove can do for a living in this town?" she asked flippantly and smiled her old, practiced smile. When he frowned, she figured he was probably worrying that she would ask him to give her some money. "Never mind," she said quickly. "A bad joke." She stood. "I'd better be going."

He put his hand on her arm again. "Sit down. Meribah's on her way with the tray." His wife served her a cup of coffee. Angel's hands were shaking as she took it. She tried to steady herself, feeling Joseph's perusal. Meribah offered her some cake. Angel declined. Joseph's mother had finished her sweeping and joined them. Angel wished she hadn't set foot in the place. With the censure of three pairs of eyes, she felt herself withering inside. They talked about the flood, and rebuilding and stocking the store. Though they didn't ask personal questions, she could feel their inquiring looks.

A customer came in, and Meribah went to serve him. Another came in, and Rebekkah, seeing Joseph had no intention of taking care of him, excused herself.

"Have you a room?" he asked.

"Not yet," Angel said. She raised her chin. "But it shouldn't be too hard."

"You're going to stay here," he said. She looked past exhaustion.

"What are your wife and mother going to say to that?" she asked sardonically, unaware of the little-girl-lost look in her eyes.

"They'd wonder more if I sent you off with no place to go. We can't offer you grand accommodations, but we can give you a clean cot and blankets and kosher food. What do you say?"

She chewed on her lip and looked at the two women.

He slapped his hands on his thighs and stood. "They won't

mind." And even if they did, he intended to make sure they kept their reservations to themselves. It was late enough that he could close the store a little earlier than usual.

Angel sat with them at the upstairs dining-room table. She pushed her food around on her plate, pretending to eat but having no appetite. Meribah and Rebekkah didn't ask her any probing questions, but she could feel their deep curiosity. When Meribah cleared the table, Angel rose and helped. Joseph and his mother began talking in low agitated tones as soon as she was through the door. They stopped when she came back in for the rest of the dishes. When she stacked them, she paused.

"I don't have to stay longer than tonight," she said. "If it's going to cause trouble between you, I'll leave first thing in the morning."

"You'll stay as long as Joseph says you will," Rebekkah said in a tone that invited no argument. "He's going to put your cot next to the wood stove downstairs. You'll be warm there."

Joseph set up her cot. He came back upstairs and told Meribah he was going out for a while. He would be back in a few hours. Surprised, Meribah didn't question him. "He never goes out at night," she said as he closed the door behind him. She took up some embroidery.

"Business," Rebekkah said, knitting rapidly.

Angel sat with the two women in the parlor. The only sound in the room was the ticking of the clock on the mantel and Rebekkah's clacking needles.

"If you don't mind, I think I'll go to bed," Angel said at last. Rebekkah nodded approval. Angel closed the door behind her and paused. The two women began talking in earnest. Probably about her. She went downstairs and lay on the cot in the darkness. She slept fitfully, dreaming of Duke.

Rebekkah came down at dawn. Angel awakened and dressed quickly. "You didn't sleep well, did you?" Rebekkah said as she watched her gather her things.

"I was fine. Thank you for letting me stay last night." She folded the blankets away and closed up the cot, tucking it into a narrow space between shelves. She could feel Rebekkah's dark eyes watching her every move.

"Joseph said you're looking for work," Rebekkah said. "We've plenty for you to do around here."

Angel straightened in surprise and faced her. "You're asking me to work for *you*?"

Rebekkah drew herself up. "Unless you have something better in mind."

"Oh, no. I didn't," Angel said quickly. "What would you like me to do?" Rebekkah briskly gave her a list.

Angel washed windows and swept out the store. She stacked canned goods and folded red flannel shirts. She hung tack on the walls. When men approached her, Meribah or Rebekkah intercepted them, answering their questions and showing them merchandise. Rebekkah asked her to carry boxes in from the storeroom and stock the shelves behind the counters. Angel worked hard, stopping for the noon meal and then returning to her labor until Joseph closed and locked the door after dusk.

Rebekkah handed her an envelope over dinner. "Your wages," she said simply, and Angel blinked, feeling her throat close up. She looked at Joseph and Meribah, then back at Rebekkah. Rebekkah nodded at her son. "She's a good worker." Angel hung her head, unable to speak. Rebekkah set a dish of potatoes beside her. "Eat. You need some meat on your bones."

Later that night, Angel sat on her cot, a lantern burning, and counted her earnings. She had made more in a half hour at the Palace, but she had never felt so clean and proud.

The next day Rebekkah asked her to measure out beans into five-pound sacks, then tie and stack them. When she finished, Angel straightened the bolts of fabric and stood them up rather than stack them. Meribah came over and said the display looked very nice and it would be much easier to handle the bolts that way. "Joseph just got a shipment of tubs. Would you help me bring them in? We can stack them in the back corner."

Each day Rebekkah gave her duties to perform, and each evening when the door was locked and the CLOSED sign put out, Rebekkah paid her.

"Look what just arrived," Joseph said, patting a crate.

Angel set her broom aside and tucked several strands of hair beneath the scarf covering her head. "What is it?"

"Michael's stove."

Her heart leaped into her throat at the mention of his name. "I'd better finish sweeping," she said. Joseph watched her for a long moment and then went back to his own work.

Angel was distracted at dinner. As soon as the dishes were cleared and washed, she excused herself. Meribah came downstairs a short time later. "Joseph and Rebekkah are going over the accounts," she said. She hesitated. "You hardly ate anything at dinner. Are you feeling well?"

"I'm fine." Angel couldn't stop thinking about Michael. As long as she was moving and working, she could hold the longing at bay. She looked at the big crate against the wall. Word would have to be sent, and then Michael would come and get his stove.

*I'll have to leave before he comes.*

Meribah sat on a box and warmed her hands near the Franklin stove. "You're thinking about leaving, aren't you?"

Angel glanced up. "Yes."

"You're not happy with the work?"

"It's not the work. It's..." What could she say? Sighing, she nodded toward the big crate. "Michael's stove. He'll come for it soon."

"And you don't want to see him?"

"I can't."

"Was it so terrible?"

It was so wonderful. Too wonderful to last. "It's just better if I don't."

"Where will you go?"

She shrugged. "San Francisco. I don't know. It doesn't matter."

Meribah folded her hands in her lap. "Joseph thinks a great deal of your husband."

Angel nodded and looked away. "I know." Just his name roused so many feelings inside her. She thought the longing would diminish. She thought distance would dissolve her feelings for him. She had been away from him for three weeks, and she ached for him more now than she had the night she left.

"I was married once before," Meribah said. "To a very difficult man. My mother died when I was young, and Papa wanted me well settled before his time came. So he picked a man who, for all outward appearances, was prosperous and kind. My husband was neither. I used to pray that God would deliver me from him. And he did." She paused. "Then I learned how cruel life can treat a woman alone."

"I've been alone all my life," Angel said simply.

"If your husband is even half the man Joseph thinks he is, you should go back and work things out with him."

Angel retreated. "Don't 'should' on me," she said defensively. "You don't know anything about my life or where I've been." Meribah was silent for a long moment, and Angel regretted her harshness.

"You're right," Meribah said finally. "I don't know all the circumstances, but I do know the little Joseph told me."

"What did he tell you?" Angel said, hearing the brittle tone in her voice but unable to ease it.

Troubled, Meribah looked at her sadly. "That your husband took you out of a brothel. He fell in love with you the first time he saw you and probably loves you still."

Her words sent a shaft of pain through Angel. "Love doesn't last." She didn't know how much showed in her pale face.

Meribah's face softened. "Sometimes it does. If it's the right kind."

Angel lay in the darkness after Meribah left and worked over what she had said. Mama had worked to keep Alex Stafford's love alive. She had tried everything to please him and keep his passion alive. Angel wondered now if it hadn't been those very efforts that served to drive him away. Mama had been so hungry for his love. Her entire life had revolved around Alex Stafford's coming to the small cottage. Her happiness depended solely on him. It had been an obsession.

How was what she was feeling for Michael any different? She couldn't stop thinking about him. Her heart longed to be near him, to hear his voice, to see his eyes light up when he looked at her. Her body ached for him, for his warmth and his touch. Her emotions were in turmoil.

She told Joseph in the morning that she was leaving. "You can't go," he said, clearly very upset with her. "Meribah hurt her back last night. Didn't you, Meribah?" Meribah looked confused. "You can admit it," he told her. She spread her hands. "See?" Joseph said. "And I've got a shipment out back. I can't get it all out on the tables by myself."

"All right, Joseph," Angel gave in, "but as soon as that's done, I have to leave."

She set to work immediately, in a hurry to finish the project and be on her way. Joseph kept telling her to take it easy, he didn't need another woman with a pulled back. When they stopped for dinner, he poked over his food for so long, Angel was exasperated. When she got up to go back to work, he told her to sit down and finish her coffee. If he was in such a dither about getting his merchandise out, why was he wasting so much time? And nothing seemed wrong with Meribah's back when she rose and took the heavy platter from the table.

When they set back to work, he said he changed his mind about where he had put some lanterns and wanted to move them to the other side of the store. The merchandise on the table he chose had to be moved, too. She did as he said, feeling more and more tense as the day went on.

**Get out of here, Angel. Go. Now.**

But she stayed, working with Joseph, wanting to finish what they had started, even if he was changing his mind every half-hour. What was wrong with him today?

Joseph laid his hand on her shoulder. "That'll do for the day. Why don't you close up?"

"It's early, isn't it?"

"Late enough," he said and smiled. He signaled for Meribah and his mother to come, and they went through the back curtain together. Frowning, Angel turned.

Michael was standing in the open doorway.

# Twenty-three

*You are all fair, my love;*
*there is no flaw in you.*

SONG OF SOLOMON 4:7

Angel froze in shock as Michael walked toward her. He was covered with road dust, his face lined and grim. "Joseph sent word you were here."

Her heart was galloping. "Why did you come?"

"To take you home."

She backed away from him. "I don't want to go back," she said, wanting to sound firm and indifferent and sounding neither as her voice shook.

He kept coming. She bumped into a table of boots, sending several thudding to the floor. "I knew you wouldn't go back to Pair-a-Dice," he said.

She gripped the table behind her for support and stood her ground. "What made you so sure?" she mocked. He didn't answer. She couldn't read the look in his eyes. When he reached out, she held her breath. He touched her cheek tentatively, and she pressed her lips tightly together to keep them from trembling.

"I just knew, Amanda."

Unable to bear the rush of emotions, she pushed past him frantically. "You don't even know why I left you."

Michael caught hold of her and swung her around. "Oh, yes, I do!" He pulled her into his arms. "You left because of this." He covered her mouth with his. When she tried to push free, he cupped the back of her head. She struggled harder as the betraying warmth stole over her.

When she stilled finally, Michael slipped the bandanna off her hair. Pulling the ribbon loose, he raked his fingers into her hair and tipped her head back. She could feel the fierce pounding of his heart beneath her palms.

"That was it, wasn't it?" he said hoarsely. Ashamed, she tried to turn away, but he wouldn't let her. "*Wasn't* it?"

"I don't want to feel this way," she whispered brokenly.

Someone cleared his throat. "Is the store still open?"

Michael turned, his hands sliding down her arms. He squeezed her hands gently before releasing her. "No, it's not. Sorry." He crossed the room and politely showed the prospective customer out the door. He closed it firmly after him, set the lock, and flipped over the sign in the window.

When Michael turned, he saw Amanda at the back of the store. She stooped over for something near the Franklin stove. He followed and saw she had a carpetbag and was gathering her few things together. His mouth tipped. "We'll go home in the morning."

She wouldn't look at him. "You go home. I'm going to San Francisco."

He clenched his teeth, striving for patience. Her face was so white and strained. When he tried to touch her again, she moved quickly, putting a barrel between them. She was stuffing her clothes into the bag frantically. "You're in love with me," he said. "Do you think you can run away from that?"

At the words, Angel froze, her head down, her hands gripping the bag tightly. She was shaking violently; the effect he had on her was shattering. She began stuffing her clothes into the bag again. The sooner she got away from him the better. She was trying to stuff her feelings in along with them. "I told you I would never let myself fall in love with anyone, and I meant it!"

"But miracle of miracles, you did, didn't you?" he said, as determined and relentless as ever.

"Go away, Michael."

"Not a chance."

"Just leave me alone!" She rolled up the last skirt and jammed it in with the rest of her things. She snapped the bag shut and glared up at him. "You want to know what love feels like to me? It feels like you're ripping my heart out."

His eyes flashed. "It started feeling that way when you *left*. Not when you were with me." She tried to move past him, and he blocked her way. "I saw the way you started looking at me, Amanda. I felt the way you responded that last night. I felt it all the way through me."

"And it gave you a sense of power, didn't it? *Didn't it?*"

"Yes!" he admitted roughly and caught her arm when she would have retreated to the back door. "But it's not a power I'm going to use against you."

"You're right," she said, trying to tug free. "I'm not going to give you the chance!"

He yanked the bag from her hand and sent it bouncing off the back wall. "I'm not your father! I'm not Duke! I'm not some gent paying for half an hour in your bed!" His hands tightened on her arms. "I'm your *husband*! I don't take what you feel lightly. I love you. You're my wife!"

Biting her lip, Angel forced the tears back.

Michael gentled. He cupped her face so she couldn't look away from him and saw her heartbreaking struggle against her emotions. Emotion had always been her enemy. She couldn't allow herself to feel if she were going to survive. He understood that, but he had to make her see that it wasn't an enemy anymore.

"Amanda, I knew the day I saw you that you belonged with me."

"Do you know how many times men have said that to me?" she said, wanting to drive him away.

He went on doggedly as though her words hadn't stabbed at him. "I've loved watching you grow and change. You're never the same. I love the way you take on new things, your drive to learn. I love how you work, how you have this little-girl look on your face when you finish something you've never tried before. I love watching you skip across the meadow with Ruth. I love seeing you laugh with Miriam and hang on Elizabeth's wisdom. I love the whole idea of growing old with you and waking up to you every morning for the rest of my life."

"Don't," she whispered brokenly.

"I haven't even started." He shook her tenderly. "Amanda, I loved giving you pleasure. I loved feeling you melt. I loved hearing you say my name." She blushed, and he kissed her. "Love cleanses, beloved. It doesn't beat you down. It doesn't cast blame." He kissed her again, wishing he had the right words to say what he felt. Words would never be enough to show her what he meant. "My love isn't a weapon. It's a lifeline. Reach out and take hold, and don't let go."

When he drew her into his arms this time, she didn't struggle. When she put her arms around him, he sighed, the stress of the past weeks dissolving. "This feels good, doesn't it? And right."

"I couldn't stop thinking about you," she said miserably, pressing closer, inhaling the sweet scent of his body. She had missed this feeling of safety that only came when she was with him. He was so determined to have her. Well, why not let him? Wasn't it what she wanted? To belong to him. To stay with him forever. Wasn't this what she had longed for every moment since she had left him?

"You make me hope, Michael. I don't know if that's good or not."

"It's good," he said, holding her close and rejoicing at her admission. It was a beginning.

They left at first light. Angel rode behind Michael, her hands tucked securely into his belt. He said little other than to ask how she'd made it to Sacramento. She told him in detail about old Sam Teal and his hard luck. He laughed when she told him about selling the pans at the mining camp. She laughed, too. "I didn't think I'd be good at anything."

"I'll let you handle business with Joseph next time we bring in a shipment of produce."

"Joseph's a different matter altogether. He wouldn't be so easily blinded."

"He likes you, you know."

"He does?" She was oddly pleased. "I thought he let me stay as a favor to you."

"Partly. He said he knew God had his hand on you when you walked in the door that day."

Angel didn't answer. She didn't think God had his hand on anything that had to do with her. He had washed his hands of her long ago. She slid her arms around Michael's waist and leaned her head against his strong, broad back. She was perilously close to crying. Shaking, she fought a nebulous fear gnawing at her. Michael sensed it but waited until they stopped for a rest to talk about it.

Dismounting, he lifted her down from the horse. Tipping her chin, he searched her eyes. "What is it, Amanda?"

"It was pure luck that I found Joseph when I did, Michael."

Michael knew it was far more than that, but telling her wouldn't make her believe it.

Angel didn't want to think of what might have happened if she hadn't found the storekeeper. She was so weak. It was a loathsome thing to face about herself. One day on her own, and she would have walked back into a brothel. One day. Maybe not even that long. "You saved me again," she said, striving for lightness. Embarrassed by her vulnerability, she looked away.

Michael tipped her face back. Oh, his eyes. So full of hope. So full of love. "I'm only a tool, beloved. Not your Savior."

When he took her in his arms, she went willingly. They remained until dusk and rode the rest of the way home in moonlight.

Michael set to work on the fields, making the final preparations before planting. Angel helped by toting stones and breaking up clods in the grainfields. When the day came to plant, Michael loaded the seed and Angel onto the back of the wagon. He told her how to sow the wheat, then drove back and forth over the ground. She cast the seed, doubtful anything would come of it.

Planting the corn was more work. Michael trapped fish and chopped them into large chunks to be buried with the kernels. It took from dawn to dusk to get the field planted, but when she looked out at the rich ground, she felt satisfied. The next morning, she saw a flock of birds in the wheat field. Dropping the water bucket, she ran into the field to chase them away.

Laughing, Michael rested his arms on the corral fence he was fixing and watched. "What are you doing?"

"Michael, those horrible birds! What are we going to do? They're eating every seed we planted." She threw a clod at another bird, and it fluttered off, perching in a nearby tree.

"Just leave them be. They won't take more than their share."

She marched back. "Their share? Why should they have any?"

"In fair payment. They're the guardians of the land." He pointed. "The swallows, swifts, and hawks guard the air, filling themselves on insects that would otherwise overload it. The woodpeckers, creepers, and chickadees feed on the grubs and beetles that would destroy our trees. The warblers and flycatchers feed on insects that attack the leaves. Grouse and prairie hens eat the grasshoppers that would devour our crops."

"What are those pecking out there?"

He laughed. "Blackbirds."

"Well, they're good for nothing, aren't they?"

"They guard the surface of the soil, along with the help of crows, thrushes, and larks. Snipes and woodcocks eat the bugs that burrow under the surface." He tugged her braid lightly. "Spare the birds, Amanda, or we'll lose our crops. Besides, I've got other things for you to do." He swung over the fence and swept her up in his arms.

"Michael, what if it doesn't rain?"

"It will."

"How do you know it will?"

He set her on her feet again. "You're worrying about things you can't control. Just take things one day at a time."

It did rain in the weeks that came, softly moistening the earth. "Michael, come and see!" Green sprouts came up, and Angel walked up and down the corn rows with uncontainable excitement. The plants were so small and fragile. One hot day would wither them, but Michael didn't worry. He repaired the corral fence, finished building the springhouse, and went hunting. He shot a buck and showed her how to dress it. They hung the meat in the smokehouse.

Sometimes, when Angel least expected it, Michael would find her at her chores. "Let's find a nice place in the sun," he'd whisper, putting his arms around her. "Come away with me and be my love."

They were lying in the hayloft one day when Angel heard

Miriam calling. "Oh!" she said, mortified. Michael laughed, caught her around the waist, and threw her playfully back into the hay. "Where you going?"

"What's she going to think? You and me up here in the middle of the day?"

"Maybe she'll think we're pitching hay."

"Miriam is a very bright girl."

He grinned. "Well, then maybe she'll go away."

"No, she won't." She jumped up and plucked hay from her hair.

"Tell her I'm out hunting and you were taking a nap," he said, getting up and kissing the nape of her neck. Blushing, she pushed him away.

Miriam came into the barn and saw Angel descending the ladder. "Oh, there you are."

"I was just napping," Angel said, flustered and pushing wisps of hair back.

Miriam's eyes twinkled. "Your fields are planted, too, I see."

Angel cleared her throat. "Yes."

"And growing nicely."

"Shall we go into the cabin? I'll fix some coffee."

"That sounds nice," Miriam said and burst out laughing. "Michael! Papa wants you and Mandy to come for dinner. We're going to celebrate our first planting."

Michael's answering laughter drifted down from the loft. "Tell him we'd love to."

Miriam took Angel's hand as they left the barn. "Mama's always flushed when she comes back from a long walk with Papa," she said. "The way you are right now."

Angel blushed. "You shouldn't talk about it so freely."

Miriam pulled Angel to a stop and hugged her hard. "I've missed you so much!"

Angel hugged her back, her throat tight. "I missed you, too."

Miriam drew back, eyes flooding. "Well! That wasn't so hard to admit, was it?" She looked very pleased.

The Altmans' own planting was finished, and Miriam said

she had more time for herself. The children were fine. They had seen Paul several times. He helped them dig their new well.

"Let's take our coffee outside and sit under that apple tree," Miriam said. Michael was chopping wood. Angel called out, asking if he wanted coffee, but he called back no.

"Mama's in a family way," Miriam said as they made themselves comfortable in the shade. "She always blooms when a baby's coming."

"How's your father taking it?" Angel asked, thinking of her own.

"Oh, he's very smug," Miriam said. She smiled impishly. "Are you and Michael working on a family?"

The question sent a sharp pang through Angel. She shrugged and looked away.

Miriam took Angel's hand. "Why did you leave? We were all so worried."

"I can't explain," Angel said.

"Can't or won't? Do you even know the reason yourself?"

"Partly." She wouldn't explain further. How could she and make this naive girl understand? She was so open, so free. Angel wished she could be like her.

"We never told Ruthie," Miriam said. "We just said you and Michael were very busy and we couldn't come for a while."

"Thank you," Angel said. She watched Michael stacking firewood, her heart aching.

Miriam smiled. "You're terribly in love with him, aren't you?"

"Terribly. I'm consumed with it. Sometimes he only has to look at me — " She stopped, realizing she was speaking her most private thoughts aloud.

Miriam looked at her. "Isn't that as it should be?"

"I don't know. Is it?"

"I hope so," Miriam said dreamily. "Oh, I really hope so."

Miriam brought Ruth the next time. Angel left her gardening when she saw the child racing down the flower-strewn hillside. Dashing the dirt from her hands, she came through the gate and took a couple of running steps to meet the child.

"Mandy! Mandy!" Ruthie cried joyously, and Angel swept her up in her arms and hugged her.

"Hello, darling," she said huskily, kissing the child on both cheeks and her nose. "Have you been a good girl since I saw you last?"

"Yes!" Ruth said, squeezing Angel around the neck again as though she had no intention of ever letting go. "Why did you run away? You were gone so long. Paul said you always run away and Michael just keeps going and finding you and getting you back again. He said Michael's a fool because you like your old life better than being a farmer's wife. What's your old life, Mandy? I don't want you to go back to it. I want you to stay *here*."

Angel set her down very slowly. Her stomach had dropped as soon as Ruth began parroting what she had obviously overheard. *We didn't tell Ruthie.* She couldn't look at Miriam when she came up to them.

"What's the matter?" Miriam asked. When Angel didn't speak, she looked at her baby sister. "What have you been saying?"

Angel touched Ruthie's dark head tenderly. "I love being a farmer's wife," she said very quietly, "and I don't want to go back to my old life."

Miriam's mouth fell open, and her face went dark red.

Ruthie nodded and hugged her around the legs. Angel looked at Miriam coldly.

"What's she been saying to you?" Miriam asked.

"Just what she's heard."

"Ruthie. Just what did you hear?"

"You and Paul," she said, muffled against Angel's skirt.

"Never mind," Angel said bleakly. "Just leave her alone, Miriam."

"I will not! You were eavesdropping, weren't you?" Miriam said, arms akimbo as she stared down at her little sister.

Ruthie peered at her. "Mama sent me." Her lower lip protruded. "She wanted me to fetch you."

"When was this?"

"When Paul was over. She said you were gone too long and she wanted you to come into the cabin."

Miriam blushed furiously. "And?"

"He was talking, and you were mad. I could tell 'cause you got all red in the face like it is now. You told him to take his stories home with him, and he said — "

Angel put a shaking hand to her brow, her face very pale.

"Never mind," Miriam said quickly, silencing her sister. She looked up, tears in her eyes. "Amanda..."

Angel shrugged, trembling.

Miriam pulled Ruthie away and gave her a light pat on the bottom. "Go say hello to Michael, Ruthie."

Ruthie chewed on her lower lip, tears building in her eyes. "You're not mad at me?"

She bent down. "I forgive you, now go on." She kissed her little sister. "We'll talk about it later, punkin. Go see Michael." When Ruthie reached Michael, he swung her up onto the fence.

"I'm sorry." Miriam was distressed. "Say *something*, Amanda. Don't look like that."

What was there to say? "Would you like some coffee?"

"*No*, I don't want any coffee." When Angel started walking toward the cabin, Miriam fell into step beside her. "I was not gossiping about you. I swear it."

"Neither was Paul," Angel said. "He was just telling you the way he sees things."

"How can you defend him?"

"I've hurt Michael more than once, and Paul knows it."

"That doesn't mean you'll hurt him again."

"It doesn't mean I won't."

Miriam and Ruthie stayed most of the afternoon, and all the while Angel couldn't get it out of her mind. Could she change? Was she different just because Michael loved her? Or was this just the quiet before the real storm?

Michael knew something was wrong. A month of blissful happiness and he could feel her drawing away from him again. He was afraid. Lord, don't let her pull away from me again. Help me hold onto her.

"Come here," he said, putting a blanket before the fireplace.

She came willingly enough, but there was something somber and secret in her eyes. What was tormenting her?

Angel leaned back against the solid comfort of Michael's broad, muscular chest. She loved his hands on her.

"What's wrong?" he asked, nuzzling her neck. "Something's been eating at you all evening. Did Miriam or Ruth say something to upset you?"

"Not on purpose." She didn't want to tell him about Paul. She didn't want to tell him how much words hurt. She had denied their power all her life, but each name cut. "It's just that I'm so happy," she said, her voice shaking. "I can't get over feeling that I don't deserve this."

"And you think I do?"

"What have you ever done to be ashamed of in your life, Michael? Not a blessed thing."

"I've committed murder." He felt the shock go through her at his admission. She drew away from him and turned, eyes wide.

"You?"

"A hundred times. When I came back for you the first time and saw what Magowan had done to you. And Duke. I've killed him a hundred times in a hundred ways, each worse than the last."

She relaxed, understanding. "Thinking about doing something wrong isn't the same thing as doing it."

"Isn't it? Where's the real difference? The same desire is there, feeding on itself and me." He tugged her braid lightly. "Don't you see? Neither of us *deserves* this. It's got nothing to do with whether we do or not. Every blessing comes down from the Father, not in payment for good done, but as a gift."

Michael saw that her eyes flickered at his first mention of God. He felt her growing resistance. *God*, the foul word. God, the being that had no meaning in her life other than retribution for sins committed, some not her own. She believed God was wrath and that he would continually punish her for living a life she was forced into by a seedy old drunk who didn't know what he was doing. God was unmerciful and enjoyed inflicting pain.

How could he make her see that God the Father was the only escape she had from living in hell when the only father she had ever known had wanted her ripped out of her mother's womb and thrown away?

"Show me this Father of yours, Michael," she said, unable to keep the edge out of her voice.

"I am," Michael said quietly.

"Where? I don't see him. Maybe if he stood before me, I'd believe he existed." And she could spit in his face for everything that happened to her and her mother.

"He's in me. I'm showing him to you every hour of every day, the only way I know how." And clearly not doing a good enough job.

She saw she had hurt him and softened. He was so sincere. And he loved her so much. She loved him, too, though she had fought so hard against it. He had made her love him just by being Michael. But that had nothing whatsoever to do with God. Did it?

"Love isn't enough," she said, touching his beloved face. "If it was, I should have been enough for my mother, but I wasn't. I won't be enough for you, either."

"No, you won't. And I won't be enough for you, Amanda. I don't want to be the center of your life. I want to be part of it. I want to be your husband, not your god. People can't always be there for you, no matter how much they want to be. And that includes me."

"And God is?" she said derisively. "God was *never* there for me." She moved out of his embrace and stood, retreating to the bed. He watched her loosen her hair. She looked at him and went very still. "I'm glad you like blondes," she said mildly.

She wasn't going to put him off that easily. "Your looks may have had a little to do with why I first noticed you," he admitted, standing up. He tossed the blanket over the back of the chair.

"Only a little?" she said without conceit. Until Michael, she had always looked upon herself as fodder for a man's lust.

"A little," he repeated firmly. When she raised her eyes, he gave her a solemn look that belied his mood. "Actually, I think it was your even temper, your willingness to adjust to my way of life, your constant desire to please me...." He crossed the room as he spoke and sat on the bed beside her as she laughed.

Her defenses dropped at his disarming smile. "So," she said, "you're just another bloke who rises to a challenge." Her smile faded even as the words came from her lips. Why did everything she say have to brand her with her past? She looked away again and continued to unbraid her hair. His hand rested comfortingly on her thigh. Even that light touch made her melt inside. "What do you feel now that I'm soft clay in your hands, Michael?"

"Joy," he said. "Pure joy." He saw how the pulse raced in her throat and pressed a kiss to it. He heard her soft intake of breath and felt the answering warmth spread swiftly through him. He wanted her. He would always want her. And, praise God, she wanted him as well. He felt it every time he touched her.

"Beloved," he whispered, feeling an overwhelming tenderness at the look of uncertainty in her blue eyes, "if anyone knew how or why people fall in love with one another, they'd bottle and sell it off to one of those traveling medicine wagons. It wasn't how you looked. It isn't that you smell and taste so good to me now. You know it isn't," he said, kissing her.

"It's part of it," she said with a sigh.

"God knows that's true, but it's something beyond just that. Something unseen. You cried out to me that day when you walked by, and I couldn't do anything else but answer."

"So you said before."

"And you still don't believe me."

"Oh, Michael. Life's done things to me. I'm so full of..." she paused, swallowing hard and pressing her lips tightly together, looking past him, unable to look into his eyes.

"Of what?" He stroked the tendrils of hair back from her temples.

"Shame," she managed thickly. Her eyes burned, and she struggled to push the emotions down again. She couldn't give in to tears, not even one, but she wanted him to know how she felt. "I don't know what I did wrong. I never knew, but I understood from the earliest time I can remember that I was never going to be good enough to deserve a decent life." And that her very presence took away the decency of others. Would it take away Michael's eventually as well? She couldn't bear the thought of that happening to him.

"So how do you explain this?"

She reached up and touched his face. "I don't. I can't. I just know it'll never last."

Michael's eyes filled with tears. She broke his heart. She always had. "I've never turned away from you. Nor will I ever. It's always been the other way around."

"I know, but if I gave you everything I had, it wouldn't be enough. I don't have enough for a man like you."

He took her hand and pressed it hard against his heart. "Then take what you lack from me. Let what I have make the difference."

Her heart was so full she hurt. "You're so beautiful," she whispered tremulously. How could she, of all women, be loved so much by a man like this? *Oh, God, if you are there listening, why did you do this to him?*

**For you, beloved.**

A shiver went through her body, and she felt the hair rise over her head.

*Not for me. Never for me.* She closed her mind tightly to the still, quiet voice.

"What is it?" Michael asked, seeing her sudden pallor.

He was so handsome, but she was drawn to him for something other than that. Maybe it was as he said. Something unseen. There was something inside him that drew her like a moth to flame, but it was a flame that didn't scorch or destroy. It lit something deep inside her so that she felt she was becoming part of him. He gave her life meaning. It wasn't a matter of survival anymore. It was something else she couldn't even yet define or understand, and yet it kept beckoning to her.

**And what of Paul, Angel?**

A frown flickered across her brow. Michael lay beside her and tipped her chin toward him. "Tell me."

She marveled at how he was sensitive to her every thought, but could she reveal this without driving the wedge in further between him and his friend? Paul wasn't wrong about her. He saw her as the rest of the world must, as a woman who sold her body for money and nothing more.

She shook her head. Michael kissed her as though he wanted to give her his hope. "I wish I could change things," she said sadly when he raised his head to search her eyes. "I wish I had come to you clean and whole."

"So that I would love you more than I do now?" he asked with a tender smile.

*So that I might be worthy of you.* She drew his head down and kissed him. "I can give you pleasure."

"You please me just as you are."

She wanted more than anything to please him in all ways.

**Remember all I taught you, Angel,** Duke's voice came unbidden. **Use it and use him.**

When Michael smiled at her, the dark voice lost its power. "No barriers," Michael said. "Nothing between us."

So Angel gave herself up. She had no thought for anything but Michael. She had always thought a man's body ugly. Michael was beautiful, and she worshiped him.

Michael rejoiced in her. "You're like the earth…the Sierras, the fertile valley, and the sea." He drew her up so they were sitting cross-legged on the bed, facing one another. She didn't know what he had in mind until he took her hands and bowed his head. He prayed aloud, giving thanks for the pleasure they had taken in one another.

Angel's heart hammered violently. What was his God going to think of *this*? When Michael finished praying, he smiled at her, the glow in his eyes easing her fear.

"No lightning, beloved," he said, understanding. "*All* good things come down from the Father. Even this." He lay back and drew her to him, holding her close until they both slept.

# Twenty-four

*For I tell you, unless your righteousness exceeds that of the scribes and Pharisees, you will never enter the kingdom of heaven.*

JESUS, MATTHEW 5:20

Paul sat brooding before his fireplace, a jug in his lap and his wedding picture in his hand. Tessie had been gone two years now, and he wanted to keep her memory alive. He didn't want to forget what she looked like. But lately, until he held the picture, all he could remember was that she was dark and had Michael's smile. He tried to remember what her skin felt like and how her voice sounded, but it was all fading away, all except the sweet memory of what they had shared so briefly. The empty, aching loneliness she had left behind was all that remained firm. Laying the picture aside, Paul drew long on the whiskey. Leaning his head back, he closed his eyes wearily. He hadn't seen Michael since he had come and asked him to help him find Angel. He couldn't forget that day or his own regret.

"She's run off again?"

"Yes. I have to find her."

"Let her go. You're better off without a woman like her."

Michael's eyes blazed. "When are you going to open your eyes?"

"When are *you*?" Paul shot back. "If she loved you, don't you think she'd stay? You wouldn't be able to drive her out. Michael, when are you going to see what she is?" When Michael turned his horse away, his anger had erupted. "Look for her in a bordello. Isn't that where you found her in the first place?" Swearing, he'd gone back to turning the soil with his spade, and he hadn't been able to get rid of the fallow feeling in his heart since. Not even when Michael had come back.

It was clear he hadn't found any trace of Angel. He had pitied Michael then. He wasn't sorry Michael hadn't found Angel.

He was sorry Michael was torn up about losing her. She wasn't worth grieving over.

"She does love me, Paul. She does. You just don't understand her."

Paul left it alone. He didn't want to know any more about Angel than he already did. One day in her company had been enough to sour his soul for a lifetime.

Michael stayed, and they talked about crops and the land, but it wasn't the same as it had been before Angel came into their lives. It didn't matter whether she was gone or not. She was still between them. "You're making progress," Michael said before leaving. "That field looks good."

"The work would go faster with a horse. Too bad I lost mine on the trail."

"Take this one." He took off the saddle while Paul stood dumbfounded. "As soon as your crops are in you'll have enough to buy another." Ashamed, Paul couldn't speak past the lump in his throat. Michael shouldered the saddle. "You'd do the same for me, wouldn't you, Paul?" He headed for home.

A few days later, Paul took a side of venison to the Altmans and learned Michael was on his way to Sacramento to bring Angel home. Joseph had sent word she was working in a general mercantile. A likely story. He'd bet everything she was selling herself to wintering miners. Six ounces of gold for fifteen minutes. Maybe more than that to make up for the time lost on Michael.

"You don't look very happy about the news," Miriam said, watching him closely.

"I'm sure Michael's happy," he said and went for his horse. "He's a fool," he muttered under his breath.

Miriam followed him. "He loves her very much."

"Is that what you call it?"

"What would you call it?"

He glanced back at Miriam as he slung the reins over the horse's head, but he didn't answer.

"Why don't you like Amanda?" Miriam asked.

Paul almost blurted out that her name wasn't Amanda. It was

*Angel*, and she was anything but that, but he kept his tongue. "I've got my reasons," he said. The saddle creaked as he mounted.

"You were in love with her, weren't you?" she said flatly.

Paul gave a harsh laugh, his grip tightening on the reins. "Did she tell you that?"

"No. I guessed."

"Well, you guessed wrong, little Miriam." He turned his horse before she could ask more questions.

Taking a step, she called after him, "Don't call me little Miriam! I'm sixteen years old."

He didn't need the reminder. Mocking her, he tipped his hat. "Good day, ma'am," he drawled and rode away.

She came over the next morning to invite him to dinner. "Venison steaks," she said, "and Mama is baking apple pie." She was wearing a pretty yellow dress that made him notice the slender curves of her young body. She noticed the direction of his gaze and blushed. Miriam's dark eyes had a velvety glow to them. "Well?" she said.

"Well, what?" he said uneasily.

Her mouth curved. "Will you come this afternoon?"

She had an enticing smile. Dismayed, he was terse. "No," he said and nodded toward the unplowed section of field. "I'll be working through until dusk." He clicked to the horse and pushed down hard on the plow, hoping she would take the hint and leave. Had he known she was coming over, he would have put a shirt on. As it was, he was stripped to the waist and had a dusty neckerchief tied around his forehead to keep the sweat out of his eyes. A fine sight he was for an innocent young girl.

Paul couldn't get it out of his head that if Miriam Altman had come along a few months earlier, Michael wouldn't be in the mess he was. Miriam was just right for Michael. If that harlot ran off again, which she undoubtedly would, maybe Michael would come to see it, too. This girl would come to his marriage bed a virgin and stay faithful to him to death. She wasn't the kind to cause a man grief. She would give him the children he wanted and make him happy.

"You have to eat sometime," Miriam said, walking beside him.

He didn't look at her. The less he looked at her the better.

"Papa and Mama would like to thank you."

"They said their thanks yesterday. Tell them they're welcome."

"Don't you like children?"

"Children?" he said, lost. "I like children well enough. What's that got to do with anything?"

"I just thought you didn't want to come to dinner because there are so many of us."

She walked with her hands loosely clasped behind her. His gaze swept her body and his mouth went dry.

"What was your wife like, Paul?"

The question took him off guard. "Sweet. She was very sweet."

"Was she tall?"

"About your size." Tessie had been smaller, and she'd had light brown hair rather than luxuriant black. And her eyes. He couldn't remember what color Tessie's eyes were when he looked into the deep, soft brown of Miriam's.

"Was she pretty?"

He looked at Miriam, and his heart raced.

"Your wife," she said. "Was she pretty?"

He tried to remember Tessie's face and couldn't. Not with Miriam staring at him the way she was. Her shy fascination with his body gave him a growing panic. "She was *very* pretty," he said and pulled the horse to an abrupt halt. "I think you'd better go home. I'm sure your mother's wondering why you're taking so long."

Miriam's face went red. "I'm sorry," she stammered. "I did-n't mean to keep you. Maybe you'll come for dinner another time." He saw her quick tears as she turned and hurried away. He almost reached out to her but stopped himself just in time. He clenched his hand and watched her go, an ache in the pit of his stomach. He hadn't meant to be cruel, but if he apologized, she might stay, and she was altogether too tempting for that.

Paul never expected her to come back.

He was washing at the well when he saw her coming across a grassy field. His heart jumped. Her younger sister Leah was with her this time. He pulled his shirt on and buttoned it while waiting for them to reach him and tell him what they wanted.

"Mama sent me," Miriam said apologetically. Her eyes barely touched his. She held out the basket she was carrying.

"Thanks," he said roughly, taking it. His hand lightly brushed hers, and her eyes came up. "She needn't have bothered," he said.

"Oh, it was Miriam's idea," Leah said, mortifying her older sister further.

"*Hush*, Leah," Miriam said, blushing. She took her sister's hand. "We'd better go. Enjoy your dinner, Paul."

Paul watched the gentle sway of her hips. *I've got no right to be feeling this way about a girl like her.* "Tell your mother I'll bring the basket over."

"No hurry," Miriam called back. "I'll come get it tomorrow."

That was exactly what he didn't want her to do. He would ride over at first light and leave the basket at their door. He put it down and brought up another bucket of cold water. Dousing his face, he cooled himself down. He was in bad shape when just looking at a pretty, sixteen-year-old girl made him feel this way. He ought to ride to the nearest camp and stop in at the local brothel. The very idea sickened him.

He took Miriam's basket into the cabin. The grate was cold. He lit a fire and ate. He was feeling the same emptiness he had when Tessie died. Those first months without her had been bad, but he had had the struggle to survive the Sierras to occupy his mind. When he and Michael reached this land, he poured himself into building the cabin. Then the grief had struck hard. The fierce pain of loss had been too much. He couldn't look out at the fields of wildflowers without thinking about how much Tessie would have loved it. Their own land in California had been a shared dream. It was empty and meaningless without her.

When the gold rush hit, he was ready to leave. In the beginning, he had lost himself in the excitement of working the streams, the chance of getting rich just beyond his reach. The excitement quickly wore off. Life narrowed down again to dawn-to-dusk labor. All he made was enough for food and a day in town to get drunk and go to a brothel. Even while taking his pleasure, he couldn't rid himself of the pointlessness of his life – and the shame of it. He knew what he bought was counterfeit. He knew because he had had the real thing with Tess.

Angel's words came flooding back, hard and cold. "*I know what I am, mister, but you call yourself his* brother."

When he gave up looking for gold and came back here to his land, he thought he had hit rock bottom. He had been wrong. He swore to himself he would make it up to Michael. He would leave Miriam Altman alone so that when the time came and Angel left him again, there would be a decent girl waiting for him.

He tried to sleep and couldn't. He couldn't get Miriam out of his head. He would close his eyes and see her dark, smiling eyes. Giving up, he put another log on the fire and took his wedding picture off the mantel. He stared at Tessie's face again. Although it was still precious to him, it roused no deep emotion, not as it had a year ago.

A year ago, he hadn't thought the pain would ever go away. But then, a year ago, he thought he would never fall in love again.

"Amanda!" Miriam cried out, racing down the hillside. "Come quick! It's Ruthie!"

Angel ran toward her. "What's happened?"

"She's up a tree, and I can't get her down. Help me!"

Angel raised her skirts and ran up the hill after Miriam. She was breathless when they reached the gnarled old oak. Heart in her throat, Angel looked up at the child perched twenty feet above on a thick branch. "Oh! How did you get up there, you little mouse?"

Ruthie waved down at her.

"Ruthie!" Angel cried out in alarm. "Hold on! Don't you budge! We'll get you down."

"I tried to climb, and I couldn't," Miriam said. "You give it a try."

"*Me?* I've never climbed a tree in my life!"

"Mandy, are you going to help me down?" Ruthie called down.

"You'd better hurry," Miriam said, pushing at her. "There's no time to lose." She bent and cupped her hands.

Angel's skirts got in the way. "Wait a minute. I can't do it like this." She bent over, grabbed the back hem, and pulled it up between her legs, shoving it into her belt. She climbed up onto the first branch with Miriam's help. "Don't be scared, Ruthie! Just don't move."

"I won't," Ruthie said, swinging her feet back and forth and seeming to have a wonderful time.

"What am I *doing*?" Angel muttered under her breath as she scrambled higher. She thought she heard laughter.

"Don't look down!" Miriam called up to her. "You're doing fine."

Angel wasn't sure whether Miriam was speaking to her or Ruthie as she made her way up through the branches. When she was within a few feet, she saw that Ruthie had a rope tied around her waist holding her securely to the trunk. She couldn't have fallen if she wanted to. What was worse, the little imp was grinning from ear to ear. "Isn't it fun, Mandy?"

"Ever seen your cabin from this vantage point?" Miriam said, just below her.

Angel's face flamed in anger. "You scared me half to death! What do you think you're doing?"

Miriam climbed past her and straddled on a large branch. "You said it yourself. You've never climbed a tree in your life." She grinned mischievously. "It's about time you did."

"You pulled her up by yourself? She might have been hurt."

"We helped," Jacob said, coming down from a higher branch. Andrew was just above him, and Leah peeked out from behind the trunk. They all looked so pleased with themselves, she forgot her anger and laughed. A tree full of magpies. Pulling herself up, she straddled a thick branch.

"You did real well for your first time," Andrew said, walking along a limb.

Angel gave him a mock frown. "You should be working with your father."

"He gave me the day off. He wanted to take Mama out for a walk."

Miriam laughed. "I told them *we'd* go for a walk instead." She lowered her voice so only Angel could hear. "One of the disadvantages to having a one room cabin is the lack of privacy." She leaned her head against the trunk. "When I get married, my husband and I are going to build a loft for the children, and we're going to have a nice cozy bedroom next to the kitchen."

"There's Michael!" Ruthie pointed. The children shouted and whistled until he turned and looked up the hill. He strode toward them. When he reached the tree, he looked up, fists planted on his hips. "What's this?" He saw Angel aloft and laughed. "You, too?"

"They tricked me," she said with great dignity.

Miriam winked at her and called down to him. "You're going to have to get her down. She's stuck!"

Angel laughed when she saw Michael pull his boots off and start up. When he was just beneath her, he slid his hand up her calf. "Shall I tie Ruthie's rope around you and lower you away?" he asked, knowing perfectly well she could make it down on her own.

"This would make a great swing tree," Leah said, climbing down next to him. "See that big fat branch? You could tie the rope right there."

"Hmmm, good idea," Michael said. He lowered Ruthie and sent Andrew to the tack room in the barn for rope. Climbing back up, he tied both ends around a sturdy branch and let the loop hang for a swing. "I'll fix a seat for it later," he said, dropping down.

The children squabbled excitedly over who would get the first turn, but Michael caught Angel and set her in it. "Hang on," he told her before she could stop him, and he sent her flying. The exhilarating rush made her laugh. Michael gave her another push and then headed back to the field and his work.

When everyone, including Miriam, had had a turn on the swing, Angel took the children down to the cabin and fixed them something to eat. The boys went out to watch Michael, and Leah and Ruthie went to pick flowers on the hill.

Miriam leaned against the doorjamb and looked out at her brothers perched on top of the corral fence, watching Michael working with the horse. "Michael knows how to enjoy life. He doesn't sit about brooding all the time."

Angel came to stand with her. It disturbed her the way Miriam was watching Michael. An uncomfortable feeling twisted in her stomach.

Miriam smiled. "I was thinking how wonderful it must be to love someone and have them love you back. I'll bet when Michael wants you, he does something about it." Blushing, she straightened from the doorjamb. "Mama would faint dead away if she heard me talking like this."

Angel looked out at Michael; and the pang of jealousy died down, and a tender concern filled her. She gave Miriam a thoughtful look. She loved the girl like a sister. "You want to get married, don't you?"

"Yes, but I don't want to marry just anyone," Miriam said. "I want someone wonderful. I want a man to love me the way Michael loves you. I want a man willing to fight for me. I want a man who won't let me walk away from him."

Seeing tears in Miriam's eyes, Angel took her hand. "You love Michael?"

"Of course I love him. How could I not? He's one of a kind, isn't he?" Miriam put her head back against the jamb and closed her eyes. "Others should be more like him, but they're not." She smiled. "I'll never forget the night Mama and I sang 'Amazing Grace' and talked about David. Michael had tears in his eyes, and he wasn't embarrassed about it. He didn't care who saw how much he cared." She wiped tears from her cheeks. "Michael's the only man I've ever met who isn't afraid to feel things. He doesn't bury himself alive."

Angel looked out at him. "It's too bad I met him first."

Miriam laughed. "Well, if you find the mold, would you make another like him?" She hugged Angel. "I love you *both* so much." She drew back. "And now I've embarrassed you." She bit her lip and looked uncertain. "Mama thinks I should keep my feelings to myself instead of blurting them out all the time, but I can't. It's just the way I am." She kissed Angel's cheek. "I'd better gather the wild Indians and go." She went out into the sunshine and called for her brothers and sisters.

Hugging herself, Angel leaned against the doorjamb where Miriam had been and watched them go. She worried about it all afternoon and tried to talk things over with Michael that night. "Do you think we could find a man for Miriam?"

"Miriam? She's a little young, isn't she?"

"Old enough to be in love. Could we go back to Sacramento and find someone?"

"Who?" he said, playing with her hair.

"Someone for Miriam."

"How about Paul?"

"*Paul!*" Aghast, Angel moved away. "Miriam doesn't belong with someone like him. She belongs with someone like you."

"I'm already taken. Remember?" He pulled her close. "Leave it to the Lord."

"'Leave it to the Lord,'" she muttered. "You always want to leave things to the Lord."

He could see she wasn't going to let go of it. "The Lord already has someone in mind for Miriam. I'm sure of it. Now, put it out of your head."

She almost told him that Miriam was in love with him, but thought better of it. There was nothing more tantalizing to a man than a young girl in love with him. "I just want to see her happy and settled."

Michael soothed her. "She will be, Tirzah. A girl like Miriam doesn't go without a husband for long."

A girl like Miriam. "If you hadn't found me, would you – "

"But I did, didn't I?"

"Yes, you did." She reached up and touched his face. "Have you ever been sorry?"

"A few times," he said solemnly, knowing she would expect the truth. He took her hand and turned the wedding ring, looking down at her. "You've given me some dark moments." His smile was tender. "But that's in the past." He kissed her hand and laid it against his cheek. "Tirzah, I know what I'm about, and I know who has control of my life. You and I are not an accident."

Angel pulled his head down and kissed him, loving his response, loving the way she felt when he took over. "I don't think I'll ever get enough of you, Michael Hosea. Never, as long as I live."

"Nor I of you."

The Altmans held a gathering to celebrate spring planting. When Angel and Michael arrived, the children ran to greet them. Elizabeth waved from the open doorway.

"Come see our new well," Leah said, tugging on Michael's hand.

Miriam was bringing up a bucket of water. She set it down. "Marvelous, isn't it?" she said proudly. "Paul helped us dig it a few weeks ago. I've missed having a well to sing into. Listen." She bent over and sang down into the depths. The melodious sound broadened and rose. "Rock of Ages."

Angel rested her forearms on the stone and listened. Smiling at her, Michael bent over the side and joined Miriam, his deep voice harmonizing. Angel had never heard anything more beautiful than the way Miriam's and Michael's voices blended.

"Oh, doesn't it sound wonderful!" Miriam laughed. "Let's do another. If you put your head down far enough, the sound is all around you. Sing with us this time, Amanda, and it'll be even better." She wouldn't accept no for an answer. "Don't tell me you can't. You can. If you don't know the words, just open your mouth and go *ahhhhh*. 'Rock of Ages' again. You've heard it enough to know a few words."

Angel joined in hesitantly. Before they were finished, the rest of the children were hanging over the well and singing down into it. Had Michael not caught hold of her dress, Ruth would have fallen in head first. "'Oh, Suzanna,' this time," Andrew said. From that they went to more road songs with funny verses. Laughing, they straightened.

Miriam's expression changed markedly, and her hand gripped Angel's. "Paul's coming." Heart sinking, Angel raised her head and saw him walking across the open field toward them. "He was so stiff when I invited him, I didn't think he would come," Miriam said. Angel had never seen a more grim-looking man. "I'd better go greet him, or he'll leave before he's arrived," Miriam said.

Paul watched Miriam come toward him and steeled himself. She was wearing the yellow dress again. When she smiled, a muscle jerked in his cheek. "I'm so glad you came, Paul." She smiled and fanned herself with her hand. "It's hot, isn't it? Come have some cider."

Too disturbed by what he felt when he looked at Miriam, Paul glanced around. Angel was looking at him. He gave her a sardonic smile, expecting her to smile back just as derisively. She didn't. He hated her so much he could taste it.

"When did you finish your planting?" Miriam asked, forcing his attention back to her.

"Yesterday afternoon." They reached the others. Michael greeted him with a handshake. His grip was firm, speaking of continued affection. He put his arm around Angel and drew her close against his side, waiting.

Angel's blue eyes flickered as she looked up at him. "Hello, Paul," she said.

Paul wanted to ignore her but knew he couldn't without offending Michael. "Amanda," he said and nodded. Her face showed no emotion whatsoever. It didn't surprise him. What would she know about feelings?

Miriam had come back with a tin cup and was watching the exchange closely. She handed him the cider and took Angel's hand. "Mandy, would you help me hide the clues to the treasure hunt?" Paul watched them go off together, hand in hand.

"Miriam's pretty, isn't she?" Michael said, smiling slightly. "Those dark eyes."

Paul drank his cider in taut silence. He hadn't expected Michael to notice so soon.

When the children ran off to find Miriam's clues to the treasure — a basket of berry tarts — Elizabeth, Miriam, and Angel set up the plank table in the yard. Angel had brought a Dutch oven full of venison, baked beans, and candied carrots. Elizabeth had roasted two fat pheasants that were stuffed with seasoned bread.

Miriam brought out two winter apple pies.

Angel was too aware of the undercurrent of hatred aimed at her from Paul to join in the jubilance. She was successful in avoiding him throughout the afternoon, but now she was seated opposite him at the table. John said grace, and when she raised her head, she encountered Paul's look. She understood all too clearly the message in his eyes: *You? Praying? What a laugh!*

She *was* a hypocrite. She bowed her head as all the others did, pretending to pray even while she held no part of it. Nor did she want to. She did it because it would hurt Michael for her to sit beside him, back rigid and head held high while grace was said. And it would embarrass the Altmans. Ruthie would ask questions. She held Paul's cold gaze.

*Can't you understand?*

If anything, he looked even more contemptuous. Resigned that he never would understand her – probably would never even try – she took a slice of pheasant and passed the platter.

"Do you want me to talk to Paul?" Michael asked her later when John was fiddling and he was dancing with her.

"No," she said, afraid she would be the cause of an even wider gulf between the two men. She had done enough damage already.

"He's a decent man, Amanda. He's stood by me through some hard times. He's confused right now."

She knew Paul wasn't confused. He was full of righteous rage and animosity. Because of her. He was hurting. Because of her. Why hadn't she thought past her own revenge that day? Couldn't she have ignored his insults? She had known he was jealous. She had known that he thought she wasn't good enough to be Michael's wife. She had known a lot of things about Paul on first sight.

"Be patient with him," Michael said.

As Michael had been patient with her. She would swallow her pride if need be. For Michael's sake, she would take whatever Paul had to throw at her.

Michael danced with Miriam, and Angel went to pour herself a cup of cider. Paul came to stand next to her, his dark eyes glinting. He nodded toward Michael whirling Miriam around. They were both laughing. "They look good together, don't they?"

Angel watched Miriam and felt the pang inside her. They did. "They like each other a great deal," she said and poured a second cup of cider. She held it out to him.

Smiling mockingly down at her, he took it. He watched Michael and Miriam again. "She should have come a few months earlier. Things would've been a lot different."

"Michael said it wouldn't have."

"Of course, he'd *say* that."

The sword thrust went deep. Angel didn't say anything.

Paul's mouth curved sardonically. "I heard you were working in a general mercantile. What were you selling?"

"A little of everything."

"Just like always, hmmm?"

Angel concealed her pain and spoke quietly. "I've no intention of hurting Michael again, Paul. I swear to you."

"But you will, won't you? It's in your nature. You'll suck him dry and then throw the empty husk away. Oh, you'll stay around for a while, just for appearances. And when the going gets rough, you'll pack up your bags and be on your merry way again."

Angel blinked and looked away. She couldn't breathe past the constriction in her chest. "I won't."

"No? Then why were you in such a hurry to get back to Pair-a-Dice? Why did you run off to Sacramento?"

"I'm sticking this time."

"For a year or two. Until you're bored with being a farmer's wife." He drank his cider and set the cup down. He watched Michael and Miriam with a frown. "You know, Angel, I haven't seen Michael smile like that in a long, long time." He walked away and stood with John.

Angel held her cup of cider clasped between her two hands. Raising her head, she watched the two people she loved most in the world dancing together and wondered if Paul wasn't right about everything.

# Twenty-five

*And after the earthquake a fire;*
*but the Lord was not in the fire,*
*and after the fire*
*a still small voice.*

1 KINGS 19:12

Paul sought to erode Angel's confidence every time they met, while Angel set herself to endure whatever he threw at her. She told herself each time he made a cutting remark or insulting prophesy about where she would be in ten years that she would make no retaliation. To fight back would only hurt Michael. And it wouldn't change how Paul felt about her. Whatever tomorrow brought, today she had Michael.

Angel refused to defend herself against Paul. What was the point? She was polite. She was silent. She stood firm even when she wanted to run away and hide in a dark place where she could curl into a tight ball.

*I'm not a harlot anymore. I'm not!*

But the way Paul looked at her made her remember and feel she still was, no matter what she did. One year did not erase ten, and Paul brought back the dark years with Duke, the years of fear and loneliness and survival. And because of it, Paul's abuse drove her further into Michael's arms. The harder Paul tried to drive her away, the tighter she held to what she had. Michael told her not to be anxious about tomorrow, and she concentrated upon wringing the life out of each moment with him. He told her not to be afraid, and she wasn't, as long as he was with her.

Michael loved her *now*, and that was all that mattered to her. He made her life meaningful and filled it with new and wondrous things. Though life was hard work from dawn to dusk, he somehow made it exciting. He opened her mind to things she hadn't noticed before. And a quiet voice in her head said over and over, **Come forth, beloved.**

Come forth from what?

She couldn't get enough of Michael. He filled her mind and heart. He was her life. He awakened her before dawn with kisses, and they lay in the quiet darkness, listening to the symphony of crickets and bullfrogs and the wind chimes. Her body trembled at his touch and sang at his possession. Every moment of every day with him was precious to her.

Spring brought a wildness of color. Bright splashes of golden poppies and purple lupines stained the green hillsides and unplowed meadowlands. Michael talked about King Solomon and how, even with all his riches, he could not clothe himself as God clothed the hillsides with simple wildflowers. "I'm not going to plow that section," Michael told her. "I'm going to leave it the way it is." Michael saw God in everything. He saw him in the wind and the rain and the earth. He saw him in the crops that were growing. He saw God in the nature of the animals that inhabited their land. He saw him in the flames of their evening fire.

Angel only saw Michael and worshiped him.

When he read aloud in the evenings before the fire, she lost herself in the deep resonance of his voice. The words washed over her like a warm, heavy wave and swept back into a distant sea. Jonathan scaling a cliff to route the Philistines. David, a shepherd boy, killing a nine-foot giant named Goliath. Jesus raising the dead. Lazarus, come forth! *Come forth!*

Michael made nonsense sound like poetry.

She took the Bible and put it back on the mantel. "Love *me*," she said, taking his hand. And Michael could do nothing else.

Elizabeth came with the children. "Paul told us about a town not ten miles from here. It's not very big and has little to offer, but they've driven in to get supplies."

Angel noticed the small bulge of Elizabeth's abdomen. She offered coffee and biscuits and then sat down to visit. Ruthie wanted to sit in her lap, and she lifted her up. "When are you going to have a baby?" Ruthie asked, bringing stinging color into Angel's cheeks and a soft, mortified gasp from Elizabeth.

"Ruth Anne Altman, you are *never* to ask things like that," her mother said, taking her from Angel's lap and setting her firmly on her feet.

"Why not?" Ruth was not the least discomforted and clearly not comprehending why her mother and Angel were.

"Because it's very personal business, young lady."

Ruth looked up at Angel, her eyes wide and surprised. "You mean you don't want to have a baby?"

Miriam suppressed a laugh and took her little sister's hand. "I think we'll go out and swing awhile," she told them.

Elizabeth sat down again and fanned her hot face. "That child just blurts out whatever she's thinking," she said and apologized.

Angel wondered whether to tell her she couldn't have children and decided against it.

"I came to ask for your help," Elizabeth said. "The baby comes in December, and I'd like you to act as my midwife."

Angel couldn't have been more stunned or aghast. "*Me?* But Elizabeth, I don't know the first thing about helping someone have a baby."

"I know what needs to be done. Miriam wants to help, but I don't think a young, impressionable girl like her should be attending a birthing. It might frighten her needlessly."

Angel was silent a moment. "I can't see that I would be any help at all."

"I've been through it before. I'll be able to tell you what to do. Back home, I had a midwife, but out here there's only John, and John simply will not do." She smiled slightly. "He can birth a calf or foal, but he's perfectly useless when it comes to bringing his own children into the world. He falls to pieces the minute I show any pain, and, well, I can't go through the whole business without some discomfort, now, can I? He fainted when Miriam was born."

"He *did*?" Somehow she couldn't imagine the stoic John passing out over anything.

"He fell right on the floor by the bed, and there I was, help-less as a turtle on its back and with my own work to handle." She laughed softly. "He came 'round when it was all over."

"Will it be very hard?" Angel asked, worried already. She remembered one girl who managed to conceal her pregnancy until it was too late to have an abortion. "Isn't there a doctor in town?"

"I suppose there might be, but by the time he arrived it would be all over. Ruth only took four hours to be born. This one may come even faster."

Angel agreed reservedly to help when the time came. "If you're absolutely sure you want me to be the one."

"I am," Elizabeth said, hugging her. She looked greatly relieved.

Angel went out to Michael when the Altmans left. Leaning on the fence, she watched him shoe a horse. "Elizabeth wants me to help birth her baby." She watched the lines deepen in his tanned cheeks as he smiled.

"Miriam told me she was going to ask you. She was a little annoyed that she wouldn't be the one helping bring her little brother or sister into the world."

"Elizabeth was worried that Miriam might be shocked," she said. "I, on the other hand, shouldn't be shocked by anything."

Michael heard the biting edge in her tone, an edge that had been missing for weeks. He glanced at her. Was it his mention of Miriam that did it? Or was she scared of this additional responsibility?

"If there's trouble, I've untangled a few colts in my time."

"She said John fainted."

Michael laughed as he drove the last nail in and cut off the end.

"It's not funny, Michael. What if something goes wrong? There was a girl in the brothel back in New York who hid her pregnancy long enough so Duke couldn't force her to have an abortion. Sally talked him into letting her stay, but when her time came, she screamed. I could hear her through the walls. It was a Sunday afternoon, and the place was busy and − " She looked at Michael's face as he straightened, and she stopped speaking. Oh, *why* had she brought all that up again?

"And what?"

"Never mind," she said and turned away.

He came to the fence. "Your past is part of you. And I love you. Remember? Now, what happened to the girl and her baby?"

Her throat closed tight, and she could hardly speak. "Sally gagged her so she wouldn't disturb anyone. It took so long. All through the night and into the next day. She was sick for days afterwards, and the baby..."

Sally had kept the other girls away but allowed Angel to come into the room with her to tend the mother and infant. The young prostitute was as white as death and silent while beside her the baby whimpered constantly and was wrapped in a pink cloth. Angel wanted to pick the baby up, but Sally hastily shoved her away. "Don't touch it!" she whispered. Angel didn't understand why until Sally carefully unwrapped it.

"What about the child?" Michael asked, pushing a loose strand of golden hair back from her pale face.

"It was a little girl. She only lived a week," she said bleakly. She didn't tell him that the baby was covered with sores or that she died without a name. The mother disappeared shortly afterward. When she asked Sally what happened to her, Sally said, "It's not for you to question what Duke does." And Angel knew the girl was dead, fodder for rats in some dark, dirty alley. Just like Rab. Just like her if she didn't obey. She shuddered.

"Elizabeth has had five children, Amanda," Michael reminded her.

"Yes," she said, "and all of them healthy."

Michael watched the color slowly come back into her cheeks. He wondered what she had been thinking of, but he didn't ask. If she wanted to talk about it, she would. If not, he would respect her silence. But she needed reassurance. He sensed that. "When a baby's time comes, there's nothing you can do to stop it."

She smiled up at him. "You know all about this, too, I suppose?"

"Not from personal experience," he said. "Tess helped deliver a baby on the wagon train. She said she didn't have to do anything except make sure it didn't fall on the floor of the wagon.

They're a little slippery when they arrive. When Elizabeth's time comes, I'll come along and hold John's hand."

Angel laughed, the tension leaving her. As long as Michael was with her, everything would be fine.

"Oh, by the way," Michael said, taking a packet from his pocket. "Miriam asked me to give this to you."

Angel had noticed Miriam leaning on the fence a long while talking with Michael. "What is it?" she asked, glancing at the neat handwriting she couldn't read. Duke had seen no reason to teach her.

"Seeds for a summer flower garden."

As spring warmth turned into summer heat, Angel learned she had her mother's gift for growing things. The flower bed she laid out around the house became a grand profusion of color. She filled the pitcher daily with pink phlox, yellow yarrow, red lamb's ear, purple delphinium and white holly-hocks. Blue flax and pristine daisies graced the mantel. But even more than the pleasure she took from the flowers was the pride she felt when she looked out at the cornfield.

She could scarcely believe that the small, shriveled kernels Michael had given her to plant had become stalks taller than he. She walked the rows, touching the towering plants and seeing the developing ears of corn. Had she really helped make this happen?

"Amanda! Where are you?" Michael called.

Laughing, she stood on tiptoe. "Over here," she called back and then ran down the row to hide.

"All right," he said, laughing. "Where did you go?"

She whistled at him from her hiding place. She and Ruthie had played hide-and-seek in the rows the day before, and she was in a joyous mood today, ready to tease Michael.

"What do I get if I find you?"

"What have you got in mind?"

"Oh, a little of this and that." He reached through a row and almost caught hold of her skirt. Laughing, she escaped again. He caught up with her at the end of the row, but she eluded him again and disappeared into the greenery. She ducked into a row and put her foot out as he passed, tripping him. Laughing, she raced back the other way.

"I'm never going to get that fence repaired," he said, coming after her. He had just caught her when someone called to them. Michael chuckled. "It's Miriam again wanting to know if Mandy can come out and play."

Miriam looked distraught when she reached them, her eyes red rimmed from crying.

"What's happened?" Angel asked in alarm. "Is it your mother?"

"Mama's fine. Everyone's fine," Miriam said, giving her a weak smile. "Michael, I need to speak with you about something. Please. It's important."

"Of course."

Miriam took Angel's hand and squeezed it. "Thanks," she said. "I won't keep him long."

Angel knew she was dismissed. "Come into the house when you're finished. I'll fix some coffee."

She watched from the window as Miriam and Michael talked together in the yard. Miriam was crying. Michael touched her shoulder, and Miriam went into his arms. Angel's stomach dropped at the sight of him holding her. A dull pain spread across her chest as she watched him stroke the girl's back and say something to her. Miriam drew back slightly and shook her head. He tipped her chin and said something more to her. She talked for a long time, and Michael stood listening. When she finished, he said something briefly. She put her arms around his neck and kissed his cheek. Then she headed for home. Michael stood watching her for a long moment. He rubbed the back of his neck and shook his head. Then he headed for the fence where he had been working earlier.

Angel waited for him to bring up what Miriam said when he came in for supper, but he didn't. Instead he talked about how the work was going on the corral and what he would be doing in the afternoon. If Miriam had told him something in trust, Angel knew he wouldn't break it.

When he came in at the end of the day, he was thoughtful.

He watched her clear the dishes. "You're very quiet," he said, coming up behind her and putting his hands around her waist as she poured hot water over the dinner dishes. He brushed her braid aside and kissed her neck. "What are you worrying about? Elizabeth?"

"Miriam." She felt his hands loosen. Turning, she looked up at him. "And you." When he blinked and said nothing, she brushed past him. He caught her and turned her firmly around to face him.

"You have no need to be jealous, though I suppose I'd be grinding my teeth if Paul came 'round and asked to talk with you privately."

"That's not likely to happen, is it?"

"No. I suppose not." He wished he had left Paul out of it. "The point is, I love *you*."

"And you're not in the least tempted by a girl who worships the ground you walk on?"

"No," he said, not denying Miriam's affection. "But I'm more a big brother to her than anything else."

Angel felt petty. She loved Miriam dearly, but seeing them together had hurt. She looked up into Michael's eyes again and couldn't doubt he loved her. He made her weak with it. Relaxing, she gave him a rueful smile. "Is she all right? What's wrong?"

"She's unhappy. She knows what she wants, a husband and children of her own, but she isn't sure how to get it. So she wanted a man's opinion."

"Well, I'm glad she didn't go to Paul," she said before she thought better of it. She turned back to the dishes. Paul would take a sweet, innocent girl like Miriam apart with his mockery.

Michael was silent.

She glanced back at him and knew she shouldn't have said anything against his friend. "I'm sorry. It's just that...." She shrugged.

"She needs a husband."

"Yes," she agreed, "but he's going to have to be something very, very special."

His mouth curved. "You love her, don't you?"

"She's the closest thing to a sister I'll ever have. Maybe that's why it hurt when I saw the two of you holding onto one another."

"I don't hold her the same way I hold you. Want to see the difference?"

Breathless and laughing, she pushed free. "You're all soggy now. Go read so I can finish my work."

He took the Bible down and sat before the fire with the book resting in his lap. He bowed his head, and Angel knew he was praying. It was a habit of his, and she no longer taunted him about it. That great black book was almost falling apart, but he looked upon it as something bound in gold and containing priceless jewels inside. He never read it without praying first. He told her once that he didn't read until his mind was open enough to receive. She didn't know what he was talking about. Sometimes his words, though plain English, made no sense to her at all. And then he would say something wonderful that filled her with warmth and dawning light. She was the blackest night, and he the starlight piercing it, creating an unfolding pattern in her life.

She finished her chores and sat beside him. He was still silent. She put her head back, listening to the crackling fire, and waited. When he finally read, she was drowsy and content. His rich, warm voice was like dark taffy, but what he read surprised her. It was the story of a bride and groom and their passion for one another. He read for a long time.

Michael put the Bible back on the mantel and placed another log on the fire. It would burn through the night and keep the cabin warm.

"Why would a virgin bride play the harlot for her husband?" Angel asked, perplexed.

Michael glanced back. He'd thought she was sleeping. "She wasn't."

"Yes, she was. She danced for him, and he was looking at her body. From the feet up. In the beginning, he was looking into her eyes."

He was amazed she had listened so carefully. "He took joy in her body, as she wanted him to, and she danced to arouse and please him."

"And your God says it's all right to entice a man?"

"It's all right to entice your husband."

Her expression clouded. She hadn't meant just any man, but he was well aware of how well trained she was at enticement. "What if they think it's enticement just because of the way you look?"

Michael nudged the log further back with his boot. "Men are always going to stare at you, Amanda. You're beautiful. There's nothing you can do about that." Even John Altman had stared at her in the beginning. And Paul. Sometimes Michael wondered what went through Paul's mind when he saw her. Did it flash back to what happened between them on the way to Pair-a-Dice? He pushed the disturbing thoughts away. Dwelling on them raised doubts that tormented him.

"Does it bother you?" she asked.

"What?"

"When men stare at me."

"Sometimes," he admitted. "When they're looking at you like an object and not a human being with feelings." His mouth tipped ruefully. "Or a wife in love with her husband."

She turned the wedding ring on her finger. "They never look at my hands, Michael."

"Maybe we should put the ring in your nose."

Glancing up, she saw his teasing smile and laughed. "Yes, or a large one around my neck. Maybe that would keep them away."

A long time later, as Michael lay sleeping beside her, Angel listened to the night breeze stirring the wind chimes outside the window. The ever changing melodies were soothing.

The new hay smelled sweet beneath her, sweeter still because it was partly due to her labor that it was there. She and Michael had harvested the hay together. What grueling work! She had been so fascinated watching Michael swing the great scythe in wide, smooth strokes, dropping the golden grasses. She raked it into piles, and they pitched it into the back of the wagon to be taken and stored in the barn. The animals would have hay through the cold winter months.

Everything Michael did had purpose. She thought of her

own life and how meaningless and miserable it had been before him. Her very reason to be alive now depended on him. And Michael depended on the earth, the rains, the warmth of the sun. And his God.

Especially his God.

*I'd be dead by now if Michael hadn't come back for me. I'd be rotting in a shallow, unmarked grave.*

She was consumed with gratitude and filled with an aching humility that this man loved *her*. Why, of all the other women of the world, had he chosen *her*? She was so undeserving. It was inconceivable.

*But I am glad, so glad he did. And I'll never again do anything to make him sorry. Oh, God, I swear....*

A sweet fragrance filled the darkened cabin, a fragrance that defied definition. She filled her lungs with it, so heady and wonderful. What was it? Where did it come from? Her mind whirled with words and phrases Michael had read to her over the past weeks and even before that, words she thought she had never heard but had somehow found their way into the deepest part of her, somewhere inside, a place she'd been unable to close off.

And then a still, quiet voice filled the room.

***I am.***

Angel sat up abruptly, eyes wide open. She looked around the cabin, but there was no one there other than Michael, who lay sleeping deeply beside her. Who had spoken? She felt fear sweep through her, and she trembled with it. Then it was gone, washed away, and she was calm again, her skin tingling strangely.

"There is nothing," she whispered. "Nothing." She awaited an answer, not moving.

But no answer came. No voice filled the stillness.

Angel lay down slowly and curled as tightly against Michael as she could.

# Twenty-six

*Give sorrow words;*
*the grief that does not speak.*
SHAKESPEARE

September came swiftly, and the corn was ready for harvesting. Michael drove the wagon between the rows and left it there. He and Angel broke the ears from the stalks and tossed them against the bang board so they dropped into the wagon bed. Soon the corncrib was full.

The Altmans gladly came to help shuck corn. It was a good excuse to get together and have some fun. They all sang songs, told stories, and laughed while working. Angel's hands blistered, and she cut them on the shucks, but she had never been happier in her life. The mound of golden ears grew about her, and she felt a sense of pride in having a part in it. There was more than enough for seed next year, and their own supply for cornmeal was replenished as well as having plenty to sell at market.

When the shucking was finished, Elizabeth sat in the shade and sipped herbal tea Angel brought to her. She was rounding nicely, her cheeks glowing with healthy color. Angel had never seen her look so well or lively.

"Do you want to feel the baby kick?" Elizabeth asked and took Angel's hand. She placed it on her swollen belly. "There. Did you feel that, Amanda?" Angel laughed, amazed. "John wants another boy," Elizabeth said.

Angel grew wistful as they talked. Elizabeth patted her hand. "Your time will come. You're young."

Angel didn't reply.

Michael and Miriam walked up the hill together to see about little Ruth, who was swinging. Elizabeth watched them with a faint frown. "She quotes Michael like gospel. I've been so hoping she would fall in love with Paul."

"Paul?" Angel looked at her in surprise.

"He's young and strong and very good-looking. He works hard on that place of his, and he'll make something of himself. I asked Miriam what she thought of him, and all she would say is he told her his wife was very pretty and he missed her. He hardly looks at her when he comes over to help John." She sighed. "I suppose he's still grieving. Too much so to notice a pretty young girl just the right age for him. And Miriam is – " She stopped as she realized what she was about to say.

"In love with Michael," Angel said.

Elizabeth blushed. "She's never said so."

"She doesn't have to, does she?"

Elizabeth wondered what damage she had done with her wandering thoughts and tongue. Sometimes she spoke with as little wisdom and tact as her children. Why hadn't she kept silent about her concerns? Amanda was too easy to talk to. "I've wondered," she admitted, seeing no way to avert the subject now. She wondered especially today, watching Miriam walk away with Michael and seeing how her daughter hung on his every word. Was Michael aware of her affection? How could he not be? Miriam never could hide anything.

Elizabeth touched Angel's hand. "Miriam would never do anything about those feelings, even if she does have them for Michael. She adores you, and she's a good girl. She's no fool, Amanda."

"Of course not." Angel watched Michael come down the hill with her friend and thought they looked very good together. They both had dark hair and were beautifully made. They had so much in common. They both believed in the same God. They loved the land. They both embraced life with zeal and joy. They gave their love without condition.

She saw Miriam loop her arm through Michael's and laugh up at him in easy camaraderie. Angel's heart contracted with a sharp stab of jealousy, but it was quickly gone, overcome by an overwhelming sadness. She watched Miriam's face carefully as they came closer.

Elizabeth was dismayed, seeing how Angel watched her daughter. "I've been a fool," she said miserably, sure she had destroyed her daughter's friendship. "I should never have said anything."

"I'm glad you did."

Elizabeth took her hand tightly. "Amanda, Michael loves you very much."

"I know," Angel said, smiling bleakly. What good would it ever do him?

"And so does Miriam."

Angel saw how distressed Elizabeth was and put her hand over hers. "I know that, too, Elizabeth. You needn't worry." Next to Michael and Ruthie, she loved Miriam better than anyone in the world. Not that she didn't also love Elizabeth. What she felt was too consuming to share.

Elizabeth's eyes filled with tears. "And now I've ruined your trust in her."

"Not at all." Oddly, Angel knew her reassurance was true. She felt secure in Michael's love. But what of Miriam? Even more unsettling, what of Michael's dreams?

Angel tried to push the disturbing thoughts away. *Michael knew what he was getting. He said so himself. So it's not my fault if he doesn't get everything he wanted. Like children.*

Angel looked at Elizabeth's abdomen and then turned her head away, pretending the grief inside her didn't exist.

Michael went to visit with Paul and was gone most of the next day. Angel wondered what he had gone to talk about and what Paul would have to say to him. She was working in the garden when Michael returned. She made no move to go out to meet him. He swung down from his horse and strode toward her purposefully. Putting his hand on the support post, he swung over the gate and caught hold of her. Pulling her into his arms, he kissed her thoroughly. When she was breathless, he relaxed his hold and grinned down at her.

"Does that set your mind at ease?"

She laughed and embraced him, relief and joy obliterating all the anxiety of the long day without him. How the mind could torment.

She went into the cabin to see to dinner while he saw to his horse. When he came in, she smiled. "Is everything all right with Paul?"

"No," he said grimly, hands shoved into his pockets as he leaned against the mantel and watched her. "Something's eating at him, and he won't talk about it. We're going to drive into town tomorrow and sell some of our produce."

Her heart sank at the thought of his being away another day, but she said nothing.

"I'll see to the stock in the morning, and you can spend the day with the Altmans," he said. "Elizabeth's putting up apple-sauce."

Angel turned to look at him. "Did you see Miriam?"

"Yes." His expression was inscrutable. "What a mess," he said almost to himself.

She didn't ask him anything more.

Paul came early. Michael was just finishing his coffee. When he stood, he put a firm hand on Paul's shoulder, pushing him down into the seat again. "Stay put. Have some coffee while I see to the stock. The wagon's already loaded. I'll give a holler when I'm ready to hitch up. We'll swing by your place to pick up your crates and then be on our way."

Paul's face was stiff, and his gaze flickered coldly to Angel when Michael went out the door. "Was it your idea we have this time alone together?"

"No. I suppose Michael hopes we'll work out our differences."

Paul drank his coffee in silence, his shoulders rigid.

She looked at him. "Have you eaten this morning? There's some mush – "

"No, thanks," he said curtly. He looked up at her sardonically. "I thought you'd be long gone by now."

It was clear he wished it so. "Would you like some more coffee?"

"So polite. So proper. Anyone would think you were raised to be a farmer's wife."

"I am a farmer's wife, Paul," she said quietly.

"No, you're a good actress. You're going through all the motions. But inside you're nowhere near what a farmer's wife should be." His hand whitened on the mug. "Don't you think Michael knows the difference every time he talks to Miriam Altman?"

She showed no sign that his words had cut deeply. "He loves me."

"He *loves* you all right," he said, and his eyes swept her body up and down in a telling way. "You know how *that* is."

How could Michael love this man like a brother? She tried to see something in him, some trace of kindness and humanity, but all she could see was his cold hatred. "Are you always going to hate me for what you did, Paul? Are you never going to forget?"

Paul shoved the mug away and scraped the chair back. His face was red, his eyes blazing. "You're blaming *me* for what happened? Did I drag you off that wagon? Did I rape you? You'd *like* to think it was my fault, wouldn't you?" He went out the door.

Angel didn't move from where she stood. She should have kept silent. She knew she had no defense.

Michael stepped in briefly to kiss her good-bye. "I'll come by Altmans' on my way home. Stay there, and we can ride home together."

Ruthie ran to meet Angel as she came across the meadow. "Paul said we could pick all his apples!" she said as she was scooped up and perched on Angel's hip. "Mama's going to make applesauce. I love applesauce. Don't you?"

Miriam was in the doorway, looking pretty in a blue gingham dress and white apron. She was smiling. "We're being put to work," she said and hugged Angel.

They took a handcart and walked the mile to the apple tree. While they picked the fruit, Miriam pointed out all the work Paul had done on his place. "He has a good crop of pumpkins coming, and he had a good crop of corn. We helped him shuck it a few days ago."

When they returned to the Altmans' cabin, they spent the rest of the morning peeling and coring apples and cutting them in pieces to cook. Elizabeth added spices as she stirred, and the sweet smell filled the cabin. While the pot simmered, she made up a picnic basket and sent them off. "The boys are already with your father, and I'll have the cabin to myself for a nap," she said when Miriam asked if she would be all right.

Ruth and Leah went with Miriam and Angel. The two younger girls waded in the cool water of the stream while Angel sat on the bank and sifted her toes through the sand. Miriam lay back, arms spread, and drank in the sun's warmth. "Sometimes I miss home," she said. She talked about the farm and the neighbors they'd had and the gatherings. She talked about the long journey west. She remembered one funny incident after another, and Angel laughed with her. Miriam made a grueling, two-thousand-mile trek sound like a pleasure trip.

"Tell me about the ship," Miriam said, rolling onto her stomach and propping her head up. "Were there many women aboard?"

"Two others besides myself. My quarters weren't much bigger than a backhouse, and it was so cold. I wore as much clothing as I could, and it still didn't help. Going around the Horn was the nearest you can get to hell. I thought I'd die of seasickness."

"What did you do when you got to San Francisco?"

"Froze and nearly starved." She clasped her knees and looked at the two little girls in the stream. "Then I started working again." She sighed. "Miriam, I don't have many funny stories to tell, and the ones I do have aren't fit for you to hear."

Miriam sat up Indian fashion. "I'm not a child, you know. You could tell me something of what it was like."

"Obscene."

"Then why didn't you run away?"

Was there faint accusation in that question? Should she tell Miriam what it was like to be eight years old and locked in a room and know that only two people had a key, a madam who brought food and replaced the chamber pot, and Duke? Should she tell her the disastrous outcome when she ran away with Johnny? "I tried, Miriam," she said simply and left it at that.

"But men wanted you. Men fell in love with you. Just once, I'd like to walk down a street and have heads turn as I went by."

"No, you wouldn't."

Miriam's eyes teared. "Just once, I'd like to be wanted by a man."

"Do you really think so? What if it was a stranger and he'd just paid someone for you and you had to do whatever he wanted, no matter how degrading? What if he was ugly? What if he hadn't bathed in a month? What if he liked to play rough? Would you think that was romantic?" She hadn't meant to speak so harshly. She was shaking.

Miriam's face was ashen. "Is that what it was like?"

"Worse," Angel said. "I wish I'd never known another man before Michael."

Miriam took her hand and didn't ask any more questions.

Michael arrived at dusk. Miriam was the first one out the door to greet him. "I thought Paul was coming back with you."

Michael jumped down. "He decided to stay in town for a day or two."

"Just like a man," Miriam said, but her gaiety was gone.

Elizabeth insisted he and Angel stay for dinner. Miriam sat on the other side of Michael and scarcely said a word through the meal. Her food was hardly touched. Angel saw Michael put his hand over hers briefly and whisper something to her. Miriam's eyes filled with tears, and she excused herself quickly and left the table.

"What's gotten into her lately?" John said, perplexed.

"Just leave it be, John." Elizabeth glanced between Angel and Michael and then passed a bowl of squash.

Michael was pensive on the wagon ride home. He took Angel's hand and held it tightly. "What I wouldn't do for a little wisdom right now," he said. "What'd Paul say to you this morning?"

"He was surprised I was still around," she said, smiling to make him think it hadn't hurt.

Michael wasn't fooled. "I brought you something from town." When they reached home, he took the items out of the back and handed them to her. She didn't know what they were at first, just thorned sticks partially bound in burlap. "Rosebushes.

The man swore they're red, but we'll find out for ourselves come spring. I'll plant them first thing in the morning. Just tell me where you want them."

Angel remembered the scent of roses drifting in a sunny parlor. "One right under the window," she said, "and the other by the front door."

When an image of her mother in a nightgown, kneeling in the moonlit garden, flashed in her mind, she quickly pushed it away.

Thanksgiving approached quickly, and Elizabeth grew so large, Angel thought she looked ready to burst. She and Miriam took over the preparations for the holiday celebration while Elizabeth watched and advised. When the day came, the table was laden with stuffed and roasted pheasant, creamed carrots and peas, potatoes and candied nuts. John had purchased a cow, and pitchers of milk sat on both ends of the table. Angel hadn't had a glass of milk in months, and this delicacy drew her more readily than all the others she had helped to cook.

"Paul went to town to celebrate," Miriam said, little inflection in her tone. "He said the other day he's thinking of going back to the streams come spring."

"There's a stream right near his house," Leah said.

Jacob gave his sister a contemptuous look. "Not with gold in it, dummy."

"That will do, Jacob," Elizabeth chided him as she set a rhubarb pie on the table. Miriam put pumpkin at the other end. When everyone was finished, the children quickly scattered before they could be drafted into kitchen duty. John and Michael went outside so John could smoke his pipe. The aroma made Elizabeth sick in her condition. Miriam went to the well for water.

Elizabeth sank wearily into a chair and rested her hand on her protruding belly. "I swear this child is carving his initials on the walls already."

"How long to go?" Angel asked, scraping leftovers from plates and putting them into the wash pan on the table.

"Too long." Elizabeth smiled. "It takes John and Miriam to get me out of bed in the morning."

Angel poured a kettle of hot water over the dirty dishes. Glancing at Elizabeth, she saw the poor woman was exhausted and half asleep. Drying her hands, she went to her and took her hand. "Elizabeth, you should lie down and rest." She helped her up and covered her with a quilt when she lay down on the bed in the second room. She was asleep almost immediately.

Angel stood by the bed for a long moment. Elizabeth was curled on her side, her knees drawn up and her hand resting protectively on her unborn child. An embrace. Angel looked down at her own flat stomach and spread her hands there. Her eyes burned, and she bit her lip. Dropping her hands to her sides, she turned away and saw Miriam standing in the doorway.

Miriam smiled wistfully. "I've wondered myself what it would be like. It's a woman's reason for being, isn't it? Our divine privilege: to bring new life into the world and nurture it." She smiled at Angel. "Sometimes I can hardly wait."

Angel saw the tears Miriam tried to hide. After all, what good was divine privilege to a virgin girl?

Or a barren woman.

# Twenty-seven

*Many are the plans in a man's heart,*
*but it is the Lord's purpose that prevails.*

PROVERBS 19:21

Before Michael went hunting, he brought several heavy sacks of dried corn into the cabin so Angel could shell it. She sat before the crackling fire and rubbed the cobs together until a few rows gave way and the rest of the kernels could be easily separated. Some fell onto her lap. Setting the bare cob aside, she picked up a kernel. Smiling, she rolled its hard shape between her fingers.

**You have to die to be reborn.**

She raised her head, listening intently. Her heart beat wildly, but the only sounds around her were the chimes stirring in the wind. She looked down at the dry, partially shriveled kernel in her palm. It was like the many she had planted last spring and out of which the forest of green had sprung. She tossed the kernel into the basket with the others and brushed the rest from her skirt.

Perhaps she was a little mad after all. The old voices seldom came anymore, but now there was this new one, quiet and still, making no sense at all. From death comes life? Impossible. But there at her feet was the basket of seed corn. She frowned slightly. Bending, she sifted her hands through it. She clenched two handfuls. So what did it mean?

"Amanda!" Miriam gasped, bursting into the cabin. "It's Mama's time."

Angel threw on her shawl and started out the door. Laughing, Miriam halted her. "You don't want to come back to a burned-down house, do you?" Angel grabbed a sack of dried corn and dragged it well away from the fireplace. Angel hurriedly lifted the seed corn to the table and swung the other sack near the bed. They ran most of the way. "Oh," Miriam said. "I didn't even think to tell Michael – "

"He'll know," Angel said, walking fast to catch her breath before she raised her skirts and ran again.

Heaving for breath, Angel plunged into the Altman cabin, Miriam on her heels. Elizabeth sat calmly before the fire, stitching on a shirt. The children glanced up from their work. They were sitting calmly around the table doing lessons.

Only John was agitated and came out of his chair like a shot. "Thank God!" he said, taking Angel's shawl quickly and tossing it in the direction of the wall hook. He lowered his voice. "Her pains are close together, but I can't get her to go in and lie down. She says she has mending to do!"

"I'm almost finished, John," Elizabeth said. She set one shirt aside and took up another. She went very still, and her face tightened in silent concentration. Angel stared at her, watching for signs of agony, waiting for a blood-curdling scream. Elizabeth closed her eyes for a long moment and then let out a soft sigh and began working again. The children scarcely noticed until their father groaned.

"Lizzie, *go to bed!*"

"When I'm finished, John."

*"Now!"* he boomed so abruptly, Angel jumped. She had never heard John Altman use such a tone on anyone in his family.

Elizabeth raised her head with dignity. "Leave me be, John. Go feed the horses or chop wood. Go muck out a stable. Go shoot something for dinner. But don't bother me right now." She said it all in such a calm voice, Angel almost laughed. John tossed up his hands and stormed out of the cabin, muttering about women. "Bar the door, Andrew."

"Mama?"

"He'll come right back in if you don't," Elizabeth said with an amused smile. The children laughed and went on with what they were doing. Miriam was tense and clearly worried.

Several more pains came, and Elizabeth stitched madly. She knotted the thread and snipped it. Another contraction came while she was folding the shirt, and Miriam was growing more pale. She looked frantically to Angel, but Angel intended to wait on Elizabeth's pleasure. If she wanted to sit there and have the baby in the chair, that was her business.

When the contraction lengthened, Angel bent down and put her hand firmly on Elizabeth's knee. "How can I help you?" she said with more steadiness than she felt.

Elizabeth said nothing, her hand clenched white on the arm of the chair. Finally, she let out a gusty breath and took Angel's hand. "Help me to the bedroom," she said softly. "Miriam, see to the children and your father."

"Yes, Mama."

"And we'll need plenty of hot water. Jacob can fetch it. And cloths. Leah, they're in the trunk. We'll need the ball of twine in the cabinet. Ruthie, you get that for me, will you, dear?"

"Yes, Mama." The children scattered to do her bidding.

Angel closed the door quietly behind her. Elizabeth sat down carefully on the edge of the bed and began to unbutton her dress. She needed help in removing it and had but a thin shift on beneath.

"It's coming now," she said. "My water broke when I went to the backhouse this morning." She laughed softly. "I was afraid for a moment that the child would drop right down into that hole." She took Angel's hand. "Don't look so worried. Everything is fine." She drew in her breath sharply, her hand tightening. Perspiration beaded on her brow. "That was a good one," she said finally.

Miriam entered the bedroom with a pitcher of water and a pan full of cloths. "Papa is bringing more water. Two buckets besides Jacob's. We've got the pot over the fire."

Elizabeth's eyes twinkled. "I suppose your Papa thinks a nice warm bath would solve everything." She kissed Miriam's cheek. "Thank you, sweetheart. I'm depending on you to take care of things. Leah was having trouble with her arithmetic, and Jacob needs to practice his letters."

The pains came more quickly and lasted longer. Elizabeth made no sound, but Angel saw the strain she was under. She was pale and sweating profusely. Wringing out a cool cloth, Angel bathed her face.

Miriam peered in an hour later. "Michael's here."

Angel let out a sigh of relief, and Elizabeth smiled. "You're doing just fine, Amanda." Blushing, Angel laughed.

Elizabeth had little to say over the next hour, and Angel respected her silence. She stroked her tenderly and held her hand when the pains came. When Elizabeth relaxed, she wrung out the cloth and dabbed her brow.

"Won't be long now," Elizabeth said following one pain that had rolled right into the next. She moaned this time, her hand clamping white on the headboard. "Oh, I didn't think it would take this long."

"Tell me what to do!" Angel said, but Elizabeth had no breath to do so. She gasped, but drew in her breath sharply again, her legs coming up. She moaned louder, her face contorting and turning bright red.

Angel didn't stop to think about modesty. She pulled the quilt back.

"Oh, Elizabeth! It's coming, darling! I can see the head." Angel supported the child as Elizabeth gave one last push. Angel went down on her knees, the newborn baby in her arms, squalling.

"A boy. Elizabeth, a boy! And he's perfect. Ten fingers, ten toes...." She got up, trembling with exhilaration and wonder.

Elizabeth wept in joy as Angel placed her son on her chest. A few moments later, with the last contractions, she relaxed completely, exhausted. "Tie the cord with the twine before you cut it," Elizabeth said wearily and smiled. "He has good lungs."

"Yes, he certainly does." Angel washed the baby carefully before wrapping him in a soft blanket and giving him to his mother. He suckled immediately, and Elizabeth smiled contentedly. Pouring warm water into a pan, Angel washed Elizabeth carefully, making every effort not to hurt her, but hurt she did, though Elizabeth didn't complain. Bending down, she kissed Elizabeth's cheek. "Thank you," she whispered to the already sleeping woman.

Angel went out quietly. Everyone was standing in the other room, waiting. "You have a beautiful new son, John. Congratulations."

"Praise the Lord." He wilted into his chair. "What'd you say his name was?"

Angel laughed, all the pent-up tension gone. "Well, I don't know, John. I think *you're* supposed to decide that."

Everyone laughed, John included, blushing beet red. Shaking his head, he went into the bedroom. Miriam and the children filed in quietly behind him.

Michael smiled at her in a way that made her heart race. "Your eyes are shining," he said.

She was so full of emotion she couldn't speak. His expression was so endearing, full of so much promise. She loved him so much she felt consumed with it. When he came to her, she lifted her face so he could brush his mouth lightly against hers. "Oh, Michael," she said, putting her arms around him.

"Someday," he said, then went cold at his cruel blunder. He held her more tightly.

Angel knew what he was thinking. They would never have a child. He drew back slightly, but she couldn't look up at him, not even when he cupped her face. "Amanda, I'm sorry," he said softly. "I didn't mean – "

"Don't apologize, Michael."

Why hadn't he thought first before saying anything? "I'll tell them we're going home." He left her long enough to congratulate the Altmans. The baby was beautiful.

Elizabeth took his hand. "Amanda was wonderful. Tell her I'd be honored to tend her when her time comes."

"I'll tell her," he said dully, knowing he couldn't.

They walked home in silence. He watched her bank the fire.

"Elizabeth said you were wonderful."

"She was magnificent," Angel said. "She could have managed with no one to help her." She glanced up at him with a sad smile. "It's what being a woman is all about, isn't it? Miriam called having children a divine privilege." She looked away. "John's seed was planted in fertile ground."

"Amanda," he said, putting his hand beneath her arm to stop her.

"Don't say anything, Michael, please...."

She didn't fight him when he drew her into his arms. He held her firmly, his hand spread over the back of her head. He wanted to take away the hurt and didn't know how. "Christmas is only a few days away."

"I didn't remember until tonight at the Altmans'." Elizabeth and Miriam had already decorated their cabin with pine bows and red ribbons. Leah and Ruthie had made a nativity scene with corn-husk dolls. Angel hadn't thought to do anything. Duke had always said Christmas was just like any other day and you slept eight hours of it.

Mama had made something of Christmas during those early years. Even when they lived on the docks and had little food and no money, Mama treated Christmas as a holy day. No men were allowed in the shack on Christmas. Mama used to tell her what Christmas was like when she was a little girl. Angel didn't like her to talk about it because it always made Mama cry.

"Christmas," Angel said and drew back from Michael.

He saw her anguish and felt he was the cause of it. "Amanda..."

She looked up at him, unable to make out his face in the darkness. "What do I give you for Christmas, Michael? What do I give you when the only thing you really want is a child?" Her chest rose and fell rapidly as she struggled against the emotion rising in her. "I wish – I wish...."

"Don't," he said brokenly.

She clenched her fist. "I wish Duke hadn't ruined me! I wish no one else had ever *touched* me! I wish I was like Miriam!"

"I love *you*." When she turned away, he yanked her back, pulling her into his arms. "I love *you*." He kissed her and felt the way she melted into him, clinging to him so desperately.

"Michael, I wish I was whole. I wish I was whole for you."

*God, why? John and Elizabeth have six children. Will I never beget even one on my wife? Why did you allow it to happen this way?*

"It doesn't matter," he said over and over. "It doesn't matter." But both of them knew it did.

# Twenty-eight

*Do nothing from selfishness or empty conceit,*
*but with humility of mind let each of you regard*
*one another as more important than himself.*

PHILIPPIANS 2:3

Paul came to the Altmans' Christmas gathering. Angel's stomach sank at the sight of him, wondering what barbs he would aim at her this time. She stayed away from him, determined that nothing would spoil this Christmas. She had never had a real Christmas, and this family wanted to include her. If Paul called her a harlot to her face, she would take it and say nothing. Besides, she knew he wouldn't do it loudly enough for the others to hear.

To her surprise, he left her alone. He seemed just as determined to stay away from her. He brought presents for the children, small brown sacks of candy from the new general store. They were delighted, all except Miriam, who looked furious when he handed her one. "Thank you, *Uncle* Paul," she said tartly and kissed his cheek. A muscle jerked in his jaw as she turned away.

Angel waited until after the huge dinner she and Miriam had prepared before dispensing the gifts from her and Michael. She had worked for two days on the rag dolls for Leah and Ruthie, and she held her breath as they unwrapped them. Their squeals made her laugh. The boys were equally exuberant about the slingshots Michael had made for them. A target was immediately set up outside.

Miriam opened her package carefully and held up the dried-flower garland Angel had made. She fingered the satin ribbons streaming from the back. "It's beautiful, Amanda," she said, tears welling in her eyes.

Angel smiled. "I kept thinking of you running down the hill through all those wildflowers. It seemed appropriate."

Miriam took her hair down quickly and shook it out so that it flowed thick and curling about her face and shoulders and down her back. She placed the garland on her head. "How does it look?"

"Wild and beautiful," Michael said.

Paul got up and went outside.

Miriam's smile dimmed slightly. "He's such a dolt," she said under her breath.

"Miriam!" Elizabeth said in surprise, the baby against her shoulder. "What a thing to say."

Miriam didn't look the least bit repentant as she glared out the door at Paul. She took the garland off and laid it in her lap. "I love it, and I'm going to wear it instead of a veil on my wedding day."

When darkness fell, the family gathered around the fire and sang carols. John handed Michael the Bible without saying what he wanted read. Michael went straight to the Christmas story. Angel listened, her arms clasped around her raised knees. Ruth sleepily nudged her. Smiling, Angel welcomed her to her lap. Ruth wiggled until she was comfortable, her head resting against Angel's breast. Angel stroked her hair. *If I love a child not my own this much, how much more would I have loved my own?*

Michael's voice was rich and deep. Everyone was silent watching him. Angel remembered her mother telling her the story of the baby Jesus being born in a manger and the shepherds and three kings coming to worship him, but from Michael's lips it was full of beauty and mystery. For all that, she couldn't find joy in it. Not as these others did. What kind of father would let his own son be born for the single purpose of being nailed to a cross?

The dark voice came unexpectedly: **You know what kind of father, Angel. You had one just like him.**

She shivered. Looking away from Michael, she saw John standing in the shadows beside Elizabeth. His hand was on her shoulder. All fathers weren't like Alex Stafford. Some were like John Altman. She looked at Michael again. He would be a wonderful father, too. Strong, loving, forgiving if it came to that. He had read her the story of the prodigal son once not long after bringing her back from Pair-a-Dice. Should his child stray, he would be a father to welcome him home again. He wouldn't be like the one who had turned her mother away.

Michael finished reading and closed the Bible. When he raised his head, he looked straight into her eyes. She smiled. He smiled back, but there was a question in his eyes.

"Miriam," John said softly. She went to her father, and he said something to her. Elizabeth handed her the baby. Miriam carried him back and placed him in Michael's arms. The baby raised its hand, and Michael brushed his finger lightly against the tiny palm, smiling as the child clasped it tightly. "So, John," he said, "have you and Elizabeth come up with a name yet?"

"We have. Benjamin Michael. After you."

Michael looked stunned and then deeply moved. His eyes glistened with unshed tears. Miriam put her hands on his shoulders and leaned down to kiss his cheek. "We hope he'll grow into the name."

Angel's heart twisted as she looked at Michael holding the baby, and Miriam with her hand still resting on his shoulder. They looked like they belonged together.

From the darkness outside, Paul was thinking the same thing.

The rose bushes Michael had brought home to Angel bloomed early. She touched the scarlet buds and thought of her mother. She was so much like Mae. She was good for growing flowers, looking pretty, and giving a man pleasure. Beyond that, what good was she?

*Michael should have children. He* wants *children.*

She knew on Christmas night what she should do, but it was unbearable to even think of leaving him, of living without him. She wanted to stay here and forget the look in his eyes when he held Benjamin. She wanted to cling to him and bask in the happiness he gave her.

It was that very selfishness that made her realize she didn't deserve him.

Michael had given her everything. She had been empty, and he had filled her to overflowing with his love. She had betrayed him, and he had taken her back and forgiven her. He had sacrificed pride to love her. How could she discard his needs after that? How could she live with herself knowing that she had ignored the desires of his heart? What of Michael? What was best for him?

The dark voice spoke often: **Stay! Don't you deserve some happiness after all the years of living in misery? He says he loves you, doesn't he? So let him prove it!**

She couldn't listen anymore. She closed her mind to it and thought of Michael instead, and she thought of Miriam, sister of her heart. She thought of the children Miriam and Michael could have, dark and beautiful, strong and loving. Down through generations to come. She reminded herself that nothing could come from her. If she stayed, Michael would remain faithful until he died, and that would be the end to him.

She couldn't let that be.

When Michael told her he was going into town with Paul, she made her decision. John had remarked only yesterday that the town had grown so big a stage came twice a day. It traveled on the high road not two miles from the cabin, just beyond the line of hills. She still had the gold she had earned from Sam Teal and Joseph Hochschild. Michael had insisted she keep it for herself. It was enough to get her to San Francisco and keep her for a time. She would not think beyond that.

*I have to think of what's best for Michael.*

When Michael came in from the fields, she had a sumptuous venison dinner ready for him. The cabin was bedecked with flowers, the mantel, the table, the bed. Michael looked around bemused. "What are we celebrating?"

"Life," she said and kissed him. She drank in the sight of him, setting every angle of his face and body to memory. She wanted him desperately, loved him so much. Would he ever know how much? She couldn't tell him. If she did, he would come looking for her. He would bring her back. Better that he think her carnal and base. But she would have this last night to remember. He would be part of her no matter where she was and even if he never knew it. She would carry the sweet memories to her grave.

"Take me up to the hill again, Michael. Take me to the place where you showed me the sunrise."

He saw the hunger in her eyes. "It's cool tonight."

"Not too cold."

He could deny her nothing, but there was a strange uneasiness in the pit of his stomach. Something was wrong. He took the quilts from the bed and led the way. Perhaps she would talk to him and tell him what preyed on her mind. Maybe she would open up to him finally.

But her mood changed, swinging from pensive to abandoned. She ran to the top of the hill ahead of him and spun around, her arms spread wide. All around her, crickets sang, and the soft breeze stirred the grasses. "It's beautiful, isn't it? The vastness of it all. I'm utterly insignificant."

"Not to me."

"Yes," she said, turning to him. "Even to you." He frowned, and she turned again. "There shall be no other gods before me," she cried out to the heavens. "None but you, my lord." She turned and looked at him. *None but you, Michael Hosea.*

He frowned. "Are you mocking me, beloved?"

"Never," she said and meant it.

She took her hair down. It spilled over her shoulders and back, white in the moonlight. "Do you remember reading to me of the Shulammite bride dancing for her husband?"

He couldn't breathe as he watched her in the moonlight. Every movement drew his gaze to her and made him aware. When he tried to take hold of her, she moved away again, her arms outstretched in invitation. Her hair floated about her, and her voice came husky and enticing in the wind.

"I'll do anything for you, Michael. Anything."

And suddenly he knew what she was doing. She was saying good-bye, just as she had the last time. She was deadening his mind with physical pleasure.

When she came close again, Michael caught hold of her. "Why are you doing this?"

"For you," she said, pulling his head down and kissing him.

Digging his fingers into her hair, he slanted his mouth across hers. He wanted to consume her. Her hands were like flame on his body.

*God, I won't let her go again. I can't!*

She moved against him, and he had no thought except for her, and it was not enough.

*God, why are you doing this to me again? Do you give only to take away?*

"Michael, Michael," she breathed, and he tasted the saltiness of his own tears on her cheeks.

"You need me." He could see her moonlit face. "You need *me*. Say it, Tirzah. Say it."

**Let her go, beloved.**

*God, no! Don't ask it of me!*

**Give her to me.**

*No!*

They clung to one another, seeking solace in sweet oblivion. But sweet oblivion doesn't last.

Michael held her tightly when it passed away. He tried to hold onto all of it, but they were two separate beings again. He had not the strength to hold them together forever.

She was trembling violently, whether from cold or spent passion he didn't know. He didn't ask. He drew the quilt around them both and still felt her resolve like a raw wound.

It was growing colder, and they needed to return. They dressed in silence, both tormented, both pretending not to be. She came to him again and put her arms around his waist, pressing herself against him as a child would, looking for comfort.

He closed his eyes against the fear uncurling in the pit of his stomach. *I love her, Lord. I can't give her up.*

**Michael, beloved. Would you have her hang on her cross forever?**

Michael let out a shuddering sigh. When she lifted her face, he saw something in it that made him want to weep. She loved him. She really loved him. And yet, there was something else in her moonlit face. A haunting sadness he couldn't take away, an emptiness he could never fill. He remembered her anguished words on the night Benjamin was born. *"I wish I was whole!"* He couldn't make her so.

Lifting her, he held her cradled in his arms. She put her arm around his neck and kissed him. He closed his eyes. *Lord, if I give her up to you now, will you ever give her back to me?*

No answer came.

*Lord, please!*

The wind stirred softly, but there was only silence.

Angel walked out to the barn with Michael the next morning and watched him saddle his horse. "When do you expect to be back?"

He glanced back at her enigmatically. "As soon as I can." Leading the horse out of the stall, he put his arm around her shoulders. She smiled up at him. Stopping, he drew her into his arms and kissed her. She kissed him back, making the most of the last opportunity she would ever have. When Michael's fingers dug into her shoulders painfully, she was surprised. "I love you," he said roughly. "I will *always* love you."

She wondered at his vehemence and touched his face tenderly. "Take care of yourself."

He didn't smile. "You do likewise." He mounted and rode away. She didn't go back into the house until he disappeared over the hill.

She wasn't going to leave until everything was properly in order. She made the bed, washed the dishes and put them away, and shook out the hearth rug. The flowers were still fresh. She banked the fire so that it would still be going when Michael returned home.

She jumped when someone tapped at the door. It was Miriam. "What are you doing here?" Angel asked in dismay.

Miriam was taken aback. "Weren't you expecting me?"

"No."

"Well, that's odd. Michael came by the house on his way to Paul's and said this was a good day for a visit."

Angel turned away and went back to her carpetbag lying open on the bed. She quickly stuffed in one of Michael's shirts and then folded a dress on top of it. Miriam watched her. "Michael didn't tell me you were going anywhere."

"He doesn't know." She snapped the bag shut and lifted it. "I'm leaving him, Miriam."

"*What?*" Miriam said, looking at her as though she had sprouted horns. "Again?"

"I'm leaving him for good this time."

"But *why?*"

"Because I have to." Angel looked around the cabin one last time. She had been happy here, but that didn't mean she should stay. She went quietly out the door.

Miriam came after her. *"Wait!"* She kept pace as Angel headed for the hills. "Amanda, I don't understand."

"You don't have to. Just go home, Miriam. Say good-bye to everyone for me."

"But where will you go?"

"West, east, it doesn't matter. I haven't decided."

"Then why are you in such a hurry? Stay here and talk things over with Michael. Whatever he's done to make you want to leave – "

Angel couldn't have her friend believing Michael was in the wrong. "Miriam, Michael has never done a thing wrong in his life."

"Then why are you doing this?"

"I don't want to talk about it." Angel kept walking, wishing Miriam would give up and leave her alone.

"You love him. I *know* you do. If you leave without any reason, what's he going to think?"

Angel knew what he would think. He would believe she had gone back to her old life. Maybe it would be better if he did believe that. It would keep him from looking for her. Only she need know that she would never go back to prostitution. Even if it meant starving to death.

Miriam argued and pleaded all the way to the road and only stopped because she was finally out of breath. Angel paced, looking for the stagecoach. It was just past noon. It should come soon. She couldn't bear this waiting much longer. Why had Michael told Miriam to come for a visit today of all days?

"I thought Michael was so perfect," Miriam said miserably, "but he can't be if you're running away from him like this."

"He's everything he seems and more, Miriam. I swear on my life he's done nothing to hurt me. He's done nothing but love me from the beginning, even when I hated the sight of him."

Miriam's eyes swam. "Then how can you leave him now?"

"Because I don't belong with him. I never did." Seeing that Miriam was going to say even more, she put her hand on the girl's arm to stop her. "*Please.* Miriam, I can't have children. Do you know what that means to a man like him? He wants children. He *deserves* them. I was ruined for all that long ago." She struggled with her pain. "I'm begging you, Miriam. Don't make this any more difficult than it already is. I'm going because it's best for Michael. Try to understand," she said brokenly. "Miriam, I have to think of what's best for *him.*"

The coach was coming at last. Angel stepped quickly into the road and waved to the driver to stop. As he drew rein on the six horses, she worked the wedding ring off her finger and held it out to Miriam. "Give this back to him for me. It belonged to his mother."

Tears pouring down her cheeks, Miriam shook her head and wouldn't take it. Angel reached out and took her hand, put the ring into it, and closed the girl's fingers around it. Turning away quickly, she handed her carpetbag up to the driver. He began lashing it down with the other cases.

Angel looked at her friend's pale, distraught face. "You love him, don't you, Miriam?"

"Yes, I love him. You know I do." She stepped closer. "You're wrong to do this. Wrong, Amanda."

Angel hugged her tightly. "Help me be strong." She held her a moment longer. "You're very dear to me." She let go and stepped quickly up into the coach.

"Don't go!" Miriam cried, putting her hands on the window opening. The coach started moving.

Angel looked down at her, fighting against the pain. "You said you loved him, Miriam. Then *love* him. And give him the children I can't."

Miriam let go in shock. Her face went fiery red and then white. "No. Oh, *no!*" She started running after the coach, but it was picking up speed and not slowing down. "Wait! Amanda, *Amanda.*"

But it was already too late. Dust swirled back, choking her, and by the time she could run again, the stagecoach was too far down the road for her to catch up. Standing in the middle of the road, she looked at the wedding ring in her hand and burst into tears.

The last thing Paul expected to see when he and Michael rode toward his cabin late that afternoon was Miriam coming out his door. His heart jumped at the sight of her and then bounded around in his chest like a rabbit when she ran toward him. What was Michael going to think about her being here?

But she ran to Michael, not him. Paul's stomach dropped like a stone. Michael dismounted.

"Amanda's gone!" Miriam said, her face pale and tear streaked. She was dusty and disheveled. "I've been waiting here all day, Michael. I knew you would come by Paul's first. You've got to go after her. She took the morning stage. You have to bring her back!"

Paul stayed on his horse. So Angel was gone again. For all her vows, she had left Michael. Just as he expected. He ought to feel glad about it. When Michael put his hand on Miriam's shoulder, a hot and completely unexpected surge of jealousy flashed through him.

Michael was pale and strained. "I'm not going after her, Miriam."

"Have you and Amanda *both* gone mad?" Miriam cried out, tears welling in her dark eyes. "You don't understand...." How could she tell him? Oh, God, what was she to do? She felt Paul watching them and couldn't tell Michael everything Amanda had said to her in confidence. "You've got to go after her. *Now!* If you don't, you may never find her again."

"I'm not going to look for her. Not this time."

"'Not this time'?"

"He means he's gone after her before and it hasn't done him any good," Paul said. "She hasn't changed since the day he met her."

Miriam turned on him, face livid. "*Stay out of this!* Go hide in your cabin! Go stick your head in the sand like you always do!"

Paul drew back, shocked by her fury.

Miriam turned back to Michael, clutching the front of his shirt. "Michael, *please*, go after her before it's too late."

He took her hands. "I can't. Miriam, if she wants to come back, she'll come back. If she doesn't, then...she doesn't."

Miriam put her hands over her face and wept.

Michael looked up at Paul and saw that he didn't intend to comfort the girl. Sighing heavily, he took Miriam in his arms. Her whole body was shaking with her sobs.

Paul stared down at them and felt a stab of pain go through his middle. This was what he wanted, wasn't it? This was what he had planned. Hadn't he been waiting for that witch to leave so Michael would turn to Miriam and have the wife he deserved? So why was it that he had never felt so lonely?

Whatever he had thought he wanted, he couldn't look at them holding onto one another now. It hurt too much. Turning his horse, he left them alone.

# Twenty-nine

*Behold a pale horse:*
*and his name that sat on him was Death,*
*and Hell followed him.*

REVELATION 6:8

San Francisco was no longer a mean little town beside a bay but a city spreading across the windswept hills. Happy Valley was no longer a tent encampment but a community of houses. Many of the ships that had been dragged ashore and turned into stores, saloons, and boardinghouses had burned down. They'd been replaced by frame structures and brick buildings. Planked sidewalks now lined the muddy streets.

The ferryman stood with his face into the wind. "Every time the city burns, they just build her back up better than ever," he told her as they crossed the bay. He warned her about the brackish water from shallow wells and said she would find better lodgings up the hill away from the docks. Angel was too tired to venture far and ended up in a small hotel on the water.

The smell of the sea and garbage reminded her of the dock shack of her childhood. It seemed a hundred years ago. She had supper in the small dining room and suffered the bold stares of a dozen young men. She ate the stew to fill the void in her stomach, but the one in her heart remained.

*I did the right thing in leaving Michael. I know I did.*

Returning to her small room, she tried to sleep on the narrow bed. The room was cold, and she couldn't get warm. She curled into a tight ball beneath the blanket and thought longingly of Michael's solid warmth beside her. She couldn't stop thinking about him. Was it only three days ago she had danced for him in the moonlight? What did he think of her now? Did he hate her? Did he curse her?

If she could cry, she might feel better, but she had no tears. She held herself tightly, aching. Closing her eyes, she tried to see

Michael's face, but the image wasn't enough. She couldn't touch him. She couldn't feel his arms around her.

Rising, she rummaged through her carpetbag to find his shirt. She lay down on the bed again and pressed her face into the wool fabric Michael had worn, breathing in the scent of his body.

"Oh, Mama," she whispered into the darkness, "the pain does make you want to die."

But a still, small voice inside her kept saying over and over again, *Live. Keep going. Don't give up.*

What was she going to do? She had a little gold left, but it wasn't going to last long. The stagecoach ride, lodgings, and the ferry ride had been more expensive than she'd expected. The going rate for this foul little hotel was far too dear. What gold she had left would keep her for another two or three days at the most. After that, she would have to find a way to earn a living.

She slept finally. The night was filled with strange, disconcerting dreams. She awakened several times, shaking violently. It was as though some malevolent force were close by, waiting.

Angel packed her few possessions and left in the morning. She wandered for hours through the streets of San Francisco. Portsmouth Square had changed dramatically. The shanty in which she had lived was gone. So were all the others, as well as the tents that had spread like a plague around the plaza. Booths were now set up, giving the square the feel of a grand bazaar. She browsed through goods from around the world.

There were several brothels, one with the elegant air of New Orleans. On the outer edge of the square were thriving hostelries, saloons, and casinos. The Parker House, Dennison's Exchange, the Crescent City, and the Empire now rose from the grime Angel remembered. On the southwest corner of Clay Street was Brown's City Hotel.

She passed doctors' and dentists' offices, attorneys' and business offices, surveying and engineering offices. She saw several new banks and a large brokerage firm. There was even a public schoolhouse with children playing tag in the yard. Angel stood watching them for a while, thinking of little Ruth and Leah and the boys. She missed them so much.

At Clay Street, men were queued up at the post office, waiting news of mail. On the corner of Washington and Grant was a new Chinese laundry. Workers scrubbed clothing in big washtubs while others stacked fresh linens into baskets. Balancing these on bamboo poles, they set off at a run to make deliveries.

By midday, Angel was famished, weary. And no closer to knowing what she was going to do to make a living. The only thing that came to mind was going back to what she knew. Every time she passed a brothel, she knew she could walk in the door and have food and shelter. She could have physical comfort. All she had to do was sell her body again – and betray Michael.

**He'll never know, Angel.**

"I'll know." A man gave her a curious look as he passed. Would she turn into a mad woman who talked to herself?

A miner stopped her and asked her to marry him. She pulled her arm free and told him to leave her alone. He said he had a cabin in the Sierras and he needed a wife. She told him to look elsewhere and hurried on.

The crush of people made her more and more nervous. Where were they all going? What did they do for a living? Her head was throbbing. Maybe it was the hunger. Maybe it was worrying about what she was going to do when her gold ran out. Maybe it was knowing she was weak and would probably go right back to being a harlot just so she could keep body and soul together.

*What am I going to do? God, I don't know what to do!*

**Go into that cafe and rest.**

Angel looked up the street and saw a small cafe. Sighing, she walked toward it and went in. She chose a table in the back corner and pushed her carpetbag behind her feet. Rubbing her temples, she wondered where she was going to spend the night.

Someone banged on the table a few feet away from her, making her jump. A wiry bearded man hollered. "What's taking so long? I've been waiting near an hour. Where's the steak I ordered?"

A small red-headed man hurried out of the back room and tried to quiet the angry patron with a whispered explanation of the delay, but that only incensed the man further. Face red, he grabbed the smaller man and held him up to his face. "Under the weather, *ha!* Drunk is what you mean!" He shoved the little man back, banging him into another table. The patron headed for the door, slamming it behind him so hard the windows rattled.

The little man ducked into the back room again, probably to escape the scrutiny of the dozen patrons still waiting for service and food. Several others got up and left. Angel didn't know whether to follow their lead or not. She was exhausted and without prospects, and sitting here was as good as sitting anywhere else. She didn't want to go out into the rush for a while anyway. Missing a meal wouldn't kill her.

Three more men gave up on waiting to find out whether food was coming or not. Angel and four others remained. The little man appeared again, his smile tense and forced. "We got biscuits and beans." The four remaining men vacated the premises with disgruntled remarks about having had enough of that fare to last a lifetime.

The little man's shoulders sagged in defeat. Not noticing Angel in the corner, he spoke to the air. "Well, that does it, Lord. I'm out of business." He walked to the front door, flipped the sign over and put his forehead against the wall.

Angel felt sorry for him. She knew what it was like to be down on her luck. "Should I leave?" she asked quietly. He turned, blushing beet red.

"I didn't know you was there. You want a biscuit and some beans?"

"Please."

He disappeared momentarily. When he returned he set a dish down in front of her and backed off. The biscuit was hard as stone, and the beans were burned. Frowning, she looked up at him. "Coffee?" he asked and poured her some in a mug. It was so strong, Angel grimaced.

"Mister, you need a new cook," she said with a dry smile, setting the mug down and pushing the plate aside.

"You asking for employment?"

Her eyes shot wide open. *"Me?"*

He took note of her surprise and looked her over again. "I guess not."

She felt the heat coming up into her face. Did her past show that clearly? Was it emblazoned on her forehead for the whole world to see? Had knowing Michael a year made no difference in her at all?

Her back stiffened. "As a matter of fact, I *was* looking for work." She gave a short laugh. "And though I'm far from the greatest cook in the world, I think I can do better than this." She winced at the congealing mass of greasy beans on her plate.

"In that case, you're hired!" He slammed the coffeepot down and stuck his hand out before she could utter a word. "My name's Virgil Harper, ma'am."

She was trying to take in the fact that she had work and that it had fallen right into her lap like a ripe plum from heaven. How had it come about? One minute she was frantic about what she was going to do to make a living; the next she was employed by a banty-rooster. "Hold on," she said, putting a hand up. "I'll need to find a place to live first. I may not even stay in San Francisco."

"You don't need to look for nothing, lady. You can have the cook's quarters as soon as he moves his things out, and he's packing right now. Your room is next to mine above the kitchen. Real cozy. Good bed, chest of drawers."

Her eyes narrowed. She should have known there was a catch.

"It's got a good lock on the door," he said. "You can check it out first if you like. Can you fix pies? We get a lot of requests for pie."

She could scarcely catch her breath he was going so fast. "How much will this room cost me?"

"Nothing," he said, genuinely surprised. "Comes with the job. Now what about the pies? Can you bake or not?"

"Yes, I can bake bread and pies," she said. Elizabeth and Miriam had taught her everything they knew. "If you can get me flour, apples, berries – "

Harper threw his head back and his hands in the air. "Lord Jesus, I love you!" He spun around and stamped his feet up and down. "I love you! I love you!"

Angel stared at him, jumping around like a grasshopper, and wondered if the poor man had gone completely off his rocker. He saw her staring and laughed. "I've been down on my knees all week wondering what I was going to do. You know what that drunk did? He relieved himself in the soup and served it all day Monday. He told me that night. I thought I'd be hanging from a post by morning, and he just laughed and said he was seasoning the broth. I won't even tell you what he did this morning."

She looked down at the bowl in front of her. "Did he do anything to the beans?"

"Nothing that I know about."

"Why don't I feel reassured?"

"Come on in the kitchen, and I'll show you what I got on hand in the way of supplies, and you can see what you can do with them. What do I call you, ma'am? I didn't even think to ask."

"Hosea," she said. "Mrs. Hosea."

Michael sank the ax deeply into the log. It went straight through and imbedded in the block. He gave it a hard tug and freed the blade again. He set up another log and split it with one swing. Over and over, he did the same thing until sections piled up around the block. He kicked them aside and set up another log. He swung again, harder than before, and the ax sliced clean through, bouncing off the block this time and narrowly missing his leg.

Shaking, Michael dropped the ax and sank to his knees. Sweat was pouring into his eyes. He wiped it away with the back of his arm. He heard something. Squinting into the sun, he saw John sitting on his horse watching him. Michael hadn't even heard him ride up. "How long you been there?" he asked, chest heaving.

"Couple of minutes."

Michael tried to get to his feet but couldn't. As soon as he had stopped the frenzied labor, all his strength had left him. He sank back again and leaned against the block. Glancing up, he gave John a wry smile. "Didn't hear you arrive. What brings you by?"

John rested his forearms on the pommel. "You got enough wood there for two winters."

"Bring a wagon over and take what you want."

The saddle creaked as John dismounted. He came and hunkered down before Michael. "Why don't you go after her?"

Michael raked a shaking hand back through his hair. "Leave it be, John." He didn't feel like talking.

"Just swallow your pride and get on your horse and go look for her. I'll watch over your place."

"It's got nothing to do with pride."

"Then what's stopping you?"

Michael leaned his head back and took a deep breath. "Good sense."

John frowned. "Then it's like Paul said."

Michael looked at him. "What did Paul say?"

"Nothing much," John hedged. "Michael, women are emotional. Sometimes they do stupid things – "

"She thought this out. It wasn't an impulse."

"How do you know that?"

Michael raked his hand into his hair. How many times had he gone over the things she had done and said that last night. He could still see her slender body in the moonlight, her pale hair floating about her. He shut his eyes. "I just know."

"Miriam blames herself for all this. She won't tell us why she thinks that, but she's mightily convinced of it."

"It's got nothing to do with her. You tell her that for me."

"I have. She tried to get Paul to go find Amanda for you and bring her back."

Michael could well guess the outcome of that conversation. At least Paul had been sensitive enough over the last weeks to not come by and gloat. "Paul never liked Angel."

"Angel?" John said blankly.

"Mara, Amanda, Tirzah...." Michael's voice cracked. He held his head. "Jesus," he said hoarsely. "Jesus." *Angel.* She never even trusted him enough to tell him her real name. Or had he been thinking of her as Angel all along without even knowing it? Was that why she left him again? *Oh, God, was that why you wanted me to let her go?*

John Altman felt helpless before the younger man's grief. He couldn't even imagine his life without Elizabeth. He had seen how much Michael loved Amanda, and Miriam swore Amanda loved him. He put his hand on Michael's shoulder. "Maybe she'll come back on her own." His words sounded hollow. Michael didn't even look up. "What can I do to help you get through this?"

"Nothing," Michael said. How many times had Angel said that very thing. *Nothing.* Had she felt as though her guts were being ripped out? Had the pain been so immense that even mentioning it made it worse? How many times had he probed her wounds, just as John was doing now? Trying to help and only drawing more blood.

"I'll come back tomorrow," John said.

Miriam came instead.

She sat with him beneath the willow tree and said nothing. He could hear her mind working, the question hanging in the air: *Why won't you do something!* But she didn't ask. She dug in her pocket and held something out for him. His stomach dropped when he saw his mother's wedding ring in the palm of her hand.

"Take it," she said.

He did. "Where did you find it?" he asked hoarsely.

Miriam's eyes filled. "She gave it to me before getting in the coach. I forgot to give it back to you the first day. Then I was...embarrassed."

He made a fist around it. "Thanks." He didn't ask her anything.

"Have you changed your mind, Michael? Are you going to try and find her?"

He looked at her steadily. "No, Miriam, and don't ask me again."

Miriam didn't stay long after that. She had said all she could the day Amanda left him and she had not persuaded him then.

Michael knew all the possible motives for Amanda's desertion. But beyond that, beyond comprehension, he knew God's will was working. "Why this way?" he cried out in anguish. "Why did you tell me to love her if you were only going to take her away from me?"

He raged at God and grieved for his wife. He stopped reading his Bible. He stopped praying. He turned inside himself seeking answers. He found none. And he dreamed, dark, confusing dreams with forces that were closing in on him.

The still, quiet voice didn't speak to him anymore, not for weeks and months. God was silent and hidden, his purpose a mystery. Life became such a barren wasteland that Michael couldn't bear it anymore, and he cried out.

"Why have you forsaken me?"

*Beloved, I am always with you, even to the end of time.*

Michael slowed his frenetic work and sought solace in God's word. *I don't understand anything anymore, Lord. Losing her is like losing half of myself. She loved me. I know she did. Why did you drive her from me?*

The answer came to him slowly, with the changing of the seasons.

*You shall have no other gods before me.*

That couldn't be right.

Michael's anger grew. "When have I worshiped anyone but you?" He raged again. "I've followed you all my life. I've *never* put anyone before you." Hands fisted, he wept. "I love her, but I never made her my god."

In the calm that followed his angry torrent of words, Michael heard – and finally understood.

*You became hers.*

Angel stood in the middle of the night-shrouded street and watched Harper's Cafe burning. Everything she had worked for over the past six months was burning with it. All she had left was the worn gingham dress she was wearing and the stained apron that covered it.

There had been so little warning. Virgil had burst into the kitchen yelling there was a fire. She didn't even have time to ask questions as he pulled her outside. Two buildings were burning a few doors away. Then a breeze came up and swept the fire right down through the remaining buildings on the block.

People were running helter-skelter, some in panic, some shouting directions, others gathering and passing water buckets frantically in an attempt to contain the fire, but it was no use. Ash and smoke filled the air, and the flames leapt higher, bright orange against the darkening evening sky.

Helpless, Angel watched the cafe collapse in an explosion of sparks and flame. Virgil wept. Business had been going well. Though their menu was limited, what they offered was excellent, and word had spread quickly.

Angel sat down on a barrel someone had rolled from a building. Men had pulled everything they could drag or carry from their buildings. The street was stacked with goods, furniture, sacks. Why hadn't she thought to do the same? She hadn't even thought to run upstairs and pack her things. She could have stuffed everything she had into her carpetbag and made it out in time.

When the fire reached the end of the street, it stopped. The breeze died down, and so did the excitement. Up and down the street people stood in despair, looking at the blaze consuming what remained of their dreams. Virgil sat on the ground, his head in his hands. Depression settled over Angel like a cold, wet blanket. Now what was she going to do? She looked around and saw that others were in the same situation she was. What would Michael do if he were here? She knew he would never give in to despair, and he would do something for these people. But what could she do? One woman, destitute herself. One thing she knew she couldn't do was stand by and watch Virgil sobbing in the street.

She sat down beside him in the dirt. "As soon as the fire dies, we'll dig through what's left and see if there's anything that can be salvaged."

"What's the use? I ain't got enough money to rebuild," he sobbed.

She put her arm around his shoulders. "The land is worth something. Maybe you can get a loan on it and start again with that."

They slept against a pile of packs using borrowed blankets. At dawn, they dug through the ash and rubble. Choking on soot, Angel found cast iron pots and pans. The stove could still be used. The utensils were melted, but many of the dishes were intact. A good scrubbing would make them usable.

Face covered with ash, her throat raw from breathing it, Angel rested. She was hungry and tired. Every muscle in her body ached, but at least Virgil was feeling more hopeful, even though he had not yet found them a place to stay. The hotels in the area were already full with paying customers and unlikely to give space in a lobby to those who couldn't. The thought of sleeping in the street with the cold bay mists was daunting, but she supposed things could be worse. Someone had given them a couple more blankets.

They worked to clear away the charred wood. Angel collected shards of glass from shattered windows in a bucket, dumping it in a pile to be carted away later. Virgil was pale with exhaustion. "I guess we'll have to camp right here until I can get the money to rebuild the place. The priest has room at the church if you want to stay there. Some of the others are going."

"No, thanks," she said. She would sleep in the mud before she went to a church for help.

Virgil nodded toward some men standing in line outside a building across the street. "Father Patrick set up a soup kitchen over there. Go get yourself something to eat."

"I'm not hungry," she lied. She wasn't going to ask a priest for anything.

But she desperately needed a drink of water. A few barrels had been put out for drinking. She wanted to wash her face, but the only other water available was in a trough. Sighing, she decided it was probably cleaner than she was. Bending over it, she cupped her hands and washed her face. The water felt refreshing.

"Hello, Angel. It's been a long, long time."

Her heart stopped. She had to be imagining that deep voice. She raised her head slowly, heart pounding, her face dripping wet.

Duke stood before her, his mouth curved in a deadly smile.

# *Thirty*

*Yea, though I walk through the valley of the shadow of death,*
*I will fear no evil,*
*for Thou art with me.*

PSALM 23:4

Duke's mocking gaze swept Angel's soiled gingham dress, his mouth curving into a sardonic smile. "I've seen you look better, my dear."

She froze at the sight of him. When he came close and touched her, she felt faint.

"It would seem no matter how far you run, you can't get away from me, can you?" He looked down over her. "You've grown into quite a beautiful woman beneath all that soot." He looked around at the burned-out buildings. "Were you working in one of these miserable little hovels?"

When he looked at her again, Angel found her voice. "I was a cook for Harper's Cafe." Her stomach was quivering.

"A cook? You?" He laughed. "Oh, that's rich, my dear. What was your specialty?" As he spoke, he looked over the men working in the burned-out buildings. "I worried about you. I was afraid you would end up with another weakling like Johnny." His eyes came to rest on Virgil digging through the rubble. "And you ended up with a little rodent instead."

She recognized that dark look and knew it boded no good for Virgil, who had shown her nothing but kindness. Her palms were sweating, but she had to take his attention off the little man who had helped her. "Surely you didn't come all the way to California just to find me. You, with so many important things to do."

"Look around you, my dear. There's a fortune to be made here." His smile was taunting. "I came to take my share."

Virgil saw them and came toward them. Her look didn't warn him away. Quite the contrary, he came all the more quickly.

He looked Duke up and down and glanced at her in concern. "You all right, ma'am? This man bothering you?"

What did the poor fool think he could do about it? "I'm fine, Virgil."

Duke gave him a cold smile. "Aren't you going to introduce us, my dear?"

She did so. Virgil had clearly heard the name before and looked stunned. "You *know* this man?"

"Angel and I are very old and dear friends."

Virgil looked at her, and she felt the need to say something more, to try to explain. But there was little she could say. "We were acquainted in New York. A long time ago."

"Not all that long ago," Duke said, his tone possessive.

"Don't you own that place across the square?" Virgil asked. "The big one?"

"Indeed," Duke drawled, amused. "Have you frequented my tables?"

"I haven't been able to afford it," Virgil said dryly.

"Shall we go, Angel?" Duke said, his hand tightening beneath her elbow.

"Go?" Virgil looked at her. "Go where?"

"I don't think that's any of your business," Duke said warningly.

Virgil drew himself up to his full five feet. "It is if she don't want to go with you."

Duke laughed.

Angel was surprised and touched that Virgil would willingly defend her, even against a man like Duke, who could plainly destroy him without much effort. "I – " She felt Duke's fingers bite into her arm and was afraid what he would do to Virgil if she even hesitated to go with him. "I'm sorry, Virgil." The poor little man looked so confused and hurt. He looked at her, and she felt she had betrayed him, too, by not being truthful from the beginning. Did she really think she could have a different life? What right had she?

"You'll have to find yourself a new cook," Duke said. "She's coming back where she belongs."

"You sure, ma'am?"

Duke's dark eyes burned with annoyance that this little cafe owner thought he could thwart him if he chose. "Perhaps I should deal with him the same way I dealt with Johnny," he said, glancing down at Angel, eyes dark with impatience.

"Johnny who?" Virgil asked, looking unruffled and ready to make a challenge. For all his lack of size, he had no lack of courage. The only thing he really lacked was common sense.

"Don't!" Angel pleaded. "Please, Duke. I'll go with you."

"You've become so polite, my dear." Benevolent once more, he smiled at Virgil. "Do you own this piece of land?"

"I do," Virgil said cautiously.

"Would you like to sell it?"

"Not on your life."

Duke laughed. "No? Well, if you need cash to rebuild, come by and we'll talk terms. If you have trouble finding another cook to replace Angel, I might even be able to help you there as well." He looked amused.

"Thanks," Virgil said, but Angel saw he wouldn't take Duke up on anything. "Mrs. Hosea, you sure about this?"

"Mrs. Hosea?" Duke said quietly, one dark brow rising as he looked down at her. Her heart was in her throat.

"Yes, Virgil, I'm sure," she said.

Duke led her away, laughing low as though at some great joke. Angel tried to think what to do, but the firm hand beneath her arm paralyzed her brain. *Michael, oh, Michael!* He had fought their way out of the saloon in Pair-a-Dice, but he wouldn't be here to fight for her this time. She was alone, and Duke was holding her so tightly she knew he didn't mean to let her get away again.

"So you married, my dear? Was it entertaining while it lasted? Or just pretense?" He ushered her into a big gaming house. Angel scarcely noticed her surroundings as he walked her between the tables. It was opulent, but then, Duke always did everything on a grand scale.

Men called greetings to him and openly stared at her in speculation. She walked with her head high, eyes straight ahead. They went up the stairs and down a richly paneled corridor. Panic rose in Angel as she remembered another corridor three thousand miles away and what had waited for her at the end of it. Duke opened a door and propelled her in ahead of him.

A beautiful brunette lay asleep in a rumpled brass bed. Duke walked over and gave her a hard slap. She came awake with a painful cry. "Get out." The young prostitute clambered off the bed, snatched up her robe, and fled. Duke smiled at Angel. "This will be your room."

She couldn't just give in. "Do I have a choice?"

"Still defiant," he drawled and came to her slowly. He gripped her face hard, staring down into her eyes. She tried to hide her fear by glaring back at him, but she couldn't fool him. He obviously knew she was pretending, and smiled. "You're home, my dear. Right back where you belong. You should be happy." His hand slid down and closed lightly on her throat. "You look so in control, but your heart is pounding like a frightened rabbit's."

He lit a cheroot and looked at her through the smoke. "You're so pale, my dear. Do you think I'm going to hurt you?" He kissed her forehead in fatherly affection, mocking her as he had always done when she dared to defy him. "Let's talk later, shall we?" He patted her cheek as though she were a child and left the room.

Michael awakened in a cold sweat. Angel had called to him. He had seen her standing in the midst of a fire, crying out his name over and over again. He couldn't get to her no matter how hard he tried, but he saw a dark figure walking through the flames toward her.

He ran shaking hands through his damp hair. Sweat was running down his bare chest, and he couldn't stop shaking. "It was just a dream."

The foreboding he felt was so heavy he was nauseated. He prayed. Then he rose from the bed and went outside. It would be dawn soon. Things would look better in the light of day. When dawn came, the sensation that something was wrong would not go away, and he prayed again, fervently. He was full of fear for his wife.

Where was she? How was she surviving? Was she hungry? Did she have shelter? How was she making her way alone?

Why didn't she come back to him?

Something ominous hung in the air all day. He could feel it like a blackness covering his soul, and he knew without a doubt it had to do with Amanda. He prayed unceasingly for her.

He knew he was helpless. There was nothing he could do if she was in trouble. He didn't know where she was or what kind of help she needed, but letting go of her was so hard. He still loved her so much. He trusted God to protect and guide him. Why couldn't he trust that the Lord would do the same for *her*?

Because he knew she didn't believe.

Angel tried the door, but it was locked. She went to the window and pushed the elegant lace curtains aside to look out. No way out there, either. Duke liked to safeguard his property.

She paced, palms sweating as she thought of what he might do to her. She wasn't fooled. He was seething with rage beneath his amiable demeanor. Leaving her alone worked in his favor. He knew she would eat herself up with all the thoughts of what he could do. "Not this time," she whispered to herself. "Not again."

Looking around, she decided she could make the bed and tidy the room. She could *do* something to keep her mind off the inevitable. Finishing those small chores, she sat at the window and watched the people milling about below. The fear rose again. Closing her eyes tightly, she wrestled with it. "Michael, Michael, show me what to do." She pictured him working in the fields. She could see him straightening, the hoe in his hand, the smile on his face. She could see him sitting before the fire, the Bible in his lap. "Trust in the Lord," he said. *"Trust in the Lord."*

The door opened, and she forced herself to sit calmly where she was as Duke entered. He was followed by a burly man. She feigned indifference as the servant gathered the other girl's things from the armoire and carried them from the room. Duke stood studying her passively. She looked up at him and smiled faintly. *You won't make me crawl, you devil. You won't turn my mind inside out this time. I'll think of Michael. I'll just keep thinking of Michael.*

A Chinese servant came in to strip the bed and put on fresh linens.

Angel sat sedately in the high-back chair, her hands resting lightly on the arms, her heart beating violently. Duke had not moved or said anything, but she knew that look, and fear grew like a knot in her belly. What retribution was he planning?

"Bring the tub up," he ordered, and the Chinese man bowed. "Make sure she has plenty of warm water." The Celestial bowed again and backed out of the room. Duke's eyes narrowed as he studied her face for a long moment. "I'll send someone to attend you." He turned and left.

Surprised, she let out her breath. He had been disturbed by her manner. She had never been able to fool him before. But then it had been almost three years since she had last seen him. Perhaps he had forgotten her ruse.

And perhaps that would only make matters worse.

A young girl came in to help her undress. She was no more than thirteen. Angel knew she wasn't Duke's mistress, though she might very well have been at one time. She was pretty enough. But Angel knew that as long as a girl was Duke's exclusively, her face was clean, she wore pastels, braids, and hair ribbons. This girl's cheeks and lips were reddened, and her hair was spilling in a curly mass over thin shoulders. She had that look of having come through hell.

Full of pity, she smiled at the young girl. "What's your name?"

"Cherry," the girl said, dumping Angel's gingham dress and underthings beside the door.

"I'd like to have those things back once they're washed."

"Duke said to throw them away."

"And one must always obey Duke." She didn't want to get the girl in trouble. "Did he bring you to California with him?"

"Me and three other girls," she said as she tested the water. "It's not too hot. You can bathe now."

Angel removed her worn underclothing. Lowering herself into the warm water, she sighed. Whatever happened, she would be clean when it came. On the outside, at least. "How long have you been here?"

"Eight months," the girl answered.

Angel frowned. She had been living within blocks of Duke all this time and never knew it. Maybe it was fate that she be with him.

"You're very beautiful," Cherry said.

Angel looked at the girl bleakly. "So are you." Such a pale, pretty girl with frightened blue eyes. She was filled with compassion.

"Would you like me to wash your hair for you?" Cherry said.

"What I would like is to find a way out of here." Cherry froze in surprise, and Angel smiled in self-mockery. "But then, that's impossible, isn't it?" She took the sponge and bar of lavender-scented soap from the girl and said nothing more.

Duke came in without knocking. Cherry jumped, her face paling. Angel put her hand on the girl's and felt how cold she was. Several satin gowns were draped over Duke's arm, and he laid them with great ceremony on the end of the bed. "Leave us, Cherry." The girl scurried out of the room.

Angry, Angel steeled all her defenses and continued with her bath as though he weren't there. He was staring at her. Uncomfortable beneath that dark scrutiny, she rose and wrapped a large towel around herself. He handed her another smaller one for her hair. She wrapped it about her head like a turban. He held a blue satin dressing gown open for her. Donning it, she tied it snugly. He put his hand on her shoulder, turning her toward him.

"You're no longer my little Angel, are you?"

"I couldn't stay a child forever," she said, chilled by his touch.

"A pity." He held a chair out for her. Breathing slowly, she forced herself to remain calm as she sat.

"You must be famished," he said and pulled the bell cord. The Chinese servant entered with a tray. As soon as it was placed on the table before her, Duke waved him out. Removing the silver covers himself, he smiled. "All your favorites, my dear."

It was a feast: a thick rare beefsteak, creamed potatoes, and mixed vegetables dripping with butter. There was even a thick slice of chocolate cake. She hadn't eaten a meal like this since leaving the New York brothel. Her mouth watered, and her stomach tightened.

Duke lifted a silver pitcher, filled a crystal glass with milk, and handed it to her. "You always did prefer it to champagne, didn't you?"

She took the glass from him. "Fattening the calf before you slaughter it, Duke?"

"The *golden* calf? Now, wouldn't I be a fool to do so?"

She hadn't eaten since before the fire, stubbornly refusing the charity offered by that priest. Eat his soup, and he would expect her to confess her soul before he told her it was beyond redemption. So she was starving now.

"I'll join you later," Duke said, surprising her again. She had expected him to stay. As soon as he was out the door, she tucked into the sumptuous meal. She hadn't tasted food this good in three years. Duke had always set a good table. She poured herself a second glass of milk.

Only when her stomach was full did she realize what she had done and shame filled her.

*Oh, Michael, I'm weak. I'm so weak! I was right to leave you. Look at me! Stuffing myself on Duke's food. I'm selling my soul for a steak and a slice of chocolate cake when I swore I'd starve before I went back to my old ways. I don't know how to be good! I could only manage it when I was with you.*

"You look distraught, my dear. What is it? Something you ate?" Duke's voice startled her. She hadn't even heard him come back into the room. "Or are you worried what my punishment will be?"

She pushed the empty plate away, her face flaming with humiliation, sick at what she had done. "I don't care what you do," she said in a flat voice. She got up and turned her back on him. Pushing the lace curtains back from the window, she looked down at the busy city street. *What's happened to all the fine moral strength I possessed while I was with you, Michael? It's gone again. I'm right back to being Angel. All in the space of a few short hours and one tray of supper!*

She closed her eyes. *God, if you are there, strike me dead. Kill me so I won't give in completely. I haven't the strength to fight this devil. I haven't any strength at all.*

"I worried about you," Duke said in a cajoling tone. She felt his hands on her shoulders, his thumbs kneading her tight muscles. "I've only your best interest at heart."

"Just as always," she said dryly.

"Did you ever have to deal with the lower classes, my dear? You only had the best. How many sixteen-year-old girls have had a senator and supreme court justice visiting them on a regular basis? Or a shipping magnate? Charles was quite devastated when you disappeared. He hired his own contacts to search for you. It was he who told me you were on a ship to California."

"Good old Charles," she said, remembering the spoiled young man. Shrugging Duke's hands off of her, she faced him. "What if I'd told you I wanted out?"

His mouth lifted slightly. "Tell me about this man Hosea."

Her muscles tensed. "Why do you want to know about him?"

"Just curious, my dear."

Maybe talking of Michael would give her the strength to resist whatever came. "He's a farmer."

"A farmer?" Duke said, surprised and amused again. "And did you learn to plow, Angel? Can you milk a cow and sew a fine seam? Did you enjoy having dirt under your fingernails?" He took her hand, turning it palm up. She remained passive. "Calluses," he said in disgust and let her go.

"Yes, calluses," she said proudly. "Even covered with dirt and sweat, I was cleaner with him than I've ever been with you."

He slapped her, and she reeled back. Straightening, she saw something in his face that made her less afraid. She wasn't sure what it was, but he didn't look so in command of himself or the situation.

"Tell me all, my dear."

She did.

"Did you love him?"

"I still love him. I'll always love him. He's the only good thing that's ever happened to me in my life, and I'll cling to that until I die."

His face darkened. "Are you in a hurry for that to happen?"

"Do what you will, Duke. Do what you please. Haven't you always?" She turned away from him again, half-expecting him to swing her around and hit her, but he didn't. She sat down on the edge of the bed and looked up at him curiously.

"So where is this paragon of virtue and manhood now?" Duke asked.

"On his farm." Perhaps he had turned to Miriam by now.

"You left him."

"Yes. I left him."

He smiled, satisfied. "Bored?"

"No. One of Michael's dreams was to have children, and as we both know, I can't have them." She couldn't keep the bitterness from her voice, nor did she try.

"So you haven't forgiven me for that yet?"

"I told Michael I couldn't have children and why. He said it made no difference to him."

"No?"

"No, but it made a difference to me. I wanted him to have all he deserved and wanted."

Duke's face hardened more with each word she spoke. She ignored the warning. She was thinking only of Michael. "It wasn't the first time I left him. I married him when I couldn't do anything else, and I left the first chance I got. I wanted no part of him. I wanted to go back and get the money that was owed me. By the time I got there, the brothel was gone. It had burned down, and the madam was gone. So I ended up working for a saloon keeper. I got a good taste there of all those lower classes you talk about with such disparagement. You know what Michael did when he found out where I was? He came and got me out. He *fought* our way out. And he took me home again. He *forgave* me."

She laughed bleakly. "But I kept running away. He made me feel things, amazing things. It was as though he was turning my whole life inside out. Loving me, always loving me no matter what he learned about my past. No matter what I did. No matter how much I hurt him. He wouldn't give up on me."

Duke gripped her chin. "Just as I haven't." His eyes burned

like coals. "Or have you forgotten you ran away from me, too, several times, and I always brought you home and forgave you."

She jerked her chin away and glared up at him. "Forgave me? You owned me. You see me as a possession. Something to be sold to the highest bidder. Something to be used. Michael *loved* me. You always thought you owned my soul. Michael showed me no one does."

"No?" He gently touched the cheek he had struck. "Don't you feel right at home here, Angel? Haven't you missed the good food, the beautiful clothes, the lavish setting, the *attention*?"

She shifted uneasily and saw him smile. "I know you," he said. "For all you protest, you love the feel of silk against your skin. You enjoy having a personal maid to attend you." He picked up the empty pitcher from the table. "You love *milk*." He laughed at her.

Angel's face was aflame. His expression was filled with malicious delight as he pressed her. "I used to watch the way you played the men who came to you. Clay in your hands. They were besotted with you."

"And that gave you power over them."

"Yes, it did," he readily admitted. "Great power." He tipped her face up roughly. "I have missed you. I have missed the power you gave me because the men I brought to you fell under your spell, and when they did, they belonged to me."

"You give me too much credit."

"No one could ever touch you."

"Michael did." She saw the flash of rage in his dark eyes. Oddly, she wasn't afraid. There was a stillness inside her. Just thinking about Michael gave her courage, but she knew it wasn't a courage that would last. Not once Duke got started. He wasn't like Magowan. He wouldn't lose control, and he would never kill her.

Duke rose. "I'll leave you for now, my dear. Rest. I'll be back to talk with you again. We have business to discuss. After all, you must earn your keep."

When he leaned down to kiss her, she turned her face away. His hard fingers clamped on her cheeks like a vice, forcing her head up. He kissed her hard. She felt no passion in him, nor did she see it when he drew back. He had tired of her in that way when she was a little older than Cherry.

Duke paused at the door. "By the way, Angel, if your Michael comes for you, I will kill him the same way I killed Johnny." He smiled slightly. "And I'm going to make you watch." Her courage withered. He saw and smiled again.

Angel heard the key turn in the lock and sank down onto the bed.

Duke didn't come back the next day or the day after that. Cherry brought her food, and a guard made sure the door was locked when the girl left.

Angel knew what Duke was doing, but knowing didn't help.

Her nightmares returned.

She was running, night closing around her. Heavy footsteps echoed in the alley behind her. Before her were the docks, ships' masts filling the horizon. She ran from one to another, pleading that they would let her come aboard. "Sorry, ma'am. All filled up," the sailors said, one after another.

She ran down the last pier and saw below her a garbage scow. The ropes were being untied. Looking back, she saw Duke. He was calling to her, his dark voice pulling at her.

Rats crawled over the refuse in the scow below her, feasting on rotting meat and vegetables. The foul smell assaulted her senses, but she jumped anyway and landed hard. Her hands sank into an oozing mass as rats squealed and scurried in all directions. She almost fainted from the foul stench but clung tightly as the scow began to move. It pulled away from the dock just as Duke reached the end.

"You can't get away. You can't get away, Angel."

Then he was gone, and she was in the middle of a storm-tossed sea. Waves crashed around her, splashing over the sides of the scow. She tried to climb to a safer haven, but there was none. She pulled herself higher to get away from the cold spray. When she reached the top, she saw Rab lying on his back. The black cord was still around his neck, and rats were tearing away his dead flesh. Crying out in fear, she slid down the heap again, huddling in the farthest corner of the scow away from him.

Shivering with cold, she covered her head. "I wish I was dead. I wish I was dead...."

"Darling, where is it?"

Angel looked up and saw her mother standing before her, shimmering in white. "Where is it, darling? Where's my rosary?"

Angel scrambled over the heap, searching frantically. "I'll find it, Mama! I'll find it!" She saw something glimmer brightly and reached for it. "It's here! Oh, it's here, Mama." The scow lurched violently and rose at one end, dumping garbage into the sea. Angel cried out, trying to reach her mother's rosary as she tumbled. Her fingertips just brushed the crucifix and beads before it slipped away, spilling over the side into the turbulent sea. Angel felt herself slipping away as well. Instinctively, she grasped hold of something, but nothing was solid enough to hold her safe. Everything was going. She splashed into the cold water, decaying debris churning around her. She kicked and fought to make the surface and when she did, it was calm. She saw a shore and swam toward it. When she reached it, she could hardly stand under the weight of the filth clinging to her. She staggered onto the beach and sank down, exhausted. Her skin was blotched with ugly sores and disgusting growths, like the baby of the young prostitute.

When she looked up, she saw Michael standing in a field. The soft wind made the wheat look like a golden sea around him. The air was sweet and clean. Miriam was walking toward him, a baby in her arms, but he paid her no attention. "Amanda!" he called out, running toward her.

"No, Michael, go back! Don't come near me!" She knew if he touched her, the foulness covering her would cover him as well. "Stay away! Stay back!"

But he would not listen. He came ahead.

She was too weak to run away. She looked down at herself and saw her flesh decaying and dropping away. Michael walked toward her without hesitation. He was so close, she could see his eyes. *Oh...*"God, let me die. Let me die for him."

*No,* came a soft voice.

She looked up and saw Michael standing before her. A small flame burned where his heart was. *No, beloved.* His mouth hadn't moved, and the voice was not his. The flame grew larger and brighter, spreading until his entire body was radiant with it. Then the light separated from Michael and came the last few feet toward her. It was a man, glorious and magnificent, light streaming from him in all directions.

"Who are you?" she whispered, terrified. "Who are you?"

*Yahweh, El Shaddai, Jehovah-mekoddishkem, El Elyon, El Olam, Elohim....*

The names kept coming, moving together like music, rushing through her blood, filling her. She trembled in fear and could not move. He reached out and touched her, and she felt warmth encompassing her and the fear dissolving away. She looked down at herself and found she was clean and clothed in white.

"Then I am dead."

*That you may live.*

Blinking, she looked up again and saw the man of light covered with her filth. "No!" she wept. "Oh, God, I'm sorry. I'm so sorry. I'll take it back. I'll do anything...." Yet even as she reached out, the defilement disappeared and he stood before her perfect again.

*I am the way, Sarah. Follow me.*

As she stepped forward and reached out for him, there was a thunder clap, and Angel awakened in darkness.

She lay still, staring upward, her heart racing. She closed her eyes tightly, wanting to go back to the dream, wanting to see it finished, but she couldn't grasp it. She could scarcely remember it now. It eluded her.

Then she heard the sound that had disturbed her sleep. It came from the next room and was so familiar it tore into her heart.

Duke was speaking in low, seductive tones.

And a child was crying.

# Thirty-one

*But now, thus says the Lord,*
*your Creator, O Jacob, and He who formed you,*
*O Israel: "Do not fear, for I have redeemed you;*
*I have called you by name; you are Mine!"*

ISAIAH 43:1

Paul knew he had to go back to the mountains. He couldn't stay on this land another week. He couldn't stay this close to Miriam and not go crazy. Better the disillusionment and drudgery of gold panning than seeing her walking across the field toward Michael's cabin.

But he needed money to buy supplies.

Swallowing his pride, he went to Michael and tried to sell his land. "I'm not asking much for it. Just enough to set me up. It's good land. It should be yours anyway, Michael. You held onto it for me when I went away the last time."

"I'm land poor," Michael said and refused the offer. "Wait until your spring crops are ready for harvest. Then take what you earn and go if you have to. The land will be waiting when you come back."

"I'm not coming back, Michael. Not this time."

Michael put his hand on Paul's arm. "Why do you torture yourself? Why do you drive yourself before any wind that blows?"

Paul tore loose, angry. "Why do you wait for a harlot who's never coming back?" He left before he said more to regret.

He had no choice now but to go to John Altman.

John invited him into the cabin. Elizabeth was rocking the baby, and Miriam was bending over the fire, stirring a bubbling stew. The sight of her made his pulse jump. She straightened and smiled at him, and his knees felt weak.

"Sit down, Paul," John said, slapping him on the back. "We haven't seen you in awhile."

Paul found his gaze drifting to Miriam again. He lost track

of what John was saying as he watched her roll out biscuit dough, cut it, and place the pieces in a cast iron pan. John's silence drew his attention again. Elizabeth was smiling at him. So was John. He could feel the heat rising in his face.

"I came to offer you my land, John." Out of the corner of his eye, he saw Miriam straighten and look at him. A muscle jerked in his jaw. "I've decided to go back to the mountains," he said with finality.

John's brows flickered.

Elizabeth frowned. "This is rather sudden, isn't it, Paul?"

"No." He could feel Miriam staring at him now, hands on her hips.

"Have you thought about what you're doing?" John asked. "You've put a lot of work into that land."

"I've thought about it. I guess I'm just not cut out to be a farmer." Miriam turned her back and slammed a lid down on the pan. Elizabeth and John jumped and glanced at her in surprise. "I'm not asking much for it," Paul said, trying to ignore her. He named his price, further shocking them.

"It's worth far more than that," John said. He rubbed his chin, troubled by the offer. "Why are you doing this?"

Miriam swung around. "Because he's a fool!"

*"Miriam!"* Elizabeth said, stunned.

"I beg your pardon, Mama. He's an idiot, a dunderhead, a blockhead, a dunce!"

"That will be enough!" John said, rising from his chair, his face darkening with outrage. "Paul is a guest in our home!"

Miriam just looked at Paul, her eyes blazing as tears ran down her pale cheeks. "I'm sorry, Papa. I guess I forgot my place. Excuse me." She hurried across the room, snatched down her shawl and opened the door. She looked back at Paul. "Go ahead. Run away to your mountains and your gold panning." She slammed the door behind her.

Paul sat motionless, shattered. He wanted to go after her and explain, but what could he say? That he was in love with her and it was driving him mad? That Michael would get over Angel and she would be wise to wait?

John sat down again. "I apologize," he said. "I don't know what's gotten into her."

"I'm sure she didn't mean it, Paul," Elizabeth said.

It would be better if she did. "What do you say, John? Do you want the place, or shall I go into town and see if anyone's interested?" The sooner he got out of here the better.

Frowning, John looked at his wife. "Let me think about it. I'll let you know by the end of the week."

Three more days. Could he stand three more days? "Thanks." Paul rose.

"Don't make yourself so scarce," John said, putting his hand on Paul's shoulder as they walked to the door. "And whatever happens, you'll always be welcome here." He walked him outside. "Whatever's bothering Miriam, she'll get over it."

Paul saw her walking across the field, heading in the direction of Michael's place. "I reckon she will." He smiled bleakly. "I'll talk to you in a few days, John." He put on his hat and headed for home.

"What do you make of that?" John asked Elizabeth when he came back inside.

"John, I haven't been able to make sense of anything since Amanda left."

They waited for Miriam to come home, hoping that she would finally confide in them as she used to. It was after dark when she came in the door. "We were worried," Elizabeth said in reprimand. They hadn't expected her to be gone so long.

"Where have you been?" John demanded.

"I went to Michael's. Then I walked. Then I sat. And then I prayed." Miriam hunched over and began to sob. John and Elizabeth looked at one another in surprise. Though their daughter was tenderhearted, she wasn't given to such outbursts of emotion.

"What is it, darling?" Elizabeth asked, putting her arm around her. "What's wrong?"

"Oh, Mama. I love him so much it hurts."

Elizabeth looked at her husband. "But he's married. You know that."

Miriam reared up, face red. "*Paul*, Mama! Not Michael."

"*Paul!*" Elizabeth said, greatly relieved. "But we thought – "

"It's *always* been Paul, and I know he loves me, too. He just too stubborn to admit it, even to himself." She looked at her father. "I can't let him leave, Papa. If you buy his land, I'll never forgive you."

"If I don't, someone else will." He tried to make sense of what was happening. "If he loves you, why would he be selling his land so he can leave?"

"I think he might be going for the same reasons Amanda left Michael."

"You never did tell us what she said to you," Elizabeth reminded her.

Miriam blushed. "I can't." She sank down into the chair and covered her face. "I just can't."

Elizabeth knelt down beside her and tried to comfort her.

"How do you propose to stop Paul from leaving?" her father asked. "He's made up his mind, Miriam, and that's the way it is."

Miriam looked up. "I could make him change his mind."

Studying his daughter's determined face, John frowned. "Just what did you have in mind?"

Miriam bit her lip and looked between her mother and father. "Something from the Bible." She wiped the tears away and sat straighter.

"What part of the Bible?" her father asked sternly.

"I know what it'll take, Papa, but you're going to have to trust me."


"How old is she, Duke?"

His mouth curved mockingly. "Jealous, Angel?"

She wanted to kill him. "Eight? Nine? She can't be much older than that, or she couldn't arouse your *interest*."

His expression became dangerous. "You'd do well to curb your nasty little tongue, my dear." He held out a chair for her. "Sit down. We have things to discuss."

Angel was dressed in a pink satin and lace confection. Though the gown fit her slender body perfectly, Angel hated it.

She hated having every curve revealed to Duke's perusal. He was checking out the merchandise, deciding how to display it to the best advantage. "Pink no longer suits you," he said, dismaying her that their thoughts could be so alike. "Red, I think. Or deep sapphire blue. Even emerald green. You will look like a goddess in those colors." He touched her bare shoulder before he took his own seat.

She faced him across the small table, schooling her face to show nothing. He studied her with a tight smile. "You've changed, Angel. You were always headstrong and aloof. It was part of your charm. But now, you are careless as well. It's not a wise thing to be in your position."

"Perhaps I don't care what happens to me anymore."

"Do you wish me to prove you wrong? I could, you know. Very easily." He tapped his fingertips together. She stared at those aristocratic hands, hands without calluses, pale and manicured. Beautifully shaped hands that were capable of unspeakable cruelty.

She remembered Michael's hands, large and strong, clearly used to hard labor. They were callused and rough. His hands had looked so cruel and yet been so gentle. His touch had healed her body and opened her heart.

Duke's eyes narrowed coldly. "Why are you smiling like that?"

"Because nothing you do to me really matters."

"Did your Michael tell you that? You've been away from me too long."

All those horrible nightmares, the secrets and guilt she had carried. Michael had said once she would have to throw away all her old baggage. That's what Duke was. Old baggage. "Oh, no, Duke. I carried you with me wherever I went." She saw his smug smile and added, "What a waste of precious time."

His mouth pressed into a hard line. "I'm going to give you a choice, my dear. You can manage the girls or become one of them."

"Take Sally's place, you mean? Whatever happened to her, Duke? I never saw her again after you moved me uptown."

"She's still in New York, making out very well for herself at the brownstone. She's still quite beautiful. Too lush for my tastes, of course."

"Poor Sally. She's loved you for years. Or did you never know? I suppose you did. You just didn't care one way or the other. She's too old for you, isn't she, Duke? Too much of a woman."

Duke came out of his chair. Grabbing her hair, he yanked her head back, and his face came down within inches of her own. "What's happened to you, my dear?" he said in a deceptively soft voice. "What will it take to bring my little Angel back?"

Her scalp was on fire, her heart in her throat. He could break her neck in an instant if he chose to. She wished he would and put an end to all of it. His dark eyes changed as he glared into hers.

Frowning slightly, he eased his grip. "You're no good to me dead." Could he read her mind so easily? He let go of her with a hard jerk and stepped away. He crossed the room, then looked back at her warily. "Don't push me, Angel. As fond as I am of you, you are not indispensable."

Angel thought of the child. "Who is manager of the keys now?" She smoothed her skirt so he wouldn't see how badly frightened she was or what her reasons for asking were. He was perplexed. That was far preferable to sadistic.

"I am." He pushed his hand into his pants and pulled out a ring of keys.

"I think I would prefer Sally's position." If she could discover which key belonged to the girl's door, perhaps she could get her out of this hellhole.

Duke was smiling, eyes laughing at her. He tossed the keys onto the table before her. "The wine cellar, pantry, linen cabinets, and costume room." He opened his collar and slipped out a gold chain. A key was on it. "This is the one you want."

Still smiling, he came to her again and rested his hands heavily on her shoulders. "I think you do need a lesson after all," he said silkily. "I'm going to introduce you this evening. You're going to wear a blue gown and leave your glorious hair down. You will be a great sensation. Every girl I have is lovely, but you are something very rare and special. Every man in the house will want you."

Angel's skin grew colder and colder as he spoke. She wanted to bolt from the chair but knew, even if she did so, she would succeed in nothing. It was wiser to sit still and wait.

"You will be the keeper of the keys next week, my dear, but for this one week, you will serve our patrons yourself. I have several in mind that will prove useful to me." He smiled. "Besides, I've kept you far too exclusive. You need a little awakening as to how well you have had it."

When he stepped away, she looked up at his face and saw he meant every word he said.

Paul awakened to find Miriam stirring the coals and adding wood to his fire. The blanket slid down his bare chest as he sat bolt upright and stared at her. He was dreaming. He must be. Rubbing his face, he looked around and saw her shawl across the back of his chair and a case on the table.

She turned toward him and smiled. "Good morning. It's almost light."

She was real all right. Panic set in. "What are you doing here?"

"I'm moving in with you."

*"What?"*

"I said I'm moving in with you." He stared at her as though she had gone out of her mind. She came and sat on the edge of his bed. He pulled the blanket up to cover his bare chest.

Miriam watched Paul, and she couldn't help but laugh at the absurdity of the situation. It was his own fault. If he weren't so stubborn...

"This isn't the least bit funny," he said through his teeth.

"No, it isn't," she agreed more solemnly. "I love you, and I'm not going to let you go off to the mountains and ruin your life." He looked endearingly confused. His hair was poking up in all directions, like a little boy's. She reached out to smooth it down, and he drew back, his eyes filled with alarm.

"Go home, Miriam," he said, desperate. He had to get her

out of there! Did she know what it did to him to have her say she loved him? If she didn't leave now, he didn't think he would be able to resist her. But she didn't move. She just sat looking at him with a patient smile. He heard a roaring in his ears and bellowed, "I said *go home!*"

"No," she said simply, "and I'm not giving you your clothes, either."

His lips parted.

She folded her hands and placed them demurely in her lap, then smiled at him. The look in her eyes made him hot all over. He could barely get his breath. This was insanity! "What are you playing at, Miriam Altman? What's your father going to say about this?"

"He already knows."

"Oh, God," he prayed aloud, wondering when John was going to burst in the door with a shotgun in his hand.

"Papa spent most of last night trying to talk me out of this and finally gave up. I would have been here sooner otherwise." Her smile hinted at mischief. "Do you remember the Book of Ruth, Paul? In the Bible? Do you remember what she did? Well, Boaz, here I am, at your very feet. Now, what are you going to do about it?" She put her hand on his thigh, and he jumped a foot.

"Don't touch me!" he said, beads of sweat breaking out on his forehead. "I'm telling you, I want you out of here right now."

"No, you don't."

"How do you know what I want?" He tried to sound angry.

"I know every time you look at me. You want *me.*"

"Don't do this," he pleaded.

"Paul," she said very gently, "I love Michael very much. He's like an older brother to me, but I'm not in love with him and never will be. I'm *in love* with you."

"You don't belong with me," he said, anguished.

"Don't be ridiculous," she said as though speaking to a recalcitrant child. "Of course I do."

"Miriam – "

She put her hand against his bare shoulder, and he drew in his breath at her touch. "I've always wanted to touch you," she said, her voice soft and husky. "That day in the field when you were plowing – "

He swallowed hard and caught her hand.

Her eyes met his. "And I've always wanted you to touch me."

"Miriam," he said hoarsely, "I'm not a saint."

"I know that. Do you think I am?" Her eyes were shimmery with tears. "This isn't easy, you know, but I am a woman, Paul, not a child, and I know what I want. I want you. As my husband. To live with for all our days."

He was shaking. "Don't do this to me." He watched a tear slide down her cheek and couldn't help himself; he reached out to brush it away. She put her hand over his, trapping it there against her cheek, but only briefly. Her skin was so soft, her hair silky. His thumb slid down, feeling the wild pulse in her throat. "Miriam. Oh, Miriam, what are you trying to do to me?"

"Nothing you haven't wanted for a long time. Admit it." Her arms slid around his neck, and she kissed him. When she raised her mouth from his, he couldn't have stopped for the world. He framed her face with his hands and kissed her, gently at first, then with all the pent-up love he'd been feeling for months.

He kissed her as the starving man he was. Her surrender to him made his senses swim. She was firm and smooth and warm, and she tasted like heaven. "I love you," he whispered, almost afraid to say the words aloud. "I've been going mad. I couldn't stand it. I had to get away from you."

"I know," she said, trembling, her hands in his hair. She started to weep. "I love you so much. Oh, Paul, I do...."

He drew back, looking down into her face, noting how her cheeks were flushed, her eyes filled with her love for him, and he thought his heart would burst. She was his. She belonged to him! He could scarcely take it in.

She saw the look burning in his eyes and reached up to touch his cheek, her face softening with tenderness. "I want us to begin right. Marry me *first*, Paul. Be my husband. I want to share everything with you without any shadows over us. Without any regrets. If you make love to me now, you'll be ashamed tomorrow.

You know you will. You won't be able to face my father and mother. You'll think you took advantage of me." She smiled tremulously. "Even though it's the other way around."

"I thought I could leave you," he said, knowing he would have carried her with him the rest of his life, a torment he would never escape. "I guess we'll have to ride up to Sacramento and see if we can find a preacher."

"No, we don't."

He looked at her, surprised.

Blushing, she smiled shyly, more the Miriam he knew and not the bold young woman who had stolen into his cabin at night.

"Papa said he would marry us himself. He was going through the trunk when I left, looking for his *Book of Common Prayer*. He was rather in a hurry, I think."

He kissed her again, unable to help himself. "I never had a chance, did I?" he said, laughing softly.

"No, you didn't." She smiled, content. "Michael always said you'd come around. I just got so tired of waiting."

From where she stood behind the curtain to the left of the stage, Angel could hear the men who jammed the casino. The place was a circus, and Duke was going to put her right in the center ring.

He had already given them a show of dancing girls, jugglers, and acrobats. Where he had found such people Angel couldn't even guess, but Duke had his ways and means. Perhaps he had waved his hand and produced them from the fire and smoke.

She moved restlessly, and the hand beneath her arm tightened. She hadn't been without a guard since Duke had put her in the upstairs room. There was no escape, and she was sick with dread and fear.

Closing her eyes, Angel fought down the nausea. Maybe she shouldn't. Maybe she should go out center stage and vomit. That would dampen the ardor Duke was inciting in the crowd. She almost laughed, but she knew if she did she would give in completely to hysteria.

She could hear him, working his audience. He had an orator's voice. It had served him well in politics – and afterward, when he decided working behind the scenes was more lucrative. He was putting a fire beneath the waiting men, rousing them. She could almost smell their lust. In a few minutes, she would face it. Hundreds of pairs of eyes staring at her, taking off her clothes, imagining whatever they wanted to do to her. And Duke would let them make those imaginings real. For a price. Anything for a high enough price.

*"For a week, you'll serve them."*

Angel closed her eyes. *God, if you're there, kill me! Please! Send a lightning bolt, and wipe me off the face of the earth. Send me into oblivion. Send fire. Turn me into a pillar of salt. Any way you want to do it. Only do it. Please, God, help me. Help me!*

"Easy, little lady," the man said, smiling down at her coldly.

*Oh, God. Oh, Jesus, please help me!*

"He's almost got them ready for you."

Then, just when she thought her heart would stop for the terror, she heard it.

**Sarah, beloved.**

It was the same soft voice she had heard in Michael's cabin. The one she'd heard in her dream....

**Be still, for I am here.**

She looked around, but only her guard and the performers were there. Her heart was racing madly, and her skin rose with goosebumps as it had that strange night in the cabin.

"Where? *Where?*" she whispered frantically.

The guard looked down at her questioningly. "What's the matter?"

"Did you hear someone speaking?"

"With all that racket out there?" he laughed.

She was shaking violently. "Are you sure?"

His hand tightened, giving her a hard jerk. "You'd better get yourself together. Pretending you're crazy isn't going to do you any good. Duke's just about ready for you to come out. Listen to those men. Sound like hungry lions, don't they?"

Angel was ready to dig in her heels, but what was the use? She closed her eyes tightly again, trying to block out the maddening crowd sitting in front of the stage, trying to focus on the frightening, quiet voice in her head that called her by a name she had heard only once in a dream since her mother died.

*What do you want me to do? Tell me. Oh, God, tell me.*

**My will.**

Despair filled her. She didn't know what that was.

"There's your signal," her guard said. "Are you going to walk on your own?"

Even if she were able to get away, where could she run? She opened her eyes, and suddenly the shaking inside her stopped. She couldn't explain it, but she felt calm. Unnaturally so. She gave the guard an imperious look. "If you let go of my arm," she said. He blinked, surprised, and let go of her. She stepped forward, and he held the curtain aside so she could walk out.

As soon as she appeared, the place went wild. Men whistled and catcalled. She kept her head up, her eyes straight ahead, and walked to the center stage where Duke stood smiling at her with malicious delight. He leaned close, his mouth near her ear so she could hear him above the din. "Feel the power, Angel? You can share it with me. We can bring them to their knees!" Then he left her standing in center stage alone.

The noise was deafening. Were they all mad? She wanted to run and hide. She wanted to die.

**Look at them.**

She forced herself to display the old arrogance and disdain as her gaze swept the crowded room.

**Look into their eyes, Sarah.**

She did, the men closest to the stage at first, then sweeping outward. They were young. There was a hollow, haunting look in their eyes. She recognized that look. Disillusionment and broken dreams, defiance. Hadn't she felt the same loneliness and desperation she saw reflected all around her? She looked at the men standing near the faro tables, staring up at her. She looked at the men lining the mahogany bar, glasses of whiskey in their hands. Was it her imagination, or was the noise quieting?

"Sing us something!" a man called from the back. Others yelled their agreement. Her mind went blank except for one song, totally inappropriate, utterly out of place. "Sing, Angel!" The noise rose again like a tidal wave, and the piano player pounded out a bawdy tune the men recognized. Some took up the tune themselves, singing raucously, laughing with abandon.

*Sing, beloved.*

She closed her eyes to shut the men out and started to sing. Not the song being played, but another song. One from long ago. And as she sang, she stood again at the well with Michael and Miriam bending over the side, singing down into it, the harmony and music rising up to envelop her. She imagined Michael and Miriam on either side of her. She could almost hear Miriam's warm laughter. *"Louder, silly. What are you afraid of? You can sing. Of course you can sing."*

And then Michael's voice echoed: *"Louder, Tirzah. Sing as though you believe it."*

*But I don't believe. I'm afraid to believe.* She stopped abruptly and opened her eyes, her mind suddenly blank. The words to the song were gone. Vanished.

The place was silent, every man staring up at her where she stood, alone on the empty stage. She could feel the burn of tears behind her eyes. *Oh, God, make me believe!*

Someone began singing for her, picking up the words where she had left off. His voice was rich and deep, so like Michael's her heart jumped. She searched for him and saw him near the bar, a tall, gray-haired man in a dark business suit.

As suddenly as they'd disappeared, the words came back to her, and she sang with him as he continued. He walked slowly through the parting crowd. He stopped below the stage and smiled up at her. She smiled back. Then she looked around at the men again, all silent now, stunned. Some couldn't meet her eyes but looked away, ashamed.

"Why are you all here?" she cried out, the tears so close she was afraid they would choke her. "Why aren't you home with your wives and children, or your mothers and sisters? Don't you know what this place is? Don't you know where you are?"

The curtains swished open behind her, and the dancing girls came racing out. The piano player began again, and the young women began singing loudly around her, kicking their bare legs up high. Some of the men began to clap and cheer. Others just stood there, silent, ashamed.

Angel walked slowly off the stage. She saw Duke waiting for her, a look in his eyes that she had never seen before. Perspiration beaded his brow, and his face was pale with fury. He grabbed her arm brutally and yanked her into the shadows. "What made you do a stupid thing like that?"

"God, I think," she said, stunned. She felt jubilation – and the presence of a power so immense she was trembling. She looked up at Duke and wasn't afraid of him anymore.

"*God?*" He spat the word out. His eyes blazed. "I'm going to kill you. I should have killed you a long time ago."

"You're afraid, aren't you? I can smell it. You're afraid of something you can't even see. And do you know why? Because what Michael has is more powerful than you ever were, ever could be."

He raised his hand to strike her, and a man spoke quietly from behind him. "You touch that young woman, and I will see you hang."

Duke swung around. The man who had sung with her was standing a few feet away. He was slightly shorter than Duke and much leaner, but there was something about him that gave him an aura of strength and authority. She looked up at Duke to see if he felt it too, and saw he did, indeed. Her heart began beating wildly.

"Would you like to leave, miss?" the stranger asked.

"Yes," she said. "Yes, I would." She didn't question his destination or intentions. It was enough that she had a way of escape, and she grasped it. She expected Duke to threaten the man for his interference, but he just stood by, silent and pale, his teeth gritted. Who *was* this man?

She would find out later. She started toward him, then halted. She couldn't leave yet. She turned to Duke. "Give me the key, Duke." Two men looked at her, one in question, the other livid with rage. And something more. Fear. "The key," she said again, holding her hand out.

When Duke didn't give it to her, she ripped open the front of his shirt, grabbed the chain, and broke it. He stared at her in shock, sweat pouring down his temples. She looked straight back into his eyes. "You can't have her." She held the key in her fist right beneath his nose. "Burn in hell, Duke." She looked at the gentleman standing silent, watching them. "Wait for me, please."

"I'm not going anywhere without you, ma'am," he said very calmly.

She hurried upstairs to the room next to hers and unlocked it. The child lying on the bed awakened immediately and sat up, her blue eyes wide with fear. She edged back, her pink dress bunching around her knees. She had pale blonde hair tied with pink satin ribbons.

Angel bit her lip. It was like looking in a mirror and seeing herself ten years ago, but she couldn't just stand here, drowning in pain. She had to get this child out of here. Now. She came forward quickly. "It's all right, sweetheart. I'm Angel, and you're coming with me." She held out her hand. "Come on now." She leaned over and took the girl's hand. "We haven't much time."

As they came out into the hallway, Angel saw Cherry standing a few feet away, her mouth open in surprise and wild hope. "Come with us," Angel said. "You don't have to stay here, but you must come *now*."

"Duke – "

"Come *now*, or you're going to spend the rest of your life in a place like this. Or something worse."

"Let me get my things – "

"Forget everything. Just leave it. Don't even look back." She hurried down the corridor. Cherry stood undecided for a moment and then raced after her. They came down the stairs together, and the stranger was there to meet them. Duke was nowhere in sight. As the gentleman looked at the two children with her, his face filled with wrath.

"I'm not going without them," she said.

"Of course not."

She nodded toward the stage door. "We can go out that way."

"No." His eyes were hard. "We're going right out on the stage and through the front doors."

*"What?"* Angel said. Was he crazy? "We can't!"

"We will. Let's move." His face was livid. "We're going to expose this man for the devil he is." The little girl was crying and clutching at Angel's blue satin skirt, and Cherry was hugging close as well. "Here, I'll carry the child," the gentleman said, but when he moved, the girl tried desperately to hide behind her.

"She won't let you touch her," Angel said, kneeling and giving her a hug. "Hold tight, sweetheart. I'm going to carry you." She looked up at the stranger and said firmly, "We won't let anyone hurt you. Duke's not going to stop us." The girl's legs clamped around her waist as Angel straightened. Her thin arms clung to Angel's neck, and she appealed to the man. "Another way would be safer."

"This way is best." He held the curtain aside.

"There are a dozen men who'll stop us."

"There isn't a man in that room who'll touch me."

"Who do you think you are? *God?*"

"No, ma'am. Just Jonathan Axle, but I do own one of the largest banks in San Francisco. Now, shall we go?"

He wasn't giving her any choice. Angel hugged the trembling child closer. "Close your eyes, sweetheart. We'll get you out of here." Or die trying.

Cherry stayed close to her side as Jonathan Axle led them out to center stage. The music came to a discordant end, and the dancing girls came to a confused stop. Angel looked around and saw the shocked expressions on men's faces. Duke was nowhere in the room. Neither was the man who had guarded her. "Let's go," Axle said quietly, his hand a firm but gentle support beneath her arm. She went down the steps into the middle of the room. The men parted before her.

Many of the patrons were staring at Cherry, dressed and made up like a fast woman though she was clearly still a child. Men moved back to open a path before her. The child's whimper seemed to fill the room.

The men began talking in low, stunned voices. Angel overheard some of the remarks as she passed. "Why would he have a little one like that in a place like this?"

Angel stopped and looked at him. "Why do you think?" she said softly, grief-stricken, and saw the man's mouth drop open in horrified comprehension.

Voices rose like a groundswell behind her, and she heard the violence in them. The men wanted blood, but not hers. She came out into the night air and let out her breath, not even aware she'd been holding it.

"This way," Axle said. "I'm sorry, but I've no carriage. It's several blocks. Can you manage?"

Angel nodded and shifted the child's weight. She followed him some distance in silence before asking, "Where are you taking us?"

"To my house."

Her eyes narrowed. "What for?"

"So my wife and daughter can see to your needs while I figure out what's to be done about that place. It should be burned, and that devil with it."

She was embarrassed for her distrust, but she didn't know anything about this man for all his apparent sympathy. The fact that he was a banker didn't mean he had goodwill in mind. She had known bankers before.

The weight of the child seemed to increase with every step. Her muscles ached, but she kept walking. Cherry kept looking back worriedly. "Do you think he'll come after us?"

"No," Angel assured her, then directed a question to Axle. "Why did you help me like that? I'm a stranger to you."

"It was what you sang. The Lord couldn't have made it any more clear that I was to get you out of there."

She glanced at him in surprise. She didn't say anything for a while, but she couldn't stop thinking about it. "Mister Axle, I've got to be honest with you."

"About what?"

"I don't believe in God." She felt a piercing pain as she said it.

*Don't you?*

The question came from deep within her, and she frowned. She had called to God in her fear, and here she was. And then there was that voice.... Had she imagined it? Axle's next words echoed her confusion.

"No? You sounded pretty convincing back there."

"I was scared to death, and it was the only song I could remember."

He smiled. "There's something in that."

"I don't believe in some little, shriveled up old man in a long white beard sitting on a throne looking over me."

He chuckled. "Neither do I. I believe in something a lot bigger than that. And I'll tell you something else." His smile was gentle. "Just because you don't believe in the Lord doesn't mean his power isn't working for you."

She blinked. Her throat closed tight, and she felt ashamed. She had tried every way to get away from Duke and been unable to accomplish it. And then tonight, a single hymn Michael had taught her had done the trick. How? It didn't make any sense. That voice had said *My will*, but all she had really done was the only thing that came into her mind. And this man had come forward from nowhere.

Words Michael had read came back to her. *"Yea, though I walk through the valley of the shadow of death, I shall fear no evil, for thou art with me."*

Duke had been afraid of *her*. She hadn't mistaken that.

*Not of you, Sarah. Of me.*

She shivered, goosebumps breaking out over her pale skin again as her heart opened wide. *O God, I've denied you so many times. How could you rescue me now?*

*Though you deny me, I love you with an everlasting love.*

*What happened back there? I don't even know. How did we get out? Oh, Jesus, I don't understand. I just don't understand how you did it.*

It began to drizzle, the heavy bay mists closing around them. Cherry hung closer to Angel as they walked. "I'm cold," she whispered.

"Is it much further, Mister Axle?" Her voice quavered, but not from cold.

"Just up the hill."

She saw a big house looming above them. He was rich all

right. The rain was coming down hard now, and the thought of shelter drove her on. Lanterns burned in the windows. She thought she saw a woman peering through a curtain. Jonathan Axle opened the gate. The door opened before he was halfway there, and a tall, slender woman with her hair pulled back severely stood before them. Angel couldn't make out the woman's face, but her heart sank. What was this lady going to say about her husband bringing home three prostitutes, regardless of the tender ages of two of them?

"Come in before you catch your death," the woman ordered. She was clearly agitated. Angel didn't know whether she was talking to Jonathan Axle or to all of them, and she stopped cold, not sure what to do. "Come in, come in," the woman said, beckoning to her.

Jonathan put his hand beneath Angel's arm. "You needn't be afraid of her," he said, amused. "She's mostly bark." Angel steeled herself as she walked forward up the path. Maybe the lady would let them dry off before she threw them out again.

She entered, Cherry right behind her, and looked around before facing the woman, who surprisingly turned out to be young and attractive, despite the unflattering bun and somber dress. "There's a fire going in through here," she said and led them into a large room with simple but comfortable furnishings. "Sit down, please."

Angel did. She looked up at the young woman and saw she was looking back at her with open curiosity. She took them all in from head to foot. "It's all right," Angel whispered to the shaking child, stroking her back soothingly. But was it?

The child relaxed in her arms and drew back enough to look around. Cherry was sitting on the settee beside her, her back straight, her face very pale and frightened. The young woman looked at Jonathan Axle for an explanation. If she was shocked by what they very clearly were, she didn't show it. "Father, what's happened?"

"My daughter, Susanna," Jonathan Axle said, and the young woman nodded and offered a tentative if confused smile. "I'm afraid I don't know your names," he said in apology.

"My name's Angel. This is Cherry, and – " She stopped, suddenly realizing she didn't even know the child's name. "Darling," she said softly, raising the girl's chin. "What's your name?" The child's lip quivered, and she whispered something before burying her head against Angel's shoulder again. "Faith," Angel said. "Her name's Faith."

"Some blankets are in order, Susanna. Would you see to that while I find your mother?"

"Mama's in the kitchen warming up your supper," she said with a smile and went hurriedly out the door.

"Excuse me for a moment," Jonathan said and left them alone.

Cherry's shoulders hunched, and she started to cry as soon as he was gone. "I'm scared. Duke's going to kill me."

"Duke's never going to touch you again." Angel took her hand. "We're all scared," she said softly, "but I think we can trust these people." They had to. What choice had they?

Jonathan came back with a small woman with bright blue eyes. Her name was Priscilla. Angel could see the resemblance between mother and daughter. Priscilla quickly took charge. "First thing we have to do is get you girls out of those wet clothes," she said, taking them upstairs. "Then you'll come down to the kitchen for a nice bite to eat with Jonathan and me."

She opened a door on the right side of the hallway showing a spacious room beyond. "You two younger ladies will share this bedroom," she said. "And Angel can share Susanna's. It's just across the hall."

Angel wondered what Susanna would have to say about that.

Priscilla produced dry clothes for all of them, surprising Angel further. Did she have wardrobes in all sizes, or did she have other daughters not yet seen? The dresses were plain, functional wool, and comfortable. Angel wadded up the dresses she, Cherry, and Faith had removed and put them in the bucket near the fireplace.

Susanna was waiting to take them downstairs to the kitchen where Priscilla served them thick beef and vegetable soup and biscuits. Jonathan ate with them. Angel declined the hot coffee in favor of a glass of fresh milk. Faith was growing drowsy beside her. Kohl was smeared below Cherry's eyes. She looked pale, but less frightened.

Priscilla put her hands gently on Cherry's shoulders and pressed her cheek to the girl's soft one. "Come on, child, you're ready for bed." She held her hand out to Faith, and amazingly the little girl took it. Angel felt a great burden lifted.

Susanna cleared the dishes. "Why don't you two go into the parlor and be comfortable, Father? Just don't discuss anything important until I join you."

"Yes, dear," Jonathan said with mock submission. He winked at Angel as he got up. "We'd better do what we're told."

Angel sat near the fire, nervous and worried. What was going to happen to all of them tomorrow? Jonathan went to a small table in the corner. She watched him pour a drink. He glanced back at her. "Would you like some cider?"

"No, thank you."

He smiled slightly and put down the decanter. He took a comfortable seat opposite her. "You're safe here."

"I know that. But for how long?" she said, surprising herself with her bluntness.

"No one is going to put you out, Angel. You can stay with us as long as you like."

Her lips parted. Her eyes burned, and she bit her lip, but she couldn't speak. He smiled. "You're very welcome," he said. She put her head back against the seat and tried to regain control of her emotions.

"I wonder what he'll do," she said almost to herself.

Jonathan didn't have to ask who was on her mind. "If he was anywhere inside that building after we walked out, he'll be hanging from a post by now. Unfortunately, I don't think he's that stupid."

"No, Duke is anything but stupid." She sighed heavily. "You're being very kind to us. Thank you."

"'For I was hungry, and you gave me something to eat; I was thirsty, and you gave me drink; I was a stranger, and you invited me in, naked, and you clothed me; I was sick, and you visited me;

I was in prison, and you came to me,'" he quoted. "Are you familiar with that?"

Michael had read those words to her once, right after he had taken the Altmans in and she had asked him why. Her memories of him were so strong, she couldn't speak.

Jonathan Axle could see great suffering in the young woman's eyes and wanted to ease it. She seemed utterly unaware of the magnitude of her actions, the courage it had taken. "You're welcome to share what we have." After all, none of it really belonged to him. He was only a steward of it.

They talked far into the night. She told him more than she had ever told another human being, even Michael. Perhaps it was because Jonathan Axle was still a benevolent stranger that she felt so free to speak. Yet he did not seem a stranger at all.

Angel leaned her head back, weary. "Where do I go from here, Mister Axle?"

"That's up to you." Jonathan smiled. "And the Lord."

Priscilla awakened when Jonathan came into their bedroom. He undressed and slid beneath the bedcovers, drawing her close. Her body was warm and soft, and her hand rested on his chest.

"I really must ask, Jonathan. What were you doing in a place like that?"

He laughed softly and kissed her forehead. "I don't really know, my love."

"But you don't drink or gamble," she said. "Whatever possessed you?"

"It was a strange day, Priss. Something gnawed at me from noon on. I couldn't put my finger on it."

"Everything's fine at the bank?"

"More than fine. I simply felt the need to walk. That's why I sent word I would be late. I was passing by that place and heard that devil making a speech. The place was in such a ruckus, I went in to hear what he was saying."

"But why? You loathe him."

"I don't know why. I just felt *compelled*. He was introducing Angel. It was obscene. It wasn't his exact words. It was his manner, the insinuation. I can't explain. I felt like I was standing in a pagan temple and he was the priest introducing a new temple prostitute."

"Why didn't you leave?"

"I thought of it, but every time I did, something told me to wait. Then Angel came out."

"She is very beautiful," Priscilla said quietly.

"It wasn't her beauty that held me, my love. She was so young, and she walked to the center of that stage with such quiet dignity. You can't even imagine it, Priss. Those men, they were like all the hounds of hell baying at her. And then she sang. She was so quiet at first, no one could hear her. Then the noise died down until the place was silent except for her."

He felt his throat constrict and tears burned. "She was singing 'Rock of Ages.'"

# Thirty-two

*God moves in mysterious ways,*
*His wonders to perform...*
WILLIAM COWPER

Miriam watched Paul brood over his supper. He had hardly eaten a bite of his stew, and his mug of coffee was cold. She didn't even need to ask what was wrong. "You've been to see Michael."

"Yes," he said bleakly. He pushed his plate back, a frown darkening his face. "I don't understand him anymore. I don't understand him at all."

Miriam waited, hoping he would say more, that this time he would explain. He was angry and frustrated, but something more was preying at him, something deep and unseen, something crippling. A cancer of the soul.

Paul spoke through gritted teeth. "When's he going to give it up? It tears at my guts to see him on his knees over that woman." He let out his breath sharply. "Miriam, I wanted to hit him." He clenched his fist. "I wanted to shake him. He was praying when I got there. Down on his knees in the barn, praying for *her.*"

She couldn't understand his animosity. "But why shouldn't he, Paul? She's his wife, and he still loves her."

His face set in hard lines. "A wife? Can't you see what she's done to him?"

"She told me she was leaving because she thought it best for him."

He scraped his chair back abruptly. "Do you believe that? You never knew her. Not really. She was cold as steel, Miriam. She was a prostitute from Pair-a-Dice. She never had any feelings for Michael other than feelings of convenience. Not in the beginning and not in the end. She hasn't got a heart. Don't be such a fool!"

Miriam's eyes welled at his attack. She had seen her father get angry many times, but he never lashed out against those who loved him. She couldn't keep silent. "You're the one who never knew her, Paul. You never even tried – "

"Don't defend her to me! I knew her," he said harshly. "I knew her better than you or Michael. You both saw what she wanted you to see. I saw what she really was."

Miriam lifted her head. She wasn't going to sit silent while he violated her friend. "You saw Amanda as some vile creature that wasn't even worthy of your slightest courtesy."

His face grew livid. "Are you reprimanding me for not falling under her spell like the rest of you? In *my own house?*"

Miriam's lips parted. He might as well have put a sword through her heart. "Then it's only your home now, even though we're married?" she said in a constricted voice. "I'm just a guest until you decide to cast me out. God help me if I do anything wrong, if I prove to be fallible."

Paul regretted his words before she even began speaking. "Miriam, I didn't – "

Her own anger was growing swiftly. "I suppose I've no right to my own thoughts or beliefs if they're contrary to your own. Is that it, Paul?" She stood and pointed to the door. "If I want to speak my mind, I have to go outside to do it. Or better yet, be sure I'm on the other side of your boundary line?"

Guilt killed his remorse. Her words struck at his conscience, and he lashed out again in defense. "You know that's not what I meant!" When she started to cry, he wilted. "Miriam, don't," he groaned.

"I don't know what you mean anymore, Paul. You're eaten up with bitterness. You carry your hatred like a banner, waving it all the time. You won't say what it was Amanda did to you to make you hate her, so it makes me wonder if you weren't a party to it!" Paul could feel the heat coming up into his face, his temper rising with it. He started to defend himself, but Miriam wasn't finished. "I would never have come to you the way I did if not for Amanda."

"What're you talking about?"

Her voice dropped. "I wouldn't have had the courage." She could see he didn't understand, and she couldn't explain. Her throat was closed tight with pain, and she just wanted to sit down and put her head in her hands. Even if she could tell him, he would never listen. He was deaf to anything that had to do with the goodness in Amanda.

Her face was crumpling like a hurt child's, and he felt his insides twisting tight in pain. "I love you," he said hoarsely. "Miriam, I love you."

"You don't act like it."

"Angel got between Michael and me. Don't let her come between us, too."

"You put her there!"

"No, I didn't," he said fiercely. "Can't you see what she does?" He wanted to beg her to listen. He couldn't bear the look on her face. "She's broken Michael," he said, his voice cracking.

"Michael's stronger now than he ever was."

"That's why he's on his knees?"

"He's fighting for her the only way he can."

"Miriam, she got her hooks into him and then ripped him to pieces."

"Are you really that blind? Michael's the one who tore through all her defenses. She *loves* him!"

"If that were the truth, wouldn't she have stayed? Nothing could have driven her away. But she didn't stay, did she? She left him just like that." He snapped his fingers. "And here you are trying to tell me she has a heart."

Miriam sat down heavily and looked up at her husband's embittered face. Had she really thought to save him by herself? What arrogance! He was further from her now than if he had gone back to the mountains to look for gold. All she knew was what she felt. "I love her, too, Paul, as much as any one of my own flesh-and-blood sisters. Whatever you think of her, I *know* her, and I'm going to pray every day of my life that she comes back."

Paul slammed the door as he stormed out.

Angel lay in bed staring up at the ceiling. She knew she had done the right thing, but sometimes her longing for Michael became so intense it was physical pain. Was he well? Was he happy? Surely he would have given up on her by now. He would have come to realize they were never meant to be together. She knew he would never forgive her, but he could go on with his life. He would have Miriam. He could have children.

She couldn't let herself dwell on it. If she did, she would drown in self-pity. It was over, finished, behind her. She had to go on. She closed her eyes, pushing the pain down. She rose and dressed, thinking over the wonderful things that had happened.

Cherry was settled with a couple who owned a bakery. She was happy and adapting to her new life. Little Faith had been adopted by a Baptist family and was now living in Monterey with her new brothers and sisters. And she was learning to read and write, for letters had come.

As much as Angel loved living with the Axles, she knew she couldn't remain with them forever. They had been far too kind already, providing her with shelter, protection, and friendship. They had even seen to a new wardrobe for her. Given the choice of what she wanted, she had asked for dove gray and brown wool in simple styles.

Susanna was the one who insisted on tutoring her. Angel despaired of learning what Susanna laid out, but her new friend insisted. "You're quick, and it'll come to you. Don't expect so much of yourself so soon." The lessons were hard, and Angel wondered if the effort would be worth the labor.

She thought about going back to work for Virgil, then dismissed it. Somehow, she knew that wasn't what she was intended to do. But what was?

Susanna took her along when she did the buying for the family. They wandered through the markets purchasing meat, vegetables, bread, and sundry items. Angel learned to bargain. It wasn't much different from selling pans to miners. She knew how to bluff. She knew how to pretend indifference. And she usually got what Susanna wanted for rock-bottom price.

"One look into your baby blue eyes and they practically hand over their goods for free. They fall all over themselves to serve you." Susanna laughed. "And imagine getting a proposal at the market."

"It wasn't a proposal, Susanna. It was a proposition. There's a big difference."

"Well, don't look so grim. You said no, and very politely, too, I might add."

Maybe if she wore sackcloth, men wouldn't notice her. Even in dove gray, men's heads turned when she passed. Few bothered her, and she suspected it was more because Susanna Axle was beside her than any credit to her new purity. The Axles were well known and highly respected in the community. Angel wondered what would happen if she were out from beneath their protective wings. At the first sign of hardship, would she weaken again? It was a thought that made her swallow her pride and accept the Axles' continued goodwill.

She even began going to church with them, feeling insulated and protected with Jonathan and Priscilla on one side and Susanna on the other. She drank in the words of salvation and redemption though she felt she had no right to them. She was so hungry and thirsty, she panted like a deer after the water of life – remembering as she listened the dream she had had in Duke's bordello in Portsmouth Square.

*Oh, God, it was you speaking to me, wasn't it? It was you. And that night in the cabin so long ago when I smelled that wonderful fragrance and thought I heard someone speaking to me, it was you.*

Everything Michael had said to her, everything he had done, made sense to her now. He had lived Christ so that she could understand.

*Oh, Lord, why was I so blind. Why couldn't I hear? Why did it take so much pain for me to see that you have been there reaching out to me all along?*

Each Sunday following the sermon, the pastor gave an invitation to anyone wanting to receive Christ as their Savior and Lord. Each time he gave the opportunity to come forward, Angel felt her nerves tighten.

The still, quiet voice beckoned tenderly.

**Come to me, beloved. Stand and come to me.**

Warmth swept over her. This was the love she'd been waiting for all her life. Yet she could not move. *Oh, Michael, if only you*

*were with me today. If only you were here to walk forward with me, maybe
then I'd have the courage.*

Each Sunday, she closed her eyes, trying to gather her nerve
to answer the call – and each Sunday she failed to do it. She sat
trembling, knowing she was unworthy, knowing that after all she
had said against God, she had no right to be his child.

On the fourth Sunday, Susanna leaned close and whispered,
"You want to go forward, don't you? You've wanted to for weeks."

Eyes stinging, throat closed tight, Angel nodded once and
hung her head, her lips pressed together. She was afraid, so afraid
she was shaking. What right had she to present herself to God and
receive mercy? What right?

"I'll walk with you," Susanna said and took her hand firmly.

It was the longest walk of Angel's life as she went down the
aisle and faced the pastor waiting at the end of it. He was smiling,
his eyes shining. She thought of Michael and felt a rush of anguish.
*Oh, Michael, I wish you were here with me now. I wish you were here to
see this. Will you ever know you struck the match and brought light into
my darkness?* Her heart filled with gratitude. *Oh, God, he loves you so.*

She didn't cry. She had years of practice containing her
emotions, and she wouldn't give in to them now before all these
people, not even with Susanna Axle at her side. She could feel the
eyes of everyone in the church upon her, watching her every
move, listening for any catch in her voice. She mustn't make a fool
of herself.

"Do you believe that Jesus is the Christ, the Son of the
Living God?" the pastor asked her.

"I believe," she said with grave dignity and closed her eyes
briefly. *Oh, God, forgive my unbelief. Make my faith larger than a mustard seed, Jesus. Let it grow. Please.*

"And do you give your life to Jesus now before these wit-
nesses? If so, would you signify by saying *I do?*"

Words meant for a wedding ceremony. A sad smile touched
her lips. With Michael she had said "Why not" rather than "I do";
she had come to the end of her endurance and felt she had no
choice. She felt that now. She had come to the end of her struggles, the end of her fight to survive on her own. She needed God.

She wanted him. He had brought her out of her old life when she had no faith. And now that she knew he really was there, he was holding out his hand to her and making a proposal.

*Oh, Michael, this is what you wanted for me, isn't it? This is what you meant when you said someday I'd have to make a choice.*

"Angel?" the pastor said, perplexed. No one breathed or moved.

"I do," she responded, smiling radiantly. "I most assuredly do."

He laughed. Turning her toward the congregation, he said, "This is Angel. A new sister in Christ. Welcome her."

And they did.

But things couldn't stay the same. She felt that in her very soul. She wasn't meant to stay in this safe bubble, protected by the Axles. Sooner or later she was going to have to leave them and find out if she could stand on her own.

First she had to figure out what she was going to do with her life.

The purchases put away in the kitchen, Angel went upstairs to her room. She took off her dark cape and hung it by the door. Priscilla had given her the bedroom Cherry and Faith had shared. It was spacious, comfortably furnished, and had a fireplace in the corner. Someone had lit the fire. Angel pushed the lace curtains aside and looked out the window.

The fog was rolling in, sending puffs of mist past the glass. She could see the wharf and a forest of ships deserted in the harbor. One by one, they were being stripped and sunk for landfill.

She remembered another day when she had stood in the upstairs window, watching Michael below as he drove out of Pair-a-Dice. She remembered hearing his voice out of the agony she had brought on herself with Magowan. She remembered Michael laughing and chasing her down in the cornfield. She remembered his compassion, his righteous rage, his tender understanding, his strength. She remembered his all-consuming love. And she knew what he would have her do to find the answers she needed. Pray. She could almost see his face as he said it. *Pray.*

Closing her eyes, she sighed wearily. "I know I've no right

to ask anything of you, Lord, but Michael said I should. So I'm doing it. Jesus, if you're listening, would you please tell me where to go from here? I don't know what to do. I can't stay here forever and live off these nice people. It's not right. I have to pay my own way in this world. What do you want me to do with the rest of my life, Jesus? I've got to do something or go mad. I'm asking. Jesus, I'm begging. What do you want me to do? Amen."

She sat for more than an hour, waiting.

No light from heaven came. No voice. Nothing.

A few days later, Susanna came to her room after dinner.

"You've been very quiet all week, Angel. What's bothering you? Are you worrying about your future?"

Angel wasn't surprised that Susanna knew what was wrong. She seemed to anticipate people's thoughts and feelings. "I have to do something," she said honestly. "I can't stay here and live off your family for the rest of my life."

"You won't."

"It's been six months, Susanna, and I'm no closer to knowing what I should do than I was the night I came here."

"Have you prayed about it?"

Angel blushed vividly.

Susanna's eyes shone, and she laughed. "Well, you needn't look as though you've been caught in an indiscretion."

"Don't look so pleased," Angel said dryly. "God didn't answer."

Susanna shrugged. "Not yet, maybe. God always answers, in his time, not in yours. You'll know what you're supposed to do when the time comes."

"I wish I could have your faith."

"You could ask for it." Susanna grinned.

Angel felt a stab of pain. "You remind me of Miriam."

"I'll take that as a compliment." Susanna's expression softened. "Faith in God hasn't come easily to me, either, whatever you may believe." She got up. "Come on. I want to show you something." She held out her hand.

They went into Susanna's bedroom where they had talked many times before. Susanna let go of Angel's hand and got down on the floor and ducked beneath the bedspread. She took out a box and put it on the bed. "I have to get down on my knees to get it," she said, dusting off her hands as she got up. "I should dust under there one of these days." She tucked a loose curl of dark hair back into her bun and sat. "Sit down," she said, patting the bed. Angel did as she was asked, looking curiously at the container between them.

Susanna put the container on her lap. "This is my God box," she said. "When problems prey on my mind, I write them down, fold them up, and put them through the slot. Once they're inside this box, they're God's problem and not mine."

Angel laughed. Susanna sat solemnly looking at her, and Angel's mirth died. "You are joking, aren't you?"

"No. I'm quite serious." She rested her hands on the box. "I know it sounds ridiculous, but it works. I'm a fixer, Angel. A worrier. I've never been able to just let things go. I want to play God, if you will." She smiled in self-mockery. "Every time I do, things go awry." She patted the box. "So I have this."

"A simple brown hatbox," Angel said dryly.

"Yes, a plain, ordinary hatbox, but it reminds me to put faith in God and not in myself. The bonus comes when I see my prayers answered." Her mouth twitched. "I can see you think I'm out of my mind. Shall I show you?" She took the top off. Inside were dozens of small papers, neatly folded. She sifted through them and took one at random, opening it.

"'Cherry needs a home,'" she read. The note was dated. "I like to know how long it takes God to answer." She laughed at herself. "Since this prayer's been answered, I won't put the note back in the box." She folded it and put it on the bedspread beside her and took out another note.

"'God, give me patience with Papa. If he brings another prospective husband to the house, I may join a convent. And you know I would make a very bad nun.'" Angel laughed with her. "I'd better leave that one in the box." She took out another. She was silent for a moment before she read, "'Please make Faith's nightmares go away. Protect her from the evil one.'" She folded it and put it back in the box. "Do you see what I mean?"

"I think so," Angel said. "What if God says no?"

The possibility didn't distress her. "Then he's got something else in mind, something better than what you would think up for yourself." She frowned and looked down at the full box. "Angel, it's not always easy to accept." She closed her eyes and let her breath out slowly. "I had everything planned out for myself at one time. As soon as I met Steven I knew exactly what I wanted and what I was going to do. He was handsome and vibrant. He was studying to be a minister, and he was full of such fire and zeal." She smiled. "We were going to go west and spread the gospel to the Indians." She shook her head, her eyes filling with pain.

"Did he leave you?"

"In a manner of speaking. He was killed. It was so senseless. He used to go down to the worst sections of the city and talk to men in the saloons. He said they needed God more than others more fortunate did. He wasn't going to be a rich man's pastor. Apparently one night a man was being badly beaten in an alley, and Steven tried to stop it. He was stabbed to death." Her face jerked, and she bit her lip.

"I'm sorry, Susanna," Angel said, feeling her friend's grief as though it were her own.

Susanna clenched her hand, tears filled her eyes and slowly trickled down her pale cheeks. "I blamed God. I was so angry. Why Steven? Why someone so good, someone with so much to offer? I was even angry at Steven. Why had he been fool enough to go down to those horrible places? Why bother with those people? They'd made their choices, hadn't they?" She sighed. "It was all such a muddle, my emotions at war. It was no comfort to me at all to know that Steven was with the Lord. I wanted him with me." She was quiet for a long moment. "I still do."

Angel took her hand and squeezed it. She knew how it felt to long for someone with your whole being and know he would forever be out of reach.

Susanna looked at her. "You said you weren't sure what you were supposed to do from here. Well, we're both in the same boat." She smiled again. "But it'll come, Angel. I know it will come."

The top of the box slipped off the bed, and she let go of Angel's hand to retrieve it. As she bent over, the box spilled notes all over the floor. Angel went down on her knees with her to help her gather them together and put them back in the hatbox. So many slips of papers, so many prayers.

Susanna picked up one and glanced at it. She sat back on her heels and smiled, the pallor leaving her cheeks and the light coming back into her eyes. Smiling, she kept it in her hand as Angel put all the others back in the box and fit the top on. Susanna slid the container back beneath the bed.

"Sometimes he answers quickly." Still smiling, she held the note out to Angel. "Read this."

Angel took it and laboriously made out the neatly scripted words. "'God, please, *PLEASE*, I need a friend I can talk to.'"

It was dated the day before Angel came home with Jonathan.

Michael loaded his wagon with bags of wheat and headed for Sacramento. There was a mill on the way where he could have the grain ground and properly sacked for market. It had been a good harvest. He would make enough to buy a few head of cattle and a couple of piglets. By next year, he would have bacon and ham for smoking and beef to sell.

He spent the night beside a stream where he and Angel had stopped. Sitting in the moonlight, looking at the pool, he was filled with thoughts of her. He could almost smell the sweet scent of her skin in the night breeze. His body tingled and grew warm. He remembered her hesitant smile and the startled look whenever he breached her considerable defenses. Sometimes it was just a word or a look that did it unexpectedly, and he had felt elation during those moments, as though he, and not God, had accomplished the impossible. Lowering his head, Michael wept.

Yes, he had learned he was powerless. He had learned a man can live after a woman breaks his heart. He had learned he could live without her. *But, oh, God, I'll miss her until I die.* He would feel this ache inside himself, wondering if she was all right, if she was taking care of herself, if she was safe from harm. Reminding himself that God was watching over her, too, didn't help. Angel's own words always came back to haunt him.

*"Oh, I know God. Do something wrong, and he'll squash you like a bug."*

Did she still believe that? Had his own faith and conviction been so weak that she couldn't see it? Had the cruelty she had suffered and her own powerlessness against it taught her nothing? Did she still think she had control of her life?

As the tormenting thoughts built in his mind, he reached back and clung to one simple Scripture. *"Trust in the Lord with all your heart, and lean not on your own understanding."* Sweat beaded his brow, and he clenched his hands. *Trust in the Lord, trust in the Lord.* He said it over and over to himself until his mind eased and his body relaxed.

And then Michael prayed for Angel, not that she would ever come back to him, but that she would find God for herself.

When he pulled out in the morning, he swore to himself that no matter the temptation, he wouldn't search for his wife when he reached Sacramento.

And he would never set foot in San Francisco.

"Angel! Angel!"

Angel's whole body jerked as someone called out her name. Why had she felt the urge to come down here to the square? She should have gone home as soon as she finished visiting with Virgil. He had fired another cook and tried to talk her into coming back to work for him. She almost wished she hadn't come and raised his hopes.

She'd found herself wandering along the streets again, passing a theater and a saloon. Her old haunting grounds. She didn't know why she was here. She had just gone out for a walk to think things through, to try to make some plans, and felt compelled to come back here. It was more than disheartening.

And now, someone from her past was pressing through the crowd and coming after her. She had the urge to run and not look back.

"Angel, wait!"

Gritting her teeth, she stopped and turned around. She recognized the young woman coming toward her immediately. And seeing her again, she could feel herself straightening up and putting on the mask of disdain and calm. "Hello, Torie," she said, tilting her chin slightly.

Torie's eyes swept her up and down. "I couldn't believe it was you. You look so *different*." She looked uncertain. "Are you still married to that farmer?"

Angel felt the pain before she could batten it down. "No, not anymore."

"Too bad. He was rather special. There was something about him...." She shrugged. "Well, that's life, I guess." She looked at Angel's doe brown dress and cape and worried her lower lip. "You aren't in the business anymore, are you?"

"No. I haven't been for over two years."

"You heard about Lucky?"

Angel nodded. Dear, dear Lucky.

"Mai Ling was in the fire, too."

"I know." She wanted to cut this conversation short and go back to the big house on the hill. She didn't want to think about the past. She didn't want to look at Torie and see how she had aged. She didn't want to recognize the hopelessness in her eyes.

"Well, at least Magowan got what he deserved," Torie said. She stared at Angel's pristine collar.

"Meg's dying of the pox," she went on. "The Duchess turned her out as soon as she found out. I used to see Meggie once in a while, sleeping in a doorway with a bottle of gin in her hand." She raised one shoulder. "Not lately though."

"Are you still with the Duchess?"

Torie gave a laugh. "Nothing ever changes. At least, for some of us." A cynical smile lingered. "It's not so bad, really. She just built a new place, and she's got a good cook. I'm doing all right. I've even got a little money laid aside for my future."

Angel felt a heaviness in her chest. Was Torie pretending she was fine when she was bleeding to death inside? Torie talked on, but Angel hardly heard a word she said. She kept looking into Torie's eyes and seeing things she had never recognized before.

And it all came back to her, everything she had ever experienced from the time she was eight years old. The pain and loneliness of it...and it was there in Torie's eyes, too.

"Well, I've kept you long enough talking about the good old times," Torie said, smiling bleakly. "I'd better get back to work. One more today and then I can relax."

As she started to turn away, Angel felt the strangest rush within her. Warmth filled her, then a burst of energy and assurance such as she had never experienced before. She reached out quickly and stopped Torie. "Have lunch with me," she said, so excited she was trembling.

"Me?" Torie was as surprised as Angel.

"Yes, you!" Angel said, smiling. She felt as though she would burst with the ideas expanding inside her. She knew! She knew what God wanted her to do. She knew *exactly* what he wanted. "I know a little cafe just around the corner." She looped her arm through Torie's and drew her along. "The proprietor's name is Virgil. You'll like him. And I know he's going to be pleased to meet you."

Torie was too stunned to protest.

"Did she say where she was going?" Jonathan asked his distraught daughter.

"No, Father. You know how restless she's been these past weeks. This morning she said she was going to go out for a walk. She wanted to go alone to think. She hasn't been back since. I think something's happened to her."

"You don't know that at all," Priscilla said. "You're letting your emotions take over. Angel knows how to take care of herself."

"Your mother's right," Jonathan agreed, but he couldn't help but wonder. If Angel wasn't home in another hour, he would take the carriage out and go looking for her.

Susanna stopped her pacing long enough to peer out the curtain. "It's getting dark. Oh! There she is. She's coming up the hill." She swung around, eyes blazing. "She smiled and waved!" She swished the lace curtains closed and marched toward the foyer. "I'm going to tell her what I think of her worrying us half sick!"

Angel burst into the house and hugged Susanna before she could utter a word of reprimand. "Oh, Susanna, you won't believe it! You just won't!" Angel laughed. "Well, I take that back. You *would* believe it." She shook her cape out and hung it up, tossing her bonnet on top with a careless air.

Jonathan noticed the difference in her immediately. Her face was aglow, and the smile she wore was one of joy. "I know what God wants me to do with my life," she said, sitting on the edge of the sofa. She clasped her hands on her knees and looked as though she was going to burst with excitement. He watched his daughter sit down slowly nearby. She looked as though she was losing her best friend. Well, maybe she was.

"I'm going to need your help," Angel said to Jonathan. "I'll never be able to repay what you've done already, but I'm going to ask you for more." She shook her head. "I'm going too fast. First I have to tell you what happened today." She told them about meeting Torie and lunching with her. She told them of the young prostitute's dejection and hopelessness and how she had felt the same way for so many years.

"She could have had a job with Virgil if she had known how to cook. As it is, he was kind enough to let her stay if I'd go down and work with her for the next few weeks until she knows what to do. She's quick. She'll be able to handle things on her own in no time."

"You're losing us," Jonathan said. The girl was so excited that she was making little sense.

"Torie said if she could find a way out, she'd take it. Virgil asked if she could cook, and she said no. And it came to me, right there in Virgil's. *Why not?*"

"Why not *what?*" Susanna said, exasperated. "You're making no sense."

"Why not give her a way out," Angel said. "Teach her to cook. Teach her to sew. Teach her to make hats. Teach her anything that would give her another way to make a living. Jonathan, I want to buy a house where someone like Torie can come and be safe and learn to earn her own living without selling her body to do it."

Jonathan grew thoughtful. "I have some friends who might help. How much money do you think you'll need to get started?"

"There's a house a couple blocks up from the docks." She told him how much it was.

His brows rose. It was a great deal of money. He glanced at Priscilla, but she gave him no help. Another look at Angel and he knew he couldn't say no and blot out the look of hope and purpose in her eyes. "We'll see to it tomorrow morning."

Eyes shining, she bent and kissed his cheek. "Thank you, dear friend."

"Father has other friends who'll help support the house," Susanna said.

Jonathan glanced at his daughter and saw the change in her expression. He hadn't seen that sparkle since Steven died. His chest tightened. *Oh, God.* The sudden insight hurt. *I'm going to lose her after all, not to a wild young zealot who intends to take her off into the wilderness and convert the heathen Indians, but to Angel and others like her.*

He wanted his girl married and settled with children of her own. He wanted her in a house close by so she could come visit frequently. He wanted her to be more like Priscilla and less like himself.

He watched Susanna pace back and forth, plans gushing forth like a fountain. Angel was laughing and tossing in her own ideas, one on top of the other. They were both so beautiful, it was hard to look at them. Light shining in the darkness.

Jonathan closed his eyes. *Oh, God, it's not the way I had things planned.*

But then, what of real, lasting value ever is?

# Thirty-three

*When I was a child, I spoke like a child,*
*I thought like a child, I reasoned like a child;*
*when I became a man, I gave up childish ways.*

1 CORINTHIANS 13:11

Paul headed for Sacramento to look for Angel. If he was going to save his marriage, he had to find the witch and bring her back. Michael clearly wasn't going to go looking for her, and Miriam wouldn't rest until she was home. Paul couldn't stand seeing Miriam grieving over Angel any longer. How she could still see good in Angel after all this time, he couldn't even imagine, but Miriam did. Maybe that's why he loved her so much. Hadn't she seen good in him?

Right now he would do anything for her, even leave their home and look for Angel, if it would make her relax and take care of her health.

He figured Angel would be plying her trade in the nearest thriving community. He sought out the brothels first, thinking with her rare beauty, she would be easily tracked down. However, "Angel" turned out to be a common name among prostitutes. He found many, but not her.

After a week, Paul left Sacramento and headed west for San Francisco. Maybe Sacramento had not been big enough for Angel. Just in case he was wrong about that, he stopped in every town along the way and asked after her. No trace.

By the time Paul reached San Francisco, he was convinced the search was fruitless. Too much time had passed since Angel left the valley. It had been almost three years. She had probably boarded a boat to New York or China by now. He didn't know whether to feel thankful for his failure or keep on searching until he found some information. Miriam had been so sure, so adamant.

"She's still in California. I know it."

Someone must have heard of her. How could a girl like Angel just disappear?

The whole situation bothered him greatly. What if he did find her? What was he going to say? *We want you to come back to the valley?* She'd know he was lying. He didn't want her to come back. He never wanted to lay eyes on her again. He couldn't imagine Michael's wanting her back either after all this time. Three years. God knew what she had been doing all that time and with whom.

But Michael did want her to come back. That was the problem. Michael still loved Angel. He would always love her. It wasn't stubbornness or pride that had kept him from going after her this time. He said she had to decide. She had to come back on her own. Well, she wouldn't. A year should have told Michael that much. Surely, two should have done the trick. When another year passed, even Miriam had given up hope that Angel would come back on her own. She said someone would have to find her.

"I want you to go, Paul," Miriam had said. "It has to be you."

Listening, he hated Angel more than ever.

At last he reached San Francisco. Fog covered the city, and Paul searched halfheartedly. Finding Angel would create more problems than not finding her. Was he supposed to drag her back to the valley the way Michael had the first time she left? What was the use? She would only leave again. And again and again. Couldn't Miriam understand? Once a prostitute, always a prostitute. Apparently, some truths came too hard for a girl as sweet and naive as his wife. Or for a man as pure as Michael. Paul loved them both so much, and he couldn't see how finding Angel would help either of them.

Why had Miriam been so insistent that he be the one to find her and bring her back? She wouldn't explain. She said he would find out for himself. At first, he'd refused, and she'd raged at him. He was stunned that his usually reasonable wife could be so fierce. Her words had been like a sword slashing him. Then she wept and said she couldn't go on this way. When she begged him to go find Angel, he couldn't bear it and gave in.

Now here he was, a hundred miles from home and missing

Miriam so much it was a physical pain. He wondered why in the name of heaven he had ever relented. Angel was better lost than found.

Distracted by his own grim resentment, he wandered aimlessly, looking around without really paying attention to what he was seeing. A young woman in gray caught his eye. She was across the street looking in the window and reminded him of Tessie. He hadn't thought of her in months, and the old sadness came up again, flooding him with pain. The girl leaned forward, and the back hem of her skirt raised enough to show worn, black, high-button shoes just like Tess had worn.

*Miriam, what am I doing here? I want to be home with you. I need you. Why did you ever send me on this mad quest?*

The girl straightened and retied her short cap. She turned and waited for a wagon to pass before she crossed the street. Paul caught a brief glimpse of her face and his heart stopped.

*Angel!*

At first, he couldn't believe it was really her. It had to be his imagination putting her face over another after all these weeks of looking. She hurried across the street and walked quickly away from him. Pushing his hat up, he stared after her, wondering if he had seen right. He must have made a mistake. It couldn't be her, not dressed like that…but he followed anyway, just to get another look.

The young woman walked briskly, her head up. Men noticed her all along the way. Some tipped their hats as she passed by. Others whistled and made bold propositions. She didn't pause or speak to anyone. She clearly had a destination. When she reached the heart of the city, she entered a grand bank on a main corner.

Paul waited outside in the cold mist for half an hour before she came out again. It *was* Angel. He was sure of it. She was with a well-dressed gentleman, a man considerably older and more prosperous than Michael. Paul's teeth clenched. He watched as the two spoke together for several minutes, and then the man kissed her cheek.

High-class clientele, Paul thought cynically. And for all her prim and proper clothing, Angel was as brazen as ever. No decent woman would let a man kiss her on a public street. Not even on the cheek.

Miriam's words haunted him. *"You've always judged her. And so wrongly."*

Paul's mouth pressed tight. Miriam wasn't here to witness this scene. She didn't know anything about women like Angel. He had never been able to convince her. She had never quite believed in the existence of a girl called Angel and what she'd done in a brothel in Pair-a-Dice. "You're not even talking about the same person," she said. But he knew what Angel was, even if Miriam and Michael never faced up to it.

What on God's green earth had they ever seen in that worthless woman, to love her with such solid, unchanging devotion? He would never understand it.

He followed Angel to a simple, two-story clapboard building not far from Portsmouth Square. There was a sign on the front door. He had to cross the street to read it. *House of Magdalena*. There it was, printed for any man to see. He had known all along. Now what was he going to do? Even if he told Miriam, she would never believe it. And convincing her would only hurt her more.

Dejected and angry, Paul walked for a long time. It was Angel's fault he was in this situation! She had been a destroyer ever since he first laid eyes on her. First she'd come between him and his money. He had thrown away gold once in a vain attempt to spend half an hour with her at the Palace. Then she came between him and Michael. Now, she was coming between him and his wife!

He spent the night in a cheap hotel. He ordered supper in the dining room and then couldn't eat it. When he went to bed, he couldn't sleep. He kept imagining Miriam's tear-streaked face. "You never even tried to understand her, Paul. And you don't understand now. Sometimes I wonder if you ever will!"

*I understand all right, and I want the witch out of my life forever! I wish she was dead, buried, and forgotten.*

Paul slept fitfully and awakened long before dawn with the decision firm in his mind to go back to the valley. He would lie to Miriam. There was no other way to spare her. He would tell her that he had looked everywhere and couldn't find Angel. Or he could tell her he found out Angel had died of fever or the pox. No, not the pox. Diphtheria. Pneumonia. Anything but the pox. Or he could say she left for the East Coast and the ship went down going around the Horn. That would be believable. But he could never tell her he had seen her go into a brothel a few blocks up from the docks.

Sickened at having to lie at all, he packed his things. All the weeks he had gone without his wife's sweet company because of Angel made him seethe. He would think of some way to convince Miriam it was a lost cause before he got home. He had to.

On his way to the ferry that would take him across the bay, he began to have doubts. Miriam would want to know the name of the ship. She would want to know the people to whom he'd spoken. She would want to know a hundred details he would have to make up. One big lie he could manage, but not a tapestry of smaller ones.

Standing in the heavy fog, a chill started from within Paul. It wouldn't work. No matter what story he conjured up, Miriam would know. She always knew. Just as Michael had known what had happened between Paul and Angel on the road without a word about it ever being spoken aloud.

Furious, he went back to the clapboard building. Seeing no reason to knock, he walked right in. Before him was a small foyer sparsely furnished with two benches and a hat rack. There were no hats on it. In fact, there was no one to ask him what he wanted, let alone whom.

He heard women talking. Removing his hat, he entered a large sitting room and froze. It was filled with women, mostly young, and all staring right at him. Heat filled his face.

Several things came to him at once. The girls were all sitting in straight-backed wooden chairs. There were no men in the room other than himself, and the place looked more like a class-room than a brothel parlor. They were all wearing the same somber gray dresses that Angel had been wearing yesterday. Angel wasn't among them.

A tall woman standing before the others smiled at him. Her

brown eyes were alight with amusement. "Are you lost, sir? Have you come to mend your ways?" The younger women laughed.

"I...I...beg your pardon, ma'am," he stammered, confused and embarrassed. What was this place?

"He thinks this is a hotel," one of the girls said, looking at the pack slung on his back. The others laughed.

"Oh, I bet he thinks this is something else all together, don't you, honey?" another said, looking him up and down.

Someone laughed. "He's blushing! I haven't seen a man blush since '49."

"Ladies, please," the tall woman said, quieting them. She put down the piece of chalk. She brushed the white dust from her slender fingers and walked toward him. "I'm Susanna." She held out her hand, and he took it without thinking. Her fingers were cool, her grip firm. "How may I help you?"

"I'm looking for someone. Angel. Her name's Angel. At least, she used to go by that name. I thought I saw her come in here yesterday afternoon."

"Paul?"

He turned sharply and saw her standing in the doorway. She looked surprised and dismayed. "Come with me, please," she said. He followed her down a hall and into a small office. She took a seat behind a big oak desk. Papers were strewn over it, as were several books. On one corner was a plain brown hatbox with a slot in it. "Please, sit down," she said.

He sat and looked around at the simple, pristine setting. He couldn't make any sense of it. Why would a madam have an office more suited to a nun? What sort of classes were being conducted in the other room? Arithmetic problems had been written on the board, but now that he faced Angel again, he didn't think to ask. The old animosity was back in full force.

If it weren't for her, he would be home with Miriam.

Angel was looking at him with her same directness, but she was different somehow. He looked back at her coldly, trying to figure out what it was. She was still beautiful, so incredibly beautiful...but she had always been that: beautiful, cold, and hard as stone.

He frowned. That was it. The hardness. It was gone. Now

there was a softness about her. It was in her blue eyes, her faint smile, her quiet manner.

*She's serene.*

The thought stunned him, and he shook it away. *No, not serene. She just doesn't feel anything at all. She never did.* He remembered the day on the road. He couldn't exorcise it. He wanted to say something and couldn't think of a word. He was angry, resentful, depressed, but he kept reminding himself he wasn't here for himself. He was here for Miriam. The sooner he got things said, the sooner Angel could refuse to return, and he could leave in good conscience.

Angel spoke first.

"You're looking well, Paul."

He had the oddest feeling she was trying to put him at ease. Why would she want to do that? "Yes. So are you," he said, sounding stiffly polite. It was true. Even in gray, she looked good. Better than ever. She was one of those women who would be beautiful even in her sixties. A devil in disguise.

"It was a shock seeing you," she said.

"Yes. I'm sure it was."

Her eyes searched his face. "What brings you to the House of Magdalena?"

Let her sweat. "Whose house is this?"

"Mine." She didn't elaborate. She waited for him to say something.

"I saw you on the street yesterday and followed you here."

"Why didn't you come in?"

"I didn't want to interrupt anything," he said. "Do you still go by 'Angel'?" He couldn't get the edge out of his voice, and he couldn't understand the look in her eyes, as though every word he said grieved her deeply. Why should it? Nothing had ever grieved her before. It was another act.

"I still go by 'Angel,'" she said. "It seemed appropriate."

Again that directness. Straightforward, to the point, yet gentler in some way than he could ever remember her being. "You look different," he said and glanced around. "I expected you to be living in higher style than this."

"Lower, you mean." She looked amused, not defensive.

He let a sneer show on his face. "Nothing changes, does it?"

Angel studied him. He was right, in one sense. At least where his hatred of her was concerned. Not that he didn't have enough reason. Still, it hurt. "No, I guess not," she said quietly. "It's understandable." She had so much to answer for. She looked away. She couldn't stop thinking about Michael. She was afraid to ask about him, especially from this man who loved him so much and hated her with equal intensity. What was he doing here?

Paul didn't know what to say. He sensed he had hurt her. She sighed and looked at him again, and he wondered if she was as calm as she seemed, if anything really touched her. It was one of the things he had despised about her. No arrow he shot had ever drawn blood.

"Do you ever go back to the valley?" she asked.

The question caught him off guard. "I live there."

"Oh," she said, surprised.

"I never left."

She didn't rise at the accusatory tone. "Miriam told me you were planning to go back to the gold fields and try your luck again."

"Out of desperation," he said. "Miriam talked me out of it."

Angel's face softened. "Yes, I suppose she would. Miriam was always saving a soul. How is she?"

"She's going to have a baby this summer." He watched the color ebb from Angel's face and then come back slowly.

"Thank God."

*Thank God?*

She smiled, but it was sad and wistful. He had never seen her smile like that before. He wished he knew what she was thinking.

"That's wonderful news, Paul. Michael must be very happy."

"Michael?" He gave a soft laugh, confused. "Well, I suppose he is." He felt driven to say, "He's been doing real well for himself the last few years. He bought some more land and a small herd of cattle last spring. He put up a bigger barn this fall." She didn't have to know she had taken half his heart with her when she left.

Michael still had faith in God, and God would find him a good wife.

He didn't expect Angel to smile at his news, but she did. She didn't look the least bit surprised. She looked relieved and happy. "Michael will always do well."

The heartless witch. Was that all she could say? Didn't she know how much Michael loved her, how much it had ripped him up when she left?

"And you, Paul? Have you worked things out with him again?"

He hated her for the reminder of what had happened. He hated her so much he had the taste of steel in his mouth. "As soon as you left, things went back to the way they were," he said, knowing it was a lie. Michael had never held a grudge. *He* was the one who couldn't let it go. Nothing was the same. She was still a wall between them.

"I'm glad," she said and looked it. "He's always loved you, you know. He never stopped." She saw his expression and changed the subject. "You can help him build an addition on the cabin. He'll need one now."

"An addition? What for?"

"With the baby coming," she said. "He and Miriam will eventually need more room. And there will be more children in time. Michael always told me he wanted lots of children. Now he will have them."

Paul couldn't breathe. He felt cold and sick.

Angel frowned. "What's wrong?"

He saw the truth, and the feeling in the pit of his stomach was nothing to the lump of pain in his chest. *Oh, God. Oh, God! Is that why she left him?*

He could feel Miriam's presence and hear her words. *"You never understood her, Paul. You never even tried."* Miriam with tear-filled eyes. *"Maybe if you had tried, just once, things might have been different. Amanda would never let me inside. Not completely. I don't think she ever let anyone know how much pain she felt, not even Michael. Maybe you could have tried to help her!"* Miriam standing firm before his scorn. *"I never knew Angel. I only know Amanda, and if it weren't for her, I never would have had the courage to come to you."* Miriam on the day she had come to his cabin. *"I have to do what's best for you."*

Angel was searching his face. "What's the matter, Paul? What is it? There's nothing wrong with Miriam, is there?"

"Miriam is *my* wife, not Michael's."

She drew back, stunned. *"Yours?"*

"Yes, mine."

"I don't understand," she said shakily. "How can she be your wife?"

He couldn't answer. He knew what she meant. How many times had he thought he wasn't good enough for her. She was just right for Michael. He had kept thinking that, all the while he had fallen in love with her himself. He had been convinced right up to the day she had come to him in his cabin. "Angel, Michael's still waiting for you to come home."

Her face went deathly white. "It's been over three years. He can't still be waiting."

"He is."

Paul's words struck her squarely in the chest. *Oh, God.* She shut her eyes for a moment. She stood and turned away. She pushed the lace curtain back to stare out the window. It was raining. She couldn't breathe past the pain in her chest. Her eyes were on fire.

Paul saw the way her hand clutched the curtain until her knuckles were white. "I think I understand," he said bleakly. "You figured if you went away, he would turn to Miriam. Eventually he would fall in love with her and forget about you. Isn't that it?" Hadn't he expected that to happen as well? Hadn't the possibility torn at his guts?

"He would have."

She didn't even have to say it: *"If you hadn't interfered."* Once, Paul had said to Miriam that he didn't think Angel had the capacity for pain or love. Those words came back to taunt him now. How could he have been so wrong about her? When she turned and looked at him, he was ashamed.

"Miriam is perfect for him," Angel said. "She's the sort of wife he needs. She's pure and intelligent and tender. She has a tremendous capacity for love."

He heard so much more than words this time. "That's all very true, but Michael loves *you*."

"He wants children, and Miriam could have given them to him. They understand one another."

"Because they're *friends*."

Her eyes flashed. "They could have been more."

"Maybe," he conceded, facing his own selfishness. "If I'd had the courage you did and if I'd left. I didn't. I couldn't." Until this moment he'd thought it was because he loved Miriam too much, but he saw clearly now that he had loved himself more. Angel had understood a higher quality of love: sacrifice.

Leaning forward, he put his head in his hands. Now he knew why Miriam had been so insistent that he be the one to find her. "I was wrong," he groaned, "I was wrong about you the whole time." His vision blurred. He looked up again. "I've hated you, hated you so much I – " He broke off, unable to say anymore.

Angel sat down behind the desk again, saddened. "You were right about me in a lot of ways."

Her words only confirmed what he now knew. He gave a bleak laugh. "I never even came close. And I know why. That day on the road, I knew you were right. You were right. *I* betrayed him."

Her eyes filled. "I could've said no."

"Did you know that then?"

She didn't speak for a moment. "Some part of me must have known. Maybe I just didn't want to. Maybe it was my way to draw your blood. I don't know anymore. It was so long ago. I never wanted to think about it again, and then every time I saw you, there it was. I couldn't get away from it."

She remembered the darkness in which she had lived. She remembered all those months that Paul had stayed away and how his absence had hurt Michael. She could imagine Paul's pain at the separation as well, and his shame. And the horrible guilt of it all. Hadn't she kept company with her own?

It was on her head. She had allowed it to happen. For whatever reason. What did it matter now? She couldn't cast blame on anyone but herself. The choice had been hers. She had never even thought of consequences. The repercussions had been like a stone flung into smooth water. The splash, then the widening circles. It was a long time before the water was smooth again. And the stone was always there, lying cold and hard in the silent pool. Michael. Paul. Herself. Ruptured souls desperate to be put together again.

The torment and rift between Paul and Michael had grown wider, not because Michael couldn't forgive, but because Paul couldn't forgive himself. Wasn't that just what she had felt most of her life? That everything that had ever happened to her had somehow been her fault, that she was guilty even of being born? She had learned in the last few years that she wasn't alone in those feelings. She heard them every day from other women who had experienced the same abuses she had. Forgiving others for what they had done to her had come far easier than forgiving herself. There were still moments of struggle.

Her mouth trembled. "Paul, I'm so sorry for the pain I've caused you. Truly, I am."

He sat for a long time, unable to speak, thinking of all the time and all the persecution she had endured. From him. And now *she* was apologizing. He had plotted her destruction and destroyed himself in the process. From that time, he had been consumed by hatred, blinded by it. *I have been insufferable and self-righteous and cruel.* The revelation was bitter and painful, but a relief, too. There was an odd sort of freedom in standing before a mirror and seeing himself clearly. For the first time in his life.

If it hadn't been for Miriam, what would he have become? Loving her had softened him. She had seen something in him he'd never imagined anyone but Tess could see. And she'd seen something in Angel he couldn't. He had wondered at it but had stubbornly held to his own convictions. Michael's wife had always been Angel to him, the high-priced soiled dove from Pair-a-Dice – and he had always treated her accordingly.

Now that he thought back, he couldn't remember one time when she had defended herself. Why hadn't she? He knew the answer to that as well. She had just given it to him when she said he was right about her. It hadn't been disdain or arrogance that had kept her silent, it had been shame. She believed everything he said about her. She believed she was soiled and unworthy, fit only to be used.

*And I helped convince her. I filled the role Michael refused to play.*

Remorse overwhelmed him. It hurt to look at her. It hurt even more to see the truth – that he was greatly to blame for Michael's pain as well. If he had reached out just once as Miriam had said, maybe things would have been different, but he had been too proud, too sure he was right.

"*I'm* sorry," he said. "So very sorry. Can you forgive me?"

She wondered if he knew tears were pouring down his face, and she felt a sudden, inexplicable warmth toward this man. Michael's brother, *her* brother. "I forgave you a long time ago, Paul. I left the valley and Michael of my own free will. Don't lay blame for that on yourself."

She leaned forward, her hands clasped tightly on the desk blotter. "Let's leave all that behind us. Please. Tell me everything that's happened since I left." She smiled slightly, teasing him gently. "Especially how a man like you ever managed to win a girl like Miriam?"

He laughed for the first time in months. "God only knows," he said, shaking his head. He sighed heavily and relaxed. "She loves me. She told me she knew the first time she met me she was going to marry me." Talking about Miriam made the warmth come flowing back. "I'd watch her and want her so much and find every kind of reason why I wasn't good enough to kiss the hem of her skirt. Then she came to me one dawn in my cabin. She said she was moving in with me, and set about convincing me how much I needed her. I didn't have the strength to send her home."

Angel laughed softly. "I can't imagine Miriam being that bold."

"She told me she learned courage from you." He hadn't known what she meant then. Now he did. Angel had loved Michael enough to leave him when she thought it was in his best interest. Miriam had come to him for the same reasons. If she hadn't, he would have gone back to the goldfields and drinking and spending time in the brothels – and he probably would have died up there with his face in the mud.

"Miriam sent me to find you. Amanda, I want to take you home." He meant it.

*Amanda.* Her throat closed, and she smiled. Another burden lifted, and she was grateful, but it wasn't that easy or simple. She couldn't let it be. "I can't go back, Paul. Not ever."

"Why not?"

How much did he have to know to understand and become her ally? "There's a lot about me you still don't know."

"Then tell me."

She chewed on her lip. How much was enough? "I was sold into prostitution when I was eight," she said slowly, staring down at nothing. "I never knew any other way of life until Michael married me." She looked at him again. "And I never understood him, not the way he hoped I would. I can't change who I was. I can't undo the things that happened."

Paul leaned forward. "You're the one who still doesn't understand, Amanda. There's something I didn't even comprehend until now because I was too stubborn and jealous and proud.... Michael *chose* you. With all your past, with all your frailties, with everything. He knew from the beginning where you came from, and it didn't make any difference to him. There were plenty of women back home who would have jumped at the chance to marry him. Sweet, sensible virgin girls from God-fearing families. He never fell in love with any of them. He took one look at you, and he *knew*. Right from the beginning. You. No one else. He told me all that, but I thought it was sex. Now I know it wasn't. It was something else."

"A crazy accident – "

"I think it's because he knew how much you needed him."

She shook her head, not wanting to hear it, but Paul was determined. "Amanda, he bought you out of bondage with his own sweat and blood, and you know it. Don't tell me now you can't go back to him."

It hurt too much because she still loved and needed him. Sometimes she thought she would die without the sound of

Michael's voice. She would close her eyes and see his face and how he walked and how he had smiled at her. He had taught her how to play and sing and rejoice, things she had never known. And the sweetness of those memories was agonizing; the separation, unbearable.

Sometimes she tried not to think about him at all because the pain was so great. But the hunger for him was always there, the endless, aching hunger. Only he had opened himself to be used in her life by Christ. Through him, Christ had been able to fill her until she was overflowing. Michael had always said it was God; now she knew that was true.

And the knowledge that he'd been the bridge between her and her Savior only made her long for Michael all the more.

She couldn't allow herself to think of all that. She had to think of what was good for him, not of what she wanted for herself. She had purpose now and satisfaction in her life. She wasn't plagued by nightmares and self-doubt. At least, not until now. And she had to tell Paul the complete truth so he would understand.

"I can't have his children, Paul. Never. Something was done to me when I was very young. To make sure." She had to stop and look away briefly before she could go on. "Michael wants to have children. You know that. It's his dream." She faced him again. "Can you understand now why I can't go back? I know he would take me back again. I know I would still be his wife. But it wouldn't be fair, would it? Not for a man like him."

She struggled to control the tears that were so often near the surface lately. She would not give in. She couldn't. If she did, she would cry until she melted away into nothing.

Paul didn't know what to say.

"Please," she said. "When you go back, don't tell Miriam you saw me. Say anything. Say I left the country. Say I died." He cringed inwardly hearing his own thoughts come back to haunt him.

"Please, Paul. If you tell her, she would only tell Michael, and he would feel he had to come and get me again. Don't let him find out where I am."

"You needn't fear that. He told Miriam he wouldn't drag

you back this time. He said it was your decision, that you had to come back on your own or you'd never really understand that you were free." He wanted more than anything now to convince her she had to come home again. "Did you ever tell him you couldn't have children?"

"Yes," she said quietly.

"What did he say?"

She shook her head, dismissing it. "You know Michael."

Indeed, he did. He stood up and put his hands on the desk. "He married you, Amanda. For better or worse, and for as long as you both are alive, and that's how long he'll wait for you, and past that, if I know Michael. If you only knew how much he's hurting – "

"Don't."

"You know him. Did he ever give up on you before? He won't give up waiting for you now. He'll never give up."

She shook her head, pale and distraught. "I can't go back."

Paul straightened. He didn't know whether he had given her something to think about or just caused her more pain. "I've said all I can. It's up to you, Amanda. Just don't take too long making up your mind. I miss my wife." He wrote down the name and address of the hotel where he stayed the night before. "I'd like to leave by nine tomorrow. Send word what you decide."

He picked up his pack and shouldered it. "What is this place anyway? A boardinghouse?"

She looked up at him, pulled back from her dilemma. "In a way. It's a home for fallen women, women like me who want to change their lives. We've been very fortunate. Several wealthy citizens gave us financial help."

*The man at the bank,* Paul thought. *God, forgive me. What a fool I've been.* "You started it, didn't you?"

"Not all by myself. I've had a lot of help along the way."

"What do you teach them in there?" He nodded toward the big room through the door and down the hall.

"Reading, writing, and ciphering; cooking, sewing, how to run a small business. As soon as they're ready, we find positions for them. We've developed a way to accomplish that with the help of several churches."

Father Patrick had been to see her often. Some Catholic priests were a lot like Michael. Devoted to God, humble, patient, and loving.

She hesitated. "Magdalena is one of the things I need to think about, Paul. They need me here."

"No matter how good a cause, it's just an excuse now. Pass the torch to someone else. That tall lady with the laughing eyes looked like she could take care of things." He went to the door. "Your first obligation is to Michael." He had said all he could. "I'll wait until noon tomorrow at the latest. Then I'm going home."

Angel sat for a long time thinking after he left. The sun went down, and she didn't light the lamp. She remembered sitting on the hill a mile from the farmhouse and Michael's saying, "This is the life I want to give you." And he had.

How could he know what he had done for her? How could he even guess that her life was new because he had shown her the way to live?

Paul thought she had gone back to prostitution. What if Michael believed the same thing? She couldn't bear for him to believe that. It would make everything he had ever done for her meaningless, and it had meant everything.

*God, was I wrong? Should I go back? How can I face him again after all this time? How can I see him and walk away again? What do you want me to do? I know what I want. Oh, God, I know. But what do you want me to do?*

She held herself and rocked, biting her lips and fighting the grief. *How can I not say thank you to him? Did I ever really explain what he did for me? What have I ever given him back but grief?* But she had gifts to offer him now. She had stood firm against Duke. She had walked the road Michael had taught her. Because of it, people had trusted her and backed her in building the House of Magdalena. She was doing good with her life, and it was all because of him, because of what she had seen in him. "Seek and ye shall find," he'd read to her, and she had. Maybe if she found a way to tell him, it would give him peace.

**Sarah, beloved.**

*God, I won't ask for more than that.* She closed her eyes tightly.
*I won't ask you for more.*

Classes were long over when she left the office. The girls
had finished supper and retired to their rooms. Angel went up the
stairs. She saw light beneath Susanna's door and tapped.

"Come in."

Angel entered.

"What's happened?" Susanna asked, getting up from bed
and coming to her. She took her hands. "You look so pale. We
missed you at dinner. Who was that man?"

"A friend. Susanna, I want you to run Magdalena for me."

"Me?" she said, astounded. She looked less assured than
Angel ever remembered. She let go of her hands and stepped back.
"You can't mean it. I couldn't!"

"I mean it, and, yes, you can." Susanna was more than capable of handling things. She just didn't know it yet. She would walk
through the fire and come out the other side even stronger than
now. Angel was suddenly very sure of that.

"But why? Where are you going?"

"Home," Angel said. "I'm going home."

# *Thirty-four*

*Come, let us return to the Lord;*
*for he has torn, that he may heal us;*
*he has stricken, and he will bind us up.*

HOSEA 6:1

"Paul!" Miriam flew from the cabin to throw her arms around his neck, weeping in joy. "Oh, I've missed you so much!" She kissed every part of his face she could reach. He laughed and kissed her mouth, feeling the pieces inside himself come back together again. He was home! All the tension of the past weeks, the guilt of the months before evaporated. She pressed closer to him, and other emotions surged through his body. Having Miriam in his arms again was heady indeed.

When he released her, she was flushed and breathless. She had never looked so beautiful to him. He looked her over and saw her pregnancy was beginning to show. "My, how you've grown," he said, rubbing the bulge.

She laughed and put her hand over his. "Did you find her?"

"In San Francisco." His heart lightened even more at the look in Miriam's eyes.

She smiled up at him tenderly. "I can see things worked out." She looked relieved and delighted. Her anger with him was completely forgotten. "Where is she?" she asked, looking past him.

"She wanted to sit for a few minutes up the road. I think she's preparing herself for an ordeal. She's hardly said a word the last two days traveling. She's changed, Miriam."

She searched his eyes and smiled. "So have you, my love. You've made your peace with yourself, haven't you?"

"I had help along the way."

Miriam saw Amanda then and left him standing while she ran up the road, arms outstretched, to meet her. The two women embraced warmly, and Paul smiled. When Miriam let go, she was chattering on gaily, tears streaming down her cheeks. Angel looked pale and strained, not at all at ease. She glanced toward Michael's land, and Paul understood why. Amanda was afraid to face Michael after all this time.

*Lord, make it right for her and Michael. Please. I'd see it as a personal favor.*

"I'll bring water up, and you can have a bath," Miriam was saying, looping her arm through Amanda's as they walked toward him. "I made bread this morning, and there's soup simmering. You must be famished after your trip."

"I can't stay, Miriam."

Miriam stopped. "You can't? But why?"

"I have to go to Michael."

"Well, of course, you do, but you can rest a few minutes and wash up. We can talk it over."

"I can't," Angel said. "If I wait any longer, I may not be able to go at all." Her smile was weak.

Miriam searched her face. She glanced at Paul and then back again. She hugged her tightly. "We'll walk with you." She beseeched Paul with her look.

"Sure we will," he agreed readily, and Angel nodded. Now that the moment was at hand, they were all afraid of what would happen. Just how long was Michael's patience? Worse, would he be angry with them for interfering and taking things into their own hands? Or had they been doing God's will all along?

When they were within sight of Michael's homestead, Angel stopped. "I have to go the rest of the way alone," she told them. "Thank you for coming this far with me."

Miriam looked ready to argue. When she looked to Paul to agree, he shook his head. Amanda was right.

Angel kissed Miriam's cheek and hugged her. "Thank you for sending Paul," she whispered.

They watched her walk away alone.

Paul put his arm around Miriam's shoulders and watched Amanda. He remembered how Angel had always walked, head high, back straight. Arrogance, he had thought, but it had been pride that had held her together for so long, and pride that had kept her separate. She had a quiet grace about her now, a beautiful humility.

"She's afraid," he said quietly.

"She's always been afraid," Miriam said, leaning against him. "Do you think we did the right thing, Paul? Maybe we should have let her come back on her own."

It was the first time he had heard Miriam uncertain. "She wouldn't have. She had made up her mind. She thought you were married to him."

"Because she told me to. She said she wanted me to have his children." She looked up at him, her eyes swimming with tears. "But I only wanted yours."

"Oh, my love." He held her close. "We'll have to remember the man Michael is."

"Yes." She put her arms around him. "It's really up to them now, isn't it?"

Paul turned her face to him and kissed her with all the longing he had felt during the weeks of their separation. "I don't know what I'd do without you."

She reached up and pulled his head down to kiss him back. It was a lover's kiss this time. "Let's go home."

Angel could see Michael working in the field. She was so full of conflicting emotions she could hardly bear it. Self-doubt, self-hatred, struggling pride, and fear. All the things that had sent her running so long ago and some that had kept her from going to him before now. She couldn't allow them to stop her again.

*Oh, God, give me strength. Please. Walk with me. Help me. I don't know if I can go through this.*

**I have not given you a heart of fear.**

She knew the moment Michael saw her. He glanced up as she was crossing the meadow. He stood very still, staring at her in the distance.

*I mustn't cry. I mustn't.*

She kept walking toward him. He didn't move. Doubt stirred again, but she fought it down. She wanted to shed all the barriers that had kept her from him, all those months of defiance and fear and uncertainty. She wanted to discard the horrible memories of her childhood and the guilt she had taken on herself for things she had been powerless to stop.

If only things had been different. She wanted so desperately to be clean for him, to be new. She wanted to please him. She would give the rest of her life to that end if he would let her. She wanted to strip away her past. Oh, if she could only be Eve again, a new creature in Paradise. Before the Fall.

With trembling hands, she removed the trappings of the world. She dropped her shawl and took off the woolen jacket. She worked at the tiny buttons of the shirtwaist. She shrugged it off and let it drop as she walked. She unhooked her skirt and let it slide down over her hips and to the ground. She stepped out of it.

Without faltering, she walked toward him.

She had never said all she should have. He didn't know what he had done for her. He had been like the sea, sometimes storm-cast, with waves crashing against a cliff wall; other times he was like the steady, lapping surf. Always he had been like the tide, washing her shore, reshaping her coastline.

*Lord, no matter what he does or says, I have to thank him. He was always your good and faithful servant, and I never thanked him. Not enough. Oh, God, never, never enough.*

She removed the camisole and slips, the corset cover and corset and pantalets. With each garment she removed and dropped, she cast away anger, fear, and her blindness to the multitudes of joy in life, her own desperate pride. She had one single, abiding purpose: to show Michael she loved him, and she peeled away the layers of pride one by one until she was humbled by her own nakedness. Last of all, she stepped out of her thin leather shoes and drew the pins that held her hair.

As she came close, she saw the gray at his temples and the new lines in his beloved face. When she looked into his eyes, everything she felt spilled over. She had always known her own pain and loneliness, her own need. Now she came to face his.

Oh, what had she done to him in denying her love, in turning away? She had played God and done what she thought best for him, and all she had done was cause him pain. She thought he was too strong to be hurt, too wise to wait. How much had her martyrdom cost him?

All her carefully planned words fled. So many words to say a simple, heartfelt thing: *I love you, and I'm sorry.* She could not even speak. The tears that had been frozen inside her all her life came, and the last bastion melted away in a flood.

Weeping, Angel sank to her knees. Hot tears fell on his boots. She wiped them away with her hair. She bent over, heartbroken, and put her hands on his feet. "Oh, Michael, Michael, I'm sorry...."

*Oh, God, forgive me.*

She felt his hand on her head. "My love," he said. He took hold of her and drew her up again. She couldn't look into his face, wanting to hide her own. Michael took off his shirt and put it around her shoulders. When he tipped her chin up, she had no choice but to look into his eyes again. They were wet like hers but filled with light. "I hoped you would come home someday," he said and smiled.

"There's so much I have to say. So many things to tell you."

He combed his fingers into her flowing hair and tilted her head back. "We have the rest of our lives."

She knew then that she had doubted he would forgive her again, but he already had. She could live with him forever and not know his depths. *Oh, Lord, thank you, thank you!* She went into his arms, spreading her hands on his strong back, pressing herself as close as she could, her gratitude so strong she could hardly bear it. He was warmth and light and life. She wanted to be flesh of his flesh, blood of his blood. Forever. Closing her eyes, she inhaled the sweet scent of him and felt she was finally home again.

She thought she had been saved by his love for her, and in part she had been. It had cleansed her, never casting blame. But that had been only the beginning. It was loving him in return that had brought her up out of the darkness. *What can I give him more than that? I would give him anything.*

"Amanda," Michael said, holding her tenderly. "Tirzah..."

**Sarah,** came the still, soft voice, and she knew the one gift she had to offer. Herself. Angel drew back from Michael and looked up at him. "Sarah, Michael. My name is Sarah. I don't know the rest of it. Only that much. Sarah."

Michael blinked. His whole body flooded with joy. The name fit her so well. A wanderer in foreign lands, a barren woman filled with doubt. Yet Sarah of old had become a symbol of trust in God and ultimately the mother of a nation. Sarah. A benediction. Sarah. A barren woman who conceived a son. His beautiful, cherished wife who would someday give him a child.

*It's a promise, Lord, isn't it?* Michael felt the warmth and assurance of it enter every cell of his body.

He held out his hand. "Hello, Sarah." She looked endearingly confused as she placed her hand in his. He shook it and grinned down at her. "I'm very pleased to meet you. Finally."

She laughed. "You are such a crazy, crazy man, Michael."

Michael laughed with her and pulled her into his arms to kiss her. He felt her arms around him as she kissed him back. She was home for good this time. Not even death would part them.

When they drew breath, Michael swung her around and lifted her above him joyously. She threw back her head and spread her arms wide to embrace the sky, tears of celebration streaming down her cheeks.

Michael had once read to her how God had cast a man and woman out of Paradise. Yet, for all their human faults and failures, God had shown them the way back in.

*Love the Lord your God, and love one another. Love one another as he loves. Love with strength and purpose and passion and no matter what comes against you. Don't weaken. Stand against the darkness, and love. That's the way back into Eden. That's the way back to life.*

# Epilogue

*Weeping may last for the night,*
*But a shout of joy comes in the morning.*
PSALM 30:5B

Sarah and Michael shared many happy years together. On their seventh anniversary, their prayers were answered with the birth of a son, Stephen. Stephen was followed by Luke, Lydia, and Esther. Miriam and Paul also remained happy and had three sons, Mark, David, and Nathan.

Both families prospered and remained lifelong friends. Together they built a community church and school and welcomed many more settlers to their valley.

Susanna Axle remained at the House of Magdalena until her death in 1892. With her help, dozens of young women once trapped into prostitution crossed the threshold to better lives. Several married well and became leading citizens.

Though Sarah's family grew rich and famous – eventually including doctors, ambassadors, missionaries, and even a much-decorated veteran of San Juan Hill – she returned for one week each year to the House of Magdalena. As long as she was physically able, she walked through the Barbary Coast and down to the docks, talking with young prostitutes and encouraging them to change their lives. When asked why, she said, "I never want to forget where I came from and all God has done for me." She frequently returned from the docks to the House of Magdalena holding an Angel by the hand.

After sixty-eight years of marriage, Michael was laid to rest. Sarah followed within a month. According to their wishes, only simple wooden crosses marked their graves. However, a few days after Sarah's burial, an epitaph was found scratched into her marker.

> Though fallen low
> God raised her up
> An angel.

Many born-again Christians talk about a single conversion experience that changed their lives forever. They can tell you the day and the hour they made their decision to live for the Lord. I can't do that.

I was reared in a Christian home. I went to Sunday school and church camp. I attended youth groups. When I filled out various forms that asked what religion I was, I checked the box that said "Protestant." Yet, for me, my actual conversion came slowly – like the changing of seasons – and with a power that still humbles me.

I will not go into details about the mistakes I made. Suffice it to say I was burdened and soul-hungry, and so was my husband Rick. We both had burdens – enough to sink a marriage had not God wanted it otherwise.

Writing was my escape from the world and hard times. It was always the one area of my life where I believed (mistakenly) that I had complete control. I could create characters and stories to suit me. I wrote romances for the secular market and I read them voraciously.

Rick once said, "If you had to choose between me and the children or your writing, you would take your writing." At the time he said it, it was sadly true. I frequently contemplated how much easier it would be to live by myself in a cabin away from everyone, with an electric typewriter as my only company.

Before long, Rick and I decided we needed to make some changes in our lives. We never do anything by half-measure, so we sold our house, gave away half of our furnishings, and moved north to Sonoma County to start a new business. All external changes, you will note, not internal ones of the heart. Though the business flourished, our relationship was disintegrating.

Yet, even through the hardest times, I can look back and see that God showed His love and concern for us. He was constantly holding out His arms and saying, "Come to me." One such message came through a little boy who lived in the house next door. We arrived with our U-Haul and were carrying in boxes to the small rental house in Sebastopol when little Eric came over to welcome us and help out. "Have I got a church for you!" he said, and Rick and I rolled our eyes and wished he would go bother someone else.

Out of curiosity, a few weeks later I attended Eric's church. After all, I had found no peace in anything else. Well, our little neighbor was right! The warmth and love I felt in the congregation drew me the moment I walked in the front door. I heard the Word of God being preached; I felt God's truth and love in action all around me. Many churches seem to be mere museums for plastic saints, or they preach fulfillment from the world's point of view – a "prosperity gospel." This church was different. It was a hospital for repentant sinners; their only blueprint for life was the Bible, which everyone was carrying and – most amazing of all – reading! The church wasn't connected to an organization. They went by the name of "Christians," and said living according to Christ's example is a lifetime process.

I started taking the children to church with me. Then Rick started coming. Our lives began to change, not from the outside, but from the inside out. We were all baptized by immersion, not just in water, but in the Spirit. It did not happen quickly, and we still have struggles, but we belong to the Lord and He is molding and making us according to His will.

I believe we all serve someone in this life. For the first thirty-eight years of mine, I served myself. My conversion was not a highly emotional experience. It was a conscious, thought-out decision that changed my focus, my direction, my heart, my life. But I don't want to mislead anyone. It was not all peace and light afterward. The first thing that happened was that I couldn't write. Oh, I tried, but it didn't feel right. Writing just didn't work for me anymore. I couldn't escape into it. I had given myself to the Lord, and He had something else in mind. I finally accepted that it might not even be in His plan that I ever write again. And I surrendered. What I came to understand was that He wanted me to get to know Him first. He wanted no other gods in my life – not my family, not my writing. Nothing.

I started craving the Word of God. I read page by page, cover to cover and cover to cover and cover to cover. I started to pray. I started to listen and learn. God's Word is like food and clean, clear water. It filled the emptiness inside me. It renewed me. It opened my eyes and ears and mind and heart and filled me with joy.

We opened our house for a home Bible study, and our pastor began a study on the gospels. Then we did a study on materialism. Then we began a study on the minor prophets. We eventually came to the Book of Hosea. That portion of God's Word hit me so profoundly that I knew this was the love story the Lord wanted me to write! His story, a deeply moving story of His passionate love for each of us – unconditional, forgiving, unchanging, everlasting, self-sacrificing – the kind of love for which most people hunger their entire lives, yet never find.

Writing *Redeeming Love* was a form of worship for me. Through it, I was able to thank God for loving me even when I was defiant, rebellious, contemptuous of what I thought being a Christian meant, and afraid to give my heart away. I had wanted to be my own god and have control of my life the way Eve did in the Garden of Eden. Now I know to be loved by Christ is the ultimate joy and fulfillment. Everything in *Redeeming Love* was a gift from the Lord: plot, characters, theme. None of it is mine to claim.

There are many who struggle to survive in life, many who have been used and abused in the name of love, many who have been sacrificed on the altars of pleasure and "freedom." But the freedom the world offers is, in reality, false. Too many have awakened one day to discover they are in bondage, and they have no idea how to escape. It is for people such as these that I wrote *Redeeming Love* – people who fight, as I did, to be their own gods, only to find in the end that they are lost, desperate, and terribly alone. I want to bring the truth to those trapped in lies and darkness, to tell them that God is there, He is real, and He loves them – no matter what.

I used to believe the purpose in life is to find happiness. I don't believe that anymore. I believe we are all given gifts from our Father, and that our purpose is to offer them to Him. He knows how He wants us to use them. I used to struggle to find happiness. I used to work hard to attain it. By the world's standards, I was successful. But it was all meaningless vanity. Now, I have joy. I have everything I ever wanted or dreamed of having: a love that is so precious I can find no words to describe it. I haven't achieved this through my own efforts. I certainly have done nothing worthy to earn it or even deserve it. I have received it as a free gift from the Lord, the everlasting God. It is the same gift He offers you, every minute, every hour, every day of your life.

I hope this story will help you see who Jesus is and how much He loves you. And may the Lord draw you to Him.